Praise for

THE PENAL COLONY

"The writer obviously excels in research. His characters come to life and are liked and disliked on their actions. A very well put together book."

The West Coast Review of Books

"Great escapism."

The Toronto Globe & Mail

"An action-filled drama it is. . . . A well written and memorable story of chilling adventure."

Lake Oswego Review

"A gripping novel, as thriller or novel of ideas."

Library Journal

Also by Richard Herley
Published by Ballantine Books:

THE PAGANS, a trilogy

THE STONE ARROW
THE FLINT LORD
THE EARTH GODDESS

THE PENAL
COLONY

Richard Herley

BALLANTINE BOOKS • NEW YORK

Library of Congress Catalog Card Number: 87-21336

ISBN 0-345-35875-9

This edition published by arrangement with William Morrow and Company, Inc.

Printed in Canada

First Ballantine Books Edition: June 1989

FOR MY MOTHER

SERT

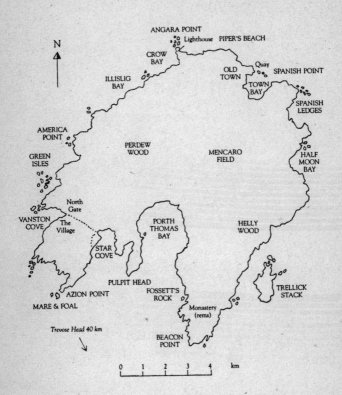

N

ANGARA POINT
Lighthouse · PIPER'S BEACH
CROW BAY
OLD TOWN
Quay
SPANISH POINT
TOWN BAY
ILLISLIG BAY
SPANISH LEDGES
AMERICA POINT
PERDEW WOOD
MENCARO FIELD
HALF MOON BAY
GREEN ISLES
North Gate
VANSTON COVE
The Village
PORTH THOMAS BAY
HELLY WOOD
STAR COVE
PULPIT HEAD
AZION POINT
FOSSETT'S ROCK
TRELLICK STACK
MARE & FOAL
Monastery (rema)
Trevose Head 40 km
BEACON POINT

0 1 2 3 4   km

PART ONE

1

Routledge became conscious. A foul taste was on his tongue; he felt nauseous, drug-sick, and at first he thought he was emerging not from sleep, but from anesthesia. It followed that he must be in hospital, in pajamas, but his skin and limbs returned a contrary sensation. He was fully and heavily clad; and hospitals smelled of disinfectant, while this place smelled of damp wood, and stone, and salt air, and an unpleasant acridity which he could not quite recognize.

Then he remembered a recent fragment of dream. He must after all have been asleep: was he dreaming still?

Above him, dimly illuminated, as if by a single candle some distance away, he could make out the form of a low ceiling, crudely made of rough laths and bundles of rushes. The quality of his sight was unmistakably real. This was no dream.

He had been placed on a low bed or pallet, on a mattress made of dried heather or bracken. He became aware that he was completely helpless: he had been zipped into a tightly fitting sleeping-bag and his wrists felt as if they had been bound together.

At that moment he understood where he was and what must have happened to him. The preceding days in the workroom, supper last night, had given no inkling of this; there had been no unusual taste in his food. Each day had followed the same routine, the routine that had been established from

3

the morning of his induction over six months before. During those days he had foolishly begun to feel safe, to imagine, somehow, that he was not after all to be placed in Category Z.

A noise to his left made him turn to the side. The interior extended for three or four meters, ending at a sort of hearth, without a fire. Here a large man was sitting, his back to Routledge, seemingly intent on making or repairing something in his lap. Beside him, on an upturned crate, burned the small oil lamp which was giving its glow to the room.

The fireplace and the walls had been fashioned from irregular blocks of gray stone. Above the hearth, supported on brackets driven into the interstices, ran a warped plank which, laden with a jumble of cans, bits of netting, feathers, plastic canisters, paperbacks, and some dried stalks in a wine bottle, served as the mantelshelf. Similar clutter filled a series of shelves to the right. Between them and the low doorway in the corner there were three or four pegs, each hung with a bulky mass of clothing, including a trawlerman's black plastic raincoat, much the worse for wear.

The man appeared to be sewing.

Perhaps in his terror Routledge had made a slight sound; perhaps the rhythm of his breathing had changed; or perhaps the man had felt, at the nape of his neck, the pressure of Routledge's gaze. Whatever the cause, he glanced over his shoulder and, seeing Routledge awake, immediately got up.

With the lamp behind him, the man was in shadow, but Routledge could see enough to tell that he was of late middle age, bearded, long-haired, balding from the forehead, wearing a tattered pepper-and-salt rollneck sweater and shapeless corduroy trousers.

He came nearer. The acrid smell grew stronger. He stopped at a safe distance and, resting a hand on one of the posts supporting the ceiling, bent forward slightly to examine his captive more closely.

"Welcome to Paradise." He spoke in a mild, educated voice, and Routledge began to feel slightly less afraid. "What's your name?"

"Routledge."

"First name?"

"Anthony."

"Good. It's on your papers, but I have to ask you. You were at Exeter, right?"

"Yes."

"Do you know where you are now?"

"Lundy?"

"No. Sert."

Routledge shut his eyes. Christ, O Christ.

"Do you think you can manage to walk?"

"Yes. I think so."

"You've got to see Mr. Appleton."

"Who's Mr. Appleton?"

The question was not answered. In a more business-like tone, the man said, "If I let you out of your sleeping-bag you won't try anything, will you?"

Routledge did not fully understand. What was there to "try"? But he nodded, and, apparently satisfied with this response, the man unzipped the bag and helped Routledge to his feet.

As soon as Routledge tried to stand unaided his legs gave way. He sat down heavily on the bed, overcome by giddiness, wanting to fight back the burning taste rising in his throat; but it was no use. The struggle was lost even before it had started. He was too weak, too frightened, too stunned by the realization of what had happened to him. He could not help himself.

Bending forward, he retched repeatedly, succeeding only in bringing up a few viscid strings. There was nothing in his stomach.

"You might have told me you were going to do that."

"I'm sorry," Routledge tried to say. He was shivering so badly that he wondered whether he were truly ill. A new fit of retching overtook him.

"Mr. Appleton won't see a man who's smelling of vomit."

Whatever they had poisoned him with, it must have been a massive dose. "The bastards," Routledge said to himself. "The bastards." For weeks past, months, he had been struggling to contain his outrage and despair. It had been bad

enough before, but since landing in that cell at Exeter with
those two animals his self-control had been stretched beyond
human endurance. And now that he was here, now that the
worst had finally befallen him, there could no longer be any
bottom to his grief.

He began to cry.

The futile attempt to void his stomach had already filled
his eyes with hot tears. Now these were supplanted by a
fresher and more copious flow. His wrists had been so firmly
bound with nylon cord that he was unable properly to cover
his eyes with his hands. This minor indignity alone, heaped
on top of all the others, was enough to move him to further
self-pitying sobs.

Routledge thought he heard the man say something sympathetic. He felt an awkward hand placed momentarily on
his shoulder.

Sniffing and wiping his face, Routledge managed to re-
cover himself slightly. The man's voice was cultured, the
voice of someone who had read books and listened to music,
someone whom one could address in the old language that
Routledge had been learning to keep hidden from view. "I'm
sorry," he said, two or three times. "Forgive me."

The man fetched a can of water and, with a rag, wiped the
mess from Routledge's clothes. Routledge saw that his prison
uniform had disappeared: instead he was dressed in an ill-
fitting black sweater, a threadbare shirt, and a pair of patched
and baggy dark twill trousers. "Take the rag," the man said.
"Clean your face up a bit."

While Routledge did as he had been told, the man brought
a comb from the mantelshelf. With his wrists bound together, it was no easy matter for Routledge to comb his hair.
His awkwardness, the reason for it, the nature of his surroundings, the future that awaited him—all these suddenly
conspired to reveal the absurdity of rearranging his hair in
this way, to set it in a pattern devised and approved by a
society which for him would never exist again. It almost
began to seem funny. He realized then how near he must be
to mental exhaustion, emotional collapse, outright madness.

There was nothing funny about his predicament. Nothing whatever.

"That'll do," the man said, half gruffly, as if he were ashamed of having displayed a trace of sentiment just now. "Do you think you'll be able to walk all right this time?"

Routledge nodded reluctantly. He was dreading what was coming next, his interview with the ominous Mr. Appleton. From what he had read and seen on television, he knew a little about the organization of the penal colonies, of which Sert had by far the worst reputation. There were no warders, no guards: the authorities never set foot on these islands, using helicopters to drop supplies or fresh prisoners. He himself must have been flown out from Exeter this morning or last night and dumped, unconscious, for Mr. Appleton and his henchmen to find. For presumably, and judging from the note of awe in the man's voice when he had mentioned the name, this Appleton had set himself up as leader, or chieftain, and Routledge was about to be presented for his approval or otherwise. If the interview went well, Routledge would have a chance of surviving. If it didn't, he would soon be dead. That much he had already guessed. But, whether it went well or badly, the outcome was really just the same. The lawcourts would have been kinder and less hypocritical to have hanged him. The punishment he faced now, with Mr. Appleton or alone, was infinitely worse.

These were the thoughts he had entertained for the past months, waiting for this to happen, hoping against all reason that his status would be revised, that he would be put in some other category. In prison he had decided to commit suicide if he were sent to one of these places. The decision then had seemed absolutely unshakable; but now he found he had already abandoned it. As the man took his elbow, Routledge understood why it is that human beings can so readily be made to dig their own graves.

"By the way," the man said. "My name's King. Brian King."

"How do you do," Routledge said.

The door, such as it was, consisted of what looked like odd planks of driftwood held together by two crosspieces.

King lifted it open on its rope hinges, and went back to extinguish the lamp before leaving.

The night was extremely dark, unseasonably cool and fresh, with heavy cloud. Yesterday had been wet; perhaps today also. "I wonder," Routledge said, taking the first steps beyond the threshold, "I wonder if I might . . ." and he searched his vocabulary for an appropriate phrase, ". . . take a slash before we . . ."

"Yes, of course. Anywhere there. Off the path."

"Thanks." The urge to urinate had been almost the first thing he had been conscious of on awakening; indeed, that urge may of itself have brought him around.

"I'll have to keep hold of your jersey."

Routledge clumsily unzipped his fly. Much as he wanted to relieve his bladder, nothing would come. So long as King continued to clutch the back of his sweater, Routledge knew he would be unable to do it. He needed privacy.

"What are you waiting for?"

"Nothing."

Then Routledge saw that he could no longer afford such niceties. His bladder was giving him a plain signal. For its own good, for the welfare of his body as a whole, it was demanding to be emptied at once. He was holding back for no sensible reason, for a reason that had nothing to do with survival or self-preservation.

Consciously he abandoned his inhibition, let it go, and immediately the flow of urine began to fall, unimpeded, into the darkness.

Routledge took the opportunity to look about him. Little could be seen. The bothy or shack from which they had just emerged seemed to be one of a group, perhaps a dozen, perhaps more, loosely clustered about the central precinct where he was now standing. In several, dim yellow lights were flickering at cracks in doors or shuttered windows. Across the precinct stood a more imposing building, almost a bungalow, within which much whiter, stronger lights were burning. Routledge's apprehension grew. Was then Appleton so important, so powerful, so much above the run of his subjects, that he had electricity, while they burned feeble lamp-oil?

"Is that where Mr. Appleton lives?"

Again the question went unanswered. It was as if Routledge hadn't spoken, or as if he had made some solecism which superior breeding bade his companion overlook.

On closer inspection Routledge saw that the building was indeed a bungalow, professionally constructed. The path to it across the precinct felt and sounded underfoot like shale. In front of the house it gave on to a broad area that seemed to be paved with slabs of stone. From the slabs, a flight of low steps led up to a porch or veranda where a man, barely visible in the light seeping from a window-shutter at the left, was seated by the door. He rose at their approach.

"Who's that? King?"

"Yes."

"Got the new boy with you?"

"He came round just now."

The guard appeared to be armed with a club. He knocked lightly at the door and said, "New boy's here." His accent had its origins in the East End of London; his manner and bearing exuded authority, privilege. Routledge's apprehension grew yet more.

"Come on, Stamper, open up!"

There was a sound of bolts being drawn back. The door opened, releasing a widening shaft of light which spilled across the boards of the veranda and illuminated the guard, a man in his twenties with curly dark hair. The club he was holding was in fact an iron bar, the sort with a pointed end used for digging post-holes. Besides this, attached to the belt of his corduroy jeans, he was equipped with a machete in a broad leather scabbard. His plaid shirt looked new, much better than any of King's clothes, and on his feet was a pair of workman's boots with heavy-duty rubber soles.

"Right, you," he said, addressing Routledge. "Inside."

2

As if in a nightmare Routledge stood facing the panel, or tribunal, at whose center sat the graying, middle-aged man who had just opened the proceedings by introducing himself, politely enough, as "Appleton." "On my right is Mr. Mitchell, and this is Mr. Stamper. Mr. King you already know, of course. Mr. King: your report, please."

King nervously prepared himself to speak. He was standing a little way to Routledge's left.

The two men had spent half an hour waiting to be summoned to Appleton's presence, sitting in a small, stuffy, and drably furnished room deep inside the bungalow. The hint of sympathy that Routledge had first detected in King had been confirmed by his subsequent demeanor. He had struck Routledge as a genial, essentially harmless man who seemed incapable of committing any crime at all, still less one that could have landed him in Category Z. In other circumstances Routledge might have tried to make more conversation with him. As it was, they had sat in virtual silence. The single question that Routledge had ventured to ask had been answered: the bungalow, King had explained, had been erected for the warden in the days when Sert had been a nature reserve. Apart from the lighthouse, and the ruined cottages of Old Town—the former fishing village—it was the only proper building on the island, and certainly the only one fit to be lived in.

Routledge knew, for his own sake, that he should have questioned King more, pumped him about Appleton, but he had felt too ill and frightened to make a start. Then the one called Stamper, the one who had first let them in, had conducted King and Routledge to this considerably larger room, formerly, perhaps, a reception area for visitors or a laboratory for the biologists who must have stayed on the island.

The room was about six meters square, lined on two sides with fitted cupboards faced with gray laminate. The floor was of parquet, much worn and scuffed but, like everything in the house, scrupulously clean. Faded floral curtains hung at the three large windows, one of which ran behind the inquisitors' trestle table.

Routledge had been mistaken about the lighting. There was no electricity; the bungalow was instead lit with incandescent pressure lamps running on gasoline or kerosene. Three were burning in this room, hissing softly, two hanging from the ceiling and a third standing near the center of the table, just in front of Appleton and to his left.

In the pool of light under this lamp Routledge saw a flimsy sheaf of papers—possibly relating to himself—next to which was a quantity of clothing, neatly folded and arranged.

"He gave his name correctly when asked," King began.

"Did you tell him where he's been sent?"

"Yes, Mr. Appleton."

"Anything more?"

"No." King checked himself. "I did tell him how this house came to be here."

"That was a mistake, Mr. King."

"Yes. I'm sorry. I also told him that the lighthouse exists, and the houses at Old Town. Nothing more. Just that they exist."

"Very well." Appleton's expressionless brown eyes examined Routledge for a moment. "Go on. Did he talk in his sleep?"

"Yes, but nothing made any sense. He said 'Louise' once or twice."

With a confirming forefinger Appleton briefly consulted his papers. Routledge wondered what else Appleton knew about him, besides the name of his wife. "What happened when he awoke?"

"He threw up, or tried to. Then he started to cry."

"Was this after you'd told him where he is?"

"Yes."

"Anything else?"

"Only that he wanted a piss."

"Yes, well." Appleton glanced from side to side. It appeared that neither Mitchell nor Stamper wanted to contribute to this part of the interrogation.

"Will that be all?" King said.

"Yes. Yes, thank you. We're most grateful to you, Mr. King."

King moved obsequiously to the door and let himself out. Routledge was sorry to see him go.

Appleton picked up the papers and absently scanned the top sheet. "Anthony John Routledge. Born April sixth, 1960. Late of Exeter Prison."

Routledge had been standing for some time now. He began to fear his legs would give way again.

"Sentenced last year for the rape and murder of one Jacqueline Lister."

"I didn't do it."

"It says here you're married with one child."

"Yes. That's right."

"The 'Louise' you mentioned in your sleep. Your wife?"

"Yes."

"Are you a homosexual?"

"No. Of course not."

"Ever had any homosexual tendencies or encounters?"

"No."

"Sure?"

"I'm sure."

"It also says you were a quantity surveyor."

"Do you mind if I sit down? I'm not feeling very well."

Appleton looked from side to side, as if to say, "Any objections?" There were none, so he motioned Routledge to help himself to one of the plastic chairs by the door.

"A quantity surveyor," Appleton went on. "Working where?"

"London, most of the time."

"Ever go abroad?"

"Yes."

"Please be more forthcoming."

"I worked in the Middle East. In Qatar. And Kuwait."

"Doing what?"

"Building a hospital in one, roads in another."

"Senior position?"

"Yes. Fairly."

"Meaning?"

"I was resident quantity surveyor on site."

"So you know a bit about civil engineering?"

"You could say that. But only the theory. I know more about materials and measurement."

Appleton made a pencil note on the topmost sheet. "What were your hobbies?"

"I played golf."

"Any interest in, say, electronics? Radio, computers, that sort of thing?"

"No. We used computers at work, of course."

"Ever write any professional software?"

"No. I mean, I couldn't. It's beyond me."

"What about do-it-yourself? Woodwork?"

Routledge shook his head. "I'm sorry," he said. "I haven't got any skills you'd find useful."

"That's for us to decide," Appleton said, so coldly that Routledge feared he had made a major blunder. The interview was going wrong, badly wrong: Routledge had been unable to take the initiative, and now it was all slipping further and further from his grasp. In the intense, unhealthy glare of the lamps the room seemed more than ever a scene from a nightmare. He noticed that Appleton and the others, like the guard on the door, were wearing relatively new clothes. Appleton's were the newest and best-fitting. Stamper and Mitchell seemed by their very postures to defer to him; Routledge wondered whether they were to take any active part in the proceedings at all.

Appleton gave the papers a further leisurely examination.
He finally looked up. "Since you are in Category Z, we can
assume you enjoy good health. You are thirty-seven years of
age and a man of some intelligence and education. Apart
from your conviction, you have no criminal record. It is in
my discretion to recommend that you be offered a place in
the Community. Before considering such an offer, you will
naturally want to know what the Community is and the terms
on which you will be admitted to it."

Routledge did not know whether he was expected to respond. He looked from Appleton to Stamper and then to
Mitchell. "Yes," he said. "On the mainland . . ."

"On the mainland they tell many lies," Appleton said.
"Mr. Mitchell, kindly explain the objects of the Community."

Almost imperceptibly, Mitchell became more upright in
his seat. He was about thirty, with dark, close features. The
skin on his face bore the ancient scars of severe acne.
"Well," he said, in a rather thick and husky voice; and with
that one word Routledge placed him in a social class the
advertising industry might have called "C plus." Routledge
suddenly realized that, as an Englishman, he had been con-
ditioned throughout his life to categorize everyone in this
way. King, the guard, Stamper, Appleton—whom he had
judged to be on a level marginally superior to his own, and
now Mitchell: Routledge had done it to them all.

"On Sert at any one time are about five hundred men,"
Mitchell said. "Of these, at present, one hundred and eighty-
three belong to the Community. We live here in the Village
in houses built by cooperative labor. We grow our own produce and keep livestock. We organize expeditions to catch
the wild goats on the island, to collect seabirds and eggs,
and to salvage anything useful that gets washed up on the
beach. We run educational classes. Some people attend the
church. But whether they are religious or not, everyone here
tries to make the best of it." He paused; he seemed to have
reached the end of his set speech, for such, Routledge had
guessed, it was.

Routledge was completely nonplussed. The idea of the

convicts attending church was so far removed from the stories he had heard that he began to doubt the validity of any of his preconceptions.

Appleton now resumed talking. "We also liaise with the Prison Service. Not because we wish to have any truck with them, but because they provide things that are useful to us. It is part of my duty, for example, to interview new arrivals and keep a ledger. If a body is found we are asked to identify it and let the Prison Service know. To help us with this, they send particulars with each prisoner." He tapped his pencil on the papers. "These particulars have told us something about you, Mr. Anthony John Routledge, but we don't take too much notice of that. They are mainland particulars, compiled by mainland men. Our opinion of you is and will be, of necessity, based on different criteria altogether. As Mr. Mitchell has rightly said, everyone here tries to make the best of it. In this we are aided by each other. We have nothing else but that. Before we admit a man to our midst, therefore, we must be reasonably certain of his character and his propensities. Much as we would like to extend a hand to those outside the Community, the exigencies of survival on Sert deny us that pleasure." Appleton sat back, elbows on the arms of his chair, holding his green pencil lightly at each end. "Mr. Stamper, will you go on?"

Stamper, a round-shouldered man of forty-five or fifty with spectacles, blue jowls and wet, red lips, bore a resemblance to an unpopular physics master who had taught at Routledge's old school. His voice, though, grating and harsh, was quite different.

"The rules of the Community are these. You will work as directed by the Father. You will not intentionally injure any member of the Community or damage Community property. You will not lie, steal, cheat, or engage in deviant sexual practices. As there are no women here, that means you are allowed to do nothing to anyone or anything but yourself. Do you understand the rules?"

Routledge was slowly becoming convinced that he was after all dreaming; or had gone mad. "Who . . . who is the Father?" he said, looking at Appleton.

"All in good time," Appleton said.

"The advantages of life in the Community are self-evident," Stamper continued, "as you will doubtless discover. The greatest, perhaps, is the opportunity to be a man."

Appleton broke in. "One of the Father's sayings. You will understand it in due course."

"Breach of the rules is punished by expulsion," Stamper said, and folded his arms, as if to indicate both the finality of his utterance and the end of his speech.

"Don't get the idea that we are Communists here," Appleton said, smiling faintly. "The Father is in control of the Village. Absolute control. It is he who decides who stays in and who stays out. The Father has examined your papers, and indeed inspected you when you arrived. He has authorized me to make this offer and, within the limits decided by him, to set the terms."

Routledge remained silent.

"Every man in the Community must earn the right to be here. He must demonstrate that he can look after himself and will not be a burden on the others. The way he does this is to remain outside the Community for a specified period of time. The standard period in July is ten days, more if we have doubts about him, fewer if we do not. The Father also recognizes that a man's age and former mode of life play a part in determining how long he can survive alone. You had a fairly sedentary sort of job, are not yet middle-aged, and, on the face of it, might be a useful member of the Community. I have therefore decided that you will remain outside for six days."

Mitchell and Stamper gave barely perceptible signs of approval.

"One hundred and forty-four hours after you leave here tonight, a bell will summon you to the main gate. If you then wish and are able to ask for a place in the Community, and present yourself within one hour of the bell, you will be taken to the Father. You will prostrate yourself before him, renounce all rights, and humbly beg for admittance. Is that clear?"

Routledge nodded.

Appleton pointed at the pile of clothing next to the lamp. "This is what you arrived in. The rest of your property is in a cardboard box in the corner, courtesy of the Prison Service. The whole issue consists of enough clothing to last you about two years, some vegetable seeds, and sundry hand-tools. You may take all or part of it now, or leave it here for safe-keeping, in which case you will be given a receipt. What do you wish to do?"

Routledge involuntarily looked down at the old clothes he was wearing.

"They are a gift to you from the Father," Appleton said. "You are under no obligation to return them at the end of the six days."

"What . . . what do you suggest I do?"

"That is not for me to say."

"Is there a waterproof jacket in the issue?"

"Yes. One waxed cotton and one PVC."

"The PVC. I'll take that."

Appleton made a pencil note.

Routledge said, "What happens if I'm not accepted?"

"We keep it all."

Routledge began to grasp the full implication of his impending ordeal. "Do you mind if I look through the box? See what else I might need?"

"It's your property."

At Appleton's request, Mitchell brought the box and put it on the table. There was more clothing than Routledge might have expected, and of a better quality than mainland prisoners wore. The tools were mostly for gardening: a hoe head, a hand-fork, a small trowel, but there was also a long sheath-knife, which Routledge decided to take.

Right at the bottom of the box was a slim pad of yellow forms. Mitchell took it out and gave it to Stamper.

"These are your requisition slips," Stamper said. "You are allowed five requisitions a year. Each requisition is in two parts. In the first you can ask the Prison Service for certain articles of hardware or clothing. It tells you on the back what you can have and how often. The second part is forwarded to your friends or relatives, if you have any. You can ask them for luxuries like extra food, books, toiletries, and so on. Anything, provided the Prison Service agrees, and provided it can go into a parcel no greater than twenty-five liters in volume and twenty kilos in weight. Luxury parcels are delivered in strict rotation. They come over on the next available helicopter, as soon as there's space. Drops are made every Tuesday, weather permitting, or on the first suitable day thereafter." Stamper reached into his breast pocket and brought out a ballpoint pen, which, together with the pad of slips, he proffered to Routledge. "Will you sign them, please? All of them."

Routledge hesitated.

"Perhaps we should explain in more detail," Appleton said to Stamper.

Stamper, immediately acceding, continued in the same matter-of-fact tone as before. "If you remain outside," he said, "you won't be having any requisitions. Outsiders are not allowed near the drop zone. If you enter the Community your slips will of course be returned to you. Signing will cost you nothing, and will be regarded as a token of good faith by the Father. Alternatively, you are entirely free to take them with you. You understand that, if you remain outside and have taken your slips, you will immediately be reported dead so that another prisoner can be received. On the other hand, if you are outside but have left your slips, you will officially remain alive until they are all used up."

"I'll sign."

With the pad on his knee, Routledge began the task of signing each of the numbered slips in turn, making on it the unique set of marks with which, in his former life, he had solemnized and authorized all his dealings with the world. After several repetitions his signature started to appear increasingly unfamiliar, a meaningless scribble of black ballpen on yellow government paper. The yellow itself was of an artificial shade which soon began to have a peculiar effect on his eyesight, such that the black ink seemed to be acquiring a progressively browner tinge, which was also imparted somehow to the surrounding view—his knee, his hand, the floor: he did not pause in his work or dare to look up.

As Routledge continued signing, Appleton resumed talking. "It goes without saying that, in the event of your failing to join us, your slips will be used only for requisitions on the Prison Service. By accepting the terms of our offer, you have already become a probationary member of the Community. All property left by an individual on his death is taken into Community ownership. The resources budgeted by the State for your upkeep here are your property, because they come from contributions made by you during mainland life. They are therefore legitimately transferred to the Community if you remain outside, since those outside are regarded as dead."

The signing was over; Routledge was relieved of the pad and pen. Mitchell gave him the PVC jacket and sheath-knife and a receipt for his remaining property.

"Good," Appleton said. "That's it. You've got six days." He stood up, and the others did the same.

Routledge remained seated. "What do you mean, that's it?"

"Exactly what I say. You will now leave the Village."

Routledge was afraid, but he was also beginning to get angry. "At night? Now? Without even anything to eat or drink? Without any proper explanation of what I'm up against?"

"Mr. Mitchell, get Mr. Myers."

Myers, he supposed, was one of the guards. "Wait," Routledge said. "Wait—please. At least tell me somewhere safe I can go till morning. You owe me that, if nothing else. You've got my stuff. I signed the slips, like you asked."

"Mr. Mitchell."

Mitchell, ignoring Routledge's pleas and protestations, went to the door and called into the corridor.

"No," Routledge said, before Myers had had a chance to appear. "It's all right. I'm going. Just show me the way."

3

At dawn Routledge saw the cliffs for the first time and, in spite of everything, could not contain a gasp of wonder, and of a feeling, in some deep, secret, and unacknowledged corner of his heart, of excitement that now and forever he was sentenced to live in such a dreadful place.

He came upon them almost unexpectedly, in the middle of fighting his way through the dense scrub of stunted willow, gorse, and holly which blanketed this part of the island. Where the trunks of the trees were exposed to the full force of the Atlantic gales they were burnished to silvery gray; the lower branches were hung with gray-green lichens in a profusion he had never seen before. Underfoot were clumps of flowerless bluebells and many other plants whose names he did not know and, in damp hollows, thick tufts of giant woodrush. He heard and saw no birds except one, a big black crow, perhaps a raven, which passed overhead just a few yards to seaward.

A moment later he was at the very brink of the land, where the vegetation yielded and the reddish earth of the clifftop lay exposed. Sections of ground had crumbled and fallen here: he drew back a little and took firm grip on the wrist-thick bole of a dwarfed rowan tree.

"My God."

The cliffs were at least a hundred and fifty meters high. He was standing at one side of a large cove, curving outward to his right, making a shallow bay terminated by a jagged stack. Beyond this, repeating the same formation but on an even more majestic scale, another bay stretched into the half-light. At the farther stack the shoreline turned and there was nothing but the dark, dawn-misted expanse of sea.

Most impressive of all was the suddenness with which the cliffs fell away. In places they appeared almost vertical. The rock was stratified, consisting of thick, perpendicular layers, each one aligned in the same direction and pointing slantwise out to sea, so that, in the middle of the cove, it presented a torn and uneven face, but at either side the open layers made an overlapping series of smooth, artificial-looking expanses of stone.

Especially in the middle of the cove, slabs of rock had calved off and crashed, littering the shore with colossal rubble. Against and among these slabs, and on short stretches of stony dark beach, the sea broke with a dutiful sort of monotony, swilling through the channels and crevices and occasionally throwing up a listless shower of spray. A dozen meters out and directly below the place where Routledge was standing, a ridge of rock lay athwart the tide. With each incoming wave the sea poured over the ridge, making a seething waterfall; and as each wave returned it poured back, making now a waterfall on the other side. Elsewhere were ridges that as yet were too high for the tide, or others that had already been submerged, only their peaks jutting above the surface of the foam.

A single white canister, perhaps an old plastic bleach-bottle, lay washed up on the beach. Except for this there was no trace of human life, no evidence whatever of civilization or mankind. Bleach-bottle apart, the view from this spot could not have changed materially in the past three thousand years.

After gazing for a moment longer, Routledge remembered himself and turned back into the scrub. He was searching for a suitable place to hide, somewhere he could safely sleep.

He was no more than two kilometers from the Village here, on part of the coast facing west. As far as he could tell, the Village was sited on a peninsula at the south-western corner of the island, isolated from the rest of Sert by a fortified border made from two young thorn hedges with an intervening no-man's-land of stakes, concrete rubble, rusty barbed wire, and other materials retrieved from the ruined lighthouse, perhaps, or from wartime defenses on the beaches, or both. The gate through which he had been expelled last night was sited at the western end of the border, and was itself fortified even more heavily than the rest. Three men had been on guard, armed with clubs and machetes; one had been carrying an ax.

Routledge had spent the night, cold, hungry, and desperately thirsty, lying in the bracken a few hundred meters from the gate. It had been too dark to go further without risk of injury. As it was, he had fallen over several times, and had nearly sprained his ankle in a rabbit hole.

In the very first grayness of morning he had begun to move away, in line with the coast, first climbing some rising ground to see what he could of the Village and of the island where he was destined to spend, as the judge had told him, the remaining term of his natural life.

The light had been too poor to see much. The vegetation was composed of rough grassland and scrub, with bracken, gorse, and, especially near the cliffs, expanses of dwarfed, scrubby woodland. The soil seemed poor and overgrazed; Routledge recalled that Sert had once been used for sheep farming. A hazily remembered television documentary about Sert—there had been a national outcry when this, and the other islands, had been taken over by the Home Office—had traced its occupancy from the Middle Ages, when it had been the site of a monastery, through to the final decline of the farming population in 1930 or so, concluding with the subsequent importance of Sert as a nature reserve. Sitting in front of his TV set—how long ago had that been?—in his comfortable, complacent living room, Louise beside him on the sofa, the pale blue display of the video blinking discreetly in the soft, lamplit gloom under the screen, what would have been his thoughts had he known what he was really watching?

He wished he had taken more of it in. Now all he remembered was that the vegetation of the island, this vista of impoverished scrub, was a legacy of too many sheep and too much grazing. And rabbits, introduced no doubt by the monks.

His survey had not lasted long: he had been too frightened of being seen. He had made out the border fence disappearing across the hill, the gateway, the roof of the bungalow, and the form of a number of other buildings in the Village. Most looked pretty crude, like King's shack. The Village was larger than he had thought, and was probably larger still, with much of it hidden by the contours of the land.

Unless he had been mistaken, he had glimpsed the movement of two or three men patrolling inside the border, approaching his vantage point. He had not waited to see more.

During the night he had feared that he would be unable to find water, but, almost immediately after his brief survey, he had come across a tiny rill springing from the rock and making its way down to the cliffs. The rill was scarcely more than a trickle, and at first he had not known how to get enough to drink. He had tried lying full length with his mouth open and his cheek pressed hard against the stone, but that had not worked. Then, despite the cold, he had started to take off his shirt, in order to soak the water up and squeeze it into a depression made in the back of his PVC jacket; when a better idea had occurred to him. Using the cuff of the jacket as a scoop, and with the sleeve twisted higher up, he had simply collected as much as he had wanted. Contaminated as it had been by the flavor of plastic, the first full gulp of water had seemed to Routledge the most wonderful he had ever tasted.

The most pressing of his problems, water, had thus been solved. Food was not so important. If necessary, he could survive for the whole six-day period without eating anything at all, although he felt that this would not do his cause much good when he returned to the Village. In order to score maximum points, in order to win the greatest possible respect and thereby the best chance of advancing himself in the Community, he had guessed that he had not merely to survive the ordeal, but to survive it with ease and style.

Going over what he had discovered during his time in the

Village, he saw that he had actually, despite Appleton's efforts, learned quite a lot. The mere fact that Appleton, doubtless following the rules laid down by the "Father," had tried to send Routledge out in total ignorance of the conditions awaiting him, this fact alone was extremely revealing about the mentality of the people he was, in the long term, up against.

From King's demeanor in front of the triumvirate, as well as from differences in clothing and a number of other clues, Routledge had surmised that, in the Community, status was all. The high status—measured by his clothing and by his failure to call Stamper "Mr."—of the guard at the bungalow door seemed to show that status was achieved principally, if not solely, by closeness or usefulness to the Father. Repellent as the idea was, Routledge saw that his only chance of future comfort was indeed to gain admittance to the Community and once there to do everything in his power to achieve high status.

If the inmates of the Village really lived by their own code, then he could assume that none of them had told him a lie. It followed that the figures Mitchell had given of the island's population could be believed. He had said that one hundred and eighty-three men lived in the Village out of a population of about five hundred in all. That meant there were something like three hundred and twenty convicts living outside the Community, a fact which Routledge had seized upon the instant the words had escaped Mitchell's lips.

These three hundred and twenty were the essence of Routledge's short-term problems. The clubs, machetes, and iron bars; the general air of security surrounding the Village; and the sheer labor and discipline required to plant, construct, maintain and patrol the boundary fence: all this spoke eloquently of the behavior of the outsiders. Or rather, "Outsiders," for that was almost the way Stamper had said the word. Presumably they were the hard-core crazies whom not even a society like the Community could digest. Presumably, too, they were disorganized, or spent their time fighting among themselves; otherwise, combined, they would surely have already mounted an irresistible assault on the Village, if only to gain their rightful access to the helicopter drops.

Appleton had criticized King for having revealed the origins of the bungalow and the existence of the lighthouse and the houses at Old Town. Why? What significance did such information have? Was Old Town where the outsiders lived? Or the lighthouse? Or both? It seemed possible. Why then had King, who by all appearances was no stranger to the combined task of nursemaid and watchman to new arrivals, why had he said what he had? Perhaps he had felt a genuine sympathy for Routledge, a sympathy which in different circumstances might have been a precursor of friendship. Perhaps he had wanted to warn him. Or perhaps it was more subtle than that. But no. "That was a mistake," Appleton had said. Routledge had already had to assume that Appleton and the others lived by their own moral code, which meant that Appleton had not lied to King.

The need to avoid all contact with the outsiders was paramount. King had as good as warned him to keep away from Old Town and the lighthouse. In order to do that, Routledge had to find out where on the island those places were. By its name, Old Town must have been an early settlement on Sert and thus must have had some sort of harbor. So Old Town was probably on the shore or close by it. The western and northern coasts would take the full brunt of the weather. Hence the harbor, if there was one, was probably on the east or south coast. But the Village was at the south-west corner of the island, which made the east coast more likely. As for the lighthouse, that might be almost anywhere along the cliffs.

This was all the most tenuous guesswork, but it looked as if Routledge would be safer keeping to the western part of the island—indeed, as close to the Village as he reasonably could. He did not suppose that all three hundred and twenty of the outsiders lived at Old Town and the lighthouse, or that they were incapable of roaming the rest of Sert, but he had nothing else to go on.

He did not even know how big the island was. From what

he had seen already, it seemed to be at least five kilometers in diameter, and maybe more.

Besides keeping clear of the outsiders, his predicament resolved itself into three distinct components: finding water, food, and shelter. Water he had already found. For food he would try catching rabbits, or birds, or even fish, though he had no idea how to go about such a task. This immediate area near the Village might provide him with enough to eat; otherwise, he would have to wander further and increase his chances of an encounter with the outsiders.

The more urgent necessity, however, was shelter, a base. He had entered the scrub with the hope of finding somewhere, and now, turning away from the cliffs, he resumed his search.

The various conclusions he had drawn had been the product of a lucid, detached rationality which bore little relation to the way he was actually feeling. During the hours of darkness, lying awake in the bracken, he had more than once caught himself being surprised by his ability to think clearly in such circumstances. For that, he supposed, he had to thank his education, and the head for detail needed in his work. For the rest, his former life had left him completely unprepared. He was not even particularly fit. Except as an impersonal exercise in logic, the uncertainty about the next few days—never mind the time after that—was too much for him to contemplate. As soon as the awareness that it all applied to him threatened to intrude, he tried to push it aside before terror overwhelmed him. For he was terrified, truly terrified. He thought he had been frightened last night, in King's shack, in the bungalow afterwards; he thought he had been terrified in custody, and standing in the dock, and at Exeter; but all that had been nothing. Now he knew what terror meant. As he forced his way through the branches, a phrase flashed unbidden through his mind, making worse the sensation, in his thorax, that he would soon be entirely unable to breathe. *This is real.*

It was dawn in July. At this corresponding instant last year he had almost certainly been asleep in bed, four hundred kilometers away at his house in Rickmansworth. At this instant now, all over the country, men such as he had been were also asleep in bed. Yet he, Anthony Routledge, was here on this island forty kilometers off the north Cornish coast, and, dirty, unshaven, hungry, wanted for the moment nothing more than to find a lair among the clifftop scrub.

The wind coming off the Atlantic was the authentic ocean wind, unbreathed as yet by anyone but himself. Its smell was the authentic ocean smell; the muffled roar of the surge was the authentic ocean sound. These obstructive branches were authentic too, wild, uncultivated, growing without human interference or restraint. And in just the same way his plight was authentic. All his life there had been, at bottom, the possibility of help from someone else in an emergency. No longer.

Thirty meters from the cliff edge he came across an especially dense thornbush with its branches forming a partial dome. The ground under the bush had apparently subsided, leaving a smoothly contoured hollow thinly covered with grasses. He stopped and looked around. The slope of the land was such that this spot would be visible only from the sea or from the more inaccessible parts of the surrounding cliffs. Beyond the thornbush the scrub extended for another thirty or forty meters before giving way to more open ground.

Routledge got down on his haunches and examined the hollow more closely. It did not look very inviting; he had known better hostelries than this. But it was safe, and it was relatively dry.

Rubbing a hand across his stubble, he hesitated before going further, still unable to rid himself of an irrational, self-conscious feeling that he was being watched.

He looked up, directly overhead. The thought had just occurred to him that he was indeed being watched. They might well have a satellite in orbit for precisely this purpose.

He considered sticking out his tongue, or thumbing his nose, or making some rather more emphatic gesture. But that was not his way, and it would merely give them something else to smile about. If they were watching. And if they weren't, the gesture would not only be futile, but also, somehow, the act of a man in the very earliest stages of madness.

Like talking to himself. He had been doing it consistently now, under his breath as if he were afraid of being overheard; and it was time to stop.

However sophisticated their cameras, they would be unable to see through the overarching foliage of the bush. He crawled into the hollow and after a few experiments found the most comfortable way to lie down, with his head given as much shelter as possible. Yes. This would do.

He told himself he ought to make a start on finding food. He would go back to the rabbit warren and try there, see if he could find a young one out on its own, or else rig up some sort of trap.

But he did not move. He was very tired. The drugged sleep he had awoken from in King's shack had left him feeling utterly drained. His subsequent terrors and exertions had drained him still more, and now, before facing the next part of the onslaught, all he wanted was a little time to recuperate.

He shut his eyes.

Enclosed by the branches, enclosed within himself, the difficulties he had just been facing, out there in the daylight, seemed immediately to recede. They belonged again to some other person, not to himself.

Routledge heard the wind in the leaves. He heard the distant waves, and, a little while later, the deep, throaty *prronk* of a raven's cry. It came only once, and was instantly swept away on the wind. He listened for it again, drifting in and out of his thoughts, thinking of all that had happened and all that would be.

Forgetting to listen, he abandoned himself completely, let himself go, and fell at last into a heavy, unhappy, and dreamless sleep.

4

"GAZZER. OVER HERE."

"What you found?"

"He must have came this way."

Routledge was instantly awake, his heart pounding so hard that he had difficulty in hearing. Two men, at least two, were very close to his lair. The first who had spoken sounded like a black man, the other, Gazzer, a white.

They were searching for someone. For him.

What an imbecile he was! They would have seen the helicopter; they would know that a new prisoner would probably have been landed; they would know the procedure. Where more logical to look for the new man, and his clothes, and anything else he might have, than in the vicinity of the gate? From the gate he would have left a clear trail through the bracken and across the wet grassland. They would have seen the places where he had stumbled, the flattened bracken where he had spent the night. They would have seen where he had drunk from the rill, and then . . . then the trail into the scrub.

So. This was how he was going to die.

The sun had come out. From the look of the light, it seemed that it was now mid-morning. He must have been asleep for several hours. The wind had softened and become warmer.

"No sign of him."

29

"I tell you he been past here. Four, five hours since."

The voices were even closer now, coming from somewhere over his left shoulder. Two meters away. No more. He was paralyzed: if he moved he knew he would make a sound and that would be the end.

There came a long silence. Finally the white man said, "Let's go on."

More vegetation was parted and crushed. They were leaving.

And then it happened.

In a conversational tone the white man said, "What's this?"

Routledge looked around. A human male, a thing, a creature of about twenty-five, hands on knees, was half bending, head cocked, and peering into the space under the bush.

"Jackpot."

Routledge sat up.

"Been asleep?"

The man's hair could not have been cut or washed for several months at least; his beard not for many more. In his right hand he was holding half a meter of rusty angle-iron. He was dressed in tattered jeans, almost rags, and a sleeveless jacket, an outlandish jerkin of what Routledge guessed was goatskin, black and brown and white. "Like Robinson Crusoe," Routledge thought. "No: Ben Gunn." Dangling from his neck was a string of assorted shells. His arms and face were, under the filth, deeply tanned. As the man began a slow smile, Routledge saw that his few remaining teeth were rotten, but his eyes, in contrast with his skin, shone with a clear, intense, maniacal healthiness.

"I said, 'Been asleep?' "

"Yes," Routledge said. "Yes, I've been asleep."

"We thought you was. Didn't we, Winston?"

The black appeared. "I'm warnin' you, Gazzer. Don't call me that."

"Just a joke."

"You been to the Village?" the black said to Routledge. He did not seem quite as tall as the white; his clothes were no better. His chief garment was a stained and grimy cotton blouson, originally pale cream. Under this he was wearing a blue T-shirt with the faded remnants of a circular yellow logo, now illegible. His dungarees, green corduroy, were too short, revealing bare ankles in a pair of grubby trainers. He looked about forty. Instead of angle-iron, he was armed with a heavy wooden club, much carved and polished.

"Course he's been to the Village," the white man said. "What's your name?"

"Anthony. Tony."

"Get here yesterday, Tony?"

"Yes."

"Have a nice ride on the 'copter? Yeah? What d'you reckon to our little island, then? Nice, innit?"

There could be no escape. They were being careful to block the only way out, and even if he did get past them they would catch him in the scrub, bring him down, and kill him. From the impudent way they were standing he could tell they knew he was soft and weak, fresh from the mainland, while they, veteran survivors, were as fit and hard and ruthless as any man could be. In their faces he could see their thoughts about his life, his job, his background, his money.

"I said it's nice."

"Yes."

"Where was you? Dartmoor?"

"Exeter."

"What you here for?"

"I . . . I . . ."

"He's here for wanking his cat," the black man said. "Who gives a shit? We're wasting time. We want fun, right?"

"You goin' to come out of there?" Gazzer said.

Routledge began to make his mind work. He started to crawl into the open.

"Don't forget your jacket, Tony."

Once, on a Harrow street corner, he had been mugged by three blacks. He had made the mistake then of trying to appease them, of answering their insolent questions, of telling them the time when asked, of revealing his wristwatch and the way he spoke. And now he had begun to do exactly the same thing again. Also a mistake.

"You want to ream him first?" the black man said, as Routledge emerged.

The white man did not answer. His hand had gone to his fly. He grinned at Routledge, looked at the black man, looked back at Routledge. "Get down on your knees and pucker up."

"That's it, Gazzer," the black man said. "That's it. Give it to him like th—"

He interrupted himself with a scream.

Routledge had no idea what he was doing. In the next instant, having already, somehow, lunging forward, managed to slash his sheath-knife across the exposed, obscenely semi-erect length of the white man's penis, he turned and with all his strength thrust the blade into the black man's chest. He was momentarily too astonished to resist; the point entered somewhere near the middle of his left breast pocket. After a fleeting resistance, as if the steel had been delayed by intervening bone or cartilage, the knife slid in as far as it would go. Routledge felt the molded brass of the guard hurting the upper joint of his thumb; he pushed even harder, clutching with his left hand at his victim's collar.

In the corner of his eye Routledge saw the white man standing immobile, his angle-iron club dropped and forgotten, hands held apart and slightly spread, staring downwards, his wild, mad, tangle-bearded face a pantomime mask of incredulity. His penis had been all but severed. Almost no time had elapsed: yet the wound, in the richly vascular substance of his erectile tissue, was already spouting blood.

The fetid smell of the black man's clothing filled Routledge's mouth and nostrils, his face pressed hard into the shoulder of the blouson. Close by his right ear came a gurgling sound, and he felt the sudden wetness of blood or mucus or saliva penetrating his hair.

The black let his club drop. Already dead, the whole weight of his body toppled forward on the knife. His arms closed Routledge in a heavy embrace. Routledge began to fear he would be unable to get the knife out: the sheer weight of the corpse was threatening to overwhelm him, but he gave a vigorous tug, and another, and the blade came free. Routledge twisted aside, allowing the body to fall forwards, and turned back to face the white man.

His jeans were soaked and splashed with red, yet still he had not moved; still he had not uttered a sound. He looked down at what had been done to him and looked up again.

In his eyes Routledge saw an expression of stupefied resignation, from almost the same source as that which appears in the eyes of a rabbit about to be killed; but this was essentially human, and, addressed at a far deeper level than mere language, directly to another man's heart, made a primal and uncomprehending plea for mercy.

The man took a step backwards. Holding Routledge's gaze for as long as possible, he turned and, half bending, holding out one hand in protection, began to crash his way through the scrub.

Routledge's first instinct was to let him go. The man would surely bleed to death anyway. But then again, he might not. And he might be found by other outsiders, who, for all Routledge knew, were also out searching for the new arrival.

He bent down, retrieved the angle-iron club, and, with the knife in his left hand, set off in pursuit.

An hour later it was finished. With much physical difficulty, wearing the PVC jacket to help protect the rest of his clothes, he had managed to drag both bodies to the edge of the cliffs. The black man's had tumbled loosely, hitting an outcrop a glancing blow and then falling almost unhindered to the beach. The other had struck a ledge halfway down and was now lying, spread-eagled, in full view. That could not be helped.

The wounded man had put up a fight. Routledge had hit him many times with the angle-iron club, in the face, on the head.

Now it was over.

Routledge felt cold. His hands were trembling. Images of what had just happened kept repeating themselves in his brain.

He was in a state of profound shock. As he crouched by the rill, trying to wash the blood from the jacket, he wondered how much longer he could tolerate the knowledge of what he had done.

In the space of a single hour his whole view of himself had been defiled. He had actually become what everyone else believed him to be. And this time he had murdered not just one, but two of his fellow human beings.

The sun had grown even warmer. Routledge felt its heat: on the back of his hands, being absorbed by the dark fibers of his sweater. The water was pure, crystal-clear. The instant it came into contact with the blood it flowed slightly back and then onward in swirling patterns of alternately lighter and darker, translucent, maroon.

As he handled the jacket he realized that, for several minutes past, he had become increasingly conscious of texture and color, shadow and contrast, of the sheer volume of detail being returned to him by his eyesight. His hearing had become more acute and detailed, too; his sense of touch, everything. It was as though he had never used his body before, except somehow at second hand.

With a twig he tried to clean the blood from the stitching on one of the big black buttons. This. Essentially this. This jacket. They were going to kill him for this.

He supposed he should now be feeling sick, but it was far more complicated than that. His main sensation was disgust, with himself, and with them for having forced him into it. He felt dirty as well as nauseous, ashamed, guilty; but he also felt glad, and relieved, and lucky. And at bottom he felt surprised, and proud, of his own strength and daring, and of the decisive way he had behaved once it had become obvious where his only course of action lay.

He was still alive, physically unhurt. He was up here; they were down there. He was still in possession of the jacket. In short, he had won, and they, they who had brought violence upon themselves, had lost.

"You want to ream him first?"

That's what the black man had said. There had been no doubt about it. "We want fun." Afterwards they would have killed him. With the angle-iron, or with the wooden club, or with both together. They would have taken his jacket, his sweater, shirt, trousers, underpants, his boots and socks. Gazzer would have put the trousers on at once and thrown his old jeans down next to the body. Winston—whatever his true name had been; Routledge might never know—would have raised an argument. One sock each.

"Have a nice ride on the 'copter? Yeah? What d'you reckon to our little island, then?"

The reality was far worse than anything Routledge had foreseen. He could not survive much more of this. Perhaps he had been right before. Suicide was the only rational answer to a place like Sert. For, even if he got into the Village, he knew it would not end there.

He discovered that he had been scrubbing mechanically at the same place on the jacket. He stopped.

The flow in the rill was barely adequate, but he lay down and tried to wash his hair, especially on the side where he had felt the black's slobber. He had been scrupulously careful so far not to touch it or to put his fingers to his lips or eyes. The same with the blood. Especially the blood.

When he had finished he stood up. Using its pop-stud, he fastened the sheath of his knife to one of the belt loops on his trouserband—the Father had not given him a belt. The sheath itself he tucked inside his trousers, leaving the handle protruding at a ready angle. Once, twice, he made an experimental grab at the knife. It came out quickly and cleanly.

The wooden club seemed a handier weapon than the angle-iron, which he now hid in the bracken just above the rill. He had no plans to come back here, but plainly the angle-iron was too valuable to be hurled away at random. The rill he had contaminated: he could not drink from it again. This spot was anyway too near the Village; and, of more importance, the area bore too many signs of activity. He had already delayed dangerously long. Besides, sooner or later he would have to solve the problem of food.

Behind the outcrop where the rill emerged, the ground rose in a fern-clad slope to a broken ridge where more of the native rock lay exposed. Up there, more of the island would be visible, and he could make a better decision about where to go next.

Except for the breeze, and the rill, and the sound of the sea, the air was utterly silent. For the first time, he noticed an absence of the vast generalized roar—of traffic, aeroplanes, factories, washing machines, refrigerators, the background noise of hundreds and thousands of people going about their daily lives—which had been his constant companion on the mainland. Even in his cell at Exeter, even during the worst and deepest part of the night, the sound had come at him from the direction of the city. Now it had ceased. Forever.

He skirted the outcrop and started pushing a way uphill through the forest of chest-high bracken.

There was something almost menacing about its luxuriance. This hillside belonged to the bracken's kingdom, and it brooked no intrusion, especially from a foreigner, a soft white mainlander like himself. The green fronds made a sea; in the half-light at ground level the stems were tough and snagged mercilessly at his ankles. The soil consisted of a dry, tobacco-like mulch, the legacy of countless generations of fern. Mingled with the summer's heat, it had taken into itself, absorbed, and corrupted the pungent smell of the fresh foliage, and now, like a giant radiator, was slowly giving it back.

There was no path of any kind, no record of the passage of human or animal feet. Routledge was having to make his own path, one that could be clearly seen and followed; but for the moment that could not very well be avoided.

The ground climbed steeply. Meter after unrelenting meter, the gradient drained the strength from his legs and from the whole of his body. With each step he became more conscious of the solid, the lifeless tons of soil and rock of which the hill was made. He was not used to physical exertion. His heart seemed to be beating dangerously fast, and with every intake of breath his throat burned. Despite the fact that he had already removed his jersey and rolled up his shirtsleeves, he was sweating profusely. The sweat attracted still more the swarms of flies he was disturbing as he went. The flies on the cliffs had been horrible black things, like huge, shiny mosquitoes; these were more like houseflies, but smaller and drabber and more persistent. He decided to break off a fern frond to use as a whisk.

"Get here yesterday, Tony?"

The voice had sounded so real that he abruptly stopped and looked around. He was three hundred meters from the cliff edge here; the place where it had happened was already indistinguishable from the rest of the clifftop scrub. The cliffs themselves, their beach, their newly acquired jetsam, were of course invisible. From the imagined position of the bodies, foreshortened somewhat by his present elevation, the blue, mist-hazed surface of the sea extended smoothly to the horizon. There were no other islands to be seen, no ships. Discounting surveillance by satellite, which he now thought unlikely, the only eyes exposed to the evidence of his crime were those of an indolent gull, floating past on the updraught.

No—it didn't happen. None of this is happening.

Sometimes, at home, in the real world to which he knew he would at any moment return, he had been awoken in the early hours by a crash, as if made by burglars downstairs. After lying in the dark for five or ten minutes, his heart thudding, he would get up and venture to the top of the stairs. Standing in his pajamas, getting progressively colder, he would listen and listen. He was standing like that now, waiting for the equivalent of the innocent creak, the noise of contracting wood or metal, that would let him accept the crash purely as a product of his own imagination and return to bed. He was waiting for some proof that this was all an illusion.

A fly alighted on his lips and in an instant he spat it away, brushing a hand across his face. He felt the stubble there. This was no illusion.

"He's here for wanking his cat."

"Shut up!" he said, out loud. "I will not go mad. I refuse to go mad. I will die the way I want to die. I will die as myself." But wasn't this already the beginning of madness, to be talking like this?

"I haven't got a cat. Can't stand the bloody things." Couldn't stand their superior attitude, their cruelty, their selfishness.

Why had the black said it? Because, because, in a poetical sense, he had been absolutely right. That's exactly why Routledge had ended up taking a ride on the 'copter. Wanking his cat: the sum total of his life before the arrest.

"That's not true!"

Yes it is.

"Stop it! Stop it!" Get a grip, you silly bastard! O Sweet Jesus, they'd done it to him this time all right! First the police, the courts, the jailers, and now last night. They could have taken him into the Village straightaway. They must have seen what sort of bloke he was. But no, they'd sent him out, the bastards, the evil rotten bastards. Like an overgrown Boy Scout, that Appleton bastard had loved every minute, they all had. And now they'd done it. It was their fault, what had happened. *No: it hadn't happened. It couldn't have happened.*

Routledge could bear it no more.

Flailing the black man's club, slashing blindly at the bracken and the flies, he began to run uphill, stumbling through the ferns, making for the ridge.

5

THE ONLY NATURAL HARBOR OF ANY SIZE ON SERT LAY AT the north-eastern corner of the island. A small, deep bay, protected from the open ocean by a scattering of rocky islands at its mouth, the harbor was edged on its inner side by a strip of fine, white sand called Town Beach: for, almost adjoining the beach, stood the remains of what had once been Sert's principal settlement.

In the five years since the island had first been used as a penal colony, Old Town had been wrecked almost beyond recognition. Never prosperous, even in its nineteenth-century heyday, the settlement had at least been characterized by a certain neat neighborliness springing from the simple, God-fearing existence led by its inhabitants. The fifty or sixty dwellings, made of stone and roofed with slate, and each with its own stone-walled garden to front and rear, had mostly been built facing the beach, along the cart-track joining the minister's house with the stone and concrete quay.

Some of the houses had been burned down, others demolished in the search for slates or useful blocks of stone. None was now much more than a blackened shell.

The largest of those still standing had been the steward's house, used for many years after the war as a small hotel for the naturalists and holidaymakers who had visited Sert. To the front was a stone terrace overlooking the quay; to the rear, the gardens and arboretum on which the hotelier had expended so much time and labor. The greenhouse had long since collapsed, every pane of glass removed or smashed. The kitchen garden, the hedges and lawns, were now a jungle. The exotic palms had been uprooted, every tree cut down.

After the evacuation, Home Office gangs had cleared the hotel, as well as the rest of Sert, of anything likely to aid an escape attempt. Officially this meant any object that might be used in the construction of a boat. In practice it gave the gangs license to destroy whatever they felt like destroying. Of all the buildings on the island, only the warden's bungalow had escaped the spree, and then only because he had remained there until the last possible moment.

The hotel had served the Home Office men as a billet, so it had not fared as badly as, for example, the lighthouse. Nonetheless, before leaving, they had removed entirely the upper floor and, as a parting gesture, had set fire to the remainder.

Since then the hotel had been assailed by the inmates themselves. That so much had survived this long was due in large measure to the old-fashioned values of the craftsmen who had built it, and in the rest to the fact that it had quite early been taken over by Alexander Peto for his residence.

Peto sat down on his bench overlooking the quay. Once he was seated, Obie, Desborough and Brookes sat down too, at their accustomed places, on the boulders set there for the purpose.

This was where Peto held his council, in imitation, Obie supposed, of the Father, the hated Franks. Not that anyone in Old Town cared what Peto or his council said. All that could be claimed for Peto's town was that its inhabitants had reached the unspoken agreement that, while actually there, they tried to refrain from attacking one another. The same agreement obtained in Houlihan's rival camp at the lighthouse.

The population of each camp varied between a hundred and a hundred and fifty. Men went from one to the other just as they pleased; or joined the utter outcasts who, alone or in pairs, lived wild.

Obadiah Walker had managed to survive in Peto's shadow. For a while he had been his reluctant bed-mate; but now Desborough had come along and that had changed.

Peto squinted down at the harbor, at the pale line of beach curving away to the right. From here virtually the whole town could be seen. What could not be seen, behind the hotel and the hillside rising above it, two and a half kilometers away around the coast, was the stained white tower of the light-house; but Obie could guess well enough what Peto was thinking.

Without moving his head, Peto said, "Houlihan's gone too far."

Obie silently agreed. He was surprised how well Peto was managing to contain his rage.

"We's going to have to do something."

"He wants us to, of course."

"And after all that shite last spring," Desborough said, meaning the protracted negotiations about territory and graz-ing.

"I say get him back," Brookes said. "Go direct. Just take him."

Peto treated him to a moment's disdain. "The question is, if we don't do nothing, what'll he do next?"

Obie had made the discovery earlier this morning. Peto's prize billy had been stolen from behind the hotel, its tether cleanly cut. Peto doted on the animal, and had even bestowed on it a name—"Billy." This, while none too imaginative, in Obie's view, was a measure of Peto's fondness, for none of the other goats had been so honored. Peto liked to watch Billy in action and drew vicarious pleasure from his perfor-mances. Billy's offspring always received preferential treat-ment, and indeed he had contributed in no small measure to the steady improvement in the Old Town flock. And now he was gone.

There were four possible explanations. The first was that one or more of the wild men had taken him. But the wild men did not breed goats. They hunted the goats which, like themselves, roamed wild. It would be an act of senseless bravado for a wild man to enter Peto's private ground to steal something he could come by at no risk.

Alternatively, Billy might have been stolen by a raiding party from the Village. Even Peto admitted, though, that the Village stock was in every way superior to his own, Billy included. Although Franks was capable of anything, and the possibility could not be dismissed out of hand, there was no obvious reason for the villagers to have taken Billy.

The third explanation was that someone in Old Town itself was responsible. That presupposed there was a way of keeping Billy or his remains concealed from Peto's view, which there wasn't. Besides, no one else in Old Town bred goats or took an interest in stock. Outside the Village, the only other man on the island who did that was Houlihan.

There could be little doubt that it had been an act of deliberate provocation. Obie could even see an amusing side to it: dark, bizarre, grotesque, typical of Houlihan. But more than this, the development was ominous. It was tantamount to another declaration of war. The truce seemed to be coming to an end.

"Get Martinson and Gazzer," Peto told Obie. "Go over the light and see what you can see."

"Gazzer's not here, Alex," Obie said, apologetically. "He went up Perdew Wood. Him and Tortuga."

"Who else went up?"

"Bruno, Zombie, Barry, couple of others."

"Where's Martinson?"

"In his place."

"Get him, then. And you, Jez. You go."

"Take the binocs?" Obie said.

"Sure."

Obie stood up. "Reckon they got the new meat yet?"

"Keep an eye out for that and all."

Routledge did not stop until, having scrambled across the warm slabs and boulders of the final outcrop, he had arrived at the ridge. The climb had exhausted him. His pulse was racing, fluttering, his heart palpitating, all his internal warning-systems far into the red zone. In the frenzy of his ascent he had somehow managed to convert a little of his mental distress into its physical counterpart, and that was easier by far to handle.

Panting, wiping his brow, he found himself looking out over two kilometers or so of uneven gorse and bracken extending towards the interior of the island. Stretching away gently downhill, the scrub thickened to a distant stand of trees, slightly less stunted and windformed than those on the cliffs; but the main impression was one of desolation.

He had been hoping for something different: he was not sure what. By now his hunger was making him light-headed. This was not a landscape which promised easy pickings.

He had two choices. He could go inland, or he could stay with the coast. The sea, if only he could get down to it, might offer rockpools with crabs, or limpets which could be pried off with the knife. And wasn't seaweed supposed to be edible? There might also be birds' eggs on the cliffs: Mitchell, the third man in the triumvirate, had said something about that. But surely by now the breeding season was over. Was there a better chance of finding food inland? Rabbits, perhaps, though they were also to be found on the cliffs. Last night he had already come across one warren.

On balance, he decided, the coast would give more opportunities for finding food. Following the coast would also enable him to explore the island more systematically and get an accurate idea of its size. The terrain on the clifftops seemed marginally easier to traverse.

Unfortunately, for this same reason there was a greater danger of encountering further outsiders on the cliffs. The cliffs themselves, by cutting off one line of retreat, would make it harder for him to evade capture.

A mewing cry above him and to his left caused him to look up. A large, ragged bird of prey, brown and paler brown, was soaring on broad, slotted wings, sailing in circles fifty meters over the scrub. Then he saw there was another beyond, and another. The first bird was joined by the others and for half a minute all three engaged in a sort of aerial display during which some question of pairing or territory seemed to be settled. As the party split up, one of the birds flew directly over his position, examining him briefly as it passed.

Routledge realized that, for the last half-minute, while watching the birds—at first he had taken them for eagles, but now he thought they must be buzzards—his mind had been relieved of its preoccupations. For that short but merciful period he had been allowed to forget himself. The likelihood that he had already taken leave of his sanity appeared to have receded; there was still a chance that he would not go mad.

He watched the buzzard's lazy course towards the south. With one last wide, graceful circle, it vanished behind a rise in the land.

Even in the short time since he had left the rill, a faint white haze had robbed the sky of its clarity. The sun had become an amorphous region of brilliance, too bright to be looked at. The breeze had dropped. Without it the air felt close and sticky.

The Village lay in that direction, south. He considered returning to the outskirts to do what he should have done at dawn—make a thorough reconnaissance. What difference would it make if he were observed by the guards? But then that was where the outsiders would be concentrating their efforts. Reconnaissance of the Village could wait a day or two until things had died down.

He did not know what to do. Still he had no plan, beyond searching for something to eat.

"Logic," he said aloud. The cliffs: food, but danger. Inland: less danger, food uncertain. What was easier to face at the moment? Hunger, or the chance of getting caught and killed?

It was easy, after all. Logic dictated that he should go inland.

Just as he began to move forward again he noticed that the knife had disappeared.

The sheath was empty. With mounting panic he searched the pockets of the jacket, knowing perfectly well the knife would not be there. He saw himself once more down by the rill, making practice grabs at the hilt, playing the Red Indian:

hadn't that been at the back of it? God, how ridiculous he was! Without the knife there was no possibility of food, or of defending himself from another attack. No self-respecting savage—not even one of his friends under the cliff—would have made such an elementary blunder. He had let the bracken take away his most valuable possession.

He could have dropped it anywhere. There was no choice but to go back and look. That meant exposing himself to view for at least three times as long as he should; it meant leaving a trail three times as prominent as it need have been; and, what seemed at this moment infinitely worse, it meant making all over again the wearisome ascent of the hillside. And at the end of it there was no guarantee he would even be getting the knife back.

He was again close to tears, but was so angry with himself that he refused to allow them to come. He could see that, until now, he had been indulging himself like a child. They were dead, those two. They'd asked for it, and he'd given it to them. That was all. It was not in his nature to go around killing people: there was no need to regard himself as a murderer. No need for remorse, or self-pity, or anything but relief that he had been strong and quick enough when the moment came.

Above all, there was no need to let scum like that bring him down. He was determined to get into the Village. That was his goal, and they weren't going to stop him.

Yes. He found he had made the decision to survive. Perhaps he had made it just now, or perhaps it had been formed last night, when he had awoken in King's shack, or when he had decided to let his urine flow, or on the cliffs, when he had successfully defended himself against murder. Perhaps the decision had been reached in stages.

However it had happened, it had changed entirely the way he perceived his plight. He saw now that state of mind was just as important as the means of finding physical subsistence, if not more so. Loneliness, guilt, fear: all these weakened the will to survive. Even more corrosive was the stupidity which had already cost him his knife.

As he retraced his path he wondered how many more such

body-blows there would be to his self-esteem. Even after his experiences in prison, the Anthony Routledge who had landed here yesterday had been a man of insufferable conceit. He was conceited still; so conceited that he was pluming himself with the thought that he was beginning to come to terms with his fate. There was no reason to suppose he was doing anything of the kind, or that the violent fluctuations in his mental state would not continue or get worse, plunging him yet deeper into derangement and despair.

The idiocy with which he had behaved so far appalled him. First, he had muffed the interview with Appleton. No—even before that, he had wasted the time he had spent with King. Then he had failed to make a proper reconnaissance of the Village. After that he had literally allowed two outsiders to catch him napping. Finally, and most shameful of all, he had lost the knife.

Was this the same man who had held such a high opinion of himself on the mainland, who had silently sneered at and looked down on everyone else? What must he have been like at home, with Louise? Or in the office? In his everyday dealings with people in shops, on the telephone, everywhere?

The bracken was not menacing, or merciless, or anything but a living organism doing its best to look after its own interests. It had not taken his knife. He had, moron that he was, simply gone and lost it, and now he was having to pay the price.

6

To be entrusted with Peto's binoculars was a sign of high rank at Old Town. Obie, lying flat on his stomach, Martinson on his left, Brookes on his right, was making the most of it.

The binoculars had once belonged to a man named Barratt; Peto had acquired them during the war with Franks. They were small and squat, covered in green rubber. A red badge on the front said *Leitz* in white script. They magnified by a factor of eight, and even now, having circuitously arrived in Peto's hands, and after several subsequent years of hard use, they were in perfect working order. More than once the binoculars had saved Peto's skin, or given him advantage over Houlihan or one of the others who had been and gone.

Obie turned the focusing wheel and again brought the lenses and prisms to bear on the rooms below the gallery.

"Let's have a go," Brookes said.

"In a bit."

Obie and his two companions had taken up a position on the cliffs overlooking Angara Point and the lighthouse, four hundred meters east of the light and about a hundred above it. Seen from here, the upper part of the structure was set against the sea, the rest against the brambles, turf and granite of the cliffs. The base of the lighthouse was about fifty meters above high-water mark. In front of it, the rest of Angara

47

Point extended, in a broken group of outcrops and islands, another three hundred meters out to sea.

Once pure white, the walls of the lighthouse were now streaked and stained with rust from the twisted remnants of the gallery, and blotched with scabrous patches where the rendering had fallen away; none of the windows in the turret had survived.

At one time a deep-cut concrete road had led up to the light from a jetty in Crow Bay, but Houlihan had half filled the road with rocks to make it impassable and secure his defenses on that side. A number of sheds and other buildings, more or less temporary, had surrounded the lighthouse. All had been demolished or burnt.

"In't that Feely?" Martinson said.

"Where?"

"On the helicopter pad."

Obie switched to the old asphalt landing pad, now covered with weeds and tufts of grass. A bald man in a red shirt was climbing the steps leading to the lighthouse door.

"Yeah. That's him."

Martinson's eyesight was impressive. Obie looked aside from the binoculars. Without them he could hardly even make out Feely at all.

"The old stonk," Martinson said.

"I wouldn't put it past him to have had that goat," Brookes said.

"Boffed him, you mean?" Martinson said. "No, I wouldn't put it past him, neither."

Feely, so named for his wandering fingers, belonged to what Houlihan called his "brain gang," three or four advisers who lived with him in the lighthouse itself.

The rest of the lighthouse citizens were consigned to the "tombs"—small, dome-shaped dwellings made of stone, scrap iron or timber, roofed with wood and turf. Nineteen of these structures were grouped around the light, and another thirty-two a little further down, by the well. They varied in size, housing between one and five men: most held two or three. At any one time about a quarter were in disrepair.

Billy was not on view. There was nothing unusual about

the scene, nor even any clue that the atrocity had been committed. Two men were prodding with hoes at Houlihan's vegetable garden; another had just milked his white goats. The rest of the lighthouse goats were feeding on the cliffs above Crow Bay and in the designated areas beyond. Billy was not among them.

"They've got him under cover," Brookes said.

"My turn," Martinson said, holding out his right hand for the glasses.

Obie, and Brookes, decided not to argue. Like a number of people on the island, Martinson was a psychopath: at least, that was the conclusion Obie had reached after long acquaintance with the man. He was supposed to have murdered seventeen women, though the total kept increasing. Martinson himself had never spoken of his crimes, and no one wanted to ask.

Obie watched him adjusting the focus. Despite his usual laconic, easygoing manner, Martinson was one of the few white men Obie really feared. He was well over one ninety, more like one ninety-five, with massive shoulders and long, powerful arms and legs. The word was that he had Swedish blood, even though he had reddish-blond hair and a pale complexion, rather like Franks, who came from County Cork. Martinson could well have been Irish too, though he spoke with a Birmingham accent. Or perhaps he was of Danish origins. The way he wore his hair, in flowing locks tied up with leather braids, and the abundance of his mattress-like beard, reminded Obie of the lunatic death-dealing Norsemen, insanely brave, whose longboats had brought terror to the English coast. His taste in garments had something of the Viking about it too. He would have looked good in a horned helmet, carrying off the headman's daughter.

Obie had never known Martinson to have anything to do with sex. He lived alone in his hut. For food he relied mainly on hunting. Rabbits he chased and killed with a mallet, an amazing feat of agility for so big a man. In season he ate eggs, young puffins and shearwaters, and fulmars, kittiwakes and murres from the cliffs. He also made regular excursions to the Village to steal their stock. In addition he received, from the other towners, occasional Danegeld of oatmeal or vegetables.

Martinson was one of the first convicts to have arrived on Sert. During the war with Franks he had sided first with Barratt, then Houlihan, then Tompkins, then gone over to Peto, and so had never even been invited to join the Community or given Franks a chance to kick him out. Barratt and Tompkins were dead now, the first murdered by Peto and the second beaten to death by his own men. Since the present state had been established Martinson had shown no interest in telling others what to do, though he was regularly employed by Peto as a bodyguard or to discharge missions, such as the present one, which contained an element of danger. To that end Martinson maintained in his hut an alarming array of weapons: most fearsome, perhaps, was a captured Village crossbow, one of several built for Franks by Randal Thaine.

This morning the crossbow had remained behind. Obie's brief was simply to try to establish that it was indeed Houlihan who had taken Billy.

"See anything?" he asked Martinson.

"No. We're going to have to go down."

Obie agreed. "Jez," he said, accepting the binoculars from Martinson and handing them to Brookes, "you wait here. If we aren't come back by noon, go and tell Alex. Right?"

"Sure thing, Obie."

They passed unchallenged among the upper tombs; Obie even paused to talk to a former towner who had fallen out with Peto and moved. At the helicopter pad, though, they were stopped, disarmed, and questioned by three of Houlihan's retinue, and only then were they admitted to the tower.

The double oak doors at the main entrance were set at the top of a low flight of reinforced concrete steps. Painted bright green, the woodwork was now flaking, the bare patches weathering to silvery gray. Inside the threshold was a storm lobby, and beyond this lay the large ground-floor room which had been the communications center. Two doors led off to the kitchen and mess; an iron staircase gave access to the upper floors. Under the staircase, an open hatchway led down to the cellar.

"Wait here," said McGrath, one of the guards. "I'll get Himself."

Obie had not been inside the lighthouse for three months, not since the grazing agreement had been reached. Nothing much seemed to have changed.

None of the windows, set deep in the thickness of the walls, had more than half a pane of double glazing left, and the steel shutters had gone. There was nothing to keep out the ferocious northerly and westerly gales of winter: the cellar, its drainage blocked, was almost permanently flooded with black bilge. The smell, together with the universal stink of stale fulmar oil, pervaded the whole building. Obie would have known where he was with his eyes closed.

The lighthouse also smelled of burned wood; the white-painted interior walls had been scorched and blackened by a series of both accidental and wanton fires. Houlihan's personal apartments, though, were said to be relatively habitable. He occupied the two floors above this one.

"Yes?" said Feely, appearing on the staircase.

"We want to talk to Houlihan," Obie said.

"Well you can't."

Feely was one of the few lighthousers who shaved, using a cutthroat razor which he honed on his belt. Like Martinson, and Houlihan himself, he was a founder member, a child killer who had almost been too old for Category Z. What remained of his hair was gray. He had lost his dentures last year, so that he could no longer eat raw meat and had become virtually dependent on cooking. That meant he was dependent on Houlihan, since Franks wouldn't have him in the Village, Peto hated his guts, and wild men seldom had the means or opportunity to cook their food. Feely had been a professor or something on the mainland. He was clever. He was also a homosexual by preference. Obie despised him.

"It's important," Obie said.

"If Peto wants to talk, he can come himself. Whatever you've got to say, you can say to me."

Obie glanced at Martinson, who gave a slight shrug.

"It's just," Obie began, "it's just that Alex's billy has disappeared."

" 'Disappeared'?"

"Last night," Martinson said. "He thinks Archie might know something about it. He thought, seeing as how Archie's his friend, Archie wouldn't mind if we had a quick look round."

"Are you accusing Mr. Houlihan of stealing Peto's goat?"

"No, course not. It's just that, like Obie says, Billy's disappeared. He might have wandered this way, like. One of youse lot might have taken him in, not knowing who he was. That's all we're saying, in't it, Obie?"

"That's right."

"I seem to remember Mr. Houlihan giving his word of honor on the goat question last April. I seem to remember him and Peto making a covenant. He gave his word, which is to say, his sacred bond. And now you two come here with a demand to search his property."

"It's not like that, F—" Obie began, just stopping himself in time. "It's not like that, Harold."

Feely crooked his finger at McGrath. "Show these men the way back to Old Town." Then, ignoring Obie, he addressed his final remark to Martinson. "If you two pillocks come round here again, you'll be sorry."

Martinson saw him first.

"Hello," he said.

"What is it?"

"Quick. Give us them glasses."

After leaving the lighthouse, Obie and Martinson had returned to the cliff to collect Brookes before continuing with their mission. Since Houlihan, through Feely, had denied the charge so strongly, Martinson had suggested that it might be worth taking a look at the Village stock, just in case Franks had, after all, been responsible for stealing the goat. They had now followed the coastline as far south as Illislig Bay.

Martinson raised the binoculars to his eyes. "That's it, dummy," he said. "Go on. Show us what you got."

"What?" Brookes said. "What is it?"

"If I in't mistaken, I'm looking at the new meat. Buggeration, the way he's looning about he must want to get caught."

Obie took the binoculars. "Where? I can't see nothing."

"Inland, about a kilo from the crest. In line with Pulpit Head."

Among the low gorse and bracken scrub a distant figure came suddenly into Obie's view: a dark-haired man in a blue shirt and dark trousers, clutching some black clothing in one hand and something else—perhaps a stick—in the other. It seemed he had just come down from the ridge and was making his way towards Perdew Wood and the middle of the island. Even at this range it was apparent, both from his general demeanor and from the mere fact that he was crossing such a visible stretch of ground, that he was completely ignorant of the basic rules of Sert. Either he was a wild man gone off his rocker, or he was, as Martinson had surmised, the new meat.

"How do you want to play it?" Obie said: for it was Martinson's privilege, having found the quarry, to decide.

"It could just be a trap," Martinson said. "It could be wild men. They could've seen us coming. Still, he's clean-faced. It's got to be him." He smiled at Obie. "We'll get him in the wood. If someone else don't get to him first."

At least seven men from Old Town, and probably a similar number from the lighthouse, had set out to look for yesterday's arrival. The Prison Service helicopter had touched down at its usual hour, in the early afternoon, and Bruno had reported a prisoner deposited for Franks's people to find.

The landing place was well inside the Village boundary, impossible to get at from outside, an expanse of close-cropped turf where the pilot was guaranteed a clear view in all directions. From the hedge, Bruno had watched the usual routine of boxes and sacks of stores being left, and had seen the full plastic canisters of mail unloaded and the empty ones taken away.

During this process the pilot always kept the rotors turning. Despite the cozy agreement with Franks, the crewmen never wasted any time on the ground. As soon as they could they would scramble into the hatch, the turbines screaming and a widening gap already appearing between the under-carriage and the turf, leaving, as often as not, one more unfortunate wretch to join the population of Sert.

But new meat was new meat: the only source, outside the Village, of factory-made clothing, boots, and news of the world at large. Thanks to the system of initiation Franks had adopted, the outsiders had at least a chance of exploiting this one commodity.

The weekly or fortnightly hunt was becoming something of a sporting occasion. Obie had even detected a certain ri-valry between the towners and the light. Because of Franks's terror of AIDS and HVC, if and when new meat was caught, the growing custom among the more rampant stonks was to make sure it failed the medical examination performed at bell-time by Sibley, the Village vet.

Quite often the hunt drew a blank. Occasionally the wild men got there first and only a corpse, perhaps mutilated, would be found.

Martinson did not normally deign to participate. Kept sup-plied with island-mades by Peto, he had little need of factory clothes, and very few new arrivals wore boots large enough for Martinson's feet. As for the outside world, Martinson was interested in that not at all. Like anyone, though, Martinson presumably saw the value of catching the meat as far as rank was concerned. It would do him no harm with Peto and the others to bring back the spoils.

Perdew Wood occupied part of Sert's central plain. The wood was merely a continuation and intensification of the scrub on its northern and western sides. In few places did it attain the status of real woodland; few of its rowans, thorns, and oaks could be classified as more than stunted versions of mainland trees. However, the wood provided the largest single area of cover on the island. For that reason it was almost invariably the choice of new arrivals, especially when they were not too bright; and, inevitably, the wood attracted the largest numbers of hunters.

As it was so late in the day it seemed likely that most of the hunters had by now given up or gone elsewhere. This, at least, was the hope Brookes had expressed on entering the wood; certainly there was no sign of any competition.

Among all the men at Old Town—and at the lighthouse too, for that matter—Martinson had developed the most formidable outdoor skills. He had adapted completely to his new life; it was unimaginable that he could ever go back to the way he must have been before. On those few occasions when he had accompanied Martinson on food-gathering expeditions, Obie had been able to observe at first hand Martinson's awesome tracking ability.

He found the trail without difficulty, separating it from those made earlier by the passage of other legs through the undergrowth. After striking for the middle of the wood, the trail turned more to the north, passing through a glade of gnarled oaks and rowans scarcely more than head-high. The undergrowth here contained clumps of bluebells as well as brambles and bear's-garlic and male fern. Martinson squatted to examine the color and texture of some damaged leaves. Then, from the soil nearby, he plucked a tiny brown toadstool. It had been trodden on: the cap was bruised, and colorless juice had seeped from the stem.

He arose, grinning malevolently, and presented the toadstool to Obie.

"Ten minutes?" Obie guessed.

"Five." Martinson raised a forefinger and touched his lips. "Listen."

Almost on cue came the sound of a dead branch snapping underfoot, like a dull pistol-shot echoing through the trees.

It was followed by more sounds of clumsy progress, no more than two hundred meters ahead.

7

THE SEARCH FOR HIS KNIFE HAD TAKEN ROUTLEDGE AS FAR down as the rill. It had not been there, so he had again turned back on himself and eventually, after a meticulous examination of every centimeter of ground, had found it not fifty paces from the ridge. The knife had fallen and been caught by the bracken in such a way that, the point uppermost, it had scarcely been visible to someone coming down the hill.

He estimated he had wasted at least two hours on the search. The sky had clouded over completely by the time he had returned to the ridge and set out, down across the bracken and gorse to this area of more imposing scrub, even woodland, wind-shaped and flattened when seen from above, greenly gloomy and claustrophobic once inside. The undergrowth, deprived of light, was relatively sparse and easy to get through.

He had dug up a few bulbs and roots and had cautiously tasted them. The first he had spat out instantly: it had tasted vile, like concentrate of garlic. Even the leaves of this plant, resembling those of lily-of-the-valley, generated a revolting musk. He had got some sap on his fingers and now could not rid himself of the smell. None of the other roots had been edible.

He had never been really hungry before. His stomach hurt; he felt dizzy. For the first time in his life he began to know what hunger meant.

He crouched and turned over a flat rock, looking for he knew not what. A woodlouse scuttled away from the light;

three more were clinging on blindly. A small, pale brown slug. Two blue-black beetles. In Africa the natives ate termites, or their larvae, or something, by pushing a twig into the nest. The twig, with its cargo of grubs, was carefully extracted and then pulled between the lips. In France they ate snails. What was a slug, if not a snail without its shell?

Routledge put the rock back.

The decision to forage inland was already looking like a mistake. There was nothing in these woods for him. He should have trusted his instinct and stuck with the coast. There had to be easier ways of finding food than this. Real food: rabbits, seabirds, shellfish.

Several times since retrieving it, he had taken the knife out of its sheath and examined the details of its construction. The banded pattern, fawn and brown and black, of the hilt; the brass guard, the long, strong steel of the blade, were the products of a technology which, compared with anything available to him now, was fantastically advanced. On the mainland he would scarcely have looked at the thing twice. Now he admired it as a collector might admire his most coveted possession. The knife belonged to him: it was his. He valued it, in a way he had not known since his childhood. And the knife was already his accomplice, his trusted friend. It knew his secret. On his service its point had entered and breached a human heart.

He stood up. He would definitely take his chances and go back to the coast.

"You won't be needing that," the white man said.

He was the tallest of the three, the heaviest and the most frightening in appearance, with ginger hair tied in a ponytail, a huge red beard, and a goatskin jacket which in style owed more to the Visigoths than to contemporary Britain. Only his incongruous Birmingham accent gave him away.

His two companions were younger, both black, dressed in ragged jeans and sweatshirts. The first, who also wore a skimpy and much stained leather waistcoat, was wiry and small, carrying a spear, a length of reinforcing steel rod sharpened to a point, below which hung a bunch of seagull quills. Round his neck Routledge was amazed to see a pair of rubber-armored roof prism binoculars costing, at current prices, some six hundred pounds. The second black, of average build, with a sheepskin headband and wristlets, had a felling ax at the ready, held across his chest. His expression indicated that he would not mind using it.

It was impossible that the three of them could have crept up behind him in total silence; yet that was exactly what had happened.

This time there would be no escape. The white man was armed with an S-shaped crowbar.

"Chuck your blade down here," he said, and Routledge complied.

"Standard issue, that," said Spear, giving it to the white man.

"Now the club," the white man said.

Felling Ax retrieved it. "Here, this is Tortuga's kerry." He looked up at Routledge. "Where d'you get this?"

"I found it on the cli—I found it."

"On the cliff. Was that what you was going to say?"

"Yes. No. I just found it."

Keeping the club. That too had been monumentally stupid. Now they would kill him for sure, in revenge, if nothing else.

"Look on his knees, Obie. It's blood. He's croted Tortuga."

"Gazzer and all," said the first black, Obie, the one with the spear.

The white man uttered a quiet, inward laugh. "What's your name?"

Routledge decided to lie. "Roger," he said, borrowing the identity of a former colleague. "Jenkins."

"Well, Roger, you done a naughty thing there, croting our two stonky mates." He laughed again. "He don't look the part, do he, Obie?"

"Looks like a bit of a sperm artist, if you ask me. Talks like one, too."

"What about their stuff?" said Felling Ax.

"The meat's mine," the white man said. "That makes their stuff mine and all."

"He's right, Jez," said the one called Obie.

Routledge did not fully understand what was going on, but it seemed that he was the "meat." It also seemed that they were not after all unduly exercised by the revelation that he had "croted" the first two. What concerned them more was the ultimate destination of the dead men's "stuff."

"Did they slake their jakes?" said the one called Jez. When it became apparent that Routledge hadn't understood, he rephrased the question. "Did they prong you?"

Routledge feigned incomprehension.

"You ever been plugged?"

"Shut up, Jez," the white man said. "Where's your stuff, Roger?"

"I'm sorry . . ."

"Where'd you put the rest of your issue? What they give you in the Village. The clobber and that."

"This is all I took."

"Just the knife and the jacket?"

"Yes."

"Want to get in there, do we? That Franks." He sneered. "How long d'they give you outside?"

"Nine days."

"He's lying," Jez said. "Where'd you hide your stuff, bastard?"

"No," the white man said. "He in't lying. You wouldn't tell us no fibs, would you, Roger? Thought not. You're coming with us now, Roger. This is Obie, this Jez. Me I'm Martinson. Ain't got no first name, have I, Obie?" He smirked again. "Let's go."

With the spear at his back, Routledge was made to walk. Martinson led the way.

As they passed through the undergrowth, Routledge remembered the newsreels he had seen of prisoners forced to appear before the cameras and recant, not knowing whether in the next moment they would be shot or beaten or merely dragged away once more and thrown into their cells. While watching he had been more or less indifferent; but now he found the faces of those men returning to haunt him. Was that how he looked now, at this moment, not in the forests of Vietnam or Central America, but on an island a mere forty kilometers from mainland Cornwall?

"Don't try and run, Roger," Martinson said over his shoulder. "We won't like it if you do."

"Where are we going?" Routledge made himself say.

"Mystery tour."

It came fully home to him then just how barbarous was the policy his peers had adopted to rid themselves of murderers, rapists, terrorists. No man slept on Sert who was not a fully paid-up member of Category Z. Only the helicopter's tenuous touch remained to link him with the past. His sentence was final, inexorable. His future was this, indivisible from the present. It was as though he was already dead. With this one difference: part of him, the part determined to survive, refused to acknowledge it.

That tiny corner of his mind had not forgotten the resolution he had made on the ridge. It enabled him to take in details of the journey, and remained sufficiently functional to file away information for later use. The white man, Martinson, appeared to be in charge. Obie he treated with respect; the other one, possibly a homosexual, he didn't. Routledge he virtually ignored, except, from time to time, for telling him to keep up: even had Routledge not been weak from hunger and lack of proper sleep he would have found the pace grueling.

Martinson, in particular, seemed to pass over rough ground almost as easily as one might walk through a shopping mall. He rapidly led them to the edge of the wood and out across the thorn scrub.

The land sloped generally downhill. After a few minutes they came to an area of more open heath, with more bracken, where Routledge noticed another buzzard in the sky. The bracken gave way to vegetation more open yet: a wide expanse of low heather, dusty purplish and just coming into bloom.

If Martinson ignored the captive, Obie did the opposite. As they walked, with Jez bringing up the rear, he badgered Routledge with questions about the mainland. His interest centered on the fortunes of Tottenham Hotspurs Football Club, about which Routledge was able to provide no information whatever. He then asked, with similar success, how preparations for next year's World Cup were coming along.

"Ain't you interested in football, then?"

"No. I'm afraid not."

"Franks's got radios. Got a telly too."

"I expect he does the pools and all," Jez said.

"Who is Franks?" Routledge brought himself to say.

"Don't you know? In the Village. The 'Father,' he calls himself. That's so his boys have to use his shit for toothpaste. Ain't that right, Jim?"

"That's right." Martinson glanced over his shoulder. "Leave the meat alone now, Obie. You can see he's puffed out."

For that Routledge found himself grateful.

The heather came at last to an end, replaced by rough turf with scattered outcrops of rock and scree. The ground began to rise once more, the grass dotted with minute yellow flowers. By now Martinson had joined a distinct path worn in the soil. It threaded its way over a ridge and into a large, bowl-shaped depression, a kind of natural amphitheater where a flock of scrawny and ill-kempt goats was feeding. The flock was being guarded by four armed men, three whites and a mulatto, wearing much the same rags and skins as the other outsiders Routledge had seen.

The goatherds were lounging on the ground, one with a hat over his face. The mulatto sat up as Martinson's party appeared.

"Who got it?" he said, referring no doubt to Routledge.

"Martinson," Obie said. "Why four of you, Beanpole?"

"Alex doubled the guard. What happened at the light?"

"Tell you later."

"Yeah. OK."

The smell of the goats was so abominable that in the midst of the flock Routledge felt his gorge rise.

"Nearly home now," Obie said. "Nearly time for you to tell us what you done with Gazzer and Tortuga."

"Who? . . . I'm sorry . . ."

"I bet you're sorry."

Martinson gave another quiet laugh. Routledge's flimsy belief that they were going to overlook his possession of the club had suddenly evaporated.

"No need to look so glum, Roger," Martinson said, as they reached the edge of the bowl and came into full sight of the sea and, below, the primitive assortment of sheds and

tents which was their apparent destination. "Be like our mate
Gazzer. Always try to look on the bright side."

Close to, the outsiders' settlement was even more appalling
than the descent of the hillside had led Routledge to expect.
The main street, or what passed for a street, was littered with
bones and shells and malodorous garbage including fish
waste, the rotting corpses of seabirds, piles of human feces.
Most of the dwellings were sited among the ruined walls and
foundations of former buildings. This was surely the "Old
Town" he had been obliquely warned about last night.

Some of the inhabitants were already on view. Others
emerged to inspect him. Shocked as he had been by the first
sight of the two on the cliffs, Routledge now saw that, compared with some of these creatures, Gazzer had been little
short of a Regency fop. At least three of the men who appeared at the doorways, or rather the mouths, of their shacks
had the unmistakable beginnings of the facial chancres that
marked active cases of HVC; Routledge noticed that they,
unlike not a few of the others, hung well back and neither
congratulated Martinson nor tried to touch and examine the
captive. Even here, in hell, they were shunned, like lepers.
What happened to them when the disease became conta-
gious? Were they allowed to reach that stage? Routledge
thought again of the black man's saliva in his hair, of the
dried blood which still clung to his trousers.

Beyond the ruined plots and houses, to the right, beyond
the shallow slope of debris-littered beach, spread a sac-
shaped bay with a scattering of islands at its mouth, bounded
at east and west by low headlands. Compared with those on
the other side of the island, the cliffs here were nothing. The
bay made an almost perfect natural harbor; the waves were
no more than knee-high, fumbling their approach and col-
lapsing early into shoals of weed-polluted, sluggish foam.

At the end of the street stood the ruins of a comparatively
large building, which Obie said was the "hotel." Canopies
and lean-tos of driftwood and plastic covered about half the
floor area, compensating for the lack of an upper story; the
rest was open to the sky.

In front of the main entrance, overlooking an old stone and concrete jetty, was a stone terrace with the evidence of an elegant balustrade and steps leading down to the beach. Here, hemmed in by Jez and a number of others who had joined the procession along the road, Routledge was made to wait while Obie and Martinson went inside.

As soon as they had gone, the attentions of the group became more insistent and impertinent. Routledge found himself being questioned on several sides at once, unable to settle one demand before another was made. The questions at first concerned news and happenings on the mainland; they soon became more and more menacing and priapic. Was he married? What was her name? What was she like in bed? When had they last done it? In detail, what were her favorite perversions? And his? During this he became aware of the leers of two men in particular, one middle-aged, the other younger, both with the same unconcealed interest in his person. The older one was the first to translate intent into action, reaching out a hand to stroke his neck.

Routledge reacted instantaneously, pulling himself away.

"Leave it, Curtis," Jez warned the man, giving his words greater emphasis with the ax.

"I didn't mean no harm."

"All you stonks. Piss off out of it."

"You can't stop us, Brookes."

"D'you want to take it up with Martinson?"

"I wouldn't mind," said the younger of the two men, at which there was laughter. "He'll have to give in some day."

"Say that to his face."

At that moment Martinson appeared in what had been the porch of the hotel. He descended the low flight of steps to the terrace.

"All right, boys," he said. "You've had your eyeful. I've got a special surprise. Something new. Be here tomorrow morning. Bring anything you got worth having. I've decided to auction the meat."

"What d'you mean, 'auction'?"

"Just what I say. You've got till morning to raise the ante. Then he goes to the highest bidder."

8

Martinson disappeared for the rest of the afternoon. In the early evening he returned to take custody of the captive. He was with Obie and Jez, who both elected to remain behind with Peto in order to report the outcome of whatever errand they had been engaged upon.

Having tied Routledge's wrists with an old length of twine, Martinson led him along the main street and towards his hut.

Routledge had spent all the intervening hours in the hotel, being questioned by Peto and his henchmen. They had wanted to know everything he had seen and heard in the Village, and then they had interrogated him on his life and background and on news from the mainland. Several other men had come in from time to time to watch, listen, or pose questions of their own. The questioning had dwelt at length on the disappearance of Gazzer and his companion Tortuga. Routledge maintained throughout that he knew nothing whatever about it, and insisted that he had found Tortuga's club by chance on the clifftop.

Nobody believed him, and apart from one Negro who heatedly swore revenge and had to be ejected, nobody seemed to care. In this respect at least, Martinson and Obie had been making fun of him.

For a time Routledge had hoped that the proposed auction was also one of Martinson's jokes, but no. It became evident that, where profit was involved, Martinson lacked all sense of humor. He was not a homosexual, nor did he want a slave; therefore he had no use for Routledge. What could be more logical than to sell his new acquisition to someone who did? The idea, apparently, broke new ground, and Peto said he wished he had thought of it himself. During much comment and speculation the name "Jones" was mentioned. If Jones won the bidding, Routledge could expect to be the subject of a "party," which he understood to mean a multiple rape.

It could have been very much worse; the auction could have been held immediately. Had it not been for Martinson's desire to raise as much interest as possible, and had he not been called away to finish his errand for Peto, the sale might already have taken place. The delay introduced an element of hope. Thoughts of evasion and escape were taking form in Routledge's mind. For now, he allowed himself to be led along, the model prisoner.

Martinson's hut stood on rising ground at some distance from the hotel, commanding a broad view of the town and the beach below. Turf and slates covered the roof, which sloped back from the doorway. The rear and two side walls were sturdily constructed of stacked rocks and solid timbers—driftwood pallets and packing cases and old joists and floorboards—while the front wall, with its single window-aperture and doorway, was made of wattle and daub. Nearby was one other hut, quite derelict; behind it rose the slope.

"Just in time for cocoa," Martinson said. From his tunic he took an oddly shaped sliver of wood, a key which he used to unfasten an ingeniously carved wooden catch holding shut the wattle-and-daub door. Satisfied that his domain had not been entered during his absence, he motioned Routledge inside.

There was no floor; in the middle of the main chamber the rock had been dug out to make a hearth from which, presumably, the smoke escaped as best it could. A large, blackened cooking pot—a saucepan which had neither lid nor handle—stood on one of the shelves which covered the whole height of the left-hand wall. Martinson took the pot down, together with an old plastic measuring-jug.

"Sit on that box, where I can see you."

Routledge complied. Apart from this wooden beer-crate, the furniture in the room comprised a makeshift table under the window, another, larger crate, and, in the far corner, a peculiar low sofa made of goatskin stuffed with heather.

This main chamber occupied the front half of the hut; the rear had been solidly partitioned off into two small rooms, each with its own narrow doorway.

The interior of the hotel had been squalid enough, but this was worse. Martinson's possessions, heaped on the shelves or merely thrown down against the walls, appeared to consist mainly of the rubbish he had collected from the tideline: tangled nylon mesh, potentially useful lumps of wood, assorted articles of plastic like yogurt pots and fishing floats, and bolts, nails, brackets, strip metal and similar bits and pieces saved from packing cases or other wooden objects washed ashore.

Routledge suddenly noticed, among the many small fittings heaped in a polythene tray on the shelf beside him, a rusty woodscrew about seven centimeters long. He immediately looked away, resuming his examination of Martinson's kitchen.

In the corner stood the water tank, a large translucent drum which might once have held industrial chemicals. There was no tap, only a length of water-filled plastic tubing fed through a hole in the lid, one end touching the bottom and the other fitted with a clip which allowed small quantities to be siphoned off, as Routledge now observed.

"Want some grub?"

"Yes. Please."

"It'll be cold. I can't be bothered with no fire."

Routledge did not object. During the whole time at the hotel, he had been offered nothing to eat or drink. He watched, almost in disbelief, as Martinson began preparing an evening meal. Many of the ingredients were wrapped in thick white polythene, sections cut from an old fertilizer sack that must have drifted ashore from the mainland. From one of these Martinson produced a lump of goat's cheese.

"Have a bit of this while we're waiting."

Routledge did his best to restrain himself. The cheese was

rank, unrefrigerated, the sort of thing Louise would have buried in the compost heap. It tasted fantastic.

"You can tell me," Martinson said. "Secret, like. Which was the first to get it? Gazzer or Tortuga?"

"I kept telling them at the hotel, I don't know anything about it."

"Do you want some supper or not?"

"I can't tell you what I don't know."

"You croted them two tossers all right. Cut them, I reckon." He emptied some oatmeal into the pot. "How you done it is a mystery, but you done it. Good riddance, that's what I say. Congratulations, Roger. It's earned you with Peto. Earned you with me and all."

Martinson turned his back to find something on his larder shelf. It was the first chance Routledge had had. Reaching out both his bound hands, he took the rusty woodscrew and just managed to insinuate it into the top of his right trouser-pocket before Martinson turned back, holding a medium-sized polythene bag.

"Dried puffin," he said. "You'll like it. This is my special scoobie-doo." He added a generous portion to the pot: dehydrated flakes of dark meat. From a jam jar he sprinkled crystals of sea salt, stirred them in with a stick. The resulting stew he poured into two ill-assorted bowls, one an old aluminum pie-dish, the other a plastic tub still marked PUTTY.

Routledge devoured a second helping, Martinson a third. During the course of the meal, which he spent sprawled on the goatskin sofa, Martinson asked about Routledge's past life and the reason he had been put in Category Z. "They all say that," he said, when Routledge protested his innocence. About his own history, Martinson divulged nothing.

The evening cloud had become heavy and low. By the time they had finished eating, the light had begun to fade.

Martinson arose. "Beddy-byes now," he said. "I'm going to have to tie you up. I know you'll understand. You're a valuable property, see?" He jerked a thumb at the left-hand door. "You can have my room. Don't bother getting no ideas about breaking out of it, not unless you've got an ax. I'll sleep out here. I get up at first light. I like lots of sleep and

I don't like being disturbed. Right? No noise. Don't even fart." He took a handful of nylon cord from a low shelf, and from his belt drew Routledge's own knife. "First of all we'll get rid of this," he said, and carefully cut through the knot of Routledge's bonds. He then began to bundle Routledge's arms behind his back.

"Wait," Routledge said. "I ought to go to the lavatory first."

"Good thinking, Roger. Can't have you wetting my bed, can we?"

"It's not just that. I think I want to . . . to . . ."

"Do number twos? Why didn't you say so, then?"

Martinson chose him a place a few meters from the doorway.

"Do you have to stand there watching me like that?"

"I don't get no thrill out of it, if that's what you mean. Just get on with it."

"Can't you at least stand by the door? I won't get very far with my trousers round my ankles."

Martinson shrugged and moved back. Routledge squatted for half a minute or so, knowing full well there would be no result.

"Hope this in't no criticism of my puffin porridge," Martinson said.

Routledge had already transferred the woodscrew to his right hand. As he stood and pulled up his trousers, he tucked in his shirt and simultaneously slipped the screw beneath his underpants and between his buttocks. He had only a moment: the position had to be just right, neither too low, so that he couldn't reach the screw when the time came, nor too high, so that he would be unable to grip it inconspicuously as he walked.

It felt as if the act of keeping the screw in place was altering his entire gait. He was convinced Martinson would notice and become suspicious.

"Remember what I said. I don't appreciate being woken up."

He tied Routledge's hands behind his back, tied his ankles, and tied both sets of bonds together. When he had finished,

Routledge, lying on the noisome feather-filled mattress which served his host as a bed, could hardly move.

The room was a bare, timber-lined cubicle a couple of meters across, with no window. As the door shut behind him, Routledge heard something heavy being wedged into place.

What little light there was gained access through cracks in the walls and around the door, which was also made of solid planking. Even as Routledge's eye dwelt on the doorframe, he heard Martinson hanging a curtain on the other side and the cracks there were abruptly obscured.

By raising his feet as far as he could, Routledge was just able to free his hands enough to get at his shirt-tail. Fraction by fraction, able to use only the tips of his thumbs and fore-fingers, he struggled to pull it from his trousers. As he worked, he listened intently to the noises coming from the other side of the door. He heard the dishes being picked up, objects being returned to the shelves. He heard water trickling into a vessel and the sound of Martinson washing himself. Presently the outer door was pulled shut. The goatskin sofa creaked.

"Sweet dreams!" Martinson called out.

Routledge did not reply. He had managed to free his shirt-tail and was now trying to reach the screw itself. The nylon cord bit deeply into his wrists. He grimaced, bared his teeth, pulled his legs back even further. Finally, with both his fore-fingers fully extended, and his thumbs forcing down the material of the waistband, he almost made contact. With a supreme effort, he pushed his fingers further and got a slender hold on the threads: he had put the screw in the wrong way up, head downwards.

He was concentrating so much on withdrawing the screw without dropping it that he only half heard a faint scraping sound from the adjoining room. He halted in order to listen. Had Martinson lifted open the outer door just then?

No. Routledge thought he heard breathing, which meant Martinson was still there.

He went on with his work.

* * *

The rain began just before dusk, a slow, relentless drizzle drifting in from the west. By the time Martinson had reached the cliffs above Crow Bay, his tunic and leggings were drenched. He disliked this warm summer rain. It made the rocks greasy. He would be coming back in the dark, on an easier section, it was true, but on these cliffs there was no such thing as an easy climb. The conditions tonight were too dangerous. Maybe he ought leave it until tomorrow. But no. Now had to be the time. And tomorrow might be wetter still.

"So what," he breathed, digging in his climbing-pick for the first hand-hold. "If I go, I go."

Now had to be the time because of the psychological element. After leaving the new meat with Peto for questioning, as was customary, he and Obie and Jez had gone on to the Village to check out Franks's stock. Billy, of course, had not been there, for the simple reason that Martinson had killed the goat himself last night and tipped the carcass over the cliffs.

Martinson was very pleased with his performance today, especially at the lighthouse. The words had come of themselves, sowing just the right seeds of suspicion and resentment in Feely's, and hence also Houlihan's, mind. Obie, he was certain, had been taken in completely. It was all turning out just the way he had planned.

Houlihan might send an emissary from his brain gang, demanding an explanation which Peto would be unable to give. But that was unlikely. From past experience, Martinson knew precisely what was going to happen. Today's visit to the lighthouse would have set Houlihan thinking. He would have perceived Peto's behavior as initial weakness. Later tonight, or tomorrow morning, he would discover how Peto—who else?—had changed his mind and retaliated.

Houlihan's indignant counterattack would come tomorrow afternoon, once he had assembled and armed his troops. The towners would be taken by surprise. Peto would see the assault as completely unprovoked, a further act of aggression to add to the theft of Billy. His mistakenly feeble response to Billy's disappearance, he would tell himself later, had been interpreted by Houlihan as a virtual invitation to step things up. The battle would be violent, with several scraggings, and then the war would begin again.

At bottom, neither Houlihan nor Peto would be sorry. The peace had lasted too long already. It was just that Peto wasn't prepared to resume hostilities yet, and that would give Houlihan the advantage.

Martinson had been monitoring the situation very carefully. He had shown superhuman patience and restraint, and taken a tremendous amount of shit from Peto. He wasn't going to let a bit of rain stop him now.

Besides, he had rehearsed this climb three times without mishap. On the last occasion, the day before yesterday, he had even reached the landing pad and overheard Houlihan's voice from the window above. There wasn't that much risk; much less than was entailed by an approach from the east, where the guards might expect an intruder to come. Not that they were expecting him.

The main problem was to get down there unseen. In the dark the retreat would be simple.

As he climbed, he couldn't help himself smiling. Long-term plans or no, he would have done this anyway, just to relieve his boredom. He only wished he could be there to see Houlihan's face.

There were several possible eventual outcomes. The best would be if it went through exactly as planned, but he did not really care which way it turned out. As long as, in the end, Franks got what was coming to him, Martinson would die happy. Sometimes he pictured the helicopter in flames. Sometimes he pictured Franks in various attitudes of torture and death. The torture would be administered by himself. Subsidiary images of Peto—for some reason, usually involving crucifixion—impinged on these fantasies, and then he thought of all three of them on crosses, as at Golgotha, with Franks in the middle, Houlihan the one to repent. He, Martinson, would offer up the sponge soaked in vinegar.

"Eli, Eli, lama sabach-thani?" he whispered, and rammed the pick into another crevice, tested it, and gave it his weight. Those apocalyptic words uttered on the verge of death, flung into the supernatural thunderous gloom. Only Mark and

Matthew had had the bottle to report them. *My God, my God, why hast thou forsaken me?* The other Evangelists had kept their traps shut, falsified the record. Knew what was best for the family firm.

At the age of thirteen, in the backstreets, he had been a Crusader, well versed in the scriptures, primed by his grandmother to sing hymns in the white-emulsioned hall which had smelled musty, like old suitcases. The man in charge, he now realized, had been a closet grunt. Those words, when he had been old enough to understand them, had explained a lot. They certainly explained this island and its colonists.

It was blasphemy. But then so was everything. "Eli, Eli," he whispered again, the evening rain trickling down his neck, his hands covered in mud and grit. "Well you may say, Liam Franks. And you, my fine friend," he told himself. "And you."

When he reached the bottom it was dark. The only guards seemed to be those on the approach path from the upper tombs.

He found Houlihan's milk-white billy in the covered pen behind the lighthouse. The other goats stirred uneasily and bleated a little as he led it away, but the billy itself came quietly and, calmed by stroking and soothing words, did not have time to react when Martinson, with a sudden upward stroke, plunged the blade into its throat, up through the thinnest part of the skull and into the brain.

The new meat's sheath-knife was sharp and quickly cut through the muscles and bones of the neck. Martinson felt the hot, sacrificial gush of blood across his hands.

Holding one of the horns, allowing the weight to dangle easily from his fingers, Martinson mounted the landing pad and left the head on the lighthouse steps. A moment later, soft and silent as a shadow, he melted into the night.

9

AT LAST ROUTLEDGE DECIDED TO RISK CALLING OUT.

"Martinson! Martinson!"

No answer.

"Martinson, are you there?"

Routledge had not decided what he would do if the man responded to his call and came in. There was nothing in the room to serve as a weapon; his only advantages were surprise and his own desperation. For he knew this was probably his last chance. If the auction went ahead in the morning, he would be killed. He had nothing left to lose.

It had taken him at least an hour, perhaps more, to get free of his bonds. The hardest part had been to sever the length binding together his wrists and ankles. Strand by strand, he had picked at the cord with the blunt edges of the screw-threads. At one stage he had thought he would never do it. The pain had been almost intolerable: of the agonizing contortion needed to manipulate the screw, and of the screw-head biting into the flesh of his fingers and thumbs. Quite early on he had begun to bleed.

When his wrists had parted from his ankles he had rested for a while before continuing. Only the fact that the screw was seven, rather than six, centimeters long had allowed him to fray the cord holding his wrists. Even so, it had been relatively slower and much more awkward than the first part of the operation. He had thought, just before the miraculous feeling of relief when his hands had come free, that this too would be impossible.

He had untied his ankles without difficulty, and then, in the dark, had started to explore the room. Moving with infinite slowness and caution to preserve the silence, he had groped his way around the walls, getting several wood-splinters in his fingers. On reaching the door he had remembered the faint scraping sound he had heard earlier, and had put his ear to the boards to listen for Martinson's breathing.

The dimmest of dim lamplight was showing at a narrow crevice in the wall. He was not able to see into the room.

The lamplight did not necessarily mean that Martinson was awake. Just before Martinson had cleared away the dishes, Routledge had heard what he now guessed was the noise of flint striking steel. In the absence of electricity or matches, with a prisoner under his roof and a possible need for light at any moment, Martinson would, Routledge supposed, keep a flame burning all night.

Try as he might, Routledge could hear nothing from the adjoining room. His hearing may not have been as good as he imagined; the curtain Martinson had hung there may have been acting as a muffle; or Martinson may have been able to sleep without making the least sound.

There was one other possibility.

Since the moment of his arrest, Routledge had felt his life accursed. Everything that could have gone wrong had gone wrong. At every turn, in his choice of counsel, in the lottery of the bench, in the abysmal standard of discernment collectively possessed by the jury, and, most of all, in the fabricated evidence and breathtaking lies of the police and their expert witnesses, luck had turned its face away. There had been no deviation in his long, long decline, only an unrelenting increase in speed and momentum. Finally, landing here in Martinson's hut, he had reached bottom. Tomorrow he would die.

The possibility that the next room was empty, that Martinson had gone elsewhere, was at first simply too remote for him to grasp. The fact that he had already managed to escape from his bonds did not for a few seconds yet strike him as a favorable omen: he had not seriously expected any advantage from his labors.

Then it began to dawn on him.

"Martinson!" he said again, more loudly. "Martinson!"

Still no reply.

Where had he gone? To the hotel? To some other hut? Was he so confident of the security of his prisoner? If Routledge was indeed a valuable property, why had Martinson risked losing him for something as trivial as social entertainment?

But surely Martinson had been planning all along to leave him unattended. Why else the curtain hung across the door? Why else the elaborate charade about his need for silence?

So Routledge had not been mistaken about the sound of the outer door scraping open. Martinson had been absent since then, throughout the whole time Routledge had been struggling with the screw. And he might be back at any moment.

Routledge eventually, after trying to force the door and attempting to kick out planks in the walls, started to attack the roof. The laths were just above head height. He found the weakest and broke it, then broke those on either side. Once the first slate was loose, it was relatively easy to dislodge others. Above the slates he found a thick layer of turf, the earth heavy with water. Routledge clawed it away with his fingers, burrowing vertically, face averted and eyes shut against the cascade of wet soil and pebbles.

He realized he had made an opening when he smelled fresh air and felt the softness of the rain. There was nothing in the room to stand on except the mattress, which he now rolled into a ball.

When he had enlarged the hole sufficiently, he reached up and spread his hands on the surface of the roof.

It was not easy to hoist himself out. Even discounting his fatigue and all the privations he had endured, he was just not strong enough. His arms were those of a quantity surveyor, a man who had spent most of his working hours behind a desk. The heaviest thing he had lifted then was a hundred-meter tape measure. But fear lent him strength: once out, he crawled to the edge of the roof and let himself down.

He had done it. He was free.

All his instincts told him to run away, into the dark, to get as far from this place as he could before Martinson came back. That, however, would represent the waste of an opportunity, an act of timidity. Survival did not go to the timid or wasteful. It went to the strong.

He found a rock and hammered at the catch on the outer door. At the fourth attempt he broke it and flung the door aside.

The lamp was standing on the table under the window. It consisted of a ketchup jar with a doubled length of canvas for a wick, held in place with a wedge.

Routledge enlarged the flame and, lifting the lamp, entered the second of the two rear chambers, which he had, correctly, taken to be Martinson's storeroom.

The two side walls were lined with untidy shelves and racks of boxes, canisters, bags of food. The far wall appeared to be devoted to weapons, more carefully arranged: axes, machetes, flails, hammers, spears, clubs, knives, each hanging on its own peg. In pride of place, suspended stock-downwards, was a crossbow. Hanging beside it he found a kind of tool-roll containing ten steel bolts and a curiously shaped metal stirrup.

His own PVC jacket had been thrown down on top of the pile of clothes which occupied part of one corner. He put it on. More clothing, mainly of goatskin, hung from pegs on the wall. He hurriedly selected a sheepskin waistcoat, too large for him, but worth taking anyway, and a broad-brimmed goatskin hat, which fitted reasonably well. On another peg he found a crude haversack. The contents—bundled twine formed into loops, perhaps snares of some sort—he tipped out, and immediately began filling the haversack with food from the shelves, scarcely bothering to look what was inside each bag. He took oatmeal, hard cheese, two polythene packets of salted fish, some beetroots, a bag of carrots. In the kitchen he found a small joint of cooked goat's flesh, and a flat gin-bottle with a screw cap, which he filled with water from the tank. When the haversack was almost full he slipped three knives into it, added a machete, the tool-roll, and fastened the straps.

He took down the crossbow. It was much heavier than he had expected, and he wondered whether he would be able to work it; that was something he could discover at his leisure.

His plunder of Martinson's hut had been brief but effective. He returned the lamp to the kitchen table and pocketed the flint and steel firemaking pouch he found there.

Ten seconds later he was outside, in the rain, climbing the slope, leaving Old Town behind.

He passed the night in the scrub behind the town, huddled against the rain, wrapped in the PVC jacket and with Martinson's hat pulled down over his eyes. Towards the middle hours he slept, dreaming again of Louise and of Christopher, his seven-year-old son, and also of Martinson and the two men on the cliff. The woodscrew featured in the final dream, together with a consciousness of the approaching auction. "They got their screw, after all," his own voice said, waking him up.

He felt wretched. His limbs were stiff and his joints ached with the cold and damp. He sniffed at his armpits and then at his crotch. He could not remember having been unwashed for so long before. The previous day he had noticed that the skin under his clothes was sprinkled with tiny red insect-bites, probably acquired in the bracken. The irritation was now very much worse, as was the itching of his rapidly growing beard.

Dawn came slowly, warm and wet, with a lethargic south-westerly wind. As soon as it was light enough to see, he circled around behind the bay and headed south, along the east coast. The tide was low, just about to turn; at the next cove he clambered down to the beach, which here was of predominantly gray shingle.

He began walking at the very water's edge. Two hundred meters on, he climbed back into the scrub and continued moving south, keeping to open ground, treading wherever he could on bare rock. After ten minutes of this he returned to the beach, followed the surf once more and then, well before the next headland made the beach impassable, climbed back to the scrub. Switching back and forth like this, using the cover of the bushes when in the scrub, he pursued an irregular path southwards, finally going back to the beach and staying with it.

He had learned his lesson yesterday, and would do his best to leave no tracks for Martinson to find. For undoubtedly Martinson would not be pleased, especially by the loss of his crossbow.

Routledge did not fully appreciate what he had stolen until much later in the morning when, having put about six kilometers between himself and Old Town, he felt it would be safe to stop and rest. A little farther along he found a suitable place, an overhang of rock hidden from view but impossible to approach unseen. He sat down, sheltered from the rain, faced by the emptiness and quiet surging of the sea.

From Old Town southwards, the east coast had become gradually more rugged and desolate. He had passed several groups of islets. The cliffs behind him, mazed with cracks and fissures and outgrowths of scrub, rose to a height which, had he not seen the cliffs on the west coast, he would have thought imposing.

These cliffs, like the others, were of stratified rock, the plates aligned in much the same direction. Here and there the formation had collapsed, producing caves in the under-cliff. Most were small and shallow, easily invaded by the tide, but some were large and extended a long way into the rock. At one or two he had found traces of occupation: piles of bones and shells, the remains of fires. Otherwise, except for large numbers of seabirds, the east coast seemed deserted.

He had now gleaned an idea of the size of the island. It was larger than he might have guessed. At this point the coast had already begun trending towards the south-west, which indicated that the north-south length was about eight kilometers. Assuming the width of the island to be about the same, that gave an area of roughly five thousand hectares. Not allowing for bays and peninsulas, the coastline would be at least twenty-five kilometers long.

After much debate with himself, he had decided to remain as much as possible on the beach, making occasional forays inland if need be. He would find a cave, and spend most of the time in hiding, emerging at dawn and dusk to collect fresh water. It was now the seventeenth, Thursday. The Village gate would open for him on Monday evening. That was the danger point. He would have to be ready for the bell, and he did not know exactly when it would ring: about eleven, perhaps. Again he gave thanks for the fact that he had lied to Martinson about the length of his ordeal.

Just offshore he noticed something round and shiny-gray, rising and falling with the swell. It had large, dark eyes, a flattened, doglike face—a seal, watching him curiously, letting itself be carried southwards on the tide.

He unscrewed the cap of the gin-bottle. "Your health," he said under his breath, raising the bottle and taking a gulp. The seal, still watching, drifted gradually out of sight.

"Be like that, then," Routledge whispered.

He ate some cheese and meat, but postponed sampling the salted fish. He then busied himself with the contents of the haversack, sorting them into order. If he rationed himself, there would be enough food for three days at least.

Taking occasional bites from a carrot, he examined the knives and machete, and began to familiarize himself with the crossbow.

It had been designed and executed with astonishing skill. The stock had been fashioned, without decoration, from a heavy plank of densely grained wood. Whoever had made it—Martinson himself?—had had access to a comprehensive variety of woodworking tools, as well as files, hacksaws, and a vice, to make the metal parts. The propulsive power came from a springy length of shaped steel, fitted in the stock with a wedge of black heel-rubber and secured with three brass plates. The string was made of braided twine, meticulously finished and waxed, reinforced in the middle where it hooked over the nib of the trigger release. The trigger mechanism showed an especially remarkable degree of ingenuity. Spring-loaded, it consisted of two plates of case-hardened steel which, operating on two pivots, allowed an apparently smooth and jerk-free release of the string.

The trigger-nib was concealed by a shallow wooden hood which carried an adjustable, beaded back sight in brass; the brass fore sight, mounted beyond the recoil of the string, terminated in a semicircle which neatly coincided with the size of the bead.

Each of the bolts was twenty-five centimeters or so in length, cut from steel rod and flighted with small tinplate vanes. These vanes, as much as the crossbow itself, gave an overwhelming impression of ruthless utility. It was a horrible thing. At school Routledge had been told about the medieval French and the disdain and resentment their use of the crossbow had excited among the English longbowmen. The history master had regarded the crossbow as unsporting, unfair, not quite cricket.

He half smiled, almost amused by the irrelevance of his upbringing. Sert was not quite cricket either. Instead of teaching him the dates of distant battles they would have done better to have prepared him for this, for the new Dark Ages, for a Britain wallowing out of control.

The bolts slid along a V-shaped groove faced with marbled gray plastic laminate: of exactly the same pattern, Routledge realized, as that on the cupboards in the bungalow reception room. Had the crossbow been made in the Village?

Almost certainly. The intelligence and craftsmanship revealed in its construction far surpassed anything he had seen in Old Town. Even the tool-roll, made of oil-cloth or something similar, was a professional, competent piece of work. Besides the bolts and the stirrup, it contained two spare strings in their own small compartment.

Resting the butt in the pit of his stomach, he engaged the string in the stirrup and pulled. The bow was stronger than he had thought. He carefully hooked the string behind the trigger nib and, even more carefully, slid one of the bolts into place.

There was nothing particular to aim at. He did not want to lose the bolt. Fifty meters away to the left he saw a relatively large heap of seaweed. That would do, assuming the bolt got there.

Even as he squinted along the sights and made the first tentative squeeze on the trigger, the crossbow went off. He was taken completely by surprise, shocked as much by the violence of its release as by the power and efficiency of the bolt. Its trajectory was impossible for him to follow, except in the last moment before impact, when his laboring eye finally caught up: fifty meters beyond the seaweed and fifteen degrees to the left, the steel tip smashed into the shoulder of a large rock. The spray of chips and fragments registered before the clang: the bolt was sent spinning, several meters into the air, and fell to earth beyond his vision.

"Bloody hell!" And he had thought the sheath-knife an impressive piece of technology! He whispered the words again, unable to believe that Sert could have produced anything like this.

Martinson, the ignorant Martinson, dark Britain personified, was the prince of Old Town. Theft was the only way he could have got his hands on it.

Yes. Without doubt, the crossbow had been made in the Village.

And if Obie could be believed, the men in the Village had radios and a television set.

Getting to his feet, Routledge began to wonder what else they had.

10

After breakfasting with Appleton and Thaine, and attending to the most urgent of the papers on his desk, Franks could contain his patience no longer. He had to know what decision Godwin had reached. Informing the guard, he left the bungalow at the rear and went out into the clean, fresh air of this sunny Sunday morning.

The aluminum-framed french windows of his office opened on an area of crazy paving, from which a patch of lawn extended for twenty or so paces and enclosed the overgrown crater of an ornamental pond. No water remained, for the polythene liner had long ago been put to better use elsewhere.

Even in the days when the house had been inhabited by the warden of Sert the nature reserve, the back garden could not have amounted to very much. Fifteen meters wide and about thirty deep, surrounded for the most part by a chest-high stone wall lined with hedges, it seemed to have been planned with the interests of wild rather than human life in mind. The original hedges had been of cotoneaster, berberis, buddleia, and other shrubs likely to attract migrant birds or butterflies, but they had since been invaded by the more vigorous thorns and brambles from outside.

The lawn was the only one on the island. Franks had retained it out of a sneaking nostalgia for elements of his former life, although it was now kept cropped, not by a suburban husband and father, but by a couple of Mitchell's sheep.

At the end of the garden stood a belt of coniferous trees—larch, mostly, and Monterey pine—put there as a windbreak and, like the various plantations elsewhere, to supply timber at some future date. Franks had resolutely resisted the temptation to take the wood. Luckily, the best of the planted timber was on this side of the border. Before Houlihan had adopted the lighthouse as his headquarters, Franks had not hesitated to remove the windbreak there, and the results of that felling were now to be found seasoning in the Village woodyard.

Visible from the lawn, through gaps in the trees, were the slate-covered roof and the long window, set in a stone wall, of Godwin's workshop.

The gate at the end of the garden had been scrounged, as had the posts and hinges. Franks passed through the opening and, turning onto the needle-strewn path under the larches, mounted the stone step at the threshold. As he had expected, he found Godwin and Fitzmaurice already hard at work.

"Don't get up," he said, entering.

"Good morning, Father," Godwin said.

"Please," Franks said. "Be seated."

Fitzmaurice, like Godwin, resumed his place at the workbench, though he obviously felt uncomfortable to be sitting while Franks stood. Fitzmaurice was twenty-six, one of those who had made the bomb that had all but demolished the Knightsbridge Barracks. Godwin, over twice his age, a quiet, puffy-looking man with sparse gray hair, was here for poisoning his wife and sister-in-law. On the mainland he had been employed as a design engineer by the Fairburn electronics conglomerate.

His workbench always reminded Franks of a shrine, a personal altar where he observed his mysterious rites. Every pair of pliers, every screwdriver, had its own silhouette on the wall; the shelves were lined with boxes and screwtop jars, graded in size, each one labeled and inventoried in Godwin's small, crabbed script. "Grommets." "2.5 mm Jacks." "Capacitors." "Thermistors." Except when in use, each of his soldering irons was always in its allotted place on the rest, its lead snaking down to a power socket on the accumulator bank. The accumulators and soldering irons Godwin had made himself. The generator had been designed by him and built by Thaine, likewise the contraption—a wooden bicycle without wheels—at which Fitzmaurice, Godwin's acolyte, could sit pedaling in order to drive it. Normally, however, the accumulators were kept recharged at the windmill on the cliffs.

This bench, running under its pleasant window beneath the trees, more even than Franks's own desk, now represented the focal point of the entire Community. The Tilleys here burned late into the night, with no restriction on the amount of kerosene they consumed. Fitzmaurice was excused all other duties, his only brief being to learn from Godwin, to guard him and attend to his every need.

Yesterday an area of Godwin's bench had been cleared, and on it a large sheet of cartridge paper had been unrolled and pinned out. For much of the evening, Godwin, Appleton, Fitzmaurice, and Franks himself had been in discussion. Godwin had agreed to work on the question overnight and, if possible, give his answer in the morning.

"Well?" Franks said gently.

"First, the bit you'll want to hear. We've found a way to do without those transistors."

Morgan's new tape recorder, delivered on last Tuesday's drop, should have yielded the necessary parts, but its circuitry had been redesigned and produced as a number of integrated modules, a bitter disappointment to Godwin and everyone else involved.

"We've altered part of the gating unit and freed those elements for the oscillator. It should work. In fact, it'll be more reliable than the other design."

In his search for components, Godwin had requisitioned every electrical appliance on the island and, except, of necessity, at Peto's hotel, had scavenged every last millimeter of cable. The most fruitful source by far had been the lighthouse, where much of the heavier equipment had been smashed and then abandoned, including one diesel and two gasoline generators, three obsolete shortwave radios, and the fixed instruments at the weather-recording station. Godwin had even unearthed, deep in a rubbish dump behind the bungalow, an old toaster, and had lovingly stripped it of everything useful.

Tuesday's drop had also brought Loosley's flat-screen television and a pocket radio for Kennard. Within half an hour Godwin had reduced both gadgets to a heap of bits and pieces. The same with Carr's flashlight, which Godwin had simply wanted for the particular batteries it used, and with Meadows's walkman set. Despite his complaints, Godwin could even find a use for integrated circuitry. He had wanted the walkman both for its headphones and its amplifier; and so, last February, Meadows had been asked to write to his mother for it.

The sheet of cartridge paper had been divided into a grid of faint pencil-lines one centimeter apart. Superimposed on the grid was what seemed to Franks an impossibly complicated maze of tiny symbols representing the prototype of the device that had confirmed Godwin in his mind as a genius. "Give him a box of paperclips and he'll make you a 3-D telly," Appleton had said; and hadn't been so far short of the truth.

About a third of the circuit, originally drafted in pencil, had now been gone over in ink. The inked elements had been found on the island, fabricated, or cannibalized from the various mechanical and electrical devices brought over on the helicopter during the past five years.

"All right," Franks said. "What about the bit I won't want to hear?"

"The DF is no problem, but as for the rest of it, we just can't say. We still haven't finalized the design of the pulsing unit. Or the transducers. Without a computer, the calculations alone could take us six months. And even if we come up with a workable solution, how are we going to get the transducer components? You can't just put in a reck for something like that."

"But the basic notion? What you were saying last night: do you stand by it?"

"Well, yes. The finished article should work, providing we can put it all together. Providing we hit on the right model in the calculations. Father, are you sure about that computer?"

"Yes. I'm sorry."

Unknown to anyone, Franks had actually considered, in the first heady days of the Community, putting in a request for a portable computer. Perhaps, he had reasoned, the Prison Service had swallowed the story he had told about the aims and ideals of the Village, just as they'd sanctioned the request for the metalworking tools. But finally he had not dared to risk it. The granting of the tools alone had been an astounding blunder which had revealed, not only that the Service were fallible, but also how greatly they underestimated the men on the island. Springing directly from it had come the scheme that was moving towards reality on Godwin's bench.

"I was talking to Mr. Thaine this morning," Franks said. "He wants to begin."

Godwin glanced at Franks in surprise. "What, already?"

"Yes. Already."

"Is he happy with the design?"

"That's no longer the question," Franks said. "Are you happy with it?"

"The mechanics I leave to him and Mr. Appleton, but I can vouch for the profile, unless someone's changed the rules since I learned physics."

"Can't you give me any idea of when you'll be ready?"

"To be honest, Father, no."

The unifying qualities of the project were almost as important as the end result. Without a firm word from Godwin, the whole enterprise could backfire in a welter of disappointment and despair. Already Franks feared that too many people outside the Committee knew what was afoot. Something so daring and marvelous had the power to split the Community apart. Godwin appeared to understand this; hence his caution, the detestable caution of the engineer. But without him, there was no chance at all, and in that moment Franks began to see why Fitzmaurice hero-worshiped this quietly spoken Englishman.

"Well," Franks said. "I'm glad about the transistors, at least. And I'm grateful to you for your honesty." He extended his smile to include Fitzmaurice too.

"Is there any more news from Old Town?" Fitzmaurice said.

"Not this morning. Mr. Foster's out there now. We expect Peto to hit the light today."

"Those loonies," Fitzmaurice said.

"Mr. Foster puts the toll at twelve dead, and about thirty injured. Most of them got it in the big battle on Thursday."

"Do we know yet what started them off again?" Godwin said.

"Mr. Foster thinks it may be a power struggle, if you can call it that, among Houlihan's lot. Or it might just be the usual thing. Conditions outside couldn't really get much worse."

"Madness," Godwin said. "Utter madness."

Franks nodded. Privately, he was not so sure. "As long as they keep on killing each other," he said, "we've little enough to worry about. But if they ever agree among themselves for ten minutes and decide to join forces, that's when we'd better start saying our prayers."

Routledge could hear more thunder. Another storm was coming in from the west. Earlier the rain had been torrential, of almost tropical intensity, boiling the gray sea to white.

It was now Sunday afternoon. Since Thursday, he had left his cave six times. On five occasions he had taken fresh water from a stream which discharged among the cliffs a short way to the north; and once, just before dawn on Saturday, unable to tolerate himself any longer, he had briefly ventured out to wash his clothes and to bathe in the sea.

Otherwise he had remained in hiding, in the damp, stony darkness, preferring boredom and inactivity to the terrors awaiting him in the open air. Of his fellow islanders there had been no sign.

Martinson's sheepskin waistcoat had proved invaluable, especially at night. At regular intervals in the day Routledge had performed stretching exercises and made himself walk on the spot, counting the steps until he had reached two thousand. Occasionally he had sat near the mouth of the cave, hypnotized by the waves, looking out for passing seals or birds.

All he had to do was burn off the hours until Monday night, one by one, and he would be safe. It was like school detention, the "twang" errant pupils had incurred on Saturday mornings, only on an adult scale. In the darkness, his thoughts had wanted to dwell more and more on his early life, on the clean, innocent days of his boyhood. He had taken it all for granted then, everyone had.

Again and again Routledge found himself edging towards despair. He still could not believe that he was really marooned forever, that he would never see his family again.

At the age of eighteen, taking his A-level exams, he had imagined no aspiration of which he was incapable. He had planned a dazzling future, and had accepted an offer from the University of Edinburgh to read engineering science. The offer had been conditional on his examination grades. He remembered opening the envelope containing his results. Maths and physics he had passed with distinction, but in chemistry he had scored only an E, not the B they had wanted.

They had agreed to keep his place open while he resat chemistry, studying at a technical college in Harrow. Three weeks after starting the course, he came home one afternoon to find that his father, a quantity surveyor, had collapsed in London and died. With two daughters still at school, a mortgage, and no insurance worth the name, and now faced with the prospect of finding work, Routledge's mother had nonetheless wanted him to continue with his studies. But the financial position had been impossible, and so he had applied for, and, to his surprise, got, a job with his father's former employers.

Perhaps if he had passed his chemistry exam in the first place, things might have been different. Or perhaps not. That long manila envelope had been his first intimation of the gap between ambition and attainment. And although he was universally said to have "done well for himself," he found the

work of a quantity surveyor ridiculous and futile. Somebody
had to do it, he supposed. A number of his colleagues drank
more than was good for them. They kept dirty magazines in
their desks and spent their time trying to get one over on the
opposition, the client or the contractor, depending which side
they happened to be on. It was worst of all in the Middle
East, and especially in Kuwait, where, like the others, he
had become lazy and indifferent, sapped by the heat, deeply
resentful of the Arabs who were, after all, only spending the
money they had extorted from the West.

He had worked a two-year contract there, building roads,
trying to earn enough money to buy a house and get married.
Louise had written to him every day. Just as she had in the
first months of his incarceration. Her letters had become
somewhat less frequent since the failure of the final appeal,
but that was because she was so much busier now.

The food had nearly run out. Eating the last of the salted
fish, he wondered again about her photographs. They must
still be in Exeter, he thought; otherwise he would have seen
them on Appleton's table. That was another reason he had to
get into the Community. Outside the Village, there was no
mail.

Thinking about Louise was the worst possible thing he
could do. At this distance, he found his need for her had only
increased. The last time he had seen her, in June, had been
on her first and, it now transpired, her only, conjugal visit.
He could see why the visit had been granted. To give him
something to remember her by. They'd known his fate for
weeks beforehand.

Routledge finished the salted fish, every scrap. He should
have taken more. And he wished he had stolen some sort of
pannikin as well as the food, although he had been able to
use a plastic bag to mix the oatmeal with water. On Friday
his bowel movements had begun again; he had made his
midden near the back of the cave, covering it each time with
a fresh layer of seaweed.

He took a swig of water. Sunday afternoon in July. The
date: the twentieth. He mustn't forget that. As for the time,
that would be about four o'clock, or five. Tea-time.

He arose and went closer to the daylight. The sky was considerably darker. He smiled grimly. A few minutes away by helicopter, straight across there, in the shabby, second-rate resorts of the north Cornish coast, impecunious holiday-makers were at this moment huddling in public shelters, unable to return to their guest houses before the gong sounded for supper. That aspect of Britain at least, its gray, litter-strewn mediocrity, the small-mindedness typified by the sea-side hotelier, he would never have to endure again. And as for the other Britain, that no longer existed, except in the pages of tourist guides. The countryside had been wrecked; every town looked like every other; self-consciousness had invaded and destroyed the atmosphere of every bit of re-maining charm. In fact, at this remove, he could no longer understand why people chose to live in Britain at all. It was not even a particularly good place to make money. They lived there because they could think of nowhere else to go; and even if they could, the chances were it would be just as pol-luted and overpopulated as the land they were trying to es-cape.

He had never thought in these terms before, but he had at last discovered how much he loved England itself: the land-scape, the skies, the feel of the air. England was still there, buried, inaccessible. It had taken Sert to make him see it. For Sert was that great rarity, a bit of England left relatively unmolested, a few square miles of how it all used to be. It was difficult for him to find anything good in his present circumstances, but there was this, the single glimmer of ad-vantage in his prospect of despair. For a few days, at least, or months, he would have been alive in the landscape of the real England. No layers of officialdom would have been in-terposed between him and the "exigencies of survival," as Appleton had called them. When his end came, it would be genuine, and not the counterfeit death allotted to him by the State.

Abruptly the rain began pelting the beach, and beyond it the sea.

11

LATE ON MONDAY AFTERNOON ROUTLEDGE LEFT THE CAVE and continued along the coastline in order to return to the vicinity of the Village. The day was warm and humid, with frequent spells of sunshine. Just south of the cave the beach narrowed and disappeared, forcing him up the cliffs and back into the bracken scrub, which presently became denser yet, mixed with a scattering of stunted firs. He found himself following a faint path under the trees, pioneered perhaps by goats and then used from time to time by men. He decided to stay with it rather than make a completely new trail.

Although he was no longer so frightened of being caught by Martinson, he had nonetheless armed the crossbow and was proceeding as stealthily as he could, often stopping to listen and to look around. He had planned his return to the Village with care, mapping out each foreseeable detail in the safety of the cave. Only later, just before leaving, had he realized how dangerous his sanctuary might have proved. The cave had no rear exit. He had been extremely lucky to have had no need of one.

But being in the open was worse. He halted again. At the moment most of Sert was lying beneath a particularly large area of blue, herding before it vast formations of top-lit cloud. Away to the left, beyond the tree trunks and through the fresh, rain-washed green of the ferns, he could glimpse stretches of the sea. From somewhere out of sight came the yelping cries of gulls.

He felt as if someone were watching him. Except for his time in Martinson's hut and in the cave, he had had the sensation almost continuously since landing on Sert. He had attributed it to two main reasons. The first was the likelihood of satellite surveillance. The second was the feeling he had brought with him from the mainland, where it was virtually impossible to be alone in any open space and one's behavior had to be modified accordingly. Yet now the feeling of being observed had grown stronger, as if there were real grounds for it.

How long had the gulls been calling? What could they see that he could not? Was there somebody on the beach? But there was no beach.

Irrational terror gripped his heart. For all the imagined progress he had made since his arrival here, he was again close to panic. He had eaten nothing since yesterday and was light-headed. He had lost weight. It had not been himself, but a bearded madman, confused and haggard, who had returned his gaze in a rockpool near the cave. Last night he had suffered an attack of diarrhea and had awoken this morning with a chill. On more than one occasion in the cave he had suspected himself of losing track of time for greater or lesser periods; he had been making increasingly stupid and absentminded mistakes. Perhaps he had already lost his marbles. Perhaps he was dead; perhaps this was the afterlife.

"No," he thought. "Not yet."

Glancing over his shoulder once more, he went on, moving slightly downhill. The path dwindled and vanished altogether. The firs yielded to gorse, and then brambles, and then to sparser scrub where he came across the first definite sign of human settlement he had seen since leaving Old Town: a low stone tower, severely decayed, standing among the remnants of walls and foundations, all more or less overgrown. The site showed evidence of having been turfed and mown, and not too many years since: perhaps just before the evacuation. It faced the sea, almost adjoining low, grassy cliffs which sloped straight down to the rocks of the shore.

The shore seemed to curve strongly round to the right, and Routledge wondered whether he had unwittingly come almost to the end of a peninsula.

The ruins had a serene, ecclesiastical air, as if the place had centuries ago been made hallow, as if, despite the use to which Sert had since been put, this protection still held good today. Entering the rubble-strewn floor space of the tower, he noticed a niche in the eastern wall. And there, higher up, near the top, was a wide slab of stone which might have run under an arched window paned with colored glass.

This, surely, was the chapel of the old monastery.

He went outside again, imagining he could trace in the foundations the layout of the monastery buildings. This part might have been the kitchen, the broader area next to it the refectory, those the walls of the living quarters.

He tried to imagine also what sort of men had voluntarily embraced the tedium and austerity of a small island in the north Atlantic. Religious fervor had quite a bit to do with it, of course. Probably it had been no great hardship to leave the oppressions and persecutions of medieval England behind. Islands had always been a place of sanctuary. The difference today was that, in a sense, the people taking sanctuary were those on the mainland.

This was no time for such idle speculation, or for sightseeing. His examination took no more than a minute. Having established that the ruins were of no practical importance to him, he decided to change course to the right, heading westwards to see whether he had indeed walked out to the end of a peninsula. With one last glance at the tower, and holding the crossbow clear of the undergrowth, he began to move in that direction.

It was then that he knew that someone was watching him.

A moment ago, looking over the ruins, he had felt the touch of eyes more strongly still, but he had dismissed it as fanciful. He did not believe in ghosts, nor did he seriously believe, as some might have done, that a place could absorb supernatural influences from the people who had lived and died there. And besides, in his present state he no longer trusted himself.

But now he knew. Someone was behind him, hiding in the scrub.

The back of his neck tingling, Routledge moved off. Then he stopped and whirled around.

He did not really see the man. All that registered was a sense of movement, across there, beyond a big clump of brambles.

By now Routledge was trembling with fear. He only had one shot. Suppose there were several of them? No. Several would have been able to rush him. One shot, then. But suppose even that first shot missed? The machete was ready to hand. He would use that as well. The watcher must have seen the crossbow. He would want it, probably very badly. He would want the machete, the haversack, the boots and clothes.

There was the slightest movement of vegetation beyond the bramble clump. Not caused by a bird. Not by a goat or rabbit. Not by the wind. By a man. It was definite. Someone was there, trying to tempt Routledge into loosing off his single crossbow bolt.

Worst of all: the thought occurred to him that it might be Martinson. Had Martinson been silently following, waiting his chance? Was it Martinson the gulls had seen? Routledge remembered all too well how quietly Martinson and the other two had come up behind him in the woods.

Or was Routledge imagining things again? That was what he wanted to believe. He would resolutely investigate the bramble clump, just to show himself there was nothing to be afraid of.

But what if he were right? Could he afford to do something so reckless? Options, he told himself: quickly, options. You can look or you can refrain from looking. You can stay or you can go. If you go, and no one follows, that's just as good as going to look. Or better, because you avoid all risk.

And if there were someone, and he followed? The watcher had already demonstrated his ability to move in complete silence. Using the cover of the scrub, might he not circle ahead? Judging by the position of the sun, the time was now about six. There were at least four hours to go before the

Village bell rang. Martinson, anyone who lived on Sert, would know the routine. He would know that Routledge would have to wait near the gate, and that, within one hour of the bell, he would have to present himself or forever forfeit his chance of a place inside.

This situation was precisely what Routledge had been dreading, so much so that he feared he had now almost willed it into existence.

He started to move away, towards the west, as he had originally intended. He reached the edge of the monastery precincts and looked around. Nothing. The bramble clump was as before. He went on, through thicker scrub of bracken and gorse. He felt the sea wind on his face, and the solidity under his boot soles as the ground began again to climb. He wanted to look back, but didn't. Finally the desire became overwhelming. He could resist it no more.

By the tower, beyond accurate range, a shaggy figure came that instant into view: a savage, an aborigine, utterly unlike any of the men Routledge had seen in Old Town. He owed nothing whatever to civilization; he was armed with a wooden spear and clad entirely in furs and skins, crudely hung about his body or strapped in place with thongs. His feet were bare, as were his arms and shoulders, which were deeply tanned. A fur band encircled his forehead; an extensive bald patch showed plainly in the sun. Dark-haired, and about Routledge's own age and weight and height, he was nevertheless endowed with a frighteningly languid, lithe athleticism Routledge had never observed before in any Caucasian male, let alone a British one. The man saw Routledge watching him and moved the spear in a gesture without meaning.

He was deliberately loitering there, waiting for Routledge to make more ground before following.

Routledge took two steps towards him and raised the crossbow. At his leisure, the man retreated behind the stonework of the tower. He knew he was beyond range but, now that he had been discovered, it seemed he wanted to indicate the nature of the game.

Routledge did not know what to do. The important thing was to get onto open ground where he was sure of a good

all-round view. The scrub through which he had come was
no use. He could not go back that way. If he really were at
the end of a peninsula, then, unless the terrain opened out
on its western side, he was done for. And he was done for if
the man had a companion, or companions. Perhaps they were
already slowly closing in. That would explain his easy manner, his insolence.

Routledge began to wish he had put his time in the cave
to better use. He should have practiced his marksmanship.

The sun went in as he turned and continued uphill, at the
fastest rate he could, just short of breaking into a run. Each
time he looked around, the man was following, keeping up
with him exactly, maintaining the same distance. Veering
more to the right, Routledge avoided the densest area of gorse
and in ten minutes came to the top of the rise. Before him
and to his right lay a kilometer's width of sea, a deep bay
defined on its far side by serried formations of sunlit cliffs
and headlands which extended westwards for at least four
kilometers, maybe more. On top of the final headland, under
cloud but almost directly against the brightest part of the sky,
his retina briefly caught the pattern of organization: buildings, fields, walls. The Village.

He had indeed trapped himself at the end of a peninsula.
But this western side, exposed to the prevailing wind, was
more open than the way he had come. For some distance to
the right, for half a kilometer at least, he would be safe.

As he went, Routledge dropped first the sheepskin waistcoat and then the goatskin hat. He hoped the man would
pause to pick them up, that their weight would be better
carried by the pursuer than the pursued. His own PVC jacket,
which he was wearing, he decided to retain. To lose it would
cost him points when he reached the Village.

The moment he had dropped the hat he regretted his action, for it would be seen as an attempt at appeasement and
as evidence that Routledge had yet more desirable objects in
his possession. It had been a mistake. A bad mistake; but it
was too late now to change his mind.

Looking back, he saw the man bend down. The next time
Routledge looked, he was wearing the hat and carrying the

waistcoat, but still maintaining the same easy, assured, re-lentless pace.

They were crossing rough, tussocky turf interspersed with clumps of low bracken and gorse. Routledge made a detour past a broad area of heather which, spreading down the hill-side nearly to the cliff edge, almost threatened to lie in his path. By now he was beginning to tire. He felt his speed beginning to fade and angrily redoubled his efforts to keep it going. For the twentieth time he looked back. His pursuer, if anything, seemed fresher, just getting into his stride, mov-ing with a leisurely, economical gait that he could maintain all day, and all night too, if need be.

The cliffs here were not steep. A couple of hundred meters ahead, almost at their edge, lay a large outcrop of rock, and behind it another. Beyond them the ground was more shel-tered, and to his horror and consternation Routledge saw that the scrub there again became gradually thicker, much thicker, thick enough to take away the advantage of the crossbow and allow the man to catch up or circle ahead unseen. That was what he had been waiting for: that explained why he had been content to hang back till now.

In his frantic attempt to find another passage through, Routledge changed course more to the right, climbing slant-wise across the face of the slope. He got to the top of the rise before acknowledging to himself the truth of what he already feared: that there was no way out.

Either he could keep on, or he could stay and stand his ground. He knew he couldn't take much more of this exer-tion. The weight of the crossbow was becoming intolerable. He stopped and turned around. The man stopped too. By going no farther, Routledge could at least rest. He might even be able to sit down, keeping the crossbow leveled at his adversary. But for how long? What would happen when the light began to fail?

Routledge's voice cracked as he screamed his desperate, hopeless oath of dismissal.

For reply the man moved a few meters nearer, confident that Routledge's aim was being steadily impaired by fear, by exhaustion, by his pounding pulse. Routledge raised the crossbow and unsuccessfully tried to align the bead. He remembered the way the bolt had smashed the rock on the beach. There was a chance. Just a chance; but he couldn't afford to take it.

Suddenly he was making for the outcrop of rock at the cliff edge, two hundred meters away down the slope. A hundred and fifty. Fifty. A flashing backward glance told him the man was gaining fast, no longer so cocky, for he had now seen what Routledge had in mind: to get momentarily out of sight, to hide in a defensible position and thus force his pursuer to take the initiative. With the last few strides Routledge realized he had done it.

The outcrop was about half the height of a house, shaped somewhat like the end of a crude boat jutting sideways from the sparse, thrift-grown turf; the far side was split and fissured into irregular gullies. One of these gullies made a partial alcove, damp and cool, permanently concealed from the sun. Routledge pressed himself into it, and, panting, waited for whatever was going to happen next.

He could hear nothing but the wind and the sound of the surf. The man had stopped moving, or had once again switched to his silent mode of travel. Then, from the shore below him and to his left, Routledge heard the loud, quick piping of two wading-birds, rising to an ecstatic crescendo which abruptly died. The sea there looked gray: he saw the birds, black and white, with red beaks, perching on two adjacent rocks.

Still there was no sign of his companion. A minute had passed. What would he do? Which side would he come from? Or was he just going to sit it out and wait?

Routledge tried to reduce the trembling in his hands. Already he was beginning to get his breath back: his lungs no longer felt as if they were about to burst. He had to keep calm. He had to be in control of himself.

Another minute passed, and Routledge started to have second thoughts about this strategy. It was worse not being able to see him. At least in the open . . .

He had expected the attack to come from the left. Most of his attention had been directed there, with the rest directed to the right. The thought had not occurred to him, obvious though it now seemed, that it would come from above. He must have detected an inadvertent sound, or sensed slight motion in the uppermost edge of his peripheral vision: whatever the reason, he looked up and saw the man there, three meters above him, in the act of raising both arms to hurl a rock down on his head.

Later, he had no recollection of stepping back and raising the crossbow, no recollection of bringing bead and sight into line with the man's body. It all happened too fast. But he did remember, as if frozen on film, the moment when his finger, already inside the guard, began to make contact with the trigger. At that moment he had conscious control. This was not like the frenzied, automatic attack on Gazzer and Tortuga. Now he had a choice. He could shoot to wound, or he could shoot to kill.

His hand and arm and eye made the decision without further reference to his brain. The pressure of his touch, faithfully transmitted by both pivots, arrived at the waiting nib, which, more rapidly than thought, and receiving the only command it knew, smoothly descended and allowed the crossbow to let fly.

The bolt hit the man in the center of his chest, so hard that he was thrown backwards, toppling out of sight. Routledge dodged the falling rock and scrabbled in his pack for the machete, then ran to the far side of the outcrop, where it would be easier to climb.

There was no need for the machete. The case-hardened, sharpened tip of the bolt had emerged between two vertebrae. The man's spinal cord had been ruptured. The bolt would have continued on its upward path and gone right through him had it not been arrested by the vanes, which, as it was, had sliced into the musculature of his chest to a third or half their depth. He was quite dead.

Routledge came to his senses and surveyed the hillside. No evidence of another one: the man had been working alone.

Close to, the primitive nobility lent him by his beard was revealed for the illusion it was. His face had a rather ugly, stupid cast. His ears were large and angular, pierced in both lobes; the eyes, staring blankly, were bulbous and blue. His open jaw betrayed a mouth filled with dental amalgam. Tattooed on his shoulder Routledge read the five blue letters, entwined in red, of a girl's name. *Karen.* Routledge examined his hands and feet and the development of his limbs, intrigued by the changes that living wild had wrought in one of his own countrymen.

The birds on the shore resumed their piping. He stood up. The corpse was beginning to bleed. He would not waste time or risk contaminating himself by burying it, or by putting it over the cliff. He would let it remain where it had fallen, food for the gulls, perhaps, or the buzzards. There was nothing on it he wanted: the skins, the necklace of rabbit bones, were worthless. He would not bother with the spear, but Martinson's waistcoat, and the hat, both of which the man had left lying at the base of the outcrop, he would retrieve.

Before climbing down, Routledge allowed himself one last look around, making sure of the hillside and the more distant scrub to the north and west.

And, turning his eyes across the bay, he studied, at his leisure now, the pattern and appearance of the fields and walls and buildings spreading across the cloud-shadowed slope of his destination, the Village headland.

PART TWO

PART TWO

1

"BEND OVER, PLEASE."

Routledge felt his buttocks being parted.

"All right, Mr. Routledge. I'm sorry about that last bit."
Sibley switched off the flashlight and replaced it on his table.
"You can put your clothes on now." He stood up, went to
the far side of the room, and washed his hands in a polythene
bowl from which issued the smell of pine disinfectant. "We
have to make sure, you understand."

"What would have happened if . . ."

"Well, you'd have been out, I'm afraid."

"Does that happen often?"

"Quite often. But not in your case, I'm delighted to say.
In fact, as far as I can tell, you've got a clean bill of health."

Routledge pulled on his brand-new trousers, gray corduroy, with a broad canvas belt. Like the socks and underwear,
the wool-and-cotton shirt, the blue lambswool sweater, and
the workman's boots, they fitted him perfectly, part of the
issue the Prison Service had sent over with him from the
mainland.

Sibley's room, in one of the shacks annexed to the bungalow, was equipped as a kind of surgery, with even a glass-
shelved cupboard containing probes and forceps and seekers.
A pressure lamp illuminated the table and the file containing
Routledge's papers. On these Sibley, an apparently absent-

minded Welshman of about forty, had scribbled notes at various stages throughout the examination.

Routledge buckled the belt. "Are you a doctor?"

"Of sorts, now. I was a vet before. And you? A quantity surveyor, weren't you?"

"Yes. I was."

Sibley closed the file and put it under his arm. "I'm to tell you the Father will see you tonight. Hurry up and finish dressing."

To put on clean, new clothes was a pleasure more luxurious even than the showerbath they had allowed him, with soap and real shampoo and tepid water gushing from an overhead tank improvised from a plastic drum. They had offered him a razor too. This he had declined: he had never grown a beard before, and was beginning rather to like the idea.

So far he had been astonished by the courtesy and hospitality they were showing him. One of the men at the gate, the one who had escorted him to Appleton, had even said "Well done, Mr. Routledge" when he had appeared, promptly, a few minutes after the bell.

The end of his ordeal had been unexpectedly easy. From the monastery peninsula he had made his way, without encountering anyone, back to the Village boundary and the gate. Having ascertained that Martinson was nowhere to be seen, he had selected a hollow in the bracken a few hundred meters away and had sat there, clasping his knees, watching the sunset yielding to darkness. An hour or two later the bell—to be exact, an oil drum struck with a length of steel pipe—had sounded. The caution with which he had covered the remaining distance to the gate had been as immense as it had been unnecessary.

Appleton had given him hot, sweet tea and a plate of cheese sandwiches, followed by a dish of yogurt flavored with fresh raspberries. Then he had commended Routledge to the care of Sibley and his assistant.

In the shower Routledge had been able to appreciate how much weight he had lost. The slight paunch which, with each succeeding year, had been becoming almost imperceptibly more pronounced, had all but vanished. There was less fat around his waist, too. His arms, and particularly his legs, had become more rangy-looking, as had his fingers and toes. There was an empty, sick feeling in his abdomen; he had suffered another diarrhea attack on the way to the gate, and wondered whether he had poisoned himself by eating Martinson's none-too-hygienic rations. When asked, though, Sibley had told him this was quite usual in the circumstances and nothing to be concerned about.

Sibley conducted him to the bungalow veranda. The guard, different from the one Routledge had seen on his first visit last week, announced his arrival and summoned Stamper, who ushered Routledge to Appleton's small office. Appleton was not there.

"Right," Stamper said. "You'll be going in now. Don't speak unless you're spoken to. When Mr. Appleton gives you the prompt, get down on the green mat. Lie on your face and say, 'I forever renounce all rights except those invested in me hereafter by the Father. I formally recognize his absolute authority and in this recognition beg for admittance to the Community.' Got it?"

Routledge, his unease growing, needed hurried coaching before he could repeat the words without error. He was right: he had thought his treatment thus far was much too good to last. As he had suspected from the start, the Father, whoever or whatever he might turn out to be, was plainly a megalomaniac.

There was no time for further thoughts along these lines.

As soon as Routledge was word perfect, Stamper led the way to the large reception room or laboratory in which Routledge had been interrogated on that first night. "Ready?" Stamper said.

Routledge nodded.

"Good luck."

Stamper's words took him by surprise. He neither liked nor trusted any of the triumvirate who had interviewed him, but he saw that he could afford to alienate none of the inmates of the Village, especially those in power, and would pretend at least to return any small gestures of friendship.

"Thanks."

Stamper knocked lightly at the door, opened it, and motioned Routledge inside. Stamper did not follow. Routledge heard the door closing quietly and unobtrusively behind him.

As before, the room was lit by three pressure lamps, but tonight the trestle table had been pushed back to the wall. In its place stood an old-fashioned wing armchair covered in tapestry, predominantly fawn, with a repeating panel depicting what the designer had imagined to be a typical eighteenth-century scene: a bewigged man in a frilled coat, wooing his beloved under a rose arbor. Even more unexpected and bizarre, Routledge saw immediately that the oblong piece of green carpet in front of it was of precisely the same color and pattern as the hall carpet belonging to Louise's parents. The pattern had been unobtainable for ten years or more. During all that time, during all those unsuspecting Sunday afternoons, this companion-piece had been patiently awaiting him here on Sert.

Appleton was standing behind the chair and to its left. Every bit of the authority he had possessed at the first interview was relinquished to the clean-faced, humorous-looking man who now entered by the second door, went to the chair, and sat down. Crossing his legs, he began subjecting Routledge to a keen and searching appraisal through the rimless lenses of his gold-framed spectacles.

Routledge had expected someone older, heavier, more intimidating, than this fellow with his freckles and reddish-blond hair. Indeed, he was no older than Routledge himself. And yet his every movement, his very bearing, gave an unmistakable impression of physical self-assurance and self-containment; the calm, refined cast of his features gave an equally vivid impression of a strongly incisive intelligence unlike any that Routledge had ever known before.

"Good evening, Mr. Routledge." He was softly spoken, with an educated southern Irish accent. "Congratulations on passing our initiative test. I hear you came back with a crossbow."

"Yes."

"May I ask where you got it?"

"From a man named Martinson."

He gave an enigmatic smile. ''Is that where you got the rest of the stuff?''

''I'd rather not say.''

''As you wish.'' He smiled again, apparently pleased by this response. ''Now, Mr. Routledge. I have a request to make. The crossbow belonged to the Community. We lost it; it presently belongs to you. We would greatly appreciate its return.''

''By all means.''

''That's very kind. Very kind indeed. I hope you didn't object to the test too much. You understand the reasons for it?''

''To be honest, no.''

''It has two main purposes. The first is to find out what you're made of. The second is to give you practical experience of life outside the Village.''

Routledge said nothing.

''On your first day the rules of the Community were explained to you. Do you have any questions on that subject?''

''No sir, I do not.''

''Kindly do not use that word here. Turnkeys are 'sir.' Politicians are 'sir.' In the Village a man is valued for what he is, or isn't, as the case may be. Do you understand?''

''Yes.''

''Get that clear before all else.'' Still his composure had not deserted him; Routledge had to give himself a conscious order to renew his mistrust. ''On your first day you were also invited to apply for a place in the Community. I will now ask you what decision you have reached in that regard.''

''I would like to apply.''

''Then there are one or two things I feel I should explain. Depending on your background and upbringing, you will find them more or less novel. If you elect to remain with us, I hope that you will not find them too irksome to live with.''

Against his will, Routledge felt himself becoming charmed. He had entered the room in a hostile frame of mind, and yet, as the interview progressed, he was beginning to feel, despite himself, an intimation that his prejudices were in danger of slipping away. He was intrigued, fascinated not so much by the sheer magnetic force of the man's presence as by the discovery that such a phenomenon truly existed in the world and that he was susceptible to its influence.

"We have come, Mr. Routledge, all of us, from a place where hypocrisy reigns supreme. One is not allowed to say what is, only what is deemed morally fashionable. Lip service is paid to the notion that all men are born equal and deserving of equal opportunity. Much is made of people's rights, without overmuch attention to the responsibility which accompanies and in precise measure counterbalances each and every one of those rights. We have also come from an economy based on the system of money. On Sert there is no money. The only currency here is respect. Respect is accorded to those who in turn respect others' rights and interests, as well as to those who are deserving in more obvious ways. Respect automatically generates consideration, which is the essential lubricant on which the mechanics of our little community depend. Clear enough?"

"Yes."

"We are all convicted criminals, abandoned and left to rot. Yet by coming here each of us is given a completely blank sheet. If you like, we have become innocents once more. We have been denied the pleasures of the mainland, but we have also been released from its demands."

These words struck a chord: Routledge remembered his own thoughts in the darkness of the cave.

"Our leader, at present myself, is styled the 'Father.' It is only a name. The leader is not a patriarch. He is not God. The men under him are not children. Is that clear too?"

"Yes."

"Nor is this a democracy. It is a meritocracy. Each man has his place in it, determined solely by his own conduct and character. What yours will be I cannot say. You may end up plucking puffins, or you may end up as leader in my stead. Understood?"

"Yes."

"And you still wish to apply? Consider carefully now."

"Yes. I wish to apply."

Appleton gestured at the floor. Routledge hesitated before,

self-consciously, getting to his knees. Appleton gestured again, somewhat impatiently. Routledge let himself down until his face came into contact with the green tufted pile of the mat.

"Well?" said the man in the chair.

"I . . . I forever renounce all rights except those invested in me hereafter by the Father. I formally recognize . . . I . . ."

Routledge had forgotten the words.

"His absolute authority," Appleton hissed.

"I formally recognize his absolute authority and in this recognition beg for admittance to the Community."

"You are one of us now, Mr. Routledge. Please get up."

When the interview had ended and the Father had retired to his own part of the bungalow, Appleton took Routledge into his office, a square, cramped room furnished with a shaky laminate-surfaced table and lined on two sides with shelves. Appleton had brought one of the pressure lamps. He hooked the handle over a wall-bracket, motioned Routledge to be seated in the battered easy chair, and sat down himself behind the table.

"This won't take a minute," he said. "As it's so late, we'll have our main talk in the morning. Please be here at six o'clock."

His authority had returned.

"You'll find we tend to rise and go to bed earlier on Sert, especially in summer. It saves kerosene and candles."

Especially in summer. There came to Routledge's mind the first true inkling of the immense period of time, season after season, year after year, during which he would be stuck on this rock.

Appleton gave him a moment's scrutiny before going on. "I just want to mention a few points of etiquette. As the Father has told you, we have no currency in the Community, other than respect. A man's place is hard-earned and he does not take kindly to lack of recognition of that place. Certain standards of behavior have therefore evolved which are very different from those obtaining on the mainland. The Father's name is Liam Michael Franks. At no time will you call him anything but 'Father.' Address other members of the Community by their title and surname. When you know someone sufficiently well he may allow you to call him by his surname used alone, except in the presence of inferiors, when it is usual to adopt the formal mode. Intimate friends may use forenames if they wish, but this is not often done. Unless he volunteers the information, it is considered impolite to ask a man about his criminal record. When a man of superior rank enters the room, you stand up. This can be tricky in the beginning, and it will be understood if you make some mistakes. For the first twenty-four hours in the Community, you are our guest. After that you must work in accordance with the rules; in other words, as directed by the Father. If you do not work properly you will receive no food and you may be denied accommodation. If you persist in not working you will be expelled. Expulsion is final and irreversible.'' He sat back. ''I think that just about covers it for tonight.''

''May I ask a question?''

''That depends what it is. You'll have plenty of opportunity to ask questions tomorrow, and on any topic you like.''

''Did the Prison Service send over my personal effects? I had some photographs of my family.''

''They'll probably come on tomorrow's drop, or next week's.'' Tomorrow was Tuesday, helicopter day. ''Now,'' he went on, ''you'll be staying with Mr. King, your guardian, until suitable accommodation is made ready. That's one of the things we'll be talking about in the morning.'' Appleton stood up. ''Mr. King is expecting you. Your issue has already been delivered to his house. I'll take you there. You might not be able to find it in the dark.''

The shack was much as Routledge had remembered it, except that it seemed King had made an attempt to tidy up. The pallet was still there, although the sleeping-bag had been replaced with gray blankets, and another blanket, folded, had been provided as a pillow. It did not look very comfortable, but at least it seemed clean.

King said, ''Can I offer you something, Mr. Appleton?''

''No, thank you all the same, Mr. King.'' Appleton moved

back to the door and opened it. "Six o'clock, Mr. Rout-ledge. Don't forget."

"I won't."

"Mr. King has a clock. Well, good night, then."

King secured the door behind him and gave Routledge a half smile which Routledge interpreted as evidence that King, while not relishing the idea of sharing his accommodation with another, would do his best not to show it.

"You're a bit of a celebrity," King said. "Word's got around about the crossbow. They're saying you took it off James Martinson. Are they right?"

"Yes. I suppose they are."

"Did you go to Old Town? By the way, do take a seat."

Routledge decided to leave vacant the chair indicated, for it was the one King had occupied on the first night. Instead he sat down on a low stool by the hearth.

"Would you like a drink? Some Village Black Label?"

"'Black Label'?"

"Whisky. What passes for it."

Routledge was very tired; what he wanted most of all was to lie down and close his eyes. "That's very kind. But only if you're having one."

King rummaged about in a box by the wall and produced a bottle, about a third full, of what did indeed look like whisky. He then produced two glasses and poured Routledge a double measure.

"Water?"

"No thanks."

"Here's to you, Mr. Routledge."

Routledge saw that the words had been sincerely deliv-ered, and was touched. The whisky was not as bad as he had expected. In fact, he had drunk worse in pubs on the main-land.

"Mr. Thorne makes it," King said. "He's trying to get some juniper bushes on the go to try his hand at gin as well."

"It's very good." The glass was shaped like the bottom half of a jam jar: which is exactly what Routledge now re-alized it was. "This is interesting," he said. "How did you make the glasses?"

"Oh, Mr. Ojukwo makes those. People give him jars or he gets them from the shore. He ties a loop of string round the jar, wherever he wants the height. The string's soaked in kerosene, set fire to, and the glass weakens along that line. Then with a bit of careful tapping the joint breaks, and he grinds the edge down by hand." Having as expeditiously as possible discharged the duty of imparting such mundane information, King took another sip and said: "You didn't say whether you'd been to Old Town."

"I was taken there against my will. But I did manage to avoid the lighthouse." This was as close as Routledge thought he ought to come towards thanking King directly for having warned him about the two outsider towns.

"Would you prefer not to talk about it?"

"To be honest, I'm just very tired. I'll tell you anything you want to know tomorrow."

King downed the last of his whisky. "I'm pretty well knackered myself. I've got to be up early again tomorrow." He took Routledge's empty glass. "I won't wake you up: you sleep on till, say, five-fifteen. Have my alarm clock, and you'll find a bit of breakfast on the table."

2

"YOU'RE A GOOD BOY, OBADIAH WALKER," MARTINSON said.

"Got to help your mates," Obie said.

Martinson winced again. He was bleeding more profusely now. The glistening prong of splintered bone, shocking in its stark, unnatural whiteness, was still protruding from the flesh of his left calf. "Holy Jesus, Obie, get it over with."

Stretched out on his goatskin sofa, Martinson had so far borne his ordeal without complaint. Obie brought the lamp closer. Going by what he remembered from cowboy films on TV, he was trying to clean the wound before setting the break with splints and a length of old shirting; but he did not really know what he was doing. He had never seen a broken leg before, least of all anything like this.

The bone had been smashed rather than snapped. Martinson had been struck with a club and knocked down from the lighthouse gallery. Besides breaking his leg, the fall had left him concussed and with extensive heavy bruising, especially about the chest and left shoulder. The skin on his face had been badly grazed. In fact, he was in a mess. It was a miracle he had survived at all. He had lain on the asphalt, unconscious, for the whole afternoon before anyone had been able to reach him. The only reason he was alive now was that Peto had waved the white flag—not for Martinson's sake, but because he had decided to give in to Houlihan's demands. The fighting, for the moment, was over.

For Peto it had been a disaster. Besides a number of vicious skirmishes, there had been three pitched battles, the first of which, on Thursday afternoon, had been started by Houlihan. Then on Sunday, before the Old Town forces had been repulsed, Peto had attempted to set fire to the lighthouse.

The final battle, today, had again taken place at the lighthouse. Lured there by Houlihan, Peto's men had been ambushed and routed. Martinson and some others had tried to scale the tower, hoping to get their hands on Houlihan himself, but to no avail. No fewer than fifteen towners had been killed, bringing Peto's losses since Thursday to twenty-seven, with many more injured. In addition Peto had been forced to give Houlihan his whole flock of goats, his binoculars, and, most humiliating of all, a hostage to good conduct in the form of his present catamite, the blue-eyed and fair-haired Desborough. What was already happening to Desborough at the lighthouse could be imagined all too well.

Nothing had yet been said, but Peto's loss of face had been so great that Obie wondered how long it would be before his leadership was called into question. There was no sign that Peto was planning to launch the revenge attack that alone could restore him in the opinion of his men.

Martinson, however, had only enhanced his reputation, especially through the lunacy and daring of today's attack on Houlihan's quarters. If Martinson hadn't been injured, and if he held ambitions in that direction, Peto might eventually have had a serious rival to contend with.

Such matters exercised Obie only so far as his own safety was concerned. He had become identified as one of Peto's council, and although that had been at Peto's instigation rather than his own, he had readily accepted the advantages and benefits the position had conferred. By so doing he knew he had earned himself grudge in certain quarters of the town. If Peto fell he might be in trouble, for he could not go to Houlihan.

Alone perhaps at Old Town, Obie had detected a pattern

in Martinson's behavior during the fighting. On several occasions Martinson had fudged or disregarded orders which, if carried out, might have had severe consequences for the lighthouse settlement and the generality of its inhabitants. His disobedience may even have cost Peto victory. Martinson, it seemed to Obie, had been pursuing a private purpose. To the exclusion of all else he had been trying to get his hands on Houlihan himself, with the secondary goal of wiping out certain members of the brain gang which had contributed so much to Houlihan's strength and success.

Obie was beginning to wonder what Martinson was doing. It could no longer be assumed that he was unambitious. But if he were simply planning to take over from Peto there would have been a showdown, or a straightforward murder, in the time-honored way, followed by a reshuffling of power inside the town. No: he was after something larger. Obie had always known he was mad; now he suspected him of the deep capacity for cunning and foresight which psychopaths often possessed.

For if Martinson had succeeded in killing Houlihan and his closest supporters, might he not then have turned on Peto? And afterwards, in the flux of two leaderless communities, might he not have advanced himself as the leader of all?

Until now Obie had imagined that, as far as it was possible to be so on the island of Sert, Martinson was reasonably content with his lot. One or two remarks he had made, at long intervals, about the Village had led Obie to believe that Martinson's resentment of Franks went rather further than most people's. But this evening Obie had remembered that Franks, like Martinson himself, had come over on the first boat. The two men had been at Dartmoor together, and had, for a time, been on friendly terms. Yet there was no suggestion that Martinson had ever been asked to join the Village. Indeed, Martinson had been instrumental in starting the war between Franks and Barratt that had led ultimately to its foundation.

Franks had only survived this long because his opponents were in disarray. United—under Martinson, for example—

they could make life in the Village much less cozy. They might even get the helicopter back.

Obie took a third bowl of boiling seawater from the fire and soaked a fresh pad of shirting. He had used seawater for its disinfectant properties: there was nothing else, not even the whisky the cowboys always seemed to use. As he dabbed at Martinson's raw flesh, Obie prayed that Peto would remain for a while longer yet. With Martinson out of action, the way was open for Dave Nackett or Dog or one of the other hard men to issue a challenge. Whichever of those won the contest, Obie could expect unpleasantness or worse. The way things looked tonight, Peto would go eventually. If he had to have a successor, Obie wanted it to be Martinson.

That was the reason Obie was here now. The other blokes had merely dumped Martinson in his hut after the battle. Because he was in bad odor with Peto, no one had wanted to take the initiative to help him.

"I finished cleanin' it now, Jim. I got all the bits out."

"Good. That's good, me old mate."

"I'm goin' to have a go at settin' it. Hold on tight."

"Did I say you was a good boy, Obie? All the boys in this town, you're the only one what gives a toss."

"Florence Nightingale, that's me."

He made the first tentative approach towards reducing the alarming angle at which the leg was bent, and for the first time Martinson gave a low groan, which, as Obie slowly increased the pressure, intensified and became a horrible shout of pain.

Sleep was a very long time in coming. No sooner had it arrived than Routledge awoke, sweating, from a nightmare involving the man he had shot.

He thought he must have shouted himself awake, but the darkness inside the shack was utterly still. King, in the far corner, was, as before, breathing regularly and deeply, fast asleep.

Routledge was afraid of going back there, to the place he had so vividly inhabited just now, the silvery vista of rock and unreal sea, the bracken stretching forever up the hill.

Most of all he was afraid of seeing those features again, or hearing the name *Karen*, uttered in the mocking voice of her lover.

The silence was being punctured steadily, relentlessly, by the officious ticking of King's clock. Between each tick came a slight noise of springs, and beneath this, underlying the heavy silence of the night, came the faintest and most distant sound of breaking waves. Lying there, wearing only his underpants and shirt, vainly trying to ignore both the musty smell of the blankets and the acrid, indefinable, salt-laden smell which permeated every corner of the shack; vainly trying to get comfortable on the lumpy stuffing of which his mattress was made, his thoughts still resonant with the mild inflection of King's voice and the man's shabby, threadbare, and essentially pathetic appearance, Routledge was again overcome by the feeling of disbelief which had been with him since his arrival on Sert, and which had beset him with even greater force since his entry to the Village. This could not be true: like everything that had happened since the moment the police had knocked on his front door, it was impossible. Impossible that he would not wake up tomorrow in his own bed, read the paper, eat breakfast, catch the train and go to the site or the office. That he would not come home again for supper, walking from the station portico to his house, avoiding as always the shorter route along a footpath illuminated by swan-necked streetlamps striving to hold back the night. The lamp standards painted that obnoxious Metropolitan Railway green and their broad shades lined with grimy white enamel. Despite the wire grids, many of the bulbs were smashed and there were extensive intervals in the line of light. Behind the diamond-mesh fence, much holed and damaged by trespassers, lay an overgrown embankment almost buried under tin cans, candy wrappers, hamburger boxes, plastic sacks of builders' rubble. It was there that her body had been found. "Good evening, sir." The flash of a warrant card: and the nightmare had begun.

It was true that Routledge had spoken to her on the train. The witnesses said he had tried to pick her up. Not so. She had spoken first, a pleasant young woman, girl, sitting beside him in a navy blue raincoat, wearing sensible black shoes. Not overtly pretty, but sexually attractive just the same. Would he mind opening the window? The heating was on full blast. He had complied. A short conversation had ensued, a few empty exchanges. She ended it by asking him for his copy of the *Daily Mail*. He had finished with it; she said she was planning to follow the serialized diet, but had been unable to get today's edition. Routledge gave it to her. It was Louise's paper. He had only brought it to read on the train coming home. Then at Harrow-on-the-Hill a window seat on the opposite side of the carriage had become vacant. She had taken it, sat looking out into the rainy October night, at the passing lights of streets, houses, factories.

She had remained there at each stop while the carriage had slowly emptied. *Northwood Hills. Northwood. Moor Park.* And it was true, God help him, that he had fantasized about inviting her back. Louise and Christopher had gone to her parents' house for the half-term holiday. That was why he had taken the *Mail* as well as his usual *Times*. This was Friday night: an empty weekend had stretched before him. But even as the thought had entered his mind he had known it to be nonsense. He had never tried anything like that; probably never would.

At Rickmansworth he had perforce followed her along the platform. She had given in her ticket; he, just behind her, had shown his season-ticket. Leaving the portico, he had turned right. She had turned left, towards the footpath. He had never set eyes on her again.

Because Louise was not there to switch on the porch light, the front of the house was in darkness. The York stone steps up to the front path were always slippery: now they were also strewn with wet leaves. On the second step he missed his footing and fell, letting out an oath of surprise. He came down awkwardly, hitting his elbow and wrist, tearing open the skin on his left knee.

The police called on Saturday evening. Apparently they had traced him by using the newspaper. It had been found near the body, among the scattered contents of her shoulder-bag. On the margin of the front page, with a distinctive violet felt-tip pen, the newsagent had scribbled *44*, the number of his house.

There were two of them, detectives in raincoats. The younger one was the more suspicious. In the hall he craned his head, looking into the kitchen, where Routledge had just been eating baked beans and the sink was full of washing-up. Would he account for his movements on Friday evening? How had he managed to bruise his hand and wrist? Could they see the clothes he had worn on Friday?

He reacted badly. He had always feared the police, especially since the notorious Whiting case, and especially since the start of the Government's vigorous new drive to improve the figures for violent crime and hence its own figures at the polls. He said he wanted his solicitor present. The older detective said there was no need for that, they just wanted to eliminate him from their inquiries. Their inquiries into what? They were not at liberty to say. Would he be at home for the rest of the weekend? Not planning to leave the district?

On the local television news that night he saw what it was all about. Her picture was shown, an unsmiling passport photo taken in a booth. She was called Jacqueline Lister. She had been raped and strangled.

After the broadcast he rang the police station and said he felt he ought to make a statement. He did not take his solicitor.

Then on Monday the police were on the train, interviewing the commuters. One of the chief witnesses for the prosecution, a woman who had been sitting opposite, said he had been leering at the girl. That was the word she used in court. Two other passengers came forward to denounce the lecher. But this was nothing, a mere foretaste of the forensic evidence. First, the copy of the *Daily Mail*, incontrovertibly his, which none of the keen-eyed witnesses had seen him giving to the girl. Then his injuries and the damage to his trousers and sleeve. Then the seminal fluid was matched to his own comparatively uncommon blood group. And finally, the DNA typing of the sperms was declared to be identical to his own.

This last piece of evidence, which even Routledge's coun-

sel did not believe had been fabricated, was the hammer
blow. Beside it his previous good character counted for nothing. Nor did the variable quality of the testimony of the witnesses from the train. The jury, which Routledge had had
ample time to study, was composed of an all-too-represen-
tative cross-section of his peers. A gormless youth in a windcheater, wearing a digital watch which bleeped every hour,
on the hour. An Asian woman who could scarcely speak
English, let alone understand the evidence. The foreperson,
so called, was a middle-aged housewife who seemed to regard the proceedings as an entertainment devised solely to
give her an opportunity to display her wardrobe, consisting
of a variety of suits from high-street multiples. In one of
these, green velvet and beige, she had stood up to deliver the
verdict.

Have you reached a unanimous verdict? No. Then have
you reached a majority verdict? Yes. What is it? We all think
he's guilty.

Condemned by a panel of illiterates. But the judge was
not illiterate. And he was scrupulously fair. Especially to
poor student nurses who were raped and strangled while
walking home to their lodgings.

In the end, only Louise believed; and, on one visiting day
at Exeter, just after the failure of the final appeal, he began
to fear that even her support might eventually crumble.

"Louise," he breathed, drifting unwillingly at long last
towards sleep, "Louise." He did not care what happened to
him, as long as he was not separated from her, or from Christopher. If there was a God up there, which there wasn't, why
was it that he worked so hard to identify whatever thing a
man dreaded most, and, having identified it, why did he
always, always, vindictively succeed in making that very
thing come to pass?

3

WHEN THE ALARM CLOCK RANG ROUTLEDGE TOOK A MOment to realize where he was.

The inside of the shack was in semi-darkness; there were no proper windows, only two shutters covering apertures in the wall. King had gone, leaving his cot neatly covered with blankets. It was almost five-fifteen.

Routledge briefly heard voices nearby, and then they were still. The sound of a barrow being pushed over shale. Chickens some way off. Gulls overhead. Distant laughter. The wind. The barrow again.

From his bed he examined the ceiling, the pillars, the walls and floor, King's pitiful collection of furniture and belongings. His eye took in the crude sideboard, equipped with a washing-up bowl and an enamel jug, which served the shack as a bathroom. And King seemed to occupy a position of some responsibility: what would Routledge's own living quarters eventually be like?

For all that, for all his apprehensions about his future here, he allowed himself to acknowledge a sense of achievement, almost of elation. He had got in. Despite Martinson, and Peto, and Gazzer, and Tortuga, despite the man at the ruins, he had beaten all the odds and got in. Really it had been luck, mostly, that and the cave. Without the cave he couldn't have done it.

He wondered how long the Community had been in existence, how long Franks had been in charge, and how many of those in the Village had undergone the same ordeal. King, for instance. How would he have fared? Or Franks himself, or Appleton? If they had all undergone the same test, or something similar, then the Village was populated with a formidable collection of men indeed.

The test had two main objects, Franks had said: to show what a man was made of, and to give him practical knowledge of life outside. If "practical knowledge" meant a bottomless dread of the outsiders and a frantic resolve to avoid them evermore, if it meant a resolution to do everything in his power to ingratiate himself with the leadership and advance to a position of privilege in the Community, Routledge conceded that, in his case, the test had been spectacularly successful.

His arms and legs ached. He still felt deeply fatigued. His night's rest had refreshed him hardly at all. Worse, he had been dreaming again.

Anxious now for his first daylight view of the Village, he got up, pulled on his sweater and trousers, and slipped his feet into his boots.

On the table he found a plastic mug and a plastic plate with three slices of coarse bread, a blob of jam, some butter, and a hard-boiled egg. Beside the plate lay a scrap of paper bearing a penciled note written in a hasty, cursive hand. He held it up to the light. *Water in tank (in corner). Latrine behind house—corrugated iron roof. Will be in potato fields if I'm needed—B. K.*

Routledge went outside.

The sun had just risen; the sky was clear. It looked as though the day would be fine.

From what he had previously seen, he already knew quite a lot about the topography of the Village. The Village peninsula, at the south-western corner of the island, was roughly oblong in plan view and covered an area of about two hundred and fifty hectares. The border fence ran from northwest to south-east, and had two gates, one near either end. Most of the peninsula seemed to be under cultivation of one sort or another, with scattered areas of natural vegetation and here and there a barn or byre. The main concentration of buildings, assorted in size and style and huddled together for safety, was not far from the north-west gate, on fairly sheltered, sloping ground running down to the western cliffs.

King's shack was near the middle, one of about twenty grouped around the broad, shale-surfaced precinct in front of the bungalow steps. Beyond the bungalow stood a line of fir trees, more shacks, and, just visible from this angle, the posts and framework of the gate through which Routledge had entered last night.

The bungalow was not technically that, for there were two dormer windows on this side. Built of stone, with a slate roof, it had a slightly institutional appearance. The design was not the usual compromise between cost and someone's idea of domestic bliss: it achieved a close accord between its function as both a residence for the warden and headquarters for visiting scientists. The most prominent feature of its broad façade was the wide veranda, supported on stone pillars and with a teak balustrade, where even now a guard was seated by the reinforced front door, nursing a crowbar. As Routledge watched, another man, dressed in jeans and a green-and-yellow sweater, mounted the steps and engaged him in conversation. No one else was in sight.

Routledge found the latrine, which appeared to serve at least a dozen shacks, and noted with displeasure the open pit and the fenestrated plank serving as a seat. But there was no smell. Below the seat a faded polythene sack was being held open on a wickerwork frame. The sack was a third full of water; the frame allowed it to be easily lifted for emptying. A rota in ballpen was fixed to the rush-and-lath wall:

                June 1—15 Mr. Reynolds
                 ″ 16—30 Mr. King
                July 1—15 Mr. Wilson
                 ″ 16—31 Mr. Carter
              August 1—15 Mr. Wouldham
                 ″ 16—31 Mr. Rothstein
            September 1—15 Mr. Flagg
                 ″ 16—30 Mr. Ojukwo

Routledge read it as he stood there, conceding to himself that Mr. Carter was indeed doing a sterling job in keeping the place clean. There was even a new roll of the familiar iron-hard Prison Service lavatory paper, hanging from a loop of string.

He returned to the shack to wash and to eat his breakfast, leaving the door open to provide more light. Except for the two men at the bungalow, there was still no one about. The settlement of shacks seemed to be deserted, its inhabitants long since up and busy with their chores. Directed by the Father or not, the thought of emptying latrines or working in a potato field held no great appeal, especially at this hour of the morning.

Using King's old kitchen knife to spread the butter, Routledge tried to reexamine the conclusions he had drawn from last night's interview with Franks. However compelling the man's personality, however well camouflaged his motives, he had nonetheless been handing out the same old message, the one regurgitated by politicians everywhere. This society was no different from any other. It ran on self-interest, with the biggest and greediest bastards at the top of the heap. "You might end up as leader in my stead." What a joke!

While still at Exeter, Routledge had imagined that these island colonies would have no social structure at all. He had imagined each one in a state of perpetual anarchy, a veritable hell on earth for those not strong enough to resist the continual assaults and outrages of those even more deranged and criminal than themselves. Yet now that he was here, he saw that such a view took no account of human nature. The population of the island had in essence divided itself into three predictable parts. The men who were so far gone that they could tolerate no society whatever had taken to living wild. These were probably in the minority. Old Town and the lighthouse settlement represented an interim stage, and probably accounted for the largest group of the population, those who were prepared to accept certain restrictions on their behavior in return for a modicum of security. The Community was this idea taken to its civilized extreme, and as such would appeal most greatly to those who were not so much hardened, lifelong criminals as victims of circumstance. This last category would be likely to include most of the men with any of the customary social skills, automatically increasing the stability of the Community. Taken together with the ever-present threat of expulsion, this would produce a pliant population consisting of a disproportionate number of the more intelligent and disciplined convicts. Such a population was ripe to be exploited by the most intelligent and disciplined of them all: Liam Michael Franks.

It appeared that Franks had entered into some sort of pact with the authorities whereby the safety of the helicopter was guaranteed. In return, he had gained control of all the benefits the helicopter provided. This alone would make it difficult to set up a rival village elsewhere; but it seemed he had also appropriated the most suitable peninsula on the island, and only a peninsula could be successfully defended against the outsiders.

There was little alternative but to do it Franks's way. Routledge had no intention of digging potatoes for the rest of his life. If he wanted even a degree of comfort and ease, he would have to climb the ladder as quickly as he could, and that meant conforming to the rules Franks had laid down last night.

Like King's whisky, the bread was better than he had expected. The butter tasted rather strong and he guessed it was made from goat's milk; the jam seemed to be of bilberries or something of the kind.

He ate the egg, which was excellent, made himself a jam sandwich with the two remaining slices, and embarked on a more thorough examination of King's personal effects. Going to the mantelshelf, he bent his head first one way and then the other to read the thirty or so book spines. The only hardback was an ancient volume of poetry: the collected works of Spenser, much thumbed and repaired with sticky tape. Most of the other books concerned practical or technical subjects—vegetable gardening, do-it-yourself, knitting, an illustrated guide to seashore life. A battered German dictionary had lost its covers. Beside it stood two books of chess theory. There were a few fiction titles, in French and German, none in English. Holding the remains of the sandwich in his mouth, Routledge briefly examined a couple before sliding them back. He read neither French nor German, but from what he had seen had managed to advance a little further in his divination of King's personality.

He left unopened what appeared to be a bundle of letters, held together with a rubber band. The address on the outer envelope was in a woman's rounded handwriting: *B. E. King Z-160551, c/o H.M. Prison, Princetown, Devon.* The letter had been posted in Milton Keynes on the ninth of April last.

Routledge supposed he too would be getting a new number, prefixed with a Z. Did "16" mean Sert? Was King the five hundred and fifty-first man to be sent here?

There were no photographs on display, and in the rest of the objects on the mantelshelf there was no real distinction between ornament and haphazard junk. King appeared to be a humble, frugal man. From the pile of darning and mending by the hearth it appeared that he undertook work for others besides himself. He had already shown a capacity for kindness, and Routledge decided to invade his privacy no further.

Besides, it was nearly twenty to six, and Routledge was receiving indications that called for a second and more prolonged visit to the latrine.

The interview with Appleton began punctually at six o'clock.

After lengthy and detailed questioning about his education, aptitudes and career, Routledge was told how his first few weeks in the Community would be spent. He was to be billeted with King for as long as it took for suitable accommodation to be prepared. This meant a stone and timber shack, or "house," as Appleton called it. Routledge was expected to supply most of the labor himself, although the materials and help with the heavier and more skilled work would be provided. So long as he consumed no more than the materials allotted to him, the shack could be of any design approved by the Father. Once the shack was finished Routledge could live in it himself; or, if by then he had been offered a place in one of the larger houses with multiple occupancy, he could accept it and the shack would become the property of the Village.

Appleton had shown keen interest in Routledge's knowledge of the building trade, but he had been more interested still in his facility with numbers, and had even given him a test in mental arithmetic, the results of which he had checked on a solar-powered calculator.

"Sixteen point three four plus ninety-seven point two one seven. Divided by eleven. Times two."

"Twenty point six . . . Twenty point six five. Or a bit under. Say point six four five."

"Square root of eight five three."

"Between twenty-nine and thirty. On the low side: twenty-nine point two. Something like that. Nine point two one, near enough."

"That's remarkable, Mr. Routledge."

Routledge found nothing remarkable in it at all. For him, ever since he could remember, arithmetic had been easy. Both at school and in his adult career, figures, abstracted quantities, estimates, had been the daily substance of his working life. Despite the calculating machines and computers at his disposal, he explained, a QS would not get far on site without at least a basic numeracy.

"You have more than a basic numeracy," Appleton said.

Routledge didn't answer; he disagreed. Compared with the mental agility of some of the quantity surveyors he had known, his own father, for example, his was not very good.

"What about algebra?"

"I know how to do it."

"Quickly?"

"Fairly quickly."

"Calculus?"

"Yes, I know that too."

Appleton's notes were becoming copious. Routledge watched the way he held the pencil, neatly and precisely, with a straight forefinger, exerting no undue pressure as his hand traveled across the paper. The writing was equally neat and precise, pedantic, quite unlike King's.

This morning Appleton was wearing a hand-knitted fawn

cardigan, made perhaps here in the Village, for Routledge had already seen sheep. He was losing his hair from the crown: his beard still retained traces of a more youthful color. On closer acquaintance, Routledge liked him even less. In fact, he disliked all the men closest to Franks, at least, all those he had seen so far: Appleton, Mitchell, Stamper, this morning's guard at the door.

"I want to turn now to your physics background," Appleton said, looking up and again directing his brown eyes at Routledge's own. Routledge had the feeling that his character was still being assessed, ready to be reported to Franks; he was still on probation; there was no reason to suppose that his position was safe or that he would not, on Appleton's say-so and without a moment's notice, be arbitrarily turfed out. This was a time for the utmost caution.

"How much electronics do you know? Do you understand the principle, say, of the transistor?"

"Yes, but it's a long time since I learned. I'm a bit rusty."

"Did you ever do any breadboarding?"

"Only at school, and then not very much. We concentrated mainly on theory."

"Do you know the theory of piezoelectric devices?"

"Yes, I think so. Vibrating crystals and all that."

"Name some piezoelectric materials."

"God. I can't remember. Quartz. That's one. Tourmaline. Er . . ."

"That'll do. What about acoustics?"

"The same. Only to A-level."

"Optics?"

"The same."

"Now you said"—and here Appleton consulted the notes he had made during the first interview—"you said you didn't know how to write professional software. Is that right?"

"Yes."

"I assume you had a home computer."

"We had a console. An Olivetti J6. For the everyday things. Video, comms, the household accounts, the bank. My son used it as well, for games and for school."

"Did you try your hand at any programming?"

"Not very much. Just for the odd simple application."

"Which languages can you use? Anything structured?"

"Olibasic, a bit of Nerys and Fifth. And Turtle. My son liked that. Likes that."

"Low-level languages? Assembly language?"

"I couldn't really be bothered with it."

"Too difficult, or too time-consuming?"

"Both, I suppose." -

"The machines at work. What did they run?"

"Geos, and Q-Sys. And tailored packages for the client or contractor." Routledge failed to see the point of these questions: surely they had no computers here, no science laboratories.

"Were you responsible for writing tender documents?"

"As far as quantities went, yes."

"And supervising applications for interim payments?"

"Yes."

"Using Q-Sys?"

"Yes."

"Did you ever have to do it manually?"

"Now and then, when the computer went down."

"What about dayworks? Did you ever measure those?"

"Yes. I did. Only too often."

Appleton made more notes. Just before looking up, he said, "You're wondering what all this is about, aren't you?"

"Well, yes, I am rather curious."

"What I'm trying to find out, Mr. Routledge, is how much aptitude you have for structured thinking coupled with a high level of numeracy and fastidious attention to detail. There is no better training for that than programming computers, but it seems the life of a senior quantity surveyor might come a pretty close second. In some respects it's even better for the work we have in mind."

"May I ask what that work is?"

"Until I have conferred with the Father, no, you may not. The final decision must rest with him. As it is you will not mention to anyone what has been discussed here this morning."

Routledge was immediately on the alert. What were they

up to? An escape attempt? Something to do with electronics? Were they planning to freak out the helicopter and hijack it? He wanted to ask more questions; but Appleton changed the subject and made it plain that this part of the interview had reached its end.

4

At the bungalow door Appleton told Routledge that, after lunch, King would be giving him a guided tour of the Community; until then, he might like to amuse himself by looking around on his own account. He was not to go near the bungalow or the workshop at the end of the garden, and it was recommended that he should keep away from the border-line, but otherwise he was free to explore all parts of the Village headland.

As Routledge emerged, the guard on the veranda acknowledged him, which he had scarcely done before. Dark, bearded, and about thirty, in green corduroys and a predominantly white, checkered shirt, the guard was reclining in the usual chair, his boots resting on the stonework of the adjacent pillar. He was cradling a crowbar with a sharpened point; on the boards beside him lay a hatchet with a shiny-edged blade. "The name's Mr. Talbot," he said.

"Routledge."

"Glad to know you, Mr. Routledge." He squinted up at Routledge, who was standing against the sun. "Lodging with Mr. King, ain't you?"

"Yes. For the moment."

"You'll be all right with him. He's an exceptionally nice bloke, is Mr. King." He paused. "Have you met any of the other men on his street? Mr. Foster, for example, or Mr. Ojukwo?"

"No, not yet."

"You wouldn't have seen Mr. Foster, anyway. He went up Old Town. He's our undercover agent. Anything going on among the outsiders, Mr. Foster knows about it. This might interest you, Mr. Routledge, seeing as you had a run in with him—the rumor is that Martinson's dead."

"Really?" That would certainly explain why Martinson had not pursued Routledge to get the crossbow back.

"You know about the fighting? Yes?"

"Mr. Sibley told me yesterday."

"It seems Martinson was hurt pretty serious. Mr. Foster's gone to find out how serious. Totally serious, we hope. That's an evil steel-plated bastard if ever I saw one."

A man who had been approaching across the shale-covered precinct now reached the steps and began to climb them. "Who's an evil steel-plated bastard?" he said. "Are you talking about me again, Mr. Talbot?" Like Talbot, he was dark and bearded, but was considerably older, wearing fawn twill jeans and a black T-shirt whose sleeves had been removed. Routledge noticed that Talbot did not stand up: his rank was evidently greater than the newcomer's.

"Hello, Mr. Daniels. Met Mr. Routledge yet? He got in last night."

"Yes, I heard. How do you do." Daniels extended his hand; Routledge, returning the greeting, also returned the calculated firmness of the grip.

"We was just talking about Martinson," Talbot said. "They reckon he may have checked out at last." Talbot suddenly put his feet down on the boards and sat upright, allowing his eye to range over the shacks opposite, where two more men had just arrived from the direction of the fields. The younger was dressed in ragged shorts and a loose out-at-elbows blue sweater; his companion was wearing blue jeans and a white short-sleeved shirt. They waved and entered a doorway. Talbot's vigilance relaxed.

"Of course, you met our friend Martinson, didn't you?" Daniels said to Routledge. "What happened? And more to the point, how did you get the crossbow away from him?"

Talbot interjected. "You just asked, didn't you, Mr. Routledge? You said: 'May I kindly borrow your most prized weapon, Jim, the one what you took personally from your most hated foes?' To which Jim, with his customary olde worlde charm, at once replied, 'By all means, Mr. Routledge, be my guest, why don't you?' ''

Talbot's impersonation of Martinson's Birmingham accent was deadly accurate and Routledge found himself smiling. He did not know what to make of Talbot, or of Daniels for that matter. To judge by his speaking voice, Daniels came from a much better background than Talbot, whose normal utterances were littered with glottal stops and elongated vowels; but everything else, from Talbot's clothes to his confident mien, proclaimed his superiority over the older man. His vocabulary, too, was unusually rich and varied for one who spoke with such an accent. It was as if this, like his own opinion of himself, had been allowed to blossom now that he was free of the artificial constraints of mainland society.

Talbot turned amiably to Daniels. ''What do you want?'' he said.

Daniels took a piece of paper from his back pocket. ''Yesterday's beach collection. Mr. Stamper's copy.''

''Leave it with me.'' To Routledge he said, ''Mr. Daniels is in charge of beachcombing.'' He turned back to Daniels. ''Where next? Outside again?''

''This afternoon. We've got up quite a big group. We're doing Fossett's Rock and Porth Thomas. With this wind we're hoping for quite a bit. Mr. Skinner saw some drums coming in there yesterday.''

''Many?''

''Three, for sure. Aniline, they looked like.''

''Great.''

''Did you hear about the light-bulbs at Trellick Cove? Dozens of them. And oranges.''

''Just loose?''

''I'm afraid so. They're quite inedible.''

''The best we had recently,'' Talbot said, addressing Routledge, ''was this crate of Swiss cakes. The theory is a deck container broke open, else they got chucked overboard in a storm. They must have been in the sea for six months. Marzipankuchen, kirschtorte, all that, sealed in foil. Bloody ace, they was.''

"For those who got any," Daniels said. "For those with a winning raffle ticket."

"You win some, you lose some," Talbot said, smugly. "See if you can find us another lot this afternoon." He raised the piece of paper. "I'll make sure Mr. Stamper gets this."

Daniels turned to go. In Talbot's expression Routledge detected the germ of his own dismissal, and perceived at once that he too was meant to leave: for if he were to stay chatting, that would be a presumption that his status was higher than Daniels's. Talbot was trying to make him feel like a new boy at a public school, the lowest of the low, frightened of unwittingly transgressing complicated and ill-defined codes of dress and conduct. Indeed, Talbot had almost succeeded. The rules of etiquette here were a minefield which he must rapidly, for the sake of his own advancement, learn to negotiate.

His glance at Talbot produced a farewell nod. Routledge's summary of the situation had been correct.

Routledge descended the steps just behind and to one side of Daniels, not certain whether it was his place to speak.

"I'm recruiting for this afternoon's beachcombing," Daniels said. "Do you want to come along?"

"I'm sorry, I can't. Mr. King is giving me a tour of the Community."

"Yes, of course, I did know that. New men always get one. What I ought to have said was, do you want to come along with me now and meet a few people?"

"By all means. I'd like to." Although the misunderstanding had not been his fault, Routledge had not failed to notice the lack of an apology. Daniels appeared to be testing him. Daniels also appeared to be a jerk. Routledge had taken as great a dislike to him as he had to Talbot.

"It won't be much good calling on any houses. Nearly everyone's out. I think we'd better try the root fields first."

Beyond the precinct they joined a dirt track which passed directly south, through and beyond the main cluster of dwellings. At intervals, side tracks led off to join up with other tracks radiating from the bungalow, forming a grid system. There were no formal boundaries, but it seemed that each building stood on its own proportionately sized plot. Most of the houses were simple shacks, like King's, with stone walls and roofs covered with spars and slate-like slices of rock, often with a covering of turf. The standard of workmanship varied greatly. The more elaborate edifices had polythene sheeting, transparent or colored, plain or bearing the trademarks of fertilizer companies, tacked or otherwise stretched across the window apertures. Some even had little gardens with salads or vegetables. By one threshold a bright display of cornflowers and nasturtiums caught Routledge's eye.

"You didn't say about the crossbow, Mr. Routledge."

"Well, Martinson had one idea about my future, and I had another. They weren't compatible."

"Did he catch you, then?"

Routledge was about to improvise, but remembered that to lie would mean breaking one of the Community's cardinal rules, and if he were to keep his place in the Village, still more achieve one with any rank, he could not afford the mental effort needed to sustain falsehood. It was safer and less trouble to tell the truth. "Yes, he caught me. But I got away, and here I am." Routledge tried to convey by his tone that he did not wish to discuss his experiences outside, a message confirmed by the fact that he now changed the subject. "Do you use any special techniques for your beach-combing, Mr. Daniels?"

Daniels's slight hesitation showed that he had understood: and almost imperceptibly, by one or two points, perhaps, Routledge felt his status had begun to rise. "Not really. The weather and tides are important, but mostly we just search."

"How many men?"

"I have fifteen allocated, though you can usually get volunteers."

"What sort of thing do you find?"

"Rubbish, mainly. Deck waste. Waxed-paper milk cartons: we find plenty of those. Plastic canisters, bottles, really anything that floats. Wood of course, sawn, planed, or as tree trunks and branches. Particle board, ply, polyboard. String, rope, lifebelts, lifejackets, buoyancy bags, expanded polystyrene. Carrier bags. Sacks. Wellington boots. You name it. We found a trombone last year. Everything is collected, even the milk cartons. Mr. Varsani uses them as flowerpots. He's our man for saplings.''

"How do you mean?"

"For hedges, especially the border hedge, and for growing trees. The Father plants as many as he can, for future timber. Currently we're putting in about ten thousand thorn saplings a year, and a thousand trees. With milk cartons the pot can go straight into the ground. The paper rots away, so growth isn't checked. That means the planting season is extended by several months.''

"Clever,'' Routledge said, trying to make the right response.

"Not really. You know what they say about necessity. We must have something to enclose the pastures with. Dry stone walling is hard graft, as I expect you'll find out. Hedges build themselves. All they need is an annual trim.''

"What sort of animals do you keep? I've seen sheep and goats.''

"That's it, pretty well. We've also got some donkeys, a few cows and pigs. Chickens. And two horses.''

They had almost come to the edge of the Village, where the shacks looked the most recently built; ahead and to either side spread undulating gorse scrub, beyond which, a hundred meters along the road, the fields began.

In the third field Daniels took him to, clearing potato haulms, bare to the waist and already sweating under the morning sun, Routledge found King.

Martinson dead. Franks prayed it was true. But there was nothing different about this morning. He had received no intuition of the other man's death.

When he was particularly troubled, when his head hurt so badly that he thought it would burst, when the ringing in his right ear grew unbearable, Franks sometimes came to sit here for half an hour, unguarded, alone on the low cliffs at

Star Cove. Above him and to his left, across the water of the cove, rose the intimidating crags and bluffs of Pulpit Head. To his right the cliffs ran almost straight, due southwest to the end of the peninsula and the twin stacks called, on the perspex-covered map in the bungalow, Mare and Foal. This map had furnished him with all the island names, some of them darkly Celtic, making him think of Sert as almost part of the ancestral territory of his race. Illislig, Helly, Mencaro, Angara: what had these names signified in the old language of Sert? Most of the others were more easily understood. Spanish Ledges were doubtless the graveyard of a ship from the Armada. America Point faced west, towards that continent. Beacon Point, Crow Bay, Half Moon Bay, Pulpit Head: these too were self-explanatory. But who was Fossett, and why had that awesome, solitary rock been named after him?

And this vantage on the cliffs, in other times, might even have come to bear the name of Franks. Or perhaps just the cave below. It lay directly beneath this spot, his mental solace when the pain grew too much to take.

He had known about the cave for a long time. He had known of it during the war with Barratt, long before the Village had been founded.

As caves went it was nothing special, not even particularly large. There were others on the island of greater size or geological interest. But this one was uniquely, especially wonderful. In the first place, it was the biggest cave on the Village headland. And more important still, it was only a meter or two from the sea at high tide. And yet more important: the interior was entirely suitable for the project he had been nursing consciously for the past two years, and unconsciously for at least a similar period before that.

"It's perfect," Thaine had said, complicating the echoes, shining his torch from ceiling to floor.

The cave would indeed have been perfect, had it not been for the reefs guarding it for a kilometer out to sea. Much of the coast was like this: in places the reefs were even more jagged and treacherous, thrashed by the combers and creating complicated currents and undertows. Beyond the reefs there was the Magic Circle to contend with—the radar, the infrared detectors, the image intensifiers and computer-controlled pattern scanners, the network of electronics run from the two lightships and from the land station near Trevose Head. Protecting the Circle were the Prison Service helicopters and at least two hydrofoil patrol boats, and reinforcing the Prison Service were the combined resources of the Coastguard, the RAF, the Royal Marines, and His Majesty's Navy. Eighty percent. Against. Those were the most optimistic odds Appleton had been able to calculate.

The Village boundary ended at the mouth of Star Cove: outsiders had ready access to Pulpit Head and the cliffs opposite. They might well see the components being carried down the cliff path; they might hear, faintly from the mouth of the cave, the sounds of assembly and construction; and at night they might make an attempt at sabotage or, in the final stages, theft. But then again, the outsiders were idle and careless and none too observant. The nearest point in their territory was at least four hundred meters from the cave mouth. Furthermore, the anti-satellite precautions—taking the parts down only in bad light, under thick cloud, and, most of all, during fog—would equally reduce the risk of being seen by the outsiders.

Franks grimaced as a new onslaught of pain sliced at his head. He snatched off his glasses and clutched his skull with both hands, gripping as hard as he possibly could, trying to force the pain downwards and back: a moment later the worst was over, leaving only a blaring new clangor of tinnitus. He was now virtually deaf in that ear. The hearing was going in the left ear too. Yet more disturbing, his vision was deteriorating also, although, mercifully, much more slowly. Sibley could tell him nothing, give no prognosis. All he could say was that, yes, it must have been caused by a blow on the back of the head that he had received from Martinson in the wars. And, yes, if he did not get mainland treatment he might end up blind as well as deaf.

How curious that that new man, Routledge, should have retrieved the crossbow. Martinson had killed a border guard to get his hands on it.

Whenever Franks's thoughts turned to Martinson he felt a

sense of transcendent mystery, of inevitability. A Buddhist, someone who believed in rebirth, would have said that the two of them had known each other in a previous incarnation, that unfinished business had remained to be settled. Their lives were linked: they had orbited one another, slowly drawing closer. The first time he had met Martinson, Franks had instantly recognized, not the outer man, but the personality within. And he was sure it had been the same with Martinson, that feeling of familiarity, of reacquaintance after an irrelevant gap of space and time.

At Dartmoor Martinson and Franks had shared a cell. A sort of friendship had developed, superficially initiated and perpetuated by Martinson, who had seemed to fear and admire Franks in equal parts. Ostensibly, for the sake of peace, Franks had gone along with it; and yet he had also detected something dangerous and fascinating in Martinson he had found irresistible: independence, a tangential way of thinking. At its core lay whatever it was that had to be resolved. Franks was in his debt. Perhaps, a thousand years before—and Franks had an uncanny feeling that they had lived by the rugged western sea then too, had belonged to the same fierce tribe—Franks had let him down, deserted or betrayed him, sold him to the enemy, taken his woman.

They had been two months at Dartmoor. Towards the end Franks, realizing too late that Martinson was insane, had tried to shake himself free. Then had come the boat, and the first appalling months on Sert. And then the wars, the division of the island, the present precarious state.

The blow on the head and its consequences marked, Franks hoped, the resolution of his debt. It was price enough to pay. Apart from Sibley, only Appleton knew how much effort it cost him to keep his suffering hidden.

The Village was his shelter from Martinson, possibly forever. That depended on Godwin and on Randal Thaine. And on himself. He had wasted enough time here this morning. He replaced his spectacles, stood up, and started back along the path to the bungalow.

As he walked he thought again of Ireland, of the wind and tides, and of the broad, peaceful estuary of Courtmacsherry, lined on the south by pastel-painted cottages and on the north by a quiet road and cornfields. He knew exactly where the ketch could be hidden and later dismantled and burned; and at Timoleague, at the head of the estuary, in a Georgian house, there would be Siobhan and money and food and, eventually, safe conduct to Pittsburgh. For the others, for Appleton and Godwin and Thaine and eight more, there would be a forged passport and two thousand pounds apiece.

The Village had been the only way for Franks to surround himself with the people capable of bringing his scheme to fruition and to enable them to work on it unimpeded. In Thaine, Godwin, and most of all in Appleton, he had found intact the English genius for improvisation and compromise; had found intact the blend of arrogance and imagination that had once painted most of the world's map pink. His own imagination, of a different and Celtic sort, more lateral and inspired than theirs, had provided the motive power to make the whole thing work. He had long ago forgiven them for being British: they could not very well help that.

He had grown to love these men. But sometimes they needed a spot of gentle manipulation. In the past few weeks he had begun to feel that Godwin was being over-cautious about his side of the work. This Franks could no longer afford. Sooner or later the outsiders would bury their differences and launch a concerted attack.

"That new man," Franks had said to Godwin, earlier this morning. "We have our doubts about him. But he's good with figures and has a bit of science in his background. I'd rather you had your computer, but do you want to make use of him? He might speed things up."

Godwin had looked uneasy. "What sort of doubts do you mean?"

"Thinks a lot of himself. Thinks he can go it alone."

"He's trustworthy enough," Appleton had said. "I'll vouch for that."

"What was he before?"

"A quantity surveyor."

Then Franks had said, "If you're not happy about it, Godwin, we'll go on as we are."

"It's just that he'd have to do a hell of a lot to produce anything useful."

"Mr. Routledge will work hard," Franks had said, winning the point, as he had known he would. "We'll see to that. You can meet him later today."

At the bungalow Talbot stood up long before Franks reached the veranda. They exchanged a few quiet words before Franks, clapping him lightly on the shoulder, left the sunshine behind and went inside to his desk.

5

IN SUMMER, ROUTINE WORK IN THE FIELDS USUALLY STOPPED
at about eleven, continuing again in the late afternoon, leaving the middle part of the day for other work or simply for
leisure. King gave Routledge lunch sitting in the sunshine
outside his house, accompanied by Ojukwo, a large, phleg-
matic and very black man of Nigerian parentage, King's next-
door neighbor and one of the Community's carpenters. Like
Daniels, King, and a number of others he had encountered,
Routledge found that Ojukwo appeared to be impressed by
his acquisition of the crossbow. As he ate, Routledge tried
to plan the best way to capitalize on his reputation.

Lunch consisted of sandwiches of cold mutton—or goat's
flesh: he did not ask which—between slices of brown bread,
coarse in texture but with a fresh, not unpleasant flavor. The
bread was made at the Village bakery, and the Village dairy
provided the butter. To drink there was water or goat's milk.
Routledge opted for water.

When they had finished eating, his guided tour began.
Ojukwo decided to come along. They went first to the nearby
woodyard, where a prodigious quantity of driftwood had been
amassed. Most of it consisted of small oddments, variously
warped, cracked, splintered, bleached gray by sun and sea,
or bearing faded stenciling in Roman or Cyrillic characters.
Few large or useful pieces remained: and none of them bore
any metal or plastic fittings, which were always stripped,

cataloged, and stored elsewhere. This scrap wood, King explained, was used to supply charcoal for the forge, and as a free source of any small pieces that anyone might need.

Ojukwo said that driftwood was not suitable for serious structural use. Under polythene shelters, arranged in correctly sticked piles and left to season, the yard also held a supply of planks derived from the island's scanty stock of trees. The yard was deserted for lunch, its workshop empty.

Opposite the workshop a sawbench stood astride a heap of pale dust. Power was supplied by the horses which, working a windlass, could raise a huge boulder four meters into the air. As the boulder came down it turned an ingenious set of gears and hence the viciously jagged blade, providing enough force to cut a meter or more into a tree trunk.

The sawbench had been built by a man named Randal Thaine, who had utilized cogs and sprockets from machinery in the lighthouse. Thaine was also master of the metalwork shop, where King sometimes worked. This was situated next to the woodyard, looking out over the scrub to the western cliffs. The forge was not in use today. Routledge noted with surprise the professional-looking range of blacksmith's tools, many made on the island from recycled driftwood fittings. There were two anvils, one the engine block of a tractor abandoned in the evacuation, the other a rounded boulder. Neither, according to King, was really satisfactory, but so far the Prison Service had failed to respond to the Father's requests for a real one.

Once on Sert, King said, there was no getting off. Nonetheless the Community had been interpreted on the mainland as an attempt at rehabilitation, if not repentance, and the unusually liberal governor of Dartmoor Prison, under whose authority the penal colonies of Sert and Lundy lay, regarded the project with a kindly and paternal eye. Had it been up to him, Franks's original petition and subsequent requests would have been even more benevolently treated, but several tiers of regulations intervened. One of these, the Home Office rules dealing with Category Z, was anything but benevolent.

Supplies from the mainland were strictly limited. There were allowances of such provisions as kerosene, matches, and medicines, but these were by no means generous. Special requests for seed, tools, and livestock were sometimes granted, more often not. For nearly everything else the prisoners had to depend on their own ingenuity, or on their personal requisitions, and these took weeks, months, to come through and even then were often lacking or inaccurately made up.

All this King explained as they visited the recreation hut, a sort of common-room fitted with a bar, dartboard, and a number of makeshift armchairs. Here Routledge was introduced to several more men. One of them, Blackshaw, turned out to be the self-appointed chaplain. Middle-aged, bald and bespectacled, with a curiously braying voice, he wasted no time in inviting Routledge to visit the chapel, which was located on its own some little way from the Village.

"You're welcome any time, Mr. Routledge. Come to evensong, why don't you?"

"Thanks. I'll bear it in mind."

Once they were outside, King said, "Are you a religious man, Mr. Routledge?"

"Not in Mr. Blackshaw's sense."

"Glad to hear it," Ojukwo said.

From the recreation hut they went in turn to the dairy, the bakery, and the animal sheds. Leaving the Village by the western track, they came to an exposed place on the cliffs where a wooden tower, reinforced with steel guy wires, looked out over the sea. At the top of the tower, about three meters up, set one above the other, were two longitudinal scoops cut from a pair of two-hundred-liter oildrums. Even in the light early-afternoon breeze the drums were revolving quite quickly, turning a vertical driveshaft connected to a generator. From this a cable led to a large storage battery set on a cart. The windmill, like the sawbench, had been made by Randal Thaine. Technically, King said, it was called a Savonious Rotor. Another, smaller, rotor was mounted on the roof of the metalwork shop back at the Village and was used to drive directly a combination grinder, lathe, and drill.

Routledge asked whether it was Thaine who had made the crossbow.

"Yes. He's done quite a few now. We use them for border security."

After showing Routledge the interior of the hut where spares and batteries for the windmill were stored, King and Ojukwo led him along the western cliffs and so back to the fields.

The soil was extremely poor. In the early days of the Village, large areas of scrub had been cleared by machete and by concentrated grazing with goats and pigs. Once cleared, the ground had been marked out with dry stone walling or with willow hurdles, along which thousands of hawthorn and blackthorn saplings had been planted to make hedges. The fields so formed were mainly pastures consisting predominantly of the coarse clifftop grasses, food for sheep and a few cows as well as the goats. With each year, though, more of the pasture was being improved and started on a cycle of rotation which would in time provide the Community with all the cereals and root crops it would ever need.

Oil-seed rape and kale were also being grown as organic material to be plowed back into the soil. The cleared vegetation of the scrub, King explained, had not been burned, but shredded and allowed to rot down. Quantities of guano were collected in winter from the seabird cliffs and used as fertilizer; every scrap of organic matter the Village produced, from potato peelings to the sawdust in the woodyard, was kept and composted in scientifically designed and tended heaps sited in the center of the cultivated area. Even the bags from the latrines were brought here to be emptied.

"Speakin' of shitbags," Ojukwo said, "let's go wait for our good friends from the Service."

King acceded: Routledge had seen enough to get the general idea. The tour was over.

"Our good friends from the Service?" Routledge said.

"The only ones we ever see," Ojukwo said. "The boys in helmets. The helicopter. It's Tuesday today."

The drop zone was marked out with a broad circle of boulders on the turf at a place called the Warrens, on the eastern side of the peninsula. This was the least cultivated part of the headland, separated from the fields around the Village by a waste of heather and bracken. The Warrens consisted of a depression rather like the one above Old Town, but much larger and shallower, shelving down to the cliffs and extending, to the north-east, beyond the border.

A number of villagers had already gathered on the landward slope. Some were shirtless; some wore shorts. All had been working earlier in the fields or the workshops and would soon be returning there.

This was the best vantage point, three hundred meters from the edge of the zone. If anyone went closer than that, Ojukwo said, the helicopter would not touch down.

They joined the waiting men. Routledge acknowledged those he had already met and was introduced to a dozen more. He was again congratulated on surviving his period outside, and was again pressed for an account of Martinson and the crossbow. It was just as King had said last night: he had become something of a celebrity. But he was careful to play the matter down, and by his reticence indicated that he did not wish to discuss it further. This seemed to have its calculated effect, and he felt his standing with them rise accordingly. During the ensuing conversation no one ventured to address him directly. King did most of the talking. Many of the matters discussed meant little or nothing to Routledge: gossip about names he did not know, the weather and the crops, the Village darts league. A championship was in progress, and King had staked a bottle of whisky on the favorite, Gunter, whose abilities were being hotly debated by several of those present.

Ojukwo was not interested in darts. He had plucked a grass stalk and was chewing it while he reclined, head in hands, full length on the turf. Routledge, following his example, was also chewing a grass stalk, but remained leaning on one elbow, with his free hand foiling the efforts of an ant to pursue the direction it wanted to take.

The sun felt hot. The breeze from the south was soft and balmy. He gave scant attention to the talk around him. He was among people, but he was utterly alone. They were his countrymen, his peers, sharing further the common bond of Sert, but still he was alone.

From time to time in his life he had known moments of a strangely heightened, cold, and detached defiance. This was one of them. His position was hopeless. He would never leave the island alive. All his former plans and expectations had been reduced to this present moment of unreality, to this feeling of alienation and despair, and yet, and yet, somehow it did not matter. He remembered once being caught practicing on a golf course by an electric storm. Counting by seconds, the lightning had been only a mile away and coming closer. The received wisdom would have required him to humiliate himself by lying down on the ground, preferably in a bunker, getting himself not only wet but also covered in orange sand. He should also have distanced himself from his golf bag, and especially from the steel stem of his multicolored umbrella. But he had continued walking along the open fairway with the umbrella raised skywards. In that torrential downpour he had not been sure that the faint vibration of the handle had been caused by the rain; equally it might have been caused by the expectation that at any instant he would be hit with a couple of million joules. Rationality had urged him to take cover. Something else, deeper, more essentially himself, had refused to listen. "Go on, you old bastard," he had breathed, "go on, do your worst. Do your worst! See if I care!"

Well, now the worst had been done and he was still here. It was Routledge alone who had disposed of Gazzer and Tortuga, who had escaped from Martinson and employed superior intelligence and nerve to eliminate the man at the ruins. The old bastard had had nothing to do with it.

"He's comin'," Ojukwo said, without opening his eyes.

Routledge heard it then, the faint sound of approaching turboshafts and rotors.

The general conversation ceased.

Near the center of the circle lay a pile of empty kerosene canisters and buttercup-yellow mail crates, brilliant in the full glare of the sun. Mitchell was in charge of the drop, and earlier he and his gang had brought the crates and canisters from the bungalow precinct.

"There it is," Carter said, pointing a kilometer out to sea, where Routledge now discerned, gunmetal gray against ultramarine, the shape of the approaching helicopter. It was less dragonfly-like than most of its kind, with a humped back, windshields rather than a dome, and a sharp, somewhat downturned snout. Seen from this elevation, it did not even break the horizon.

"Where's it based?" Routledge said.

"Dartmoor," Ojukwo said.

All eyes were raised as the intensifying racket heralded the sweep across the cliffs and then, turning on its axis, the deceleration of the helicopter, the yellow bands on the rear rotor making a blurred circle which vanished and reappeared as the machine reached the drop zone and prepared to land.

The engines seemed impossibly loud and intrusive. Routledge made out the words *H. M. Prisons* and the numerals *3-947*, painted in white on the length of the tail. The tires hanging from the cowled main undercarriage reached for and made contact with the turf, and were followed a moment later by the nosewheel.

The pilot, sitting behind his plexiglass, could be seen checking the controls even as the hatch in the left-hand side slid open and two white-helmeted crewmen jumped out, wearing fluorescent yellow lifejackets and gray flying-suits. While the rotors kept the grass bent flat, the crewmen hurriedly unloaded the full canisters and crates and loaded the empty ones. When the loading was finished, they brought out a stretcher bearing a fair-haired man, left its contents supine on the ground and, almost as an afterthought, dumped the cardboard box containing his issue.

Just as Routledge had been, exactly a week ago, the newcomer was out cold. As far as the brain inside that head was aware, he was still a prisoner on the mainland. He had an unpleasant surprise in store.

The whole operation had lasted no longer than two minutes: the helicopter was already airborne again, its hatch sliding shut as, nose down, it gained altitude and headed out to sea.

Routledge had half expected an undisciplined rush for the mail crates. Instead, no one stirred except Mitchell and his five assistants, two of whom picked up the newly arrived convict and carried him off towards the Village. Mitchell himself examined the supplies. When satisfied that everything was in order, he issued a wave, and Routledge joined the group of twenty or so who went down to the drop zone. The mail crates remained sealed: Routledge found that he had volunteered to help carry everything back to the bungalow. He and King shared the weight of a fifty-liter plastic drum embossed with the words DANGER—HIGHLY INFLAMMABLE.

Routledge was not as strong as King. At frequent intervals he had to ask to stop and rest, and soon they fell far behind. The sun was burning the back of his neck; his hands already reeked of kerosene.

"I'm sorry," he said, as they sat down beside the track. "I can see I've got a bit of toughening up to do."

"Don't let it bother you."

"Why is the drop made where it is? Why not at the Village?"

"Two reasons, really. First, at the Warrens the helicopter has an all-round view: they're understandably nervous about anyone wanting a lift back to the mainland. At one time they used to drop at Half Moon Bay, but once the Village got going the Father persuaded them to do it here. Secondly, the official line is that supplies are shared equally among all the islanders, so we could hardly ask them to make a doorstep delivery."

"Is the island under surveillance?"

"Of course. From a geostationary satellite."

"Meaning it stays in one place with respect to the planet surface?"

King nodded. "It serves this place, Lundy, and Dartmoor for good measure. High-resolution optics, image intensifiers, the lot. The computers scan all movement and automatically alert the technicians to anything that happens. The image can be enhanced, magnified, and manipulated however they want. It's all part of the security network. Have you been told about the Magic Circle yet?''

''No,'' Routledge said. ''Not yet.''

''There used to be two lighthouses on Sert, an unmanned one at Beacon Point and the main installation at Angara Point. At the evacuation they brought in two lightships instead, one north of the island and the other to the south. Each one is stuffed with electronics. Between them they monitor the entire coast and the sea round the island to a distance of several kilometers. They're coordinated on the mainland. The whole thing forms a circle round the island. It's impossible to break it undetected. In fact, it's impossible to do anything in the open and remain undetected, day or night.''

''Has anyone ever escaped?''

''I wondered when you'd ask me that. The answer's no.''

''Has anyone ever tried?''

''No. There's no way you could build a boat without them knowing. Even if you did, it'd show on the radar as soon as you got into open water.''

''You could swim.''

''It's forty kilometers to the nearest land. The currents would make it nearer eighty. Assuming you survived the reefs. And exposure. Even in late summer you'd be unconscious in no time, and dead soon after that. But, just say you did manage to keep alive. Within a couple of minutes your body heat would register on the infrared. They have the very best equipment. However much money they spend, it still works out cheaper than running a maximum security prison for five hundred men. Outdoors, anywhere, the chances are you're being watched. The cameras probably aren't good enough to resolve faces, because the authorities rely on us to tell them who's died. At least, they appear to rely on us. It may be that they accept our figures so they can send more prisoners than the regulations would otherwise permit. Mr. Godwin says they've got cameras now that can resolve newspaper text. If that's the case, they're aware of even more than we think.''

"So they know about the outsiders and the distribution of supplies?"

"They must do. If the penal reform people found out they'd make a stink, as they would about the numbers, but then they're not privy to that information either. Unofficially, I suppose the authorities don't care. It's probably pretty much the same on all the penal colonies."

"But the outsiders—don't they object?"

King shrugged.

"Do they make trouble?"

"All the time. But then they'd make trouble whatever happened, even if we handed them everything we produced. We waste most of our energies maintaining the border. You'll find out. You'll be on night patrol in a couple of months. When you've finished building your house."

"What?" Routledge had fondly been imagining that he need have nothing more to do with the outsiders.

"We all take our turn."

"Are there many incidents?"

"Enough. There was one last night. A man was caught near the piggery. He repeatedly refused to stop when challenged."

"And?"

"Dead, I'm afraid."

Routledge looked around. He had just become aware that no one else was in sight. "Are we safe here?" he said. "It's not very far from the border."

"They haven't started attacking in daylight. Yet. I'm not criticizing the Father, but there's a certain amount of pressure in Council to change the intake procedure. The present arrangement merely tends to increase the number of outsiders. Some people are saying it would be safer to weed them out straight after the interview. The same people advocate going outside to reduce the numbers of those already here."

"Do you mean kill them?"

"Of course. We're not in Rickmansworth now, Mr. Routledge."

"So I'd noticed."

King gestured at the two handles of the canister. "Ready?"

When they reached the bungalow they found Appleton on the veranda, handing out the last of the mail and requisitions. For King there was a single letter, which he retired to his shack to read. For Routledge there was a brown envelope from Exeter Prison, containing his wristwatch, his wedding ring, and his photographs.

"I see they came, Mr. Routledge. Mr. Appleton here said you were anxious."

Franks had silently appeared on the veranda and was leaning on the rail, watching Routledge rip open the envelope and examine its contents. Behind him, Appleton observed from the shadows. In the presence of the Father, Talbot was standing, almost to attention, by his chair.

"Yes," Routledge said. "Thank you. Would you like to . . . see them?"

Franks studied the snapshots briefly but appreciatively before handing them back. "A pretty wife, Mr. Routledge. And a fine-looking boy."

"Christopher. That's his name."

"What can we say about this island of ours?" He stood upright. "I want you to come and meet someone. Mr. Appleton, will you accompany us?" To Talbot he said, "We're going to see Mr. Godwin."

6

After supper that evening, King took Routledge to the recreation hut. Quite a few men were seated outside, talking and playing cards or dice in the last of the sunshine. As he approached, Routledge detected the smell of marijuana smoke.

It was even stronger inside: the hut was crammed full, with every chair occupied and a number of men sitting on the floor. No one arose when King entered, even though a number of those present were his inferiors. King had already explained that the usual rules were relaxed here, and here only.

Under King's supervision, Routledge was served with a glass of tepid beer. No payment of any kind was demanded at the bar, but the man officiating there seemed to know precisely who was entitled to what, refusing some requests while acceding to others, occasionally keeping tally in a notebook.

Again Routledge felt his isolation. He had nothing in common with these people; he would never belong. Despite the fact that the Village had attracted an undue share of the more educated and intelligent convicts, the majority were just like those he had been forced to live with at Exeter. King, Godwin, Stamper, Appleton, Sibley, Daniels, Franks himself: these were very much the exception.

At Exeter, blacks had constituted about a quarter of the

population. At Old Town it had seemed more like half. Here, it was about a third. Most were young, in their twenties. All, black and white, belonged to the worst and most dangerous stratum of the criminal class.

Yet more introductions were made, yet more hands shaken, yet more names mentioned which Routledge instantly forgot. Until ten o'clock he was still technically a guest of the Community, and that was how he was being treated. A chair was vacated for him. He was offered a reefer, which he declined. The fumes alone, a few sips of the unexpectedly powerful beer, the crush and noise of the place, his own deep sense of exhaustion and unreality, were already combining to make him intoxicated.

"Where does the jang come from?" he asked, moving closer to King's ear and raising his voice to make himself heard.

"We grow it."

"Yes, but how did you get the seed?"

"Don't know. It's supposed to be pretty potent."

"Do you smoke it?"

"No. Bad for the brain."

Smoking cannabis went contrary to the work ethic. Routledge was surprised that Franks allowed it. But then, considering, he saw how little else the villagers had in the way of comfort or entertainment. And probably the supply was controlled to Franks's advantage. And further, any deviation in behavior caused by the drug would lead to expulsion, thus keeping its use under control. Nonetheless, Routledge was surprised.

He applied himself to his beer. The glass was again a cut-down jar, this time a marmalade jar decorated with a motif of leaves and lemons. "Is the place always this full?" he said.

"Sometimes it's fuller. There's a darts match later. Then you'll see it fill up. Mr. Gunter is playing."

"He's the champion?"

"Defending, yes."

With marijuana replacing tobacco, and the drinkers dressed in ragged work clothes and a motley assortment of leather and sheepskin jerkins, waistcoats, jackets, trousers, and shorts, wearing boots or trainers or barefoot, the atmosphere in the hut was otherwise that of a popular pub on pay night. It was almost the last thing Routledge had anticipated finding on a penal colony. Indeed, he had been totally unprepared for almost everything he had encountered so far. He was still in a state of shock.

Parrying remarks made at him by more of King's friends, he suddenly remembered that, ten minutes' walk away, one lying spreadeagled on a ledge, another on the beach below, were two cadavers, with a third, impaled by a steel crossbow bolt, almost as near in the other direction. Unless they had been moved or already picked clean by the birds, each would now be an inferno of flies. He had done that: and here he was, drinking beer as if nothing had happened.

"Fill up?" King said.

"Well . . . is there something else? Fruit juice, perhaps?"

While King was at the bar, Godwin's assistant, Fitzmaurice, came in. He acknowledged Routledge with no great enthusiasm and ignored him thereafter.

Before Franks had taken him to Godwin's workshop, Routledge had been thinking almost continuously about this morning's interview with Appleton and the mysterious project it implied. Here was a way, he had immediately realized, to advance himself in the Village hierarchy; but he had had no idea what to expect, and his introduction to the pudgy, sarcastic Godwin had enlightened him hardly at all.

With Franks watching, Godwin had given Routledge a test in arithmetic, in algebra, calculus, and various simple statistical techniques. He had tested him too on his knowledge of electronics and acoustics, and had asked him to draw a circuit diagram to show how a dimmer switch worked. Routledge had completed the tests satisfactorily, at which Godwin had signified his grudging approval.

And now Routledge had landed himself a job doing he knew not what: for the purpose of all the wiring, the soldering, the bits and pieces of apparatus on Godwin's bench, had not been explained to him. When he had asked, Franks had said that Godwin would tell him whatever he needed to know, at the time he needed to know it. Meanwhile, Routledge was forbidden to divulge details of the work to anyone, King included.

He would be starting tomorrow afternoon. His working arrangements were to be flexible, depending on what Godwin wanted. In any case he need put in no more than eight hours a day, Franks had said, not, at least, while he was building his house, although the work with Godwin was to take absolute priority. Extra labor would if necessary be supplied to finish the house on time, by the autumn.

Almost without doubt the project had something to do with the Magic Circle. That could only mean one thing. An escape attempt, a boat. The Community clearly had the technical ability to build one: the problem was launching it undetected and then getting clear away. Where would it go? The Devon or Cornish coast. Who would be on it? Franks, of course, probably Appleton, Godwin, and Fitzmaurice too. Plainly they were having trouble with designing or testing the electronics. There was no other reason they would have involved him, a newcomer, without giving themselves time properly to assess his personality and abilities. That meant they were running against some sort of deadline. Why? And most important of all, what were the chances of a place on the boat for himself?

Nil.

Even so, mental work, indoors, was vastly preferable to carting compost or scavenging along the tideline. When, eventually, he was able to begin making sense of this welter of initial impressions, he knew he would regard with satisfaction his appointment to Godwin's project.

Routledge did not stay for the darts match. Making his excuses, he left as early as he could and went to bed; but he was so tired and miserable that he again had difficulty in getting to sleep.

He lit a lamp and for a long time lay looking into his favorite picture of Louise, taken on the Thames, on a hired motorboat. She had been three months pregnant then, wearing a blue sundress and sandals, one of which she had removed in order to trail the toes of her right foot in the water.

The picnic had been her idea. He remembered everything about that afternoon: the dank, shady smell of the river, the glimpses of white houses and their lawns sloping down to the water, the island temple at Remenham, the bankside mud eroded and exposed by the wash of cabin cruisers and steamers. The Thames at Henley Reach was already a river to be reckoned with, gathering force from the heart of England as it moved towards London and the sea. Its valley was broad and rich, on the grand scale, rising northwards to the wooded Chiltern Hills, but it was in the small things that the essence of the river was to be found. The furniture of the riverbank—the gates and railings and signboards—had a peculiarly apt and English flavor. Henley the town still retained remnants of its former self. Downstream they had watched a rowing eight at practice, and seen a grebe, and heard the breeze turning the sallow leaves, and moored at some unnamed place to eat and rest. He had loved her more on that day than ever before.

Eventually he put the photograph back in its place, propped up on his makeshift bedside shelf. He shut his eyes, turned on his side, but was still awake an hour later when King returned.

King stole to the table, where Routledge had left the oil lamp burning low, and, shielding the light from Routledge's end of the room, turned up the wick slightly and began to carry the lamp towards his own pallet bed.

"It's all right, Mr. King," Routledge said.

"Did I disturb you?"

"No. Not at all." Routledge sat up. "Who won the darts?"

"Mr. Gunter."

"Did you get your whisky?"

"Not yet. That only comes if he wins the cup." King removed his sweater and began unbuttoning his shirt. "Can't you sleep?"

"Well. There's a lot to think about."

"It's best not to do too much of that."

"Yes. I'm sure."

"If you get too pissed off, let me know. That's what I'm here for. It's a cliché, but it really does help to talk."

"And you? Have you adjusted to it yet?"

"No. I don't think you ever can."

"Does it get easier?"

"In some ways. I've been here for three years. From the point of view of material comfort, the further you get from your former life the better." He poured water into the bowl and began washing himself. "I dimly remember having a bathroom with a fitted carpet. But this seems quite normal and adequate now. It's surprising what you can do without. The other things are harder to give up. The mental things." Having dried himself, King turned away, took off his trousers and climbed into bed.

"Since we'll be sharing the same roof till September," he said, after a moment, "I think you ought to know what I'm here for. Multiple murder. I killed my next-door neighbors."

An image of a newspaper photograph, a lurid headline, vaguely returned to Routledge's mind. "How many of them?"

"Three."

Sitting up in bed, his mild features made even more lugubrious by the lamplight, King then recounted a story so horrific and grotesque that Routledge forgot for the moment his own troubles and could only marvel at the depths of feeling which existed behind anonymous front doors. King had lived in Basingstoke, working by day as a languages teacher in a comprehensive school and by night tending his disabled sister. Their bungalow was the subject of a compulsory purchase order to make way for a new road. The compensation was inadequate; they could afford only a much smaller, attached, house, on a recent development outside the town. The new house was very badly built, with thin walls which transmitted every sound.

From the start there was trouble from the people next door, a couple with a nine-year-old boy. The main problem was noise, keeping King's sister awake, preventing him from concentrating on his marking and preparation. The television was left on almost permanently, at a high volume; at other times the stereo played pop music with a driving, insistent beat which penetrated every corner of the house. Requests to turn the sound down were at first complied with, then ignored, then met with abuse.

The following Christmas the boy was given a puppy as a present, a wire-haired terrier. As it grew older it learned to bark. Anything and everything set it off. Sometimes it barked for no reason at all. When the neighbors went out shopping or visiting relatives the dog was left locked in the house, and then it barked without cease. The woman used to let it out at five to six in the morning and again at a quarter past eleven at night, so that King's hours of sleep were determined by the habits of the dog. His health began to suffer.

In October the family bought a second terrier—to keep the first one company, as they explained. By the following spring King had tried to raise a petition among the other people living nearby, a prerequisite for legal action. No one had been willing to sign. The dogs did not disturb them, they said; some pretended they could not even hear them. King began to be regarded as an eccentric. He was ostracized. He tried to move house, but could find nowhere suitable.

Matters came to a head during the ensuing summer, on a muggy Sunday afternoon in June, at the height of the lawn-mowing season. The neighbors had an electric rotary mower which emitted a high-pitched whine. King was trying to mark a heap of examination scripts on his desk. Eventually, when the neighbor had gone inside, he decided to cut his own tiny lawn. He took his push-mower from the garage. As he fitted the grass-box, both terriers came out as usual and began yapping at him. The gardens were separated only by a low, white plastic picket fence.

He went back into the garage. He took a can of gasoline, which was full, and poured the contents into a polythene bucket. Before leaving the garage he made sure he had some matches and a quantity of old newspaper.

The dogs were still barking. They redoubled their efforts as he drew near. He flung the gasoline at them. Both were drenched, the older one taking the brunt. With the newspaper alight, King jumped over the fence and set them on fire.

In the few seconds left to them the dogs made instinctively for sanctuary—for the open french window—and ran indoors. Within a few minutes the whole house was blazing; all attempts by the family to put out the fire had failed.

The three of them appeared at the kitchen door. The wife had seen everything; her husband was armed with a metal vegetable rack. Shouting incoherently, he rushed at King, who easily wrested the thing away from him. The scuffle proceeded to the garage. King punched him in the face. As the man went down, King snatched a spade and hit him over the head. The wife, who had been trying to assist her husband, also received a blow, as did the boy. After that, King's mind went blank.

"By the time the police and fire brigade got there, all three were dead." He pushed a hand through his hair. "My defense tried to show provocation, but it didn't wash. It was the dogs. No jury would forgive me that. Not in England."

Routledge remained silent for a while. Finally he said, "And your sister, Mr. King?"

"King. Call me King. The firemen got her out. She had to move away, of course. She's in Milton Keynes now, in a home."

"You had a letter this afternoon."

"Yes. From her. She writes nearly every week. It's censored, but she knows that, so we've evolved a sort of code."

"In what way censored?"

"They black out whatever they feel you shouldn't know. There aren't any rules. Outgoing letters are censored more heavily still. Anything about conditions here is always expunged, anything about the Village or the outsiders. One or two men once put some messages in bottles, just to see what would happen. We didn't get any feedback."

"Couldn't you build a radio?"

"They'd know. They'd pick up the transmissions immediately. Then there'd be no more helicopter till the radio stopped. Besides, the Father wouldn't permit it. There's no point in antagonizing them."

"He's an interesting man," Routledge said, experimentally.

"The Father is more than that. Without him we'd have been lost."

"What was he before?"

"I don't know. He comes from County Cork, I think. Near Kinsale."

"Was he a terrorist?"

King said nothing. He blew out the lamp. "You've an early start tomorrow. You know you're seeing Mr. Appleton to get a plot for your house, don't you?"

"Yes."

"You're supposed to report to him at half-past five."

"Good night then, King. Sleep well."

"You too, Routledge."

7

"I LIKE LAMPERT'S IDEA, ALEX," OBIE SAID. "SWAP HIM for Des."

"Just the lines I been thinkin' along, Obie. Have to clean him up a bit, though. Give him a bit of appeal."

The new meat, naked and covered in blood and grime, had been thoroughly abused even before being brought here to Old Town and the hotel. Zombie, Curtis, and Reed, who had found him, had gone first. Then they had hired him out, cheaply enough for almost anyone to afford. After that they had lost interest and sold him to Peto.

"Zombie reckons he was a virgin," Obie said.

"What's your name, Sonny?" Peto said.

He did not speak. He was huddled in the corner, on the floor of the old dining-room, hunched up like a fetus, needlessly now trying to protect himself from the onslaught. He had not merely been raped; he had been dehumanized. His eyes, when they had been open, had registered nothing. This was the worst case Obie had ever seen, and he had seen plenty. At the lighthouse, with Houlihan, this blond-haired boy would not last long. He was pretty, prettier than Desborough, and as a bargaining counter would be worth a lot.

"If the stonks hadn't got there first I could've gone for him myself," Peto said.

Obie felt his stomach turn. He was beginning to regret

having supported the idea of a swap. But then it was vital for Peto's standing in the town that he got Desborough back.

This morning Obie had returned to Martinson's hut to find him much improved. The broken bone was giving him somewhat less pain, and it looked as if the cleaning and setting might even have worked. Obie had prepared Martinson a meal, emptied his slop bucket, and generally made himself useful before coming over to the hotel, as he usually did, towards noon. Often he would just sit around with Jez or Bubbles or Penguin or Peto himself, either outside on the terrace or in the dining-room. He might lend a hand with the goats, or do a bit of digging in the vegetable patch or among the stalks of oats or corn. Occasionally they would swim in Town Bay, or go after birds and eggs. If the helicopter had left new meat Obie might join in the hunt, though today he hadn't bothered.

The dining-room, with its old bay windows overlooking the terrace and the beach, was the best preserved part of the hotel and formed Peto's main quarters. A driftwood grid overhead was covered with fertilizer-bag plastic and turf. Most of the floorboards remained intact and only a few, mainly those near the windows, were rotten. The doors had disappeared, as had the window-frames and glass, while nearly all the plaster had fallen out of the walls, revealing crumbling laths and here and there strands of old wiring. In winter and at night Peto leaned sheets of corrugated iron against the windows. The furniture was the best Old Town could offer, extending to a pair of smelly armchairs and a settee with springs and stuffing hanging out at all angles, as well as to some hard chairs and a broken card-table from which Peto ate his meals.

Peto was slumped in one armchair, while Obie occupied the other. "Get Jez," Peto said. "You two clean him up. I'll find him somethin' to wear. Then you go over the light and talk to Houlihan."

"On my own?"

"Take a white flag."

"I want people with me."

"Penguin, then. And Jez."

"Hard people. You come, Alex."

"No chance. They'd bod me for sure."

At that moment raised voices outside in the sunshine preceded the sound of a scuffle on the steps, where Jez Brookes and Eric Craddock had joined Bubbles and Lampert on guard. There was a shriek: Obie glanced at Peto, who jumped up and grabbed the iron bar he always left leaning against the wall. A second later Dave Nackett, behind him Lampert and Bubbles and Craddock and three more, appeared in the doorway.

Nackett was holding a machete. An anglo, heavily built, with a gray beard, he had once been prominent on Peto's team. Obie saw that all his predictions were coming true; only the speed and boldness of the move had been unforeseen.

"What about you, Walker?" he said to Obie, when at last it had stopped. "You want some too?"

Obie had taken refuge by the fireplace, ignoring Peto's screams for help. While Craddock and Lampert had held Peto's arms, it was Nackett who had struck the first blow.

"I don't want no bother, Dave," Obie managed to say.

"Cut his head off," Craddock said. "Like we done to Brookes."

"Christ's sake, Dave," Obie said. "Town's yours now. I don't want it. I never did."

"That's right," Nackett said. "It's mine now." He turned to Craddock. "He was only Peto's bumboy. He knows what to expect if he makes trouble. You, Walker. Get rid of this carrion."

"Yes, Dave. Sure thing, Dave." Obie grasped Peto by what remained of his armpits and began pulling him towards the door.

"When you done that, come back and clean up the meat. We're dealin' with Houlihan now."

Godwin's workshop was much better finished than King's shack, with a flagstone floor and windows of real glass. It consisted of one large and one small room, together with

Godwin's bedroom and kitchen. For Fitzmaurice, Godwin's assistant, there was a folding bunk in the main workshop.

"This is where you'll be sitting, Mr. Routledge," Godwin said, indicating a small plywood table set against the wall. "You can have that orange chair. Fetch it, will you please." Routledge went to the bench and collected the plastic stacking chair, much faded and scuffed, taken no doubt from the laboratory in the bungalow. "Extra paper's in that cupboard. Waste as little as possible." With a motion of his hand Godwin indicated that Routledge should be seated. Already waiting on the table were a propelling pencil, a ruler, a solar-powered calculator and a pile of scrap paper.

"Something relatively easy to start with. I want you to draw some graphs. You'll have to make your own graph paper. Do it as accurately as you can. Then plot these equations. There are twenty of them."

"Right." Routledge accepted the sheet of paper and glanced at the equations, which had been numbered and written out in blue ballpoint. Below them was another, unnumbered, equation and a line of figures.

The light from the window flashed momentarily in Godwin's glasses. The style of the dark plastic frames, which held the lenses in place with a single heavy bar, was distinctly oldfashioned. He wheezed slightly when he spoke, as if he suffered from asthma or emphysema. At one time he might have smoked a pipe and worn cardigans with leather elbow-patches, and spent his evenings tinkering in a basement den.

"Now, yesterday you said you were familiar with the evaluation of definite integrals. Yes?"

"Yes."

"Do you remember Simpson's Rule?"

"Finding the area enclosed by a curve?"

"That's the one. Or you can use Dufton's Rules. However you do it, I want the areas of the curves between the ordinates x equals zero and x equals thirty-six. Two percent accuracy will do for now. Then substitute each of the equations generating the three smallest areas for theta in the master equation. Evaluate alpha for these values of x. Got it?"

Routledge nodded.

"Any questions?"

"No, Mr. Godwin. Not that I can think of."

"Fine. Give me a shout if there are."

Godwin returned to the bench, where Fitzmaurice, leaning on one elbow and cradling his temple in his fingers, had been using a pencil point to trace the flow of current in a large circuit diagram.

"It's here," he said to Godwin. "Look."

"All right. So what does that imply?"

"A glitch somewhere in the filter."

"Got to be."

They fell silent, both poring over the diagram.

Routledge turned to the sheet of equations. Theta was usually an angle. His suspicions about the nature of the project began to take more definite form. Acoustics, electronics: they were trying to build an echo sounder. Echo sounders were used to identify obstacles on the sea bed. Rocks, for example. Or to find clear channels for navigation. A boat. Franks was planning a boat. There could no longer be the slightest doubt about it.

Routledge began work. It should have been soothing beyond measure to return to the logical, clear-cut haven of mathematics. Out there the sun was beating down; in here, in the drowsy stillness of the summer afternoon, he was on safely familiar territory. But a week ago, to the minute, he had been in the bracken searching for his knife, almost out of his mind with guilt and fear. He could not stop thinking about the events of that day and, worse, of the following Monday. The images of Gazzer and Tortuga he could perhaps, in time, manage to come to terms with and absorb. The other one, the one at the chapel, was different. No conversation had been exchanged, only the primeval communication of intent between hunter and victim. The man would have killed him. It had been a question of survival, pure and simple. Routledge's conscience should have been clear. But Routledge was not a caveman. He could not rid himself in one week of ten thousand years of cultural conditioning. Where had the man been born? Where attended school? Who were his parents? And who was Karen, the name in the tattoo? Had she occupied Louise's place in the man's heart?

Routledge gave himself a conscious order to attend to the business in hand.

Two percent accuracy, Godwin had said. Twelve strips, say. Routledge opened the calculator wallet and the black bars of the liquid crystal display came instantly to life. Clear it. Press % C to scroll the instructions. Eight memory-registers. Not programmable, but plenty of functions. So. Equation One. Let x equal zero.

All this had something to do with a sound beam. Theta was the width of the beam. What could he remember about sonar? Very little. Well, what problems were they up against? Range would be a function of power. The transducers would need to be small and hence operate at high frequency. But at high frequencies there would also be high attenuation due to absorption by the water, calling for higher power. At close quarters, say when detecting a reef, that would increase reverberation. Then there would be background noise caused by the waves, as well as thermal noise and turbulence. And how would the signals be produced? How would they be synchronized and regulated?

Routledge looked up. I've already guessed what it's about, he wanted to say. Tell me exactly what I'm calculating and I'll work better and faster. I might even be able to suggest a few shortcuts.

Fitzmaurice glanced around. "Yes," he said, "is there something?"

"No—nothing. I was just thinking."

8

Only after about ten days in the Village did Rout-ledge come to appreciate just what Franks's organization had achieved. He had never before had cause to give much thought to the amount of care and labor needed to provide even the most basic municipal services. To supply the Community with clean water, for example, was a major undertaking involving hard work and strict attention to hygiene. Drinking-water was taken from two wells, one of which the Community itself had dug, while water for other purposes came from a brook which discharged over the cliffs as a small cascade. Above the cascade a pond had been hewn out of the rock to act as a reservoir. Drinking-water was distributed by donkey-cart and delivered daily to the door of each house, in a variety of found plastic canisters. Water for washing was delivered weekly; more could be collected from a central point, using one of a fleet of special wheelbarrows fitted with drums and taps.

Fuel for cooking and heating was at a premium. Much of the spare brush and driftwood was used to make charcoal for the forge, leaving a very limited supply for other purposes. At a place called Mencaro Field, however, near the center of the island, was an extensive peat bog which the Community had begun to exploit both for fuel and as a source of compost for improving the soil. To provide warm water for laundry and showers, Thaine had constructed a number of solar absorption bags from black polythene, while the bungalow was served by solar panels and an undersoil heat-exchanger inherited from its former occupants.

Besides candles and kerosene from the mainland, which were allocated by Stamper, for lighting the villagers used a spermaceti-like wax obtained from the stomach of the fulmar. The smell permeated all clothing and furnishings and papers wherever fulmar candles were burned; it was this odor which had served Routledge, on first awakening in King's house, as his introduction to Sert.

The fulmar was also collected for meat. Between April and July the cliffs around Pulpit Head, Porth Thomas Bay, Beacon Point, and other parts of the south and south-eastern coast still held large colonies of seabirds, especially fulmars, kittiwakes, puffins, and murres. A little further north, at Trellick Stack and Half Moon Bay, the colonies included razorbills too; while the triangular area between Angara Point, Perdew Wood and Old Town was home to a thousand pairs of Manx shearwaters. Formerly there had been five thousand pairs: Sert had been a seabird sanctuary of international scientific importance, but now heavy predation by the convicts had drastically reduced the numbers of all the species and restricted the cliff-nesters to the more inaccessible ledges. On Franks's orders, only a quota of seabirds was taken from the Village peninsula. The bulk of the birds was caught outside the peninsula by large, armed expeditions formerly led by Shoesmith, an expert cragsman whose mainland hobby had been rock-climbing. King showed Routledge some of the ropes, fowling-rods, and horsehair snares. Once each spring, at the neap tide, the fowlers crossed the causeway to Trellick Stack. This spring Shoesmith had slipped and fallen to his death: that, King had said, was the price of fulmar light.

In food, in clothing, and shelter, and indeed in everything else, the Village was all but self-sufficient. There were now nearly a hundred and ninety inhabitants, who had brought with them a wide range of expertise which Franks, through Appleton and Stamper and the descending layers of the hierarchy, had employed to the greatest possible effect. When knowledge was lacking, Franks sent to the mainland for books, and in this way had developed some of the more specialized skills of food production on a barren Atlantic island. The Community bred goats and sheep, and had recently begun to expand its dairy-farming, poultry-keeping, and hog-raising. It grew wheat, oats, barley, sugar beet, potatoes, and a number of other vegetables. An early enterprise was fruit-growing. Blackberries and gooseberries were native to the island and cultivated strains did well. Netting cages were put up to keep birds away from the raspberries, loganberries and black currants. More tender fruits such as strawberries were protected from the sea wind by greenhouses made of driftwood and polythene sheeting, in which salad crops were also intensively grown. Surrounding the soft-fruit area were orchards of young apple, greengage, pear, and cherry trees, and surrounding these were shelter belts of Leyland's cypress which, besides providing rapid growth, were evergreen and could eventually be harvested as lumber. Most of the produce was eaten fresh, to give the greatest dietary benefits, though a proportion was preserved for the winter.

All the processes of production in the Village were interdependent and demanded a high degree of cooperation. At busy times the men growing fruit were excused other duties, and extra labor was drafted in to pick the crops. Every member of the Community had his own area of responsibility, yet the work schedules were so well manipulated by Franks and Appleton that nothing ever seemed to be left undone. It was this aspect of life in the Village that Routledge found the most remarkable. He would not have believed it possible, least of all from a disparate bunch of convicts whose chief common trait had been an inability to function in mainland society.

The need to conform, to earn the respect of their fellows, and to avoid at all costs the specter of expulsion, had wrought equally remarkable changes in their social behavior. Routledge had scarcely begun to fathom the rules of etiquette which regulated Village life, so different were they from those of the mainland. He almost felt it would be easier to master court life in twelfth-century Japan. The business of names was endlessly delicate and subtle, the chief medium through which status was measured and made known. Paradoxically, the more times a man was addressed as "Mr.," the lower his standing. Such exalted individuals as Godwin or Thaine might be accorded one or two "Mr."'s in a conversation; but this varied according to the substance of the conversation and the status of anyone else within earshot.

Breaches of etiquette, conscious or otherwise, resulted in a lowering of a man's status which was instantly and mysteriously broadcast to the whole Community. Among these, besides clumsy use of names and unwarranted criticism of the Father and his Council, were any acts which could be construed, however remotely, as selfish or inconsiderate of others, particularly those with a lower status. Virtues which earned an increase of status included physical or mental courage, generosity, personal pride, and a capacity for hard work, especially when this was of direct value to the Father. Myers, for example, Franks's senior guard, enjoyed a status second only to Appleton's, though he was a man of comparatively low intellect and did not serve on the Council.

The granting or refusal of informality reflected on the status of both parties involved. Refusal was not necessarily a snub. Routledge's status was such that he was already on surname-only terms with two of the men who had been appointed to help him with his house. But Ojukwo, a senior carpenter, was still "Mr." Routledge had been quite wrong in thinking that the crossbow would improve his position. He was near, if not at, the bottom of the social scale.

The Village held many other surprises. The stone and driftwood chapel drew a congregation of forty or fifty men, many of them born-again fanatics like the chaplain, Blackshaw, himself. There were musical evenings, a darts league, a drama group, even a bird-watching club. King was active in the chess circle, which attracted an unexpectedly large number of devotees.

"You ought to join," he said. "It's what your game needs."

Routledge did not reply. He was staring at King's small portable board, trying to find a response, any response, to King's last move. This was the fifth time they had played: on each occasion Routledge had been thoroughly humiliated. Now he was already a rook and a knight down, and an evil-looking combination was slowly assembling against his queen.

Rain was falling outside. As it was Sunday, he had been allowed to sleep late, until seven. The time before lunch had been spent on various domestic chores; this afternoon Routledge was due at Godwin's to do some extra calculations. Each weekday he had risen at four-thirty, worked for most of the morning on the construction of his house, eaten lunch, reported to Godwin's at one and worked there until nine, when he had been left with the strength only to stumble into bed and fall asleep. He felt deeply fatigued, but the fatigue was not unwelcome: it helped him to forget.

He had not wanted to expend the mental effort needed for chess, but the alternative, the possible loss of King's company, had seemed worse.

"Do you want to put your bishop back where it was?" King said.

"No. I've moved it now."

"Then it's mate in four. You're in *Zugzwang*."

"What's that?"

"Any move you make now lands you in hot water."

"That, at least, I can see." Routledge considered for a moment longer. "I resign," he said.

"There's one chess story, doubtless apocryphal, from the Middle Ages. Nothing was said during the whole game. Suddenly one of the players leaped up, grabbed the board, and brought it down endways on his opponent's head. That's the sort of game it is." King was setting up the pieces once more. "Another?"

"I don't think my nerves can stand it." Routledge glanced at the alarm clock: the time was nearly one. "Besides, I ought to get over to Mr. Godwin's."

King closed the lid on his chess set, snapping the catch, and in that instant Routledge realized how much he liked the older man. During the past week his opinion of King had been rising steadily.

At the start of their first chess game, Routledge—who,

although he had not played since his schooldays, had always thought himself a formidable opponent—had assumed automatically that he would win. He had viewed with complacency King's quiet development of his pieces, feeling his first twinge of alarm only when he saw he had blundered straight into an elegant and silken trap. It appeared that King had judged him nicely, using his own confidence as a weapon. And so it proved in real life. Routledge now regretted and felt ashamed of his first estimate. Very little escaped King's notice. Half a dozen words were all it took for him to understand a complex idea that another man might never have seen. If Routledge wanted to keep any secrets, he knew he would have to be careful what he said. King had noted Routledge's initial opinion, and not taken offense. He mixed easily and freely with the other villagers, was popular without currying favor and, above all, showed respect for his social and mental inferiors.

This attitude was in marked contrast with the one Routledge had brought with him to Sert. Routledge had begun to see it; he had already, under King's influence, begun trying to modify his behavior. And yet, except for King, he had not met anyone remotely sympathetic. With those like himself, on the lower rungs, he had nothing in common. Franks fascinated him, but his fascination was tinged with fear. Appleton and the rest of the upper echelon were simply unpleasant, and that included Godwin, whose subtly sarcastic manner was second only to his conceit as a polluter of the atmosphere in the workshop. Fitzmaurice did not help. He had made it plain that he resented Routledge's presence and regarded his contribution as unnecessary.

"Hello," he said, as Routledge opened the door.

"Mr. Godwin not here?"

"As you can see. He left your work on the table."

Fitzmaurice insisted on saying "the table" rather than "your desk," which is what it had now become. Routledge sat down.

Suddenly he decided he had had enough. It was time to snatch up the board and bring it down on Fitzmaurice's head.

"Have you decided what sort of transducers to use?" he said.

Fitzmaurice was clearly startled. "Come again?"

"For the sonar."

"What sonar?"

"The sonar I'm helping you design. That one."

"What are you talking about?"

"Even if Mr. Appleton hadn't given the game away, I would have guessed by now."

"We're talking at cross-purposes, Mr. Routledge."

"Mr. Appleton asked me what I knew about piezoelectric devices, about electronics, acoustics. We're stuck on an island. How do you get off islands? By boat. Just what sort of idiot do you take me for?"

"I don't take you for any sort of idiot, Mr. Routledge." Fitzmaurice got up from the bench. "I've got one or two things to attend to," he said, moving towards the door. "I'll see you later."

"Tell Mr. Godwin he's not using me properly. I can do better than this. Understand?"

Routledge had stepped far beyond the bounds of safety. This was a gamble, a calculated risk. If he was ever to get anywhere in the Community, he had to start now, and the man to start with was Fitzmaurice.

No rebuke was forthcoming. Fitzmaurice donned his oilskin and opened the door. "As I say, I'll see you later."

When he saw Godwin's face, Routledge wondered whether he had indeed gone too far. Godwin took off his raincoat and hung it by the door, removed his wellington boots, and slowly, deliberately, pulled on the old tennis shoes he used in the workshop.

He had arrived without Fitzmaurice, who, Routledge supposed, was even at this moment conveying to Franks the news that their secret had been rumbled. Routledge thought of Myers, and Talbot, and regretted having spoken. Godwin might be followed to the workshop by an armed deputation, and Routledge might well end his afternoon at the bottom of the cliffs.

"Sit down, please," Godwin said.

He went to the bench and sat down himself, his back to the window, so that Routledge had difficulty in making out his features.

"Mr. Fitzmaurice tells me you believe we're not using you properly. What do you mean by that?"

"It means . . . I feel I could contribute more."

"To what?"

"To the work here."

"Isn't that for me to judge?"

"Yes, Mr. Godwin. Of course. Only . . ."

"Only what?"

Routledge swallowed. Who were these people, anyway? He looked up, directly at Godwin's face. "I think I know what you're building. If I'm right, I believe I could be of greater service to you. If I'm wrong, then I am being presumptuous and I apologize."

"I think you are being presumptuous in either event."

"A matter of opinion."

Godwin expelled his breath and glanced out of the window before speaking again. "Tell me what you think we're building."

"Ultimately, a boat. At the moment, a sonar. If the sonar can be made to work, you'll start on the boat."

"And where is this 'boat' going to go?"

"Away from Sert."

"And its destination?"

"Devon or Cornwall. Some deserted cove."

"Aren't you forgetting about the Magic Circle?"

"The sonar isn't all you're working on."

"Is that so?"

"You've found some way to beat the system."

"Have I, now?"

"I don't ask for a place on the boat, if that's what you're thinking. I'm not blackmailing anyone."

"Big of you."

"No. I just don't want to get chucked over the cliffs."

Godwin expelled another breath, more heavily this time. "Mr. Routledge," he said, after a moment. "You have a great deal to learn about the Community. No one is going to chuck you over the cliffs. You are one of us. Any man in the Village would defend you with his life. Not because he likes the color of your eyes, but because he would expect you to do the same for him.'' Against the window, Godwin's silhouette was bathed in bluish light. ''I can now do one of two things. I can remove you from the project with an admonition to say nothing about what you believe you have discovered, or I can let you in on the full details of the plan. Either way, if you reveal anything, no matter how slight, to anyone in the Village, anyone, you'll be across that border hedge so fast your feet won't touch the ground. Get the picture?''

Routledge nodded.

''You're good at sums, I'll grant you that.'' Godwin half turned and absently leafed through some papers on his bench. ''You've already proved your worth.'' He picked up a pencil and began turning it end over end against the papers, pushing it through the fingers of his right hand. After several turns he let the pencil drop. ''All right. Tell me what you know about sonar.''

''Not much, specifically. The basic idea. But I know the physics.''

''Then let me tell you what's going on here. You're right, the Father wants to build a boat. It will carry twelve men: Mr. Appleton, Mr. Thaine, me, and the Father himself. When and if he decides to go ahead with it, he will announce a lottery for the eight remaining places. Like Mr. Fitzmaurice, you will have to take your chances, assuming by then you still want to go. You're also right in thinking that without a sonar the boat would never get away from the island. Why that is, and how we hope to evade the Magic Circle, I shall not yet tell you. All you need to know about, for now, is the sonar. As you may have gathered, there are lots of problems, most of which are caused by a shortage of components. We're tackling it on three fronts. We've already made a simple system using parabolic reflectors. The transmitting reflector contains a modified radio loudspeaker fed with a high frequency blip from a loop tape. The receiver is simply a pair of microphones, each in its own reflector, connected to a stereo amplifier and headphones. From the nature of the feedback the operator deduces the profile of the bottom. It works, but the image is much too crude for safety. The second approach uses the remote-control circuitry from Mr. Appleton's flatscreen. This allows better imaging, but the range is restricted, and as water turbidity increases the image dies. Inshore it wouldn't be good enough. Does all this mean anything to you?''

''Yes. I understand.''

''The final option is a full-blown rig with single or double switched piezoelectric or electrostrictive transducers. We haven't got very far with it. Without a computer, we still can't establish the optimum beamwidth, pulse frequency or wavelength, or even the best type and configuration of transducer. In the end we may have to settle for magnetostrictive rather than piezoelectric or electrostrictive transducers, but at the moment a twin-array piezoelectric system seems the most promising. The trouble with the final option is the number of variables to consider. Each model takes about a fortnight to calculate out. Change one variable and the whole model must be worked through again. That's where you come in.''

''I see.''

''Now the cat's out of the bag you might as well look at the original papers.'' From below the bench Godwin produced a thick folder. ''If you can find any way to save time on the mathematics, I suppose my confidence in you will be justified.'' He shook his head, as if reproving himself for his own trusting credulity. ''I'll put the kettle on. When Mr. Fitzmaurice gets back, we'll have a cup of tea.''

9

By the middle of September, the structure of Routledge's house was complete. On the morning of the twenty-third, before starting at Godwin's, he was able to move in.

Since the end of August the weather had been deteriorating daily. North had entered the wind: the sea, gray and desolate, was becoming rougher than ever, at high tide this morning driving towers of spume across the rocks in Vanston Cove. At night the beam of the southern lightship turned to its slow and lonely beat, sweeping the miles to the island coast and out to the empty seas beyond. Between Vanston Cove and America lay nothing but that expanse of waves, the same each day, the same horizon. Notwithstanding all its changes in hue and aspect, in light and shade, in agitation and direction, the sea always remained the same, encircling, debarring, a manifestation of the mainland's implacable, merciless indifference to his fate. After ten weeks on the island, Routledge no longer liked even to look at it.

He was trying to turn his vision inwards. Best of all he liked fog. Except for the dismal sound of the lightship's horn, he could almost imagine then that he was on part of some continent, that to east or north lay vast tracts of terrain across which, if he only chose, he could journey on foot forever.

Luckily the plot Appleton had given him was on the landward side of the bungalow, a couple of hundred meters from King's house and looking out over as yet unpopulated ground.

178

Moving in would have been a daunting task to accomplish on his own, but in this as in the preceding weeks of work he was helped by King and by Ojukwo, who had built much of the framework, the door, the two shutters, and Routledge's bed, chair, and table.

Many others in the Village had contributed to the job: at least twenty men had been involved in one way or another. King had been the most generous of himself and his time, ensuring that Routledge kept to the schedule for completion that Appleton had laid down.

The bulk of the work, though, Routledge had had to do himself. First he had cleared the gorse by machete and dug up the roots, then used pick and shovel to level the soil and prepare for the foundations. The smaller twigs and branches had been taken by donkey-cart to the compost heaps over a kilometer away; the roots and the bigger branches had had to go to the woodyard. With the donkey-cart he had brought lumps of stone from the cliffs, and turf from Bag Head. Under the guidance of a man named Phelps he had learned how to choose and place the stones and how to pack the interstices with clay. Contrary to Routledge's first impression, the resulting walls were hard packed and extremely strong, forming a solid base for the timber framework of the roof, which was covered with overlapping plates of rock and then a layer of turf.

The interior comprised one room, five meters by six, with two windows and a fireplace. Four pillars helped to support the ceiling. In most features the accommodation resembled King's, and indeed it was King himself who had suggested the design, which, with minor variations, had been adopted for many of the single-occupancy houses in the Village.

The structure contravened nearly every code of building practice Routledge knew, but it would give him shelter and had been made as economically as possible with the materials available. For the load-bearing beams and roof members he had been given seasoned fir, but most of the lumber had arrived on Sert with the tide. In August Daniels had rescued over a ton of first-quality Swedish marine ply, in various thicknesses, and some of this had been incorporated into the shutters and door, and into the table that Routledge and Ojukwo were now bringing down from the carpentry shop, while King and Carter, carrying some shelves and the final bundle of Routledge's possessions, came behind.

There was a chill in the air. Spots of rain were one by one darkening the surface of the tabletop.

"Better be quick with that table," Carter said. "You don't want to spoil the french polish."

"I got your french polish, Carter," Ojukwo said.

Carter laughed. He was twenty-six, a white man, dark-haired and sallow. With two others, he shared Ojukwo's house. He seemed unusually close to Ojukwo; just recently Routledge had begun to wonder about them. So far in the Village he had detected no signs of homosexuality, but, not-withstanding the rules and the punishment it incurred, he was certain it must exist, if only in a sublimated form.

The house smelled of earth and of freshly sawn wood. Mounting the threshold, Routledge acknowledged in full the feeling of achievement that had been growing within him during the past weeks. Despite the crudeness of the design, the house had taken all his skill and strength to bring to completion. The interior was as yet lacking in comfort and personality, but, given time, he knew he could make it habitable. And though he did not admit it to himself, in a curious way he was even looking forward to living here, to being free at last of King's interference with the full development of his sense of grievance and self-pity.

"Where d'you want the table?" Ojukwo said.

"By the window, please."

King and Carter began placing shelves on brackets.

"Really, leave that," Routledge said. "You've done enough. I'd like to offer you all something to eat, but I've got to be at Mr. Godwin's in ten minutes. This evening. Could you come then? I've been saving a few things specially. My wife's sent me a fruitcake."

"We couldn't eat your cake," Ojukwo said. "Wouldn't be fair."

"No, honestly. I've been saving it till now. I want you to have it."

"Sort of a housewarming?" Carter said.

"Exactly. I'd like to invite everyone who helped, but there won't be enough for that. See if you can get Mr. Phelps and Mr. Johnson to come too."

"What time?" King said.

"Nine-thirty. If that's not too late."

As he sat working that afternoon, Routledge listened out for the distant drone of engines which sometimes, when the pilot came or went a certain way, announced the arrival of the helicopter.

When first he had seen the drop zone, Routledge had thought the spacing of the stone circle ridiculously extravagant, the caution of the crew exaggerated beyond reason. Later, he had learned from King that they kept a machine gun in the cabin and were equipped with riot gas. Now he saw why. The helicopter had formed a focus for his dreams: with many of the villagers it had become an obsession. What it was like for those outside he could not imagine. Those crewmen were gods, descending briefly from Olympus to the netherworld. On Olympus they could indulge in delights that, to the convicts, had become unthinkable. And not just the company of women: never again would Routledge be able to walk through the park, ride a bicycle, see a traffic signal change from amber to green. One of the hardest parts of his sentence was to realize just how many mundane activities he would never be able to sample again; and worse, to realize how many opportunities for pleasure he had allowed to pass him by.

On the mainland he had always lived in the future, always looking forward to the completion of the project in hand. When he passed his exams, got the new contract, married Louise, paid off the mortgage: when, in turn, each of these dreams was realized, then, and only then, would he be happy. All were ends, to be reached by any means expedient or possible. He saw now that there were no such things as ends, only means: for ends were phantoms that melted away when approached, only to reform into other ends further off. For most men the process was limited by death. For him, and the others on the island, the limits had been abruptly and artificially set. There could be no more ends, only the day-to-day business of survival.

Except for Franks. Through almost superhuman willpower he had created the possibility of a goal. Routledge did not know him well enough to understand his attitude towards it. Certainly, and Godwin had confirmed this, Franks and his Council perceived the project as more than a mere attempt at escape. In the period between making the details public and holding the lottery, the Village would be united as never before, paving the way for who knew what developments. Then, if the attempt succeeded, the mental relationship between the villagers and the Prison Service would have been broken forever. Until now the authorities had had it all their own way. The knowledge that escape had been achieved, and could be achieved again, would transform everything.

That was what the Council believed. Routledge was not so sure. Without Franks he doubted that another boat could be built. Most of the Village would be dismayed by the news that he and the most prominent members of his Council intended to leave.

But then the announcement of the lottery might never come. Godwin had yet to confirm that the sonar could actually be made to work.

Louise had written every week except the last. Twice she had enclosed a note from Christopher, and once, a fortnight ago, he had received a parcel containing various groceries and treats, including a Dundee cake, some bars of chocolate, and a quota of extra clothing, books, soap, and other luxuries.

The censor had so far treated Louise's correspondence with lenience, blacking out only a paragraph or two and some isolated words relating to the winding up of the legal process. In a letter from his mother Routledge had learned that money had at first been very difficult for Louise, but the house had now at last been sold and she had found a better-paid job.

The lack of a letter last week, while disappointing, had,

according to King, been nothing unusual, and would probably be followed by a double delivery today.

"Do you think the helicopter's been yet?" Godwin said.

"I haven't heard it," Fitzmaurice said.

They were still soldering, using a fine-pointed iron and a magnifying glass mounted in a wooden stand. "What about you, Mr. Routledge?" Godwin said, looking up. "Heard anything?"

"No. Not yet. Of course, he might have come another way."

"Bit more on that joint," Godwin said to Fitzmaurice.

Routledge studied them for a moment longer before returning to his calculator. He had come to loathe them both. On a personal level Routledge had found himself consistently isolated. Despite the fact that he had already contributed in no small measure to the development of the electronics, and was now also regularly undertaking figurework for Thaine, he felt he had not been accorded the respect his part in the project deserved. Neither, despite the importance of his work, had he improved his position in the Village as a whole. There was nothing he could actually pin down, but in all his dealings with others, King excepted, there was an unspoken and unpleasant reserve. He had resigned himself to the fact that he was unpopular; he did not fit in.

In his former life he had noticed that people who were capable and intelligent were often disliked for the simple reason that they could not be pitied. Their qualities made it impossible for others to feel that warm glow of superiority which the need for indulgence always generated. How else could one understand the preference given to underdogs of every kind, no matter how undeserving their case or their cause? How else could one explain the common feeling of jealousy and spite towards anyone whose own efforts had raised himself out of the gutter? For all Franks's high-flown talk of a meritocracy, just the same applied here.

From the far side of the bungalow came the dull sound of an iron bar striking a suspended oil drum, once, twice, thrice: the mail gong.

"There it is," Godwin said. "Will you go, Mr. Routledge?"

Routledge arose, scraping the legs of his chair. "Are you expecting any parcels?"

"We live in hope. There should be something for Mr. Gunter. Flashlight batteries."

"Mr. Gunter's with the fishing party."

"There's no rush. If Mr. Ross gets a parcel, let me know."

Stepping outside the workshop, Routledge again felt the keen edge of autumn. The moaning in the trees had become more insistent; a few premature larch needles were being shed. Along the garden hedge a flock of starlings rose and was flung away downwind. The french windows of the bungalow, sealed tight, returned only dull reflections: he had the feeling that Franks was at his desk, watching him keep to the concrete path, watching him cross the paving stones and turn the corner. He passed the kitchen door and mounted the side steps to the veranda, where Stamper was distributing the mail.

"Letter for Mr. Fitzmaurice," Stamper said. "And two for Mr. Godwin."

"Any for me?"

"Yes, Mr. Routledge. Just the one."

Routledge saw instantly that this was a letter from his mother. The envelope was slim, unbulky, enclosing only one or two sheets of paper. "Just this?"

"Just that."

"Could you check?"

"It's all in alphabetical order. Look. Redfern. Sibley. Nothing else for you."

Doing his best to conceal his bewilderment, Routledge said, "That parcel for Mr. Gunter. There's something in it for us."

"I know. As soon as he's had a chance to open it I'll be over."

"Was there a parcel for Mr. Ross?"

"Not today."

"Right. Thanks."

When he got back he found Fitzmaurice making the tea.

Even in this minor ritual Routledge felt himself excluded from the life of the workshop. Fitzmaurice guarded the ceremony as his own childish preserve: boiling the water, producing a tea-bag, new or secondhand, according to the state of the workshop supply, straining the milk if necessary to exclude coagulated cream, timing the infusion, pouring the finished brew. Routledge, as if to emphasize the temporary nature of his position, was always served first. After the failure of a couple of uneasy attempts to sit at or lean on the workbench during breaks, he now always retreated to the safety of his desk.

The letter from his mother said nothing about Louise, and contained only general news, some of it effaced by the censor's solid blocks of impenetrable black, all of it utterly irrelevant. She still hadn't understood. He would not be coming back. In all but the strictly biological sense, her son had died. Sert was merely an anteroom for the great black hole. She said she hoped he was keeping well. Hard though it was, she said, not knowing the first thing about it, she hoped he was coming to terms with his fate. She hoped he was not bitter. She prayed for him daily.

As he read, he framed the reply he wanted to send but knew he never would. It angered him to think that still, even now, he had to hold back, to spare her feelings. He had never told her just what he thought of the value of prayer and all the rest of the self-deluding mumbo-jumbo with which otherwise rational people tried to humanize the cosmos. Man had created God in his own image, not the other way around. He had done it through sheer terror, and who could blame him? Unfortunately he had made too good a job. The god he had invented was just as cruel and careless as man himself. Not a deity to whom one should seriously address a prayer.

It was exactly then, perhaps, at that very moment, that Routledge felt his first misgivings. Maybe there had been an administrative hitch, he told himself. Yes, without doubt: Louise's letters were stuck at Dartmoor, or had been delivered to some other Routledge on some other island. There could be no other explanation. Next week, or the week after, the backlog would come.

At the sound of the latch Routledge turned his head. The door opened and Franks entered.

"Some tea, Father?" Godwin said, once Franks had told everyone to resume his seat.

"Thank you, yes."

Franks took off his spectacles, placed them on the bench, and rubbed the bridge of his nose. For a moment he seemed pained; his eyes appeared small and weak, making him look vulnerable, but then, with a practiced movement, the rimless lenses were again set between him and the outside world. His V-necked sweater, pale gray, was new, as were his corduroy trousers and a pure white shirt. On his wrist Routledge glimpsed a flash of Rolex. "I'll get straight to the point," he said, glancing at Routledge as if to indicate that he could now be considered privy to any and all secrets of the project. "I've just had word from Courtmacsherry. It's got to be next year or never. Mr. Thaine is ready to proceed, but says it'll be tight." He accepted the mug of tea from Fitzmaurice. "I must tell him today. Yes or no."

"This is too sudden. There's still too much to be done."

For want of materials, Godwin had reluctantly opted for magnetostrictive rather than piezoelectric transducers, and had heavily modified four radio loudspeakers for the purpose. The transmitting and receiving amplifiers had been built and tested, the clock circuitry almost finished, the design of the pulsing unit finalized. They were now wiring the gating unit.

"Yes or no, Mr. Godwin."

"You're asking me to risk twelve lives, including my own."

"And mine. If we go."

"But we can't make the announcement and then hold back."

"True."

"So we'll be going whatever?"

"All else being equal. Next May. Provided we have the sonar."

"May?" Godwin said in alarm. "But the temperature differential will be dangerously high."

"High, but not unmanageable. Mr. Thaine says he can step up the flow-rate."

Godwin let out a sigh, and then an oath, a plea to the Almighty, his forehead in his hand.

"Yes or no."

"All right. Yes. I'm mad, but let's say it. Yes."

10

At ten past seven Routledge set out for the metal-work shop, where he was due to report to Thaine to do some stress calculations. The cloud had not lifted all day; the moaning in the larches had intensified to an ominously rising howl. Dusk was coming early, and on Thaine's bench an oil-lamp was already burning. But the forge was cold and dead, and when Routledge arrived he found only Chapman, drilling holes in a small steel plate.

"He had to go over the Father's," Chapman said. "That's where you'll find him."

Talbot was again on duty at the veranda. As always, he remained firmly seated at Routledge's approach.

"I've come to see Mr. Thaine. Mr. Chapman said he was here."

"Not anymore he ain't. He left about half an hour ago."

"Do you know where he went?"

"Try the windmill. Or the carpentry shop."

"Did he say anything about leaving some figures for me?"

"No."

Routledge considered asking Talbot to find out whether Stamper or Appleton, or Franks himself, might know; but decided against it. He would check the places Talbot had suggested. If that failed, he could with an easy conscience return to his house and begin getting it in order, since his stint for Godwin today was now over.

"Better take a waterproof," Talbot called after him. "Shipping forecast says we're in for a big one."

Routledge waved an acknowledgment without looking around. If he had to go out to the windmill he would indeed take his PVC jacket, but the carpentry shop was nearer. It stood on the far side of the precinct, next to the woodyard. No lights were showing: the place seemed deserted. The outer door was shut. Nevertheless, Routledge opened it and looked inside.

The two benches made areas of paler gloom. On one of them stood an unfinished frame, perhaps for a cabinet; the other was clear. Work had not long ceased, for the smell of fresh shavings and glue still hung in the air. The floor had been swept and all the tools put away.

Routledge was about to leave when, above the wind, he thought he heard a noise from the storeroom at the back. Someone was in there. Puzzled at first, and then increasingly disturbed, he listened more closely. Not just someone: two people. Two males. There could be no mistaking that bestial rhythm. Every night, in the cell at Exeter he had shared, he had been made to listen and learn from a distance of no more than two meters.

No recognizable words were being uttered, but from the timbre of one of the voices he suspected that its owner was Ojukwo. Of course: Ojukwo worked in the carpentry shop. Where else would he and Carter hold their assignations? After hours the chances of detection were slight—slight enough to be disregarded by men whose urges could no longer be denied.

The rhythm abruptly ceased.

Routledge heard a gasp, the exchange of murmurs. Ojukwo and Carter, for sure. Surprisingly, it seemed, as the Exeter argot would put it, Ojukwo and not Carter was the bitch. In a minute or two they might emerge. He had to decide what to do. The impulse to confront them could prove dangerous. They might kill him rather than face ejection from the Village.

What they were doing to each other was not only sordid and depraved but also, given the medical risks, antisocial in the extreme. His first thought was to earn himself credit with Franks by reporting them. Then he remembered that Ojukwo had acted fairly towards him at all times: and so had Carter. Ojukwo had been on Sert for five years, Carter for slightly less. Was Routledge so sure of his own sexuality that he could not find it in him to understand their desperation? Men varied in the strength of their sexual drive. Some, like himself, could deal with abstinence, forever if need be. Others were not so fortunate. Once temptation had summoned, once their desires had glimpsed the possibility of escape, all will was lost, all normal considerations were left behind. On the blind path downwards no shame or humiliation was too great to risk. Thus had it been with those two at Exeter.

However, the facts of the matter were clear. They were breaking the rules of the Community. It was his duty to report them. If thereby he gained credit with the hierarchy, that would be no less than his due.

The noises from the storeroom indicated that only a few moments of safety remained. He would leave at once, defer reaching a decision on how to handle the situation; but at any rate he wanted them to know they had been overheard. In this wind, merely leaving the door open would not be enough. From the nearer bench he silently took down the cabinet frame and used it to wedge the door open at its furthest extent, and then, as the rain began, hurried out of the workshop and across the precinct.

He found Thaine at the windmill. There had been a mixup. Stamper had forgotten to tell Talbot about the calculations Thaine had left for Routledge to collect.

"They're to do with the building molds," Thaine said. He was crouching, working by torchlight, in the final stages of some repair or adjustment to the rotor shaft. "We want to know whether the axles will take the weight. After all, she'll be virtually full of water." He glanced around, spanner in hand. "When I give the word, climb up and stick that rod in the lock, will you?"

"In there?"

"That's it. All right. Now."

With difficulty Routledge pushed the pencil-thick steel pin into place, locking the rotor to the frame and preventing it from turning. He saw that Thaine was now checking and tightening the bolts of the framework itself. The precautions were not coming a minute too soon. Heavy rain was already falling, and the wind had strengthened even in the short time since Routledge had left the Village. Darkness had taken the sky in the east. To the west, over the sea, lowering cloud still retained traces of daylight. Routledge jumped down. "Mr. Talbot said a storm was coming."

"The first of the autumn," Thaine said. " 'Force seven, backing northerly, increasing storm force eleven, imminent.' Force eleven is about a hundred kilometers an hour. It could gust to twice as much, maybe more. We don't want to burn out the generator, or lose the mill entirely." Thaine, wiping his nose with the back of his hand, finally stood up. "OK, Mr. Routledge, that'll do it," he said. "By the way, I meant to ask you. Do you know anything about sailing?"

This was a question which, for reasons which were obvious now, Appleton had not posed during the interviews.

"It depends what you mean. I did a bit of dinghy sailing at school. On the local gravel pits. Never on the sea. I remember capsizing a lot."

"What did you sail?"

"Enterprises, mainly. 5-0-5s. That kind of thing."

Thaine made a meaningless sound. Routledge took it to indicate that Thaine, as a representative of the Council, already knew all there was to know about seamanship and had asked merely on the off-chance, not expecting even the reply he had received. Routledge wondered whether he would tell Thaine about Ojukwo and Carter; and was almost on the point of deciding that he should when Thaine said, "We're starting on the hull tomorrow. We'll have lots of sums from now on. And measurements to be checked on plans, on timber, and on the finished pieces. I've asked the Father if I can use you a bit more. You'd be amenable to that, would you?"

"Certainly. Anything I can do to help."

"Thanks. It's appreciated." He gestured at the hut. "Since you're here, could you give me a hand with the tarp?"

Wired to the framework and pegged into the ground with iron stakes, the tarpaulin was used as an aerodynamic foil to deflect the worst of the buffets. The wind had already reached the point where the job was made awkward. Three men, not two, were really needed. The rain was becoming heavier. Routledge was glad of Talbot's advice about the waterproof, but Thaine, in his leather jacket and jeans, seemed indifferent to the wet.

As they fixed the first wire a tremendous gust took them unawares and tried to wrest the tarpaulin away. Thaine yelled with pain. The wire had snapped and gashed his hand. He lost his grip.

The tarpaulin, flapping wildly and suddenly filled with its own huge, mysterious, and autonomous power, was like a broad blue monster unexpectedly come to life. It wanted to head inland, across the scrub and over the potato fields. Routledge was nothing, a trifle, an afterthought. It began pulling him along. He lost his balance, fell, and found himself being dragged through the prickles of the low gorse bushes which bordered the fields here.

"Let go of it!" Thaine shouted. "Quick!"

"We'll never get it back!"

"Let go! Let go! It could take you over the cliff!"

Afterwards, Routledge was not sure why he had refused to obey. Perhaps he had had enough of the way they were treating him. Perhaps he had felt it was time to assert himself, if not over Thaine then over the tarpaulin, this entity which in its unruliness was just as unmanageable as his relations with the Village as whole. For a moment he did not actually care whether the wind did indeed change direction and pull him over the cliff. To fall then, at the onset of darkness in this early-autumn gale, would have been a resolution of sorts. During the first two or three seconds, dropping through space before taking the first of the brutal, fatal blows, he would at least have been free.

These were not thoughts. There was barely even time for them to take shape as a feeling when, just as mysteriously, the gust subsided and the tarpaulin abandoned its attempt at liberty. Routledge gathered in the folds and went back to Thaine.

"What about your hand, Mr. Thaine?"

Thaine shone the flashlight on it. The skin had been torn and there was blood, but the wound looked worse than it was. "I'll live," he said. "Let's get this thing fixed."

As they worked, Routledge decided to forbear mentioning what he had overheard in the carpentry shop.

Until now he had disliked Thaine, just as he had disliked all those on the Village Council. Like everyone except King, Thaine had made no attempt to reciprocate the subtle overtures of friendship which Routledge believed he had extended and which, at the first sign of indifference, had been withdrawn. Thaine in particular, with his self-confident manner and the technical ability that had placed him so high in the tree, had evinced not the slightest interest, rebuffing these embryonic approaches with something like rudeness. Routledge's pride would not allow him to make the next move. But he must unconsciously have craved Thaine's esteem, for he was surprised, once they had finished fixing the tarpaulin and were walking back to the Village, how gratified he was when Thaine said, "That was a brave thing to do, Mr. Routledge. You could have been killed."

"To be honest, I didn't really think. I suppose I just felt angry, if you know what I mean."

"Anyone else would have let go. I'm sorry I put you at risk. I should have secured the mill earlier. We heard the storm warning at the six o'clock news. Only the Father got an important letter from home. But you know about that, don't you?"

"In outline."

Thaine did not pursue the subject, and neither did Routledge, who, in the commonplace remarks they exchanged on the way to the precinct, was increasingly conscious that an irreversible change had taken place in the way Thaine regarded him.

"You ought to see Mr. Sibley about that cut," Routledge said, as they drew near to the bungalow. "Get some iodine or something."

"Yes, I think I will."

They paused on the shale: Routledge would be going straight on, to the veranda, to fetch the calculations. "Good night, then, Mr. Thaine."

"Be seeing you," Thaine said.

Routledge did not know how he was going to endure the housewarming which he himself had so stupidly dreamed up. The moment when Carter and Ojukwo arrived could easily have proved a disaster, but Routledge managed to carry it off and was certain they had detected no change in his attitude. As for them, they were concealing their fears remarkably well. They surely knew that someone in the Village had wedged open the workshop door. Perhaps they already suspected Routledge; perhaps they had discovered that Talbot had sent him there looking for Thaine. But that was most improbable. They would not dare make such inquiries. There was nothing they could do to alleviate the excruciating suspense of wondering when the hammer would fall. Or perhaps they thought they had not been identified; perhaps they thought they had got away with it. Was that why they seemed so nonchalant?

They were the first to arrive. "Mr. Phelps says to say he can't make it," Carter announced. "He's on patrol duty."

Routledge, acting the host, hung their dripping raincoats from the pegs by the door. "I don't envy him," he said.

"Nor me," Ojukwo said.

"It looks nice in here," Carter said.

Routledge had been busy. Two extra lamps were burning near the table, which he had spread with his meager stock of provisions: cake, assorted cookies, apples, a plum, a bar of whole-nut chocolate already divided into sections.

"Something to drink?"

"What you got?" Carter said.

At that moment, to Routledge's relief, Johnson appeared, bearing two bottles of island beer. Johnson had helped with the foundations. He looked part Asian, with a scanty beard; his summer crewcut was now growing out. Besides working on various building projects in the Village, Johnson, with his excellent eyesight and his abilities in tracking and self-concealment, acted as an assistant to Foster, the undercover agent who monitored events and trends among the outsiders. Just like Foster, Johnson maintained a robust attitude towards the threat they posed. His was one of the growing number of voices calling for direct action to reduce the outsiders' numbers: a "cull" was how he described it. Routledge wondered how he would react to the news about Carter and Ojukwo.

As Routledge opened the beer, there was a knock at the door and King arrived. The gathering was complete.

"There's been more fighting," Johnson said, once they had started on the cake. Routledge did not have enough chairs, so his guests were standing. "Mr. Foster come in about an hour ago. He reckons Nackett's in trouble. I can tell you now 'cause it'll be public tomorrow. Houlihan went for Old Town first thing this morning, before dawn."

"How many killed?" King said.

"Ten, easy."

"Prisoners?"

"Could be."

"Does it mean anything?" Routledge said.

"We don't know yet. Might just be the usual. Revenge. They're like them hillbillies. They can't even remember what the feud's about no more." Johnson accepted a bourbon biscuit. "They're good, these. We used to have these when I was a kid."

"What happens if Nackett goes?" King said.

Johnson shrugged. "One less cockroach to worry about. Don't frig around, squash the lot of them, that's what I say. Wouldn't take long. We've got blokes'd love to do it. Still, the Father knows best."

He said this in all earnestness. The other three guests silently agreed; the remark seemed to put an end to further speculation about the outsiders.

The storm had now reached its height. The house was standing up to its baptism extraordinarily well. Not a single drop of water had so far penetrated the roof or the walls. Only at the edges of the windward shutters, and in places around the door, were there slight signs of damp. Ojukwo's craftsmanship was already paying dividends.

Routledge remembered the skill and efficiency with which Ojukwo had set to work on his behalf. No payment had been asked for, none expected, yet Ojukwo had worked harder and better than any mainland carpenter. In fact, on the mainland, in his daily contact with builders, Routledge had developed a general contempt for artisans of all sorts, for their laziness and greed, for the substandard work they put in. He had forgotten just how much care even an uncomplicated piece of joinery, when properly done, demanded of the craftsman. Ojukwo was indeed a craftsman. His work was invested with and guided by the single quality most lacking on the mainland: pride.

If Routledge had still been in two minds about what to do, the memory of Ojukwo with his try-square and scratchstock would have helped recommend him to one rather than another course of action; but there was more to it than that. Ojukwo's bulk, his mildness, the sad expression in his eyes, reminded Routledge of King. He had never talked about his crime. Until today he had seemed to live largely within himself. Yet now it had emerged that he and Carter were lovers. Homosexuals, a menace to the Community, but lovers all the same.

Routledge pitied them their vice, their need for physical affection. Unless they were stopped, they would sooner or later be thrown out. If that happened the others outside would show them no mercy.

He would try to frighten them. He was no longer interested in earning points with Franks. If it was their fate to be reported, he would rather someone else got the credit, someone like Johnson, perhaps, with a sturdier and less complicated sensibility. They were lucky that it was he and not Johnson who had entered the workshop tonight.

Tomorrow, or at the first safe opportunity, he would slip a note into Ojukwo's jacket pocket at the recreation hut. He would write the note with his left hand, in disguised, thickly penciled block capitals.

As he served more beer, as the conversation turned to talk

of the storm, Routledge mentally perfected the text. Its composition gave him a curiously serene feeling. He had arrived at a new point in his experience, utterly unknown. He had undergone a change of heart. The incident with Thaine had been not a cause, but a result, of this change. He was different. He viewed his fellows in another and less critical light.

"Mr. King," he said, for he did not know how familiarly King knew Johnson. "Mr. King, help yourself to chocolate." The final version was ready. He rehearsed it again, even visualized the way it would look on paper, crumpled paper of an anonymous sort, not the kind he used at Godwin's.

I KNOW WHAT YOU & CARTER DONE IN THE CARPENTREY SHOP, YOU'D BETTER STOP NOW FOR YOU'RE OWN GOOD. NEXT TIME I TELL THE FATHER. A FREIND.

11

For a while Houlihan did not answer. Illuminated by three fulmar lights, he sat in perfect ease and silence, picking his nose with a deeply exploring forefinger, and at intervals took time to examine the spoils.

Despite the presence of Pope and Feely, Martinson watched him with a profound sense of peace. Something inevitable was coming to fruition here, prefigured perhaps a million years before, in the stars, in the rocks, in the pounding waves, in the gale against the lighthouse wall. The old feeling was coming back; had never left him. He was at one with the universe. That moment, the first time he had laid hands on that soft white neck, the look in her eyes, stood out in his memory like a marker post for this slowly unfurling future. All the psychiatrists they had produced had been unable to understand this simplest of simple ideas: the idea of destiny. Not for nothing had he been born at that particular time and place. Not for nothing had his young mind been steeped in the magnificent language of the Old Testament. The prophets had foreshadowed everything that was to come.

The struggle had lasted two thousand years, would reach its conclusion with the beginning of the third millennium. Why the third? Because three was the first in the series of numbers dedicated to darkness. Satan's strongest forces came in threes. The three crosses at Golgotha, site of the enemy's first bad mistake. *Eli, Eli.* And then, on the third day, the

Resurrection. After that it had been downhill all the way. With his gleaming shield and morningstar Satan had rained countless swingeing blows on his adversary, by sheer strength and persistence wearing him down. Now he was almost on the ground, flat out, a taloned, scaly foot about to be clamped in triumph on his face. Soon the end would come. Driven by those massive bundles of muscles and sinews, the spiked ball would be powered through its highest and most momentous arc, coming down with a force that nothing could withstand. At bottom, when it made contact, when the morningstar smashed its way below the horizon, aptly, inevitably, the lights would go out forever.

Few were those on Earth privileged to share in this final blow. Few were those to whom Armageddon and the next millennium's afterworld held out their greatest promise.

Not for nothing had he been born then. Not for nothing had his old man buggered off just before his birth. Not for nothing had his mother abandoned responsibility for baby James and left him for long periods, years at a stretch, with his grandma. Shut up for weeks in her room, he would hear only stories from the Bible. As soon as he was old enough to read, she taught him how to understand Ezekiel and Jeremiah and the Book of Revelation. She taught him the interpretation of symbols. He came to understand that, just beneath the surface, everything fitted the pattern, everything was a symbol within the larger symbolic whole.

The reason he was here on Sert was to play out his part in this stately and preordained game. Sert had become a model of the age-old struggle. The Village was the final bastion, and he had been chosen to breach it.

Sometimes he had not been sure how to proceed, and then guidance had always been provided. He saw now that Peto would never have thrown in his lot with Houlihan. The grazing treaty had stretched to the limit their powers of agreement. Peto had been an obstruction right enough, but it had been a false move last summer to set him and Houlihan against each other: the seeds of Peto's downfall had already been evident then. As punishment, and also to put him in abeyance until the proper time, Martinson had been cast down from the tower. Now, thanks to Obie, his leg was getting better: he could walk again, albeit with a limp.

Tonight he had used the cover of the storm to come here alone and put his proposition. The Irishman had listened suspiciously, his pale blue eyes giving nothing away. With his large, bald, and bony head, with his red face and the tufts of curly gray hair protruding above each ear, with the deliberation of his speech and the slowness of his movements, Houlihan seemed every inch the peatbog peasant. All this was in complete contrast to the true man, whose ruthless cunning had kept him for so long safe and sound in charge of the lighthouse.

"I don't know," he said finally, wiping his finger on his trouserleg. "There's so much bad blood, I don't know if my boys'd go for it at all."

"It's our only chance of getting him," Martinson said.

"Make no mistake. I hate that Liam Franks as much as you."

Impossible. Martinson's hatred was both personal and impersonal, specific and general. As a representative of the other side, Franks was just about ideal. And besides, it was his race of bigheads that had always infested every position of authority and ease, exploited every opportunity, imposed their will on those unable to protect themselves. They ran the world. Franks had gathered about him all those on the island who shared the same trait, like that bighead Jenkins, the one who had stolen the crossbow and wrecked his house, the one whom he would have tracked down and killed had it not been for the fracas about the goats. Jenkins was on the list too, second only to Appleton.

"What's it to be?" Martinson said. "D'you want Nackett or not?"

"I could get him myself. I nearly had him this morning."

"Yes, and five of your blokes topped in the process."

"Looking long-term, like," Houlihan said, innocently enquiring, "what happens when you get ideas?"

"I won't get no ideas. Franks is all I want."

"That's your word on it tonight. Tonight is tonight. Later is later. It could come down to it."

"You got to take a chance."

"Honest enough, anyhow." Houlihan's finger returned to his nose for a final brief visit. He glanced at Feely. "What d'you say to our friend's scheme, Harold?"

Feely shrugged and made a sputtering noise, the beginnings of a raspberry. "He's got a point about joining forces. But then we've always known that. If you draw up a list of pros and cons, the cons always outweigh. Pro: we eliminate Franks. Pro: we get our deliveries back. Pro: we get the stuff in the Village. And that's it. Con: we have to fight them. Not easy. They've got crossbows and God knows what else. They're well organized, better than us. At the moment we get no bother from them at all. If Franks goes that might change. Con: we have to risk sovereignty over the lighthouse. Con: we have to forget our differences, and, as you say, Archie, there's just too many old scores to settle for that. Then the last and biggest con of all, we have to trust the word of a nutter like Martinson here."

Yes, Feely, Martinson thought. Nutter. That's what the shrinks reckoned. And that's what you'll reckon when I'm driving in the nails.

The meeting was working out much as he had expected. The campaign would have been quicker and neater with Houlihan's cooperation, but it was by no means essential. He might have counted on Feely to put the boot into his proposals: but Pope was another matter. Pope was less of a brownnose, slightly more representative of the rest of the brain gang, more realistic and pragmatic. Martinson had been studying him closely. It was early days yet. Probably best not to make a move too soon.

"And Wayne," Houlihan said. "Your opinion, please."

After a moment, Pope said, "It be nice to say goodbye to Dave Nackett."

"This is true," Houlihan said. "This is very true. It wouldn't be your personal ambition talking, would it now, Jim?"

"I told you. I want Franks."

"And nothing else? Not even leadership of your illustrious borough? Nor even of mine? No, don't answer that again."

He scratched his pate. "Let's say you bod Mr. Nackett any-way, just to show willing. Then if your boys make you boss, we'll talk again."

"Do we want that?" Feely said, nervously. "Do we want Martinson in charge? At least we know Nackett's little ways. He's no worse than Peto."

"Be quiet, Harold."

Feely persisted. "Why not scrag Martinson now, while we've got our hands on him? Why take the risk, Archie?"

"I foreseen that possibility," Martinson said. "I've got certain sureties, like."

"Such as?" Feely said.

"You'll have to kill me to find out."

"I told you to shut up, Harold," Houlihan said. "Now, Jim. You haven't given us your answer. Will you be murder-ing Nackett for us anyhows?"

"If I do, it'll be like I said. His blokes are strong. My leg in't healed proper yet. Give it a couple of months. Three."

"Say till Christmas?"

"Yes."

"Can't you see what he's doing, Archie? It's just a trick to get us to take the pressure off Old Town."

"No it's not. Jim was one of Peto's boys. He don't care for Nackett any more than us." He looked back at Martin-son. "Right?"

"Right enough, Archie."

"So you'll do the deed? Yes?"

Now it was Martinson's turn to shrug. "Yes," he said. "Sure. What's to lose?"

"Excellent," Houlihan said. "You give Mr. Nackett his little Christmas present, then send me a card, and I'll wish you a happy new year." He arose. "No more arguments, Harold, and won't you kindly show this gentleman down-stairs?"

The easterly passage of the storm across the mainland was marked by radio reports of fallen trees, television pictures of drowned sheep, of army inflatables rescuing householders from the floods. Few of the men in the Village bothered to watch or listen: even fewer possessed radio or television sets. There was one large flatscreen at the recreation hut, owned by Appleton, powered by lithium batteries and used once or twice a week to show feature films. Godwin sometimes tuned in to BBC radio in his workshop, which was where Routledge usually heard the news. In a month's time there was to be a general election. The incumbent party were certain to be returned to office: there was no chance, however remote, of a change in policy there. Only war with the Russians, now looking less and less likely, might produce a change, and then, no doubt, it would be for the worse.

The Council monitored all bulletins and weather forecasts for anything relating to Sert. Such rare items of news were displayed by Appleton on a noticeboard at the bungalow veranda, beside which was another for announcements from the Village's various clubs and groups. On the Friday after the storm, Appleton had pinned up a notice asking as many men as possible to gather in the bungalow precinct on Sunday at noon.

"What do you reckon it's about?" Scammell said.

Routledge was sure he knew, but was not allowed to say. "We'll know in twenty minutes," he said. "I don't suppose there's much use in speculating before then."

Scammell agreed.

Routledge said, "Can I have these three, please, Mr. Tragasch?"

The Village library was located in a small room in the recreation hut, and contained about five hundred books, mostly fiction, together with a large stock of magazines and some walkman tapes, all donated by villagers. Tragasch, the librarian, a short, mild-voiced man and one of the stalwarts of the chess club, also kept a list of those titles in private possession which were available for loan. The library opened for general use on Saturday afternoons and Sundays.

Earlier this morning Routledge had visited the shack of Peagrim, the Community barber, and had received the basic Sert cut, the same Peagrim gave to everyone from Franks down. Each villager was entitled to one of Peagrim's haircuts a month. For the tenth time Routledge scratched his scalp.

Smiling but refraining from comment, Tragasch issued Routledge's three books: two thrillers and a volume of chess openings, for Routledge had now begun to attend the chess club with the ultimate object of at least defending himself with honor against King.

"See you in the precinct, then, Mr. Tragasch," Routledge said, as he made for the door and the main room of the recreation hut. "And you, Mr. Scammell."

"I'll come with you, Mr. Routledge," Scammell said, nodding a farewell at Tragasch. "If you don't mind."

"No, not at all."

Scammell's books and magazines were issued and he accompanied Routledge into the calm, clouded morning. About thirty, with lank blond hair, Scammell was a former factory hand in a car plant. Now he worked mainly with the sheep and goats and poultry, occupying a lowly place in the hierarchy. "How you doing, Mr. Routledge?" he said.

"Not so bad." Routledge was as yet on informal terms with fewer than a dozen men, and was truly friendly with none but King. He had known Scammell for several weeks, found him unobjectionable, even likeable. He decided to take a chance and risk a rebuff. "Just call me 'Routledge,' " he said.

"No. Thanks all the same. No offense. It wouldn't be right. Not yet. You don't mind me telling you this, do you? I mean, you're new."

He glanced sideways at Scammell. His respect for him had suddenly grown. For Scammell had understood that the invitation had not arisen through the natural process of mutual regard, but had been forced and was therefore unacceptable.

"I'm sorry, Mr. Scammell," Routledge said, "I didn't mean—"

"Nothing personal, Mr. Routledge."

"Even so—"

Either Scammell was not articulate enough to continue this line of conversation, or he felt the desire to move onto safer ground. "They say the Father's going to change the work rotas," he said. "That's probably what it's about. Usually something like that."

As they emerged from the lee of the recreation hut, Routledge saw that the bungalow precinct, almost deserted before, was rapidly filling with men. The stone slabs before the veranda were completely covered; newcomers were joining the back of the crowd, standing on the shale. At least a hundred and twenty villagers were already waiting, with more appearing on the tracks or leaving the doorways of their houses. The precinct was alive with the murmur of voices.

Routledge had never seen the whole population together before. Only now did he appreciate the size and vigor of the Community. Each of these men was fit and strong, or he would not have been put in Category Z. This was that oddity, a society without women, without the weak, the sick, the old. There were no practical skills these men lacked. They had of necessity dispensed with the feminine touch. They spun wool and wove cloth. They could cook, clean and do everything else that was needful to survival. But Routledge was becoming increasingly conscious of the ludicrous in all the Community's works. Men were little boys at heart, Louise had always said. They never grew up. What was Sert, if not a glorious, perennial game of Cowboys and Indians? A few of the men in the Village seemed happier here than ever they could have been on the mainland. Thaine, for one. Thaine's life now was an endless series of model railways to be built and tested and played with; he never had to wash his hands and come in for tea. Without women, men became absurd.

And yet, for all that, the things Thaine built were genuinely useful, often essential. For all that, there was no other choice open, except the downward path that led to Old Town or the lighthouse.

Sunday noon. Usually at this time Routledge would have been doing something silly in the garden, squandering yet more labor on that emblem of suburban futility, the lawn; or, more likely, drinking in the golf club, just before turning his thoughts to Sunday lunch, which Louise always professed to prefer cooking in peace, without him around.

Why hadn't she written?

The crowd had closed in behind him. Overhead the sky

had the blandly patterned appearance of mother-of-pearl. Routledge noticed three large, brown-mottled gulls passing northwestwards, towards the open ocean, where the sky deepened to a heavier gray. And, far beyond the bungalow roof and the picturesque, silhouetted line of larches, he saw the superbly independent skyward spiral of a hunting buzzard, at this distance black against the cloud. It was high over America Point, gaining altitude above the seething rocks of Green Isles and the cliffs where even now two sets of raven-picked and weather-bleached bones were lying in disarray: one on a ledge partway down, the other among the dark debris of the beach.

Scammell nodded at the veranda. The murmur of voices ceased. The front door was open. One by one, the whole Council emerged: Mitchell, Stamper, Godwin, Thaine, Sibley, Foster, Appleton, each man moving to left or right. Finally Franks himself came out.

The silence was complete. He moved to the front of the veranda, resting his hands on the rail, and again Routledge felt himself in the presence of a phenomenon. Franks's personality had imposed itself on all these men. They had wished it; they had abandoned their independence to one who was wiser and stronger, and for the first time Routledge saw why they called him "Father." Just as Franks had told him, they were not children. They were adults who knew a leader when they saw one, knew the value of what he had to offer. But there was something more at work here, something that in civilized life had been lost. As Routledge, as the whole assembly, waited for Franks to speak, he felt the surge of a common feeling with its focus the man who had made life here endurable. The feeling was impossible to define, but, as it flowed over and through him, Routledge realized for the first time that he was generating it too.

"Good morning," Franks said. "I have an important announcement to make." He looked around the congregation, including everyone in his gaze, and then, clearly, articulately, made the beginning of his speech.

"Gentlemen," he said, "we are going to build a boat."

12

On Tuesday October 28, exactly a month after Franks's announcement, Routledge took part in his fifth border patrol. His first four had been at night, and had passed off without incident. Today's had begun at dawn and would not end until the early afternoon.

The decision to patrol in daylight as well as after dark had been just one consequence of making the escape project public. Franks had explained the plans in detail, even down to the sonar. He had also explained the risks. According to Appleton's calculations, the occupants of the ketch had less than a one-in-five chance of surviving the voyage. If the attempt failed and they were lucky they would drown. If they weren't, the boat, which would carry hardly any rations, would go off course and into mid-Atlantic. If they were discovered by a patrol-boat there was every chance of being deliberately rammed and sunk.

The lottery for the remaining eight places would be held three weeks before sailing. As matters stood at the moment, departure date would be May 1, or possibly, depending on the weather, May 2 or 3. The original idea had been to sail in July or August, when sea temperatures were more favorable, but that had been prevented, Franks had said, by mainland factors.

The announcement had had a remarkable effect on the Community. The first reaction had been one of astonishment, not only at the project itself, but also at the audacity of the thinking behind it. This was followed by a polarization, not anticipated by Routledge but foreseen by the Council, of the Community into two groups: those who wanted to go, and those who didn't. Generally it was the older men who belonged to the second group, which was anyway much in the minority. For the others, the ketch and the lottery immediately became the sole topic of conversation. Then, a little later, the excitement was tempered by a realization of just how great were the odds against securing a place. To alleviate this, Franks had said that all plans, tools, and a construction diary were to be left behind so that the ketch could be duplicated.

There was also disappointment over the news that Franks, not to mention Appleton and Thaine, intended to leave. But there was little or no resentment. On the contrary. The prevailing sentiment was that the four Council members richly deserved their places. Franks had worked harder than anybody, and for longer; it was he and Appleton and Thaine and Godwin who had conceived the escape and were making it happen. The eight spare places were manna from heaven.

At first Routledge had been surprised that Franks had made the announcement so soon, and that he had gone into such detail. Franks seemed to have no fears that anyone would leak the information in a letter home. Considering this further, Routledge marveled at his own naïveté. Clearly, and there could be no other implication, all outgoing mail was secretly vetted by the Council. Routledge had hinted at the subject in conversation with King, without response.

More surprising was the Council's implicit trust that the project would not become known to the outsiders. This also implied that, between now and the launch, no one would need to be expelled from the Community. Soon after the announcement, however, this anomaly had begun to be explained.

The Council's attitude towards the outsiders had undergone a marked change. Two new arrivals, deemed to be unlikely candidates for acceptance, were rumored to have been clandestinely disposed of rather than have them swell the outsiders' ranks, though Routledge greatly doubted the truth of this. Indisputably, however, the period new arrivals were spending outside had been reduced.

Foster and Johnson now spent all their time on surveillance, and border patrols were organized around the clock.

Talbot was in charge this afternoon and carried the crossbow. He, Routledge, and a man named Huggins had been detailed to cover the eastern part of the border, from the red halfway marker rock to Star Cove.

Heavy rain was again falling, cold, miserable, an ocean rain not meant for land-based men to endure. It had hardly stopped since the weekend, since the last day of Summer Time. Darkness now arrived before five-thirty: the real autumn had begun. Until now, with the light evenings, Routledge had almost been able to believe that he was here on a temporary basis, roughing it, that when the weather turned bad he would be going home to classify the specimens he had gathered or write an account of his experiences. He could delude himself no longer. He had finally become a fully fledged prisoner of Sert. And worse: for seven whole weeks now there had been no word from Louise.

"Boring, ain't it?" Huggins said.

Routledge nodded, although he did not agree.

"Don't knock it," Talbot said.

Patrolling was irksome and tedious, but not boring. Despite the rain and cold, despite the work rotas and the demands of the Village, being out day after day in the open air, learning to be dependent on his surroundings for his food and drink and warmth, living in a thin-walled shack virtually exposed to the elements: all this, together with a sense of his own increasing physical strength and fitness, was beginning to effect a profound change in the way Routledge viewed the natural world. He had, together with most people, dismissed as overreaction the protests raised by the Greens when Sert and the other penal islands had been taken over. Now he began to understand what the protesters had been fighting for. There were interludes in his self-pity, in his gnawing anxiety about Louise, in the grim business of survival, when he became conscious not only of the heart-stopping grandeur of the island, but also of his own place within it. He knew every inch of shoreline on the Village peninsula and, after beachcombing, blackberrying and goating expeditions with Daniels and the others, much of the rest. The ruins on Beacon Point, the peninsula where he had shot the wild man, were indeed, as he had guessed, those of the old monastery. He knew now why the monks had come to Sert. Among a handful of his fellow villagers he had sensed the same unspoken feeling. Talbot shared it, Talbot whom Routledge had at first so disliked. In him the feeling took expression as a fascination with birds and plants. The South London gangster, a four-year veteran of the island, had become a naturalist.

The patrol had reached the cliffs once more, still without seeing anyone. Outsiders had too much sense to risk catching pneumonia on a day like this. They were all safely under cover. But during bad weather incursions by wild men were much more likely, and yesterday another patrol had caught and ejected a pair of them at Vanston Cove, within five hundred meters of the bungalow itself.

Talbot glanced southwards along the cliffs, towards the drop zone. ''I wonder if the 'copter's coming today.''

''Should be,'' Huggins said.

''Yeah. He comes in worse than this.''

''What's the time?''

''One o'clock.'' A rivulet was running from Talbot's sou'wester and down the back of his oilskin coat. He looked out over the sea. Routledge followed his gaze to the horizon, where, through the murk, came the distant flash, pause, flash of the southern lightship. Huggins, meanwhile, was scanning Pulpit Head with the binoculars.

''Can't see a bloody thing,'' he said. ''They're all fogged up.''

''Have you got rain on the eyepieces?''

''No, it's condensation inside.''

Each time he came to Star Cove now Routledge thought about the cave where, according to the Father's announcement, the ketch would be assembled and launched.

"Look," Talbot said to Routledge, pointing out to sea. "Killers."

With a fluttering escort of gulls, five black dorsal fins, six, seven, eight, were slicing through the outer part of the cove, all but indifferent to the swell, picking an easy course through the reefs, coming in diagonally towards the beach.

Routledge watched in amazement and alarm; he had not known that killer whales occurred in British waters.

"Holy Joe, look at 'em go," Talbot said, his sense of wonder unconcealed. "They can do twenty-five knots when they feel like it. See that tall fin, Mr. Routledge? That's a male. There's another one. Two males. The rest is females and young. It's a pod, a family group." He turned to Huggins. "What they after? Seals?"

"Could be," Huggins said, now studying the group, which was slowly spreading out, through the magnifying mist of the binoculars. "Yep. Seals. There's three, at least."

"Fancy a dip, Mr. Routledge?"

Routledge had never felt more glad to be on land.

Huggins was glued to the binoculars. "Jesus, they already got one! There's red, there's red! It's bleeding!"

The waters at the head of the cove had been turned into a maelstrom. Routledge glimpsed the piebald pattern of the larger male, the wounded seal, a big adult, in its jaws. With a toss of its head the seal was hurled several meters upwards and back, coming down with a tremendous splash among the other whales, which seemed instantly to tear it to pieces.

Two fins were almost on the beach. As they reached the shallows the enormous glistening bulk of the whales was exposed, the white oval behind the eye, the dramatic division along the flanks between black above and white below. There could be no depth left: surely the whales were already grounded, but still they were advancing.

Exploding from the surf with a terrified sideways leap, a huge bull seal scrabbled desperately up the narrow stretch of stones under the cliff. Only the middle state of the tide had allowed it to escape: with chilling, synchronized grace the two whales pursuing it turned and swam back into deeper water, rejoining their companions in the chase. "They've got

another one!'' Huggins shouted. ''God Almighty! Swallowed it whole!''

A minute later it was over and the whales were heading
out to sea, leaving only the gulls searching for scraps and the
refugee seal still cringing on the beach, its dread of man
forgotten. Beyond the foaming reefs at the mouth of the cove,
one by one, the fins dived, surfaced, dived, surfaced, and
disappeared from view.

''Opportunist feeders,'' Talbot said. ''Ever seen killers
before, Mr. Routledge?''

Stunned by what he had just witnessed, Routledge shook
his head. The sheer speed of the attack, as much as the realization that the anonymous seas surrounding Sert could
hold such monsters, had shaken him to the core. Neptune
had just shown his hand. ''How did they know the seals were
there?''

''Heard 'em fooling about, I expect. They use sonar too.''

Fleetingly he thought of the almost insuperable technical
problems of echolocation, requiring all Godwin's ingenuity
and expertise, effortlessly solved in flesh and bone by nature,
by evolution, by the Creator—whatever you wanted to call it.
''Are killer whales common here?''

''Not common. But they're about.''

''Mr. Talbot,'' Routledge said. ''This is Star Cove.''

''So?''

''This is where the boat launches.''

Talbot and Huggins exchanged glances. ''You're right,''
Talbot said. ''D'you still want to be included in that lottery,
Mr. Routledge?''

''Reckon you ought to think about dropping out,'' Huggins said.

Talbot, seeing Routledge's face, relented with a smile.
''It's all right, Mr. Routledge, don't worry about it. No one
knows why, but they don't never go for humans. Not unless
they're provoked. Maybe it's the taste, or our funny skin.''

The raid on the seals had been utterly ruthless. But then
seals showed small mercy in their dealings with the crabs
and fishes which comprised their prey. The whales, the seals,
inhabited just the same world as Routledge himself. He

thought of the man at Beacon Point, still the subject of his nightmares, emerging from the ruins of the chapel, from the ruins of civilized life, and knew that from now on the nightmares would not be the same. Eventually they might even dwindle and cease.

"Come on," Talbot said. "We can't hang about here all day. Time to get back to it."

Her letter came that afternoon, reaching him just before four. The handwriting on the envelope, in black rollertip, was even more careful and controlled than usual. *A.J. Routledge Z-160683, c/o H. M. Prison, Princetown, Devon PL2O 6SA.* Even the stamp had been stuck in its corner with meticulous precision. It bore, not the Watford district postmark carried by Rickmansworth letters, but a neat dark circle inscribed LONDON WI. This alone, documentary proof of the fact that her work now took her to the West End, would have been enough to cause him unease; but that stage had already been passed. In the last seven weeks there had been plenty of time for thought along these lines. Not long enough, though, to prepare him for the reality of the two sheets of buff paper which, seated at his desk, he now unfolded and began to read.

"Bad news?" he heard Godwin say, after a while.

"No," Routledge said, stuffing the pages back in their envelope.

In a daze he tried to resume work. The desk looked the same, the pencils, the calculator keys. Physically, everything was just as it had been before the delivery. The rain was still falling. A dismal autumn day. The same autumn rain had fallen on the helicopter which, carrying her letter deep in the darkness of its hold, had flown towards him, low over the sea, all the way from the mainland. Under Mitchell's direction the boxes had been collected, the mail innocently sorted into alphabetical order. Ross, Routledge, Sibley. Stamper had rung the gong. Fitzmaurice had offered to go. He had received a luxury parcel. "Here you are, Mr. Routledge," he had said.

Now Routledge heard him say, "Are you all right, Mr. Routledge?"

"What?"

"I asked if you wanted a chocolate toffee."

"A what? I'm sorry. I wasn't listening."

"A chocolate toffee."

Fitzmaurice must have received them in his parcel. Already eating, he thrust the bag further in Routledge's direction. Routledge saw that Godwin was chewing too.

"Not just now, thanks. Perhaps later."

"Put one behind your ear."

Briefly Routledge saw Godwin frowning at Fitzmaurice and lightly shaking his head. Routledge looked away, out of the window, at the rain in the garden, at the dull gleam of the bungalow roof.

"Letter from home?" Godwin said.

"Yes. A letter from home."

"I think you'd better pack it in for today," Godwin said.

"I'm all right. Really."

"That's an order."

Routledge went to his house. He read the letter over and over again. He lay on his bed. He stared at his photos. Towards dusk he remembered looking out towards King's place.

King did not return until nightfall, at half-past five. At six-fifteen Routledge put on his waxed-cotton jacket and went out into the rain.

He knocked on King's door. King was clearing up after his supper.

"I need your help," Routledge said. He did not know what he was doing. He had not intended to show the letter to anyone, or to speak about it. What had happened between him and Louise was the business of no one on Sert, no one in the Village. She had been, she was, the most important part of him. There was no allegiance left for anyone else.

King, suddenly concerned, took the letter and held it close to the lamp. As he read, Routledge knew, word for word, line for line, exactly what was passing before his eyes.

19th October

Dear Anthony,

This is the worst and hardest letter I have ever had to write. I do not know how to express what I must say to you. I know that I shall be hurting terribly the one person in the world who least deserves it. You have given me years of your love. The life we had together was special and unique and no one can take that away from us. You know that I love you and that I want the best for you. But we can never be together again and I, as I am sure you do, want the best for Christopher. He is at a difficult age and faces an uncertain future without a father's influence.

I do not know how to break this to you. It would be so much better to speak face to face or even on the phone. ███████████████████████████████████
███
███

           In the end one must be cruel because the truth is cruel.

What I am trying to tell you, Anthony, and have been too cowardly to tell you before, is that I have met somebody else. I met him some time ago and now he has asked me to marry him. He is a successful businessman, a widower with two young children. I know that you would like him and hope that you can find it in you to wish us well, knowing that the position for you is hopeless now. Oh Anthony we tried so hard but in the end ███████████████████████████████
███
█████████████████ I pray that you are safe on the island and every morning wait for the postman in case I hear word of you. Most of your last letter ██████████
███
███
███

This is too painful for me. I beg you to give us your blessing. Soon you will receive papers to sign from my solicitor—another one, not ███████████████████

I will continue to write, if you will let me, and send news of our son, for I know what torment you must be going through. I have already spoken to your mother and have asked her permission to introduce her to Tom.

But whatever else happens know that I love you always.

>   Forgive me.
>   Louise

PART THREE

1

THE CHRISTMAS TREE OCCUPIED MOST OF THE END WALL OF the recreation hut. It consisted of the crown of a Monterey pine, removed with the Father's permission and decorated with tinfoil stars and streamers, small fake parcels in colored paper, brightly painted papier-mâché globes. Beneath the tree stood the prizes for the Christmas raffle: beer, two bottles of Thorne's whisky, a box of cookies, and, in pride of place, the iced fruitcake sent over on yesterday's helicopter, a gift from the governor's wife.

The fairy at the pinnacle, supervising tonight's festivities, had been modeled by Venables in papier-mâché, then dressed in a pink tutu and given a pair of silver wings. The outsize head was bald and bore a face painted red, with worm-like lips, watery blue eyes, and tufts of curly gray hair extending above the ears. To Routledge, who had never seen Houlihan, the caricature meant nothing; but King had laughed when he had first seen it, the more so when Fitzmaurice observed how and with what force Venables had thrust the figure down onto the wire holder at the top of the tree.

"There's bliss for you, Archie," Fitzmaurice had said.

Fitzmaurice was one of the impromptu band. He had brought his concertina. Mountfield, Macness, and Wright, all Irishmen, were playing too. Macness played the fiddle, Mountfield a drum, Wright a penny whistle. The air was

219

thick with marijuana smoke. Routledge was already drunk, stamping his feet with the rest.

"What do you think of the music?" King shouted in his ear.

"Marvelous! Bloody marvelous!"

He had not known that Fitzmaurice, that anyone on Sert, had such music in him. Celtic music, reels and jigs, wild, flowing tunes that stirred the heart, carried along with yelps and shrieks from the band and the room full of men. As the sound filled his veins Routledge could half believe that something in his own ancestry was responding too, and not just the drink. He had been here before; had visited this epicenter of comradeship in some different life, in a purer time when the honest values were all that mattered. Who cared what a man owned or what was the color of his skin? Who cared how he spoke or where he'd been to school, just so long as he was on your bloody side when the chips were down?

"Another! Another!" King was yelling, in chorus with the rest.

Routledge, drinking moonshine from his glass, looked at him and blearily away, elated he knew not how. King was on his side all right. They all were. Even Fitzmaurice. Especially Fitzmaurice, Fitzmaurice and his Irish music. Routledge leaned over towards King. "King," he tried to say. "I want to apologize. To you. To Mr. Fitzmaurice. To the Father. Everybody."

King gave a puzzled frown. "What?"

Routledge's words were lost in the din. The band were protesting that they were dry and wanted to take a break for more beer, but that was impossible. Another tune was demanded: there was no refusing.

"Come on," King had said, a long time ago, five hours or more. Routledge held his watch towards the light. Five to twelve. Five to midnight. Yes, five hours ago. "Come on," King had said. "We're going to get you well and truly plastered." He had dragged Routledge from his house and to the recreation hut, where, during the autumn, the stocks of drink had been built up to heroic proportions. Each man had an allowance, noted by Venables in his little red book. You could drink it gradually or all at once, or give it away. The Community made beer, not too badly, and an explosive potato moonshine. It made horrible carrot wine. It made every kind of booze. Thorne's whisky was the thoroughbred. Routledge had acquired a half-bottle to give to King tomorrow morning. Christmas Day.

The twenty-third, yesterday, had been the last Tuesday before Christmas. No new prisoner had been deposited. Instead the helicopter had brought a bumper delivery of mail. A ludicrous greeting from the governor, which Appleton had pinned to the veranda noticeboard so that everyone could have a good laugh. With the greeting had come the cake. Most men had received at least one card. For Routledge there had been cards from his mother and his two sisters and their families.

From Louise, from Christopher, there had been nothing. Nothing.

"Come on," King had said.

On the mainland, Routledge's circle of friends had been small and untrustworthy, held together only by the flimsy common circumstances of their life. Without exception they had let him down in his time of need. Some he had known at school; all were just like him, middle-class, golfers mostly, members of clubs and professions, estate agents, accountants, solicitors, a dentist: all, just like him, relentlessly mediocre.

Now he had no friends whatever. Except King. Routledge was beginning to think King was the first real friend he had ever had.

His advice about Louise had been compassionate and sage. He had said that if Routledge really loved her, he would not wish to prevent her from starting a new life; he would, as the letter had asked, give her his blessing. If he couldn't bring himself to do so, then perhaps his feelings for her were not as he had imagined. That being the case, losing her was not such a tragedy after all. At least she had promised to keep in touch. Some men in the Community would have given anything for such a letter: the first they had known about their divorce was the arrival of the papers.

"Did you ever get married yourself?" Routledge had asked.

"No. That was one pitfall I managed to avoid."

"Did you ever come close?"

"Yes. I came close."

"What happened?"

"She died."

"I'm sorry."

"Don't be. I was better off alone with my sister. Women these days . . . well."

"Women these days what?"

"If you found a good one, just be thankful for the years you had."

Had he found a good one? She certainly hadn't wasted any time in finding another mug to pay the bills. That much he knew.

He had not heard from her since November, even though he had dutifully signed and promptly returned the divorce papers.

The bitch.

"Bitch," he said. "Faithless bitch."

"What?"

"Louise," Routledge said. "Bitch."

"No." King shook his head.

The band were giving in. Another tune. Fitzmaurice conferring with Macness. Beginning to play. A rapid reel. A chorus. Men starting to sing. Stamping feet. Yells and laughter. The chorus again. Routledge made out the words and joined in, louder than the rest.

> If I had a wife to beggar me life
> I tell ye what I would do
> I'd buy her a boat and put her afloat
> And paddle me own canoe

"Paddle me own canoe!" Routledge shouted, completely won over. Yes: he had to put her afloat. There was no other way. No use pretending. He had to get on with these people or he'd be dead. Buy her a boat and put her afloat. And what a canoe they were building! Bit by bit, component by component, the schedules were becoming intricate reality. He had never known such craftsmanship, such obsessive attention to detail. For it all had to work first time. There could be no tests, no trials. It all had to go together perfectly and nothing could be allowed to fail. He, Routledge, was one of the chief checkers. Every dimension of every last bit of wood had to be checked five times, written down and submitted to Appleton. The same quality control with the electronics, which Godwin and Fitzmaurice were now completing. No sea trials. Had to work first time. He wished Godwin were here so he could get him a drink and shake his hand. Brilliant, brilliant Godwin! Brilliant Thaine! Brilliant Appleton! Brilliant Father! Then he thought of the other men who weren't here tonight, who were sober on his behalf, patrolling the border, tending the stock. Foster and Johnson out there in the freezing darkness above Old Town or the lighthouse. Appleton in his office. The Father somewhere in the Village, aware of everything, bearing the entire weight of the Community's problems. A wonderful, extraordinary man. Quite extraordinary. A privilege to know someone like that, to be tolerated, to be allowed to belong. As the music died and the band took on more beer he leaned towards King to try again.

"Wish to formally apologize," he said. "Formally apologize for being such an insufferable little . . . insufferable . . . the term is I believe . . . insufferable little . . ." He did not know whether he had said the word or not. It didn't matter. For it was true. Now he belonged: he realized he belonged. After thirty-seven years of quiet desperation, of dwelling among two-faced people who were dead inside, the ineluctable workings of his destiny had brought him here and taught him the human lesson of belonging. For the first time in his entire life, Routledge knew he had outgrown the pitiable creature that had once been himself. He knew at last that he belonged.

He saw the room tilt and sway and then he was falling, losing his balance, passing out, falling with heavenly grace forwards into midnight and stupor and the beatific silence of this, his first truly happy, because selfless, Christmas Day.

Looking north from Piper's Beach, between Old Town and the lighthouse, the sea appeared almost mirror smooth. A black-backed gull and its reflection flapped in synchrony low across the water from right to left; at the curve of the headland two shags were perched on a white-squirted pinnacle of rock. The morning was frosty. Except for a haze which made the water seem even smoother, it was also bright. Here under the cliffs, out of the sun, the air felt damp and cold.

Martinson picked up a black pebble and hurled it as far as he could. The shags craned their necks anxiously, and one even made as if to depart, but at the harmless splash of the projectile fifty meters out it changed its mind and, with its companion, remained uneasily watching.

"Get a move on, Obie," Martinson muttered.

He had sent Obie to the lighthouse with a message for Houlihan.

There were currently four members of the brain gang: Feely, Wilmot, Gomm, and Wayne Pope. Pope was the only one with ambition. Wilmot and Gomm could be relied on to adapt. Feely was another matter.

This was Christmas morning. Martinson thought of the uplifting celebrations taking place all across Britain. Just about now the kids would have broken their new robots or discovered that batteries weren't included. Then, this afternoon, when it clouded over, when the whole family had pigged themselves sick on turkey and pudding, the adults' rows and sulks would begin.

He had known two Christmases with his mother. The rest he had spent with grandma, except for one, when he had been invited to the house of a rich kid he had met at Crusaders. Not rich, really, but better off than anyone else he had ever met. The parents had called him "James" and tried to make him feel at home. They had given him a plastic Darth Vader and a jigsaw-puzzle of Lake Windermere. The Christmas dinner had been pretty good. Afterwards he and the rich kid had gone upstairs. Martinson had looked around his bedroom, at all the stuff he owned, listening to him boasting about his old man. "I've had enough of this," Martinson had said. "Enough of what?" "Enough of you, dunghead."

That kid was probably some bigshot now, able in his own right to massage his conscience by patronizing what he would certainly call "disadvantaged" children. Like the shrinks and social workers and the parole board and all the rest of them. The mind-boggling arrogance of these bastards was utterly beyond belief. Martinson, flinging another pebble, told himself he was better off here.

Before the ripples had died he noticed that the shags had gone. Three figures were picking their way along the beach from the direction of the lighthouse. One was Obie. Another was Wilmot, distinctive in his yellow PVC jacket. But the third, in an island-made sheepskin coat and dreadlocks, could have been either Gomm or Pope. At least Feely wasn't among them.

As the figures drew nearer, Martinson identified the third man and again felt that sense of predestination. For it was Pope who had elected, or been ordered, to come. Or, even stranger, perhaps Pope had some ideas of his own: perhaps he was already thinking along the lines that Martinson himself intended, faintly and impressionistically, to adumbrate today.

"That's far enough!" Martinson shouted, machete in hand, when they were yet a hundred meters off.

Both of Houlihan's men were armed with iron bars.

"I'll talk to one or the other! Pope! I'll talk to you! Wilmot, you stay with Obie!"

Pope and Wilmot conferred; Pope shrugged and came forward. "What's up, man?" he said, when he was close enough to talk. "Why didn't you come to the light?"

"I got reasons."

"Obie wouldn't tell us nothing about Nackett. What happened? You scragged him yet? That's what Archie want to know."

"Nackett's still alive."

"But you said—"

"I just said I'd top him. Not when."

"You give Archie to understand it would be Christmas. He'll be disappointed. He been looking forward to it."

"And what about you, Wayne? You disappointed too?"

"Anything upset Archie upset me and all."

Martinson smiled: the sketchy beginnings of an understanding had passed between them.

"So when it going to be?"

"Soon," Martinson said. "Can I say something to you? Off the record, like? When I've done Nackett I got to be sure Archie keeps his end up. I want that bastard Franks. When we go for him it's got to be hard, and it's got to be right."

"You know you can count on Archie, Jim."

"Sure I can. But a thing like taking the Village needs planning. It needs expert work. For that, Obie's the only bloke in Old Town I can trust."

"We gots blokes you can trust."

"Like you?"

"Like me, for one." Pope glanced over his shoulder at Wilmot, who was rubbing his hands together, his iron bar tucked under his arm. "Thing is, Archie won't want to commit no resources till Nackett goes."

"I need the binoculars."

"No chance."

"Before we hit the Village I want to know everything about it. Patrol schedules, guard details, work rotas, where Franks craps. I don't want him getting away. To find out all that I need observers. If Archie says I can't have observers, then I need binoculars. With binoculars me and Obie can do it between us."

"You didn't say nothing about this before," Pope said, peevishly.

"I didn't think of it before."

"You ain't the sort of bloke what don't think of things."

"Maybe so."

"Archie'll never stand for it."

"Does he have to know?"

Pope's eyes narrowed. He was cunning: Martinson would have to be deadly careful. "How long you want them for?"

"Couple of months."

"He'd create if they went missing."

"All I'm after is Franks. I don't care about nothing else."

"What is it with you and Franks? Archie reckon you got the hots for him."

Martinson gave a sneering laugh. "Yeah, sure. Tell Archie it's the real thing." He looked directly into Pope's eyes. "And tell him this is the best way he can get the whole island for himself. The 'copter. The governor. The lot."

"You make it sound tempting, put like that."

"I'll be here at noon every day for the next three days. If you get them binocs to me, Archie'll have cause to thank you later."

"Yes," Pope said, weighing his iron bar. "I can see that, Jim."

Martinson delivered his next words with cool deliberation. "Tell him what you like about Nackett. Tell him I lost my bottle, if you want."

"I'll tell him you'll do it later. That's right, ain't it?"

"That's right. Nackett goes. Make no mistake there. But he goes when the time is right and not before."

Pope gave an emphatic nod. "Right. Leave it with me." He nodded once more, turned, and started back towards Wilmot.

"Merry Christmas to you, Wayne."

"And to you, Jim. And to you."

2

Picking up his watch from the bedside shelf, Routledge saw that he had slept almost unimaginably late. It was
well past ten o'clock. He had wasted over two hours of daylight.

His tongue felt thick and furry. His head was throbbing.

He slowly put the watch back and coaxed himself into
rising.

Standing shivering by the washbowl, he shut his eyes and
frowned. He remembered now. The evening was coming
back to him. How much had he drunk? Two months' allo-
cation, at least. He would be in debt to Venables till the end
of January.

This was Thursday, Christmas morning, a holiday. He had
volunteered to work this afternoon with Thaine in the carpentry shop; before then, he and King and several others had
been invited to Mitchell's house for lunch. Appleton was
organizing another lunch in his house, Stamper another in
his, Blackshaw another in the recreation hut, and the Father
would be presiding over the biggest of all, in two sittings, at
the bungalow.

Routledge steeled himself to wash. Luckily there was water in the jug, though he could not recollect having put it
there. Nor, now, could he recollect undressing or falling
asleep. His clothes had been neatly laid out on the chair, but

that was not the way he usually arranged them himself. King. King had put him to bed.

Routledge frowned again. It pained his skull to bend down, and the water in the jug was thinly covered by ice, but he leaned over the bowl anyway and poured the whole jugful on his head.

He put on yesterday's clothes: long underwear, plaid shirt, thin sweater, thick sweater, corduroy jeans, thin woolen socks, thick woolen socks, lace-up work boots, woolen mittens, a woolen scarf, and the woolen noddy which, having taken lessons and been given some of the yarn spun under Stamper's supervision, he had knitted for himself. After making his bed he rejected the idea of breakfast and put on his waxed-cotton coat. From the mantelshelf he took a parcel he had prepared the previous morning, and slipped it into one of his capacious outer pockets.

King was at home. He had been sitting alone with his volume of Spenser, the southern shutter laid open to admit the sunshine, a peat fire burning in the grate.

"I brought you this," Routledge said, once he had been invited inside, and handed King the half-bottle of whisky, which was tied at the neck with a bit of red ribbon. "Season's greetings."

King seemed to be moved by the gesture, but not entirely surprised. "Well, that's very nice," he said. "To use the hallowed phrase, you really shouldn't have. Whisky's far too extravagant." He went to his shelves and took down a medium-sized package done up in brown paper; a sprig of berried holly had been tucked beneath the string. "I thought you might do something like this," he said, "so I took the necessary precaution. Happy Christmas."

Carefully untying the string and removing the paper, Routledge saw that he had been given exactly what he needed: a new belt, made of supple pigskin and with a steel buckle fashioned apparently from driftwood fittings. About five centimeters wide, the leather was unstained but had been most expertly tooled with an artistic pattern of oblique bars.

"It's superb," Routledge said. "Did you make it yourself?"

"I wish I had. It's one of Mr. Caldecote's."

"I don't know what to say."

"Say you'll have a drink. Take a seat."

Despite the open shutter, the peat fire was so efficient that Routledge decided to remove his coat first. "Reading your friend Edmund again?" he said, picking up the book.

"It's a drug." He handed Routledge a glass of whisky, taken from the full-sized bottle he had won on Gunter's victory in the darts championship. "So. How are you feeling now?"

"Much better for a sip of this. I want to thank you for putting me to bed. If it was you."

"Yes, it was me, and Mr. Fitzmaurice."

"I'm afraid I was pretty far gone last night."

"That was the whole idea." King paused and raised his glass. "If you don't mind me saying so, I would now like to propose a toast. To the metamorphosis of Anthony John Routledge."

"Metamorphosis?"

"Sert makes or breaks everyone in the first few months. It's an ordeal. You've come through intact. At one time I didn't think you would, but then one can never be sure who will and who won't. To be honest, when you first arrived I was sure you wouldn't. Still, you survived outside, and that's ninety percent of it. If you can do that, there's a good chance you'll eventually be OK."

Routledge, overwhelmed by this unexpected praise, looked down at his glass. But King was right: he had come through the worst part of his punishment and been made stronger. He was stronger physically, and he was much stronger mentally, than the man who had awoken in this room last July. He had begun to learn something quite alien and new: he had begun to learn how to tolerate discomfort and pain, disappointment, bitterness, his fellow men.

"I didn't murder that nurse," he said, after a moment.

"I believe you."

"When the jury brought in their verdict I just couldn't grasp it. My legs felt like water. I had to hold on to the dock or I'd have gone down. I shouldn't be sitting here on Christmas Day. I should be at home. But I don't mind anymore. Can you understand that, King? I don't mind the injustice of it anymore. It's happened. I can't change it now. Maybe there is such a thing as fate. Maybe I was supposed to be sent to Sert.'' He thought of all the coincidences, the flimsy scraps of circumstantial evidence, one suggesting and confirming another, which together had convinced the police of his guilt. If only he hadn't taken Louise's newspaper that day; if only the nurse had got into another carriage or even another seat; if only he hadn't slipped and fallen, unseen, on his garden step; if only, if only . . . the list was almost endless, and he had been through it a hundred thousand times. ''I can't pretend I'm pleased to be spending the rest of my days in a penal colony. I'd give anything for a place on the ketch. But I have to admit there are compensations, of a sort. I've learned things here I'd never have known on the mainland. Mostly about myself.''

''There's no need to say any more,'' King said. ''Don't forget I've been through it too. Although in my case, of course, I was guilty.'' He smiled ruefully and raised his glass once more. ''I drink to yapping terriers.''

''To yapping terriers. None of which are here to plague us on Sert.'' Now it was Routledge who smiled.

''True.'' King emptied his glass. ''There are, as you say, compensations. What about a refill?''

The new cutting-lists had come last night from Appleton and were lying on the plan-table. ''This is right up your street again, Mr. Routledge,'' Thaine said, opening the master portfolio and untying the tapes. ''I want you to check these revised quantities against the plans. Include the bits we've already done. Then check that the working cutting-list tallies with the numerical cutting-list. Be especially careful that the timbers match.''

''OK. Will do.''

During lunch, cloud had slowly spread from the north-west and now the afternoon was dull, with a freshening breeze which had just begun plucking at a loose shutter on the windward side of the carpentry shop. Dusk was not far off. Two Tilleys had been lit, one spreading its light on this broad, sloping plan-table by the storeroom door.

On arrival just now Routledge had found Thaine already at work, supervising Ojukwo, Chapman, and Betteridge as they cut and finished the marked timbers whose measurements he and Appleton had already approved. These three men were the finest carpenters in the Village. Thaine excepted, only Betteridge had any experience of boatbuilding, and then only of making a dinghy from a kit. Most of the techniques of boatbuilding were new to them.

Leaving the plan-table, Thaine fastened the offending shutter before returning to Chapman, who was using a spar gauge and smoothing plane to round the bars of the two transom handgrips.

Routledge sat down and began.

During his professional life he had seen and handled many plans, but could remember none as thorough or as beautifully drawn as those Thaine had prepared for the ketch. The paper had been supplied by those villagers who received artists' materials among their luxury goods. The earliest drafts had been preserved in order to retain any useful ideas that might otherwise have been lost. They were executed in pencil. For later work Thaine had turned to felt tip, and then to Chinese ink and draftsman's pens. Lacking a proper drawing board, templates, flexible curves; lacking all aids, in fact, except compasses and a straight-edge, he had produced drawings, in plan and sectional and three-dimensional view, of such comprehensive accuracy that any competent boatyard anywhere in the world would be able to build the craft without further reference to its designer.

From what little Routledge knew about the subject, the vessel seemed to be something quite revolutionary. It was to be a fraction under eight meters in length and two and a half in the beam, chine built of larch, oak, arbor-vitae, and marine plywood, with a shallow draft and a double keel. Space inside would be extremely limited, for the boat's most striking feature was the fact that it could be all but totally submerged and still retain buoyancy. The submersion and subsequent emergence were to be achieved so simply that

Routledge, when first he had seen the plans, had shaken his head in disbelief.

It was obvious that Thaine had already assembled the ketch, in his mind, a dozen times over; had sailed it, knew the way it would handle in calm water or rough. He had incorporated each of Godwin's requirements, however demanding. To reduce the chances of detection by radar, no exposed metal was to be used anywhere on the exterior. The blocks and cleats and cringles and shackles were to be made of wood, and all screw-heads sunk and plugged. For the same reason the design avoided sharp edges, angles, and protrusions. The two masts, the spars, the rangefinder, and all the rigging would be stored in special compartments flush with the deck. To evade the infrared detectors, a wooden sprinkle-bar running the length of the boat, fed from below by a hand pump, would keep the decking at the same temperature as the surrounding sea.

To go with the drawings, Thaine had prepared a complete production schedule, with cutting-lists, tables of quantities, schedules for making and fixing the various fittings and fastenings, plans for the steam-box which now occupied one corner of the carpentry shop, and a list of the special tools, cramps, and gauges required, with designs for those which had had to be made on the island.

He had also played a part in helping Godwin with the electrics. Power for the sonar, radio direction finder, and the helmsman's address system would be supplied by four twelve-volt accumulators. For fear of detection by the Magic Circle, there could be no electric motors on board, so the pump had to be worked by hand. The sonar system-box would go in the bows; the transducers were to be mounted amidships, externally, angled vertically downwards inside fairing blocks to reduce turbulence. Twin eighty-ohm coaxial cables—taken from the aerial for Appleton's flatscreen—ran upwards and aft to the helmsman's display unit, a backlit dial registering depths to a maximum of thirty meters. The length and resistance of the coaxial cables were of crucial importance, for the cables formed an integral part of the sonar circuit.

All the specifications for the sonar had now been settled

and most of the wiring completed. Compared with even the most basic model available commercially, it would be, as Godwin freely admitted, primitive and clumsy. The transmitted signal was of medium-to-high frequency with a rapid clock speed, giving reasonable resolution at the sacrifice of range. The choice of frequency and beamwidth had been forced on Godwin by the size and limitations of his botched-up transducers. With Godwin's approval Fitzmaurice had even felt-tipped the words *M. Mouse Electronics Co.* and drawn Mickey's smiling face under the plastic lid· of the system-box. But in theory the sonar was capable not only of detecting approaching reefs but also of suggesting likely channels between them, and that was all that mattered.

Whether the thing would actually work no one knew. Neither could anyone say whether the ketch would perform as predicted. It might easily overturn or sink. The watertight glands and hatchways were to be sealed with washers and pressure-joints of fat-soaked goatskin, which might or might not be adequate in practice. They had worked in fresh water, during prolonged tests at the bottom of one of the wells, but when Thaine had asked to try them in the more realistic conditions of the sea, the Father had refused. Thaine had suggested using the cover of one fishing party to set the test-rigs and another to retrieve them, but still the Father had refused. No sea trials of any description were to be undertaken. They were too risky: if the satellite picked up anything remotely suspicious the whole project would be threatened.

It was dangerous enough that each component of the ketch had to be carried down to Star Cove. The larger and more obviously suspicious assemblies would be taken down there during fog, during the day; at night, moving figures on the cliffs might show up on the infrared. Smaller pieces would be taken down at random times and at long intervals, under cover of thick cloud and at dawn or dusk, in a strict order worked out jointly by Appleton and Thaine. Some components were already there, and the building-molds in the cave had been in position since early November.

The final assembly process had been minutely planned.

Thaine would be virtually living in the cave during the fort-night before the launch.

"Mr. Thaine," Routledge said.

Thaine approached.

"This hatch doubler. Part number 34.5."

"What about it?"

"It's down as five-mil ply on the numerical list and as larch on the cutting-list."

"How many off?"

"Two."

"Assembly 34. That'd be the for'ard bulkhead."

"Yes. The plan says ply."

"That's right. Change the cutting-list, please, Mr. Rout-ledge. It's just a clerical error. No sweat."

Ojukwo, taking long, curling shavings from a plank of larch on the other side of the workshop, briefly interrupted himself and glanced this way, showing the whites of his eyes, before returning to his jack-plane.

When, a little later, Thaine went to the bungalow, Ojukwo came and looked over Routledge's shoulder. He pulled one of the plans from the heap. It depicted the electrical system.

Routledge looked around. Since receiving his note, Ojuk-wo's manner had become even more withdrawn, not just towards him, but towards everybody. He did not know whom to suspect: but it seemed that the affair with Carter had stopped. Carter had moved out of Ojukwo's and into a single-occupancy house on the far side of the precinct.

"Pretty picture," Ojukwo said. "Think we'll ever get it together?"

"You'd know that better than me."

"Any detectors on board?"

"There's no point. If we're caught, we're caught."

"What d'you mean, 'we'?" Betteridge said. "You ain't got priority, have you, Mr. Routledge?"

"No, I haven't got priority. But I might be going. Any of us might."

"Pigs might fly," Ojukwo said, moving away.

Routledge made no comment.

So far, a hundred and thirty-nine men had put their names

forward for the lottery. The probability that any one man would win a place was about 0.058. Fewer than six chances in a hundred—of what? Going back to England?

Not England. Mexico, Brazil, Peru, perhaps: from Shannon Airport an escaper could, with forged papers, make his way across the Atlantic.

Routledge had assumed that the ketch would head for Devon or Cornwall. That was the obvious place to go: but in this, as in many of his assumptions about Franks and the Village, he had been wrong. Instead of embarking on the straightforward forty-kilometer crossing to the British coast, the ketch would make a voyage over eight times as long, across St. George's Channel to the Tuskar Rock at the southeastern corner of Ireland. It would follow the coast of counties Wexford, Waterford, and Cork, keeping out of sight of land until, after dusk, the lighthouse on the Old Head of Kinsale signaled the approach to Courtmacsherry Bay. Once in Ireland, Franks would give each man money and the opportunity to choose his own destination.

Not England; Routledge would never go back there, much as he wanted to see Christopher again. Maybe later, when he was older, Routledge would be able to get some word through, send him a ticket.

It was fantasy, all fantasy, a way of passing the time. In the first place he would never win a berth on the ketch. In the second place, even if it could be launched, the ketch would never survive in mid-ocean. It would hit a rock, spring a leak, be run down by a tanker. Or Godwin had been deluding himself and everybody else with his estimation of the Magic Circle. In his mind Routledge saw the ketch caught in the searchlights of the helicopter, heard the words "Turn back!" blared through the tannoy. Soon another helicopter would arrive, and a hydrofoil with even brighter searchlights. Probably the ketch would be sunk there and then.

On the other hand, Routledge told himself, why shouldn't it all work as planned? Franks could scarcely have found anyone better than Randal Thaine to build him a boat. Routledge thought of the astonishment he had felt when first he had loosed off a bolt from Martinson's crossbow. Compared with some of the other gadgets Thaine had made, the cross-bows were nothing. Routledge thought of the sawbench, the windmill, all the machinery in the metalwork shop. And Godwin: he wasn't exactly a cretin, either. From bits of junk he had actually made a functioning sonar.

Yes. It might all work. It really might.

And then again it might not. And even if it did, Routledge wouldn't win a place, so what did it matter anyway?

In his heart of hearts he knew he would nevermore set eyes on his family, his son, his mother, his sisters, even his wife, his soon-to-be ex-wife.

Bleakly he brushed them all aside and gave his full attention to his work. "Assembly 78, cockpit trim," he breathed. "Angled beam, part number 78.1. Four off." He scanned the working cutting-list. "Arbor-vitae. Arbor-vitae. There it is."

"Talking to yourself again, Mr. Routledge?" Betteridge said lightly.

"It beats talking to you lot," Routledge said, equally lightly, forcing himself to smile.

He caught Ojukwo's eye.

Ojukwo was not smiling back.

3

Appleton he knew. The other one, the one carrying the oil drum, he didn't think he did. They were making their way out to the end of Azion Point, at the very tip of the Village peninsula, overlooking the Mare and Foal, fifteen hundred meters from Obie's vantage place on the brow of Pulpit Head.

The wind, coming in freezing buffets from the south-west, straight at him, made it impossible to hold or even get a steady image. His eyes were streaming; he was so cold that he could no longer keep still. If only he had some proper leather gloves, with fingers, not these old holey socks he was using as mittens. They both had leather gloves, those two Village bastards, and warm coats, and scarves, and, he was sure, long woolly underwear too.

The weather was showing no sign of improving. The snow dusting the bracken had been there since New Year's Eve, and now it was the middle of January. Sert never usually got this cold. Palm trees had once grown in the hotel grounds.

Obie hated the winter. He hated everything about it, the darkness, the cold, the lack of food. In Peto's time it had been bad enough, but now Obie lacked even the smallest privilege and had to take his chances along with the rest. He had not eaten anything substantial since the day before yesterday, when he and Martinson had shared a pot of rabbit stew.

Life would get better in the spring. Not just because the seabirds came back then, but because Martinson was going to scrag Nackett, who, unfortunately for him, was too stupid to have twigged Martinson as a threat. He should have killed Martinson last summer when he had been laid up with his broken leg. The leg was better now. Martinson was almost as strong as ever.

He had not told Obie all his plans, that much Obie knew. They involved Wayne Pope, and possibly one or two others in the brain gang. Martinson had also been working, slowly and insidiously, on Nackett's people. He had already got to Bubbles; maybe to Craddock as well.

So far, Obie's part in the master plan had consisted mainly of spending long hours out here on the cliffs with the binoculars, observing the comings and goings of the villagers. Without a wristwatch, without a pencil or paper, it had been hard at first to establish any pattern, but in the past two weeks one had begun to emerge.

The border patrols, in which Martinson was greatly interested, now operated in daylight as well as after dark. Each patrol group comprised six men, divided into two parties which each covered half of the border, the center point being marked by a red rock. In addition, the two gates were manned by three men apiece, giving a total of twelve guards on duty at any one time. Shifts lasted eight hours. A minimum of four crossbows was deployed continuously, one with every group of three men.

Obie had amassed a lot of other information about the Village, usually watching either from here on Pulpit Head or from the cliffs at Vanston Cove, on the other side of the Village peninsula. On a few occasions he had gone over the border, but mostly he had left that to Martinson. He knew many of the villagers by name, as many more by sight only. He was figuring out who did what, who worked in the fields and who worked in the compound.

Like everyone outside, Obie envied and resented the men in the Village, and not just because they had appropriated the helicopter. They were warm, well fed, secure. For them the nightmare was not so bad.

In clear weather, from the eastern coast, you could see the mainland as plain as you like. With the binocs you could even see houses and sometimes the flash of sun on a windscreen.

Obie had never received a letter here. Not one. His girl friend had probably shacked up with someone else long ago, probably had a kid, two kids, three. He didn't care about her. He only cared about his mum. He would never know when she died. Still less would he be able to go to her funeral or put flowers on her stone. She might already be dead.

"That's enough," he breathed. "No more of that."

If he went on with it the emptiness and despair would get too bad to handle. He would end up jumping off the cliff. A number of blokes had done that. Especially if they weren't already gay and couldn't stomach the prospect of turning queer. Especially when they learned what the rest of the alternative to the Village was like.

He couldn't blame them, had considered it himself. The first time he had submitted to Peto he had felt his flesh crawl. Anything he could do, anything, to help Martinson get that Franks bastard, would be for Obie the sweetest imaginable labor of love.

Appleton and the other one had reached the end of the Point. They stopped walking. Obie altered the focus by a fraction and blinked, trying to sharpen his eyesight. He saw the other one setting the oil drum down. Appleton glanced up, almost guiltily, at the sky, and quickly pulled something from inside his coat—a stick, was it?

Obie had to look away and wipe his eyes. When he looked back, Appleton was holding or steadying the top of the oil drum. The other man was kneeling on the ground, his head cocked. He seemed to be using the top of the drum like a gunsight, squinting south-eastwards out to sea. Obie got a better view of his face. With a beard it was difficult to be sure, but the general build seemed familiar. A moment later the man stood up, hurriedly took something from his pocket. One hand drew away from the other with a rapid, smooth movement, and he bent over the drum. A tape measure? Was he measuring something?

What in hell's name were they doing? First the daytime patrols. Then the activity in Star Cove. Now this. Were the three connected?

Again the wind forced Obie to put the binoculars down and wipe his eyes. Afterwards it took him a moment to find the two men once more. The other one was again carrying the oil drum. He and Appleton were walking back the way they had come. They followed the path to the chapel and then, going behind the Warrens, were lost to view.

Allowing the binoculars to range over the rest of the Village headland, Obie tried to fit this new observation into the vestigial framework of what he had already seen. Something extraordinary and suspicious was going on. The previous week, in the misty pre-dawn gloom, he had watched two villagers carrying what had appeared to be a heavy wooden door down the cliff path to Star Cove. They had disappeared under an overhang of rock. So much time had elapsed before their reemergence that Obie had thought he had missed them coming out.

There was a cave down there, quite a big one, as Obie recalled.

Patrols in daytime as well as at night.

Peculiar measurements on the cliff.

Appleton.

Obie suddenly remembered the name of the man with the oil drum. Jenkins, that was it: the new meat that he, Jez and Martinson had found last summer in Perdew Wood. Jenkins was educated. Talked posh. Just like Appleton. Martinson would be interested in this. He had asked Obie to keep a special watch for Jenkins.

On the way back to Old Town, Obie turned what he had seen over and over in his mind. The business with the oil drum had intrigued him. Especially Appleton's guilty, involuntary, skyward glance. And what had Jenkins been peering at, away to the south-east?

What, Obie asked himself, lay to the south-east of Azion Point? Apart from salt water, nothing but the lightship!

The lightship. They were planning something nasty for the lightship!

Like hijacking the helicopter, this was a recurring fantasy among everyone on the island. Never mind the radar: just get a bunch of hard geezers together, swim out to one of the lightships, storm it, hold the crew hostage. Make them weigh anchor and sail to the mainland, to France, anywhere.

There were three good reasons why it had never been attempted. First, each ship was several kilometers offshore, and to get there you had to negotiate the reefs. An even better reason was the fact—made clearly known to the pioneering prisoners who had come over on the boat—that the men on the lightships, like the helicopter crews, were armed with riot gas and machine guns. Finally, no one knew for sure whether the lightships had engines. They might have been merely towed into place. Certainly they never went anywhere, never altered their positions. Just before the onset of really heavy weather the helicopter usually came to evacuate the crews.

Even so, planning an attack on a lightship had been a favorite topic of conversation in Peto's council. No one outside the Village had the balls to try it. But Franks. Franks was another matter!

That explained Star Cove. They weren't going to swim. They were building a boat, perhaps a raft. That's how they'd do it. A raft. And they were building it under cover because of the Eye.

In his excitement, Obie nearly failed to think this through to its logical conclusion; he remembered himself just in time.

Martinson returned at noon. He had nothing of interest to report. "You?"

"Not much," Obie said. "I seen that Jenkins. The one what ligged your crossbow."

"Where was he?" Martinson said, with sudden relish.

"In the fields."

"Doing what?"

"Diggin' parsnips, far as I could make out. You're goin' to get him back, ain't you, Jim?"

"No one pulls holes in my roof. No one steals my stuff. No one makes me look a herbert in front of the whole town.

Specially no jumped-up little pratt-faced stonk-fodder faggot like that.''

"That's just what I thought." Obie sat down on Martinson's sofa and with a hopeful eye scanned the vacant larder shelves. "Got any scoff?"

"Eight two seven," Routledge said, stretching Thaine's steel tape between the two outer pins of the protractor.

"Eight two seven," Appleton said, writing the number down.

They, together with a guard party consisting of Myers, Bourne, and Wilson, had come to the end of Beacon Point to take the second fix on the southern lightship. For this they were using a protractor of Routledge's design, made of two laths of plywood, hinged at one end like a pair of dividers. A wire nail ran vertically through the hinge. Another wire nail, precisely fifty centimeters from the inner or hinge nail, had been driven through the end of each limb. The inner and left-hand outer nail had been lined up with the lightship, the inner and right-hand outer nail with the tip of Azion Point, some four kilometers west. A fortnight ago Routledge and Appleton had taken a similar reading from Azion Point, with Beacon Point as the reference, giving a value of 291 millimeters.

The map of Sert in the bungalow did not show the position of the lightships. However, it did have a scale. Provided with these two readings, Routledge would be able to pinpoint the position of the southern lightship. The fixes on the northern lightship had been taken earlier: its position would be determined in the same way, hence establishing the distance between the two lightships.

Godwin had estimated the Magic Circle as effective to a range of no more than five kilometers from the island coast. Allowing as much margin for error as possible, this meant the ketch could not be allowed to surface any nearer than seven kilometers out.

Once around the Village headland, the course of the ketch would be due west. The course would be plotted by compass: but without a log the helmsman would have no way of measuring the distance covered. What was needed was a range-finder, quick and foolproof in use and guaranteed accurate.

Thaine had devised one, but Routledge had suggested another, even simpler, consisting of a T-shape in plywood. The perpendicular of the T would be thirty centimeters long; the width of the bar would be determined by schoolboy trigonometry based on the distance between the lightships. Held horizontally, with the bottom of the T touching the chin, the bar, its tips stained white on the observer's side, would be aligned with the two flashing lights. If the lights fell between the tips the ketch would be over seven kilometers from the coast and so could safely surface.

"Good," Appleton said, putting his notebook away. "Fine." He retrieved the protractor from the top of the small oil drum, brought specially by Routledge, which they had been using as a base. Appleton closed the limbs and slipped the protractor inside his coat: the fix had been accomplished in less than half a minute. There was little chance that this fix, any more than the others, had attracted the attention of the Service. For safety's sake the fixes had been spread over a period of a month.

Routledge picked up the drum and they set off, Myers leading the way, following the western path along the peninsula.

For Routledge this terrain held private memories. Here, at this rock rising boat-like from the turf: this was where he had shot the wild man. No bones were visible on the top. The birds, or foxes, or other men, had removed them.

The place seemed different now, tamer, smaller in scale. Routledge's nightmares had ceased. In fact, he found himself able to regard his former feelings about the incident with what amounted almost to detachment. The wild man had played and lost the fatal game he had himself insisted upon. As with Gazzer and Tortuga, Routledge had not wanted any part of it; had been innocent of malice. And, just as with Gazzer and Tortuga, Routledge had taken the correct and necessary steps to win.

It was hard, but then Sert itself was hard. The slack, ill-defined morality of his upbringing had no place here. He understood now and approved of the way Franks ran the Village. The initiation procedure was cruel and harsh, often, doubtless, unfair. It was wasteful of men and abilities. But, like natural selection, it worked.

In the same way, Franks's right to the helicopter drops could not be judged by fuzzy mainland standards. He got the drops because he had won that particular game. Again, hard: but not as hard as the consequences of losing.

Routledge glanced over to the right, up at the ridge which hid the ruins from view.

"What's on your mind?" Appleton said, drawing level.

"The monastery."

Appleton grunted. "There's some stone there we ought to take. Be handy for paving."

Except during his patrol duties, Appleton rarely left the Village. He had said he had come today for the exercise. Routledge felt there was another motive. Appleton may have been checking that this morning's fix, like the ones last month, was being correctly taken: his life, after all, might depend on it.

Since that excursion to Azion Point he had become much more friendly. He seemed, in tune with several others, to be responding to the changes that, difficult to define, Routledge had felt developing within himself. He had been admitted to informal terms with Tragasch, with Fitzmaurice, even with the undemonstrative Scammell.

In the past few weeks his status had risen: he did not know how far. Neither his academic abilities nor his contribution to the escape project had earned him any appreciable points. What benefit he had accrued for working for Godwin and Thaine had come because he had applied himself every day and willingly done whatever had been required of him. Neither, it now appeared, had it passed unnoticed how hard he had worked to finish his house on time.

He had revised his opinion of Appleton. The man was a stickler for what he believed to be right and true: for the interests and welfare of the Village. He cared nothing for popularity, yet was regarded with profound respect, almost veneration, by the whole Community. And, hidden below dense layers of reserve, visible only to those to whom he chose to show it, Routledge had detected in Appleton a keenly observant sense of the ridiculous.

When they got to the bungalow he accompanied Appleton to the door of Franks's office.

The visit had been arranged yesterday. Franks was expecting them. With a gentle knock on the panel, Appleton went inside and sought permission for Routledge to enter.

Franks was sitting by the window, in the tapestry-covered armchair, pencil in hand, a file in his lap, more files and papers on the low table beside him. "Good morning, Mr. Routledge."

"Good morning, Father."

Routledge had never been in this room before. It adjoined the laboratory, where the Council met and new arrivals were interviewed, and through its french windows gave Routledge an unfamiliar perspective of the back garden, the line of larches, Godwin's workshop. Godwin was there now, his head bent over his bench.

"This won't take long," Appleton said.

The left-hand wall was dominated by the warden's 1:10,000 map of the island, showing place-names, contours, tidal zones, vegetation, and the various survey stations used in studying the animals and plants.

"Do you want to take it off the wall?" Franks said.

"It'd be much easier if we did," Appleton said.

Using a screwdriver attachment on his pocket knife, Appleton unfastened the perspex sheet and with Routledge's help lifted it down. They carefully unpeeled the map.

"Shall I clear my desk?" Franks said.

"There's no need. We'll take it into the lab."

Franks came to watch. Routledge and Appleton laid the perspex sheet across two trestle tables and spread the map across it. Appleton produced his notebook.

With Thaine's tape measure and a large pair of folding-leg compasses borrowed from the carpentry shop, Routledge ascertained the distance on the paper between Azion Point and Beacon Point, 401 millimeters, and drew an arc with this radius from each of the two Points. From Azion Point he raised an arc of 663 millimeters, which was the reading taken on Beacon Point multiplied by 401 and divided by 500, the distance from the inner to the outer nail on each limb of the protractor. With a pencil and straight-edge he joined Beacon Point to the place where this arc crossed the arc he had just raised from Beacon Point. Performing the reverse operation on Azion Point left him with two straight lines which intersected somewhere out to sea about four kilometers south of Beacon Point. This was the position of the southern lightship. It actually fell beyond the edge of the map, so he took some extra paper from Franks to make an extension.

He next plotted the position of the northern lightship. Stretching the tape measure between the two points gave a converted distance of 16,060 meters.

"Say 16,100 to allow for inaccuracies," Routledge said.

Franks smiled. "I'll buy that." He turned his head. "Come in, Stamper. Come in."

The door to the corridor was ajar: Stamper had knocked on it anyway.

Stamper appeared extremely agitated. Routledge had never seen him like this before.

"Father," Stamper said. "I must have a private word."

"If it's not a personal matter, you can say anything in front of Routledge here."

For a moment Routledge did not realize the honor that had just been done him. He was too worried by Stamper's expression, by the growing premonition that something terrible had happened.

"There's an outsider on the porch," Stamper said. "He says he wants to see you."

"An outsider? How did he get into the Village?"

"Through the gate. Mr. Myers took the decision."

"Who is it?"

"Obadiah Walker. Father, he knows about the boat."

4

"THAT'S OK, WAYNE," MARTINSON SAID. "I UNDER-stand."

"Just protectin' my interests, Jim."

"Sure. Sure. I'd do the same if I was you."

" 'Nother thing. Ain't safe to push Gomm and Wilmot no more. When the time come, that time enough."

"And Feely?"

Pope grinned, showing his yellow teeth.

"Want to know a secret, Wayne?"

"Spill."

"You and me, we speak the same lingo."

This was their fifth meeting in all, the third at Piper's Beach. At the second, on the day after Boxing Day, Pope had brought the binoculars and Martinson had known that everything at last was about to go his way. Their earliest conversations had been almost like a ritual dance: elaborately wary, replete with buried meanings, of full significance only to the participants. Later, when it had become apparent that they did indeed speak the same lingo, Pope had been the first to open up.

"What's happening about the binocs?" Martinson said.

"Archie blame Des now. Reckon he leave the door unlocked. Des get a bit of a smackin'. Still, he like that anyway. He like that fine."

"Yeah? Never did before. When he was with Peto."

"Do now."

"You in't no tin roof, Wayne?"

"Me? No. Not special." Moving his hips back and forth in unison, he made a brief pumping movement with his right hand. "Any hole do Wayne. I takes it as it come."

"Why you doing this?"

"Fun, man. Laughs."

"And the island."

"That too."

"You'll be king. Wayne the First of Sert."

"Might wears purple and swaps my name. Be the Pope instead. Pope Wayne."

Martinson shook his head and smiled. Seated on a flat rock, he was popping the bladders on a strand of green-black weed. He let the waves break a few more times before speaking again. He liked the stertorous noise they made, like giants breathing. Crash. Drag. Crash.

"So I'm on me own," he said.

" 'Fraid so, Jim. 'Cept the rope. I'll do that OK."

"Comes down to the when."

"Can't be yet awhile. Not till the weather warm up."

"Don't he never take the shutter down in winter?"

"No."

"Couldn't you unfix it, like? On the night?"

"No. Couldn't do that. You got to wait, Jim. With the curtain it be easy."

"When you say warm weather, what do you mean? March?"

"April. Could be May."

"May!"

"April. Usually April."

It was now early February. Two months. Eight weeks, maybe ten. A long time to wait. But then he had been waiting five years to hear Franks, disillusioned at the last, raise a despairing voice to his Maker. If he had to wait another five years it would still be worth it. What were ten weeks, balanced in the scale of Armageddon? And he could use the interval to gather yet more intelligence about the Village, to continue probing at Nackett's boys. Bubbles was in the bag. With Bubbles he had already begun to plot and plan.

Nackett would die a rapid death. He was lucky. Unlike Pope. Pope would be taking Nackett's place. On the right hand side. Feely would be in Houlihan's place, on the left. But, unlike those of the man in the middle, their legs would be broken and for them it would be comparatively merciful.

April. When did Easter fall this year?

"All right," Martinson said. "We'll do it your way. Let's have a date."

"April 15th."

"You sure?"

" 'Pend on the weather. Could be sooner than that. Could be later. And don't forget the moon."

"We need a signal. Hang something from the gallery."

"Too chancey. I tells you what, Jim. Every day after April 15th, you look here on the beach. If'n this rock gets turned upside downside, you know that's the night to move."

Martinson bent his head to examine the rock on which he was seated. "All right."

"Till then I don't wants to see you no more. If you got a 'mergency, send Obie with some bullshitty message, then I'll knows to meets you here. If I gots one, I'll come to the town. Right?"

"Right."

Pope glanced around. No one was in view. "Like I said, if you get caught, hard shit."

"I won't get caught."

"See you in the spring, then, Jim."

"Yeah."

The pact now settled, Pope turned and started to move away.

Obie began to wonder whether he had made a mistake, the worst and last in the long chain of appalling blunders that constituted his life. The way Myers was looking at him, the way he was being kept waiting outside, the way Stamper and Myers had conversed in low tones: all this was leading him to believe that he should have listened to his own original counsel of caution and stayed away. Because, even if they acceded to his demands, the best he could eventually hope for was a faceful of TK-6 and the splattering, torrential impact of the batch of Prison Service machine-gun rounds reserved specially for him.

The prospect of escape, however remote, had been too intoxicating to resist; setting foot in the Village had instantly sobered him up. He should definitely have kept further watch and then reported everything to Jim. Definitely.

"Where d'you think you're going?" Myers said.

"Got to take a leak."

"Sit down."

Obie decided not to protest. "Cold out here," he said.

"Shut up," Myers said, flatly.

"Suck my big toe, Myers." Obie was about to say more, but Myers moved the hatchet just slightly and Obie remembered that his own weapon, one of Jim's machetes, had been confiscated at the gate. No point in antagonizing the hired help. The goons.

Obie eyed Myers's pristine boots and clothes, his warm jacket. Myers was clean. His beard was trimmed, his hair cut short. His skin looked healthy. No blotches or pimples from eating crap all winter long. Since Nackett had taken over the flock, Obie had received scarcely any milk or cheese. The villagers not only had goats, lots of them: they had cows too. Pigs, chickens. Vegetables. Fruit.

In fact, they had everything.

The door opened and Stamper came out. "All right," he said to Obie. "You can come in now."

Reluctantly, Obie rose to his feet.

"You said you wanted to see the Father, didn't you?"

"Changed my mind."

"Tough," Myers said, rising himself.

"He's waiting," Stamper said.

"I got to take a J.R."

"Later." Myers took his elbow.

Obie angrily shook himself free. "OK," he said. "Later."

He was not prepared for the inside of the bungalow. In the past five years he had forgotten what the interior of a civilized

building was like. He had learned to accept as normal the
lack of all facilities, the vandalism, the rotting boards, the
commingled stink of stale bird-oil, urine, excrement, vomit,
semen. He had almost forgotten what a window did, or what
a hinge was for. And this was just the hallway. When Stamper opened the door to the large room where Franks was
sitting with Appleton, Obie felt himself crushed by the shock
of realizing how far he had fallen and how much he had lost.
This was like the heartbreaking contrast between the cell-
block and the two minutes the parole-seeking con spent
standing in the carpeted, picture-hung coziness of the governor's office; like it, but infinitely multiplied by the knowledge that the denial of these treasures extended not just to
the end of his sentence, but forever.

"What is it you want?" Franks said, from behind the
trestle table.

He did not offer Obie a seat.

When Obie didn't answer, Franks said, "Mr. Myers tells
me you seem to think we're building a boat."

Obie had come this far. He reminded himself there was
no point in stopping now. "In Star Cove. In the cave."

"What an extraordinary notion."

"Don't give me that, Franks." Now he had started talking, Obie found himself continuing volubly, simultaneously
releasing all his pent-up thoughts and frantically trying to
say the right words to stave off what he now feared they were
going to do to him. "I know, and one of my mates knows,
and if I don't come back he's goin' to tell everyone in the
town, so don't get no ideas about boddin' me to keep me
quiet. We seen you buildin' it and me and my mate want in.
We want to get off the island much as you. That's all. That's
it. That's our price. Way I see it you ain't got no choice."

Franks seemed amused. "We have every choice. Let us
first assume that you have put the correct interpretation on
what you imagine you have seen. Let us assume that we are
not merely building a cheese store in the cave."

Cheese store? Cheese store? Obie was about to panic, but
then took strength from the memory of Appleton and Jenkins
on the cliff. And why bother to hide a cheese store from the

Eye? Why use dawn and dusk and fog to take the timber down? And why run daytime patrols to protect a few wooden shelves?

"Let us assume, as I say, that you are right. We can then either believe you when you say that you have a mate who knows, or we can disbelieve you. If we believe you, what is to stop us from grabbing your dick with a pair of pliers and squeezing till you tell us his name? What is then to stop us from going to Old Town now to find and kill him before he suspects you won't be coming back?"

"I wouldn't tell you his name. I'd tell you someone else's."

"Perhaps. Or perhaps, and which is more likely, no one else knows anything about this. Perhaps you're trying to four-flush us, Obie. What odds would you give on that, Mr. Appleton?"

"Good odds."

"Good odds, Obie. You heard Mr. Appleton. Good odds that it would be safer to kill you now. After, of course, we have grabbed your dick with our pliers and squeezed until you've told us whatever else you might know." He smiled icily. "Come to think of it, just what have you seen?"

"I seen enough. With the binocs."

"What binocs?"

"Barratt's."

Franks studied him without speaking. He sat back and looked away, apparently considering what to do. He stroked his face a few times and drew air between his teeth. Finally he decided. He raised his eyes to Myers, who was standing by the door.

"Kill him," he said.

Obie saw Myers start forward, drawing a long-bladed knife from the sheath at his belt. "No! No, wait! There's somethin' else! Somethin' more! About Jim! About Martinson!"

Franks held up his hand: the knife slowly returned to its sheath. "Let's hear it, then."

"You'll let me live?"

"I might. No promises."

"Think you're some sort of hard case, don't you, Franks?"

"You've got five seconds. Starting now."

Myers drew the knife once more. Obie looked at it, looked at Franks. He thought of what Martinson would do to him if he found out he had been betrayed.

"All right, Mr. Myers," Franks said. "Do it."

"Wait! Martinson's plannin' to hit the Village! Could be any day."

"On his own, I suppose."

"No. He's anglin' to scrag Nackett and Houlihan. When he's done that he wants to join the town and the light. He can do it, Franks. He's the cleverest bloke outside. He knows we all want the 'copter."

"And Martinson himself? What does he want?"

"He wants you. He hates you, Franks. Says he's going to crucify you. Really do it. Really goin' to nail you up. Told me yesterday. I always knew he was barmy. I always knew he had it in for you. But yesterday he told me for sure. He's out of his head. That's why I got to get off the island. That's why I'm here. When he's boss it'll make now look like the good old days. Only reason you've been safe so far is Houlihan. Houlihan won't risk fightin' the Village. He's nearly as clever as Jim, but not clever enough. You got to take me with you. Me and my mate. We'll give you all the dope."

"Why shouldn't we just go out and kill Mr. Martinson?"

" 'Cause it's bigger than him now. 'Cause he's into the brain gang. The idea's out. If you get rid of Jim one of the others'll take over. Do it my way and you get the S.P. on all his moves. Do it my way and I'll tell you how to block them."

"In return for a hypothetical place on our hypothetical boat. And one for your hypothetical mate."

"Your boat ain't hypothetical. I know. If you're worried about me and my mate, we'll do our bit when we get out there."

"Out where?"

"To the lightship."

Obie saw Appleton shoot a strange glance at Franks, whose expression remained impassive. For a second Obie did not twig what the glance meant. Then he did. "You ain't goin' to no lightship. You're goin' all the way. Right?"

"It's a shame about you, Obie. A shame you picked the wrong side. We could have used you in the Village."

"When's it going?"

"When's what going?"

"Me and my mate, we don't want gettin' left behind."

"You know what you've done, don't you, Walker?"

"What?"

"You've placed me in an impossible position. If I agree to your proposal that's as good as admitting that we have a boat. If I don't and let you go, you could still spread a rumor that we have one. It looks very much as if we're going to have to kill you after all." He paused. "On the other hand, I am interested in what you have to say concerning Martinson. I would like to know more. If we kill you that will be difficult. What do you suggest?"

"I ain't pressin' on the boat. One hand washes the other, right?"

"What if your information isn't reliable?"

"What if you go without me? I mean, us."

"You forget, Obie. In the Village we tell no lies."

"You'll take us, then?"

Appleton was evincing signs of alarm, which Franks ignored. "If, as a result of your help, Martinson is thwarted in his attempt to attack the Village and take control of the island, I will be favorably disposed towards you. How that favor will be manifested I cannot yet say."

"Not good enough."

"It's that or a knife in the guts. Choose."

Obie felt his advantage go. He had lost. Somehow, he had lost. He would have no guarantees. But he could not go back. He had already blown the whistle on Jim. This way, at least he would escape from the Village with his life. Had Franks not held up his hand just now, Obie knew he would already be dead. There was no doubt in his mind about that.

Franks went on talking. "And if you spread the word about our hypothetical boat, and if the other outsiders come to take it from us, your prospects of getting a place from them will be exactly zero. I feel I should remind you of that. Furthermore, if we lose the boat because of you, you will also have earned my extreme displeasure. The consequences of that you are familiar with from the past. So. Take your pick.''

Franks had left him nothing to choose. If Obie failed to keep his part of the bargain, Franks would get word to Martinson about this meeting. All that remained was to settle the details of the betrayal, to arrange a clandestine rendezvous where messages could be conveyed. All that remained was to hope and pray and get down on his knees and beg that Martinson didn't find out.

Yes. Obie had been right. Coming here had been a mistake, the worst in the entire blighted span of his miserable, rancid, twenty-eight years of poxy life.

5

As soon as Stamper had brought the news about the arrival of the outsider, Routledge had been sent from the bungalow. He had gone to the carpentry shop where, having calculated the required width of the rangefinder, he had sat checking and rechecking the cutting-lists. His pleasure and disbelief in his meteoric rise in status, in the realization that the Father had taken to addressing him simply as "Routledge," had been completely overshadowed by the awareness that news of the escape project had gone beyond the border hedge.

It was at the carpentry shop, half an hour later, that Routledge saw Stamper next.

"Mr. Routledge," he said, beckoning from the doorway.

Routledge rose from his seat at the plan-table. Betteridge was standing by one bench, Chapman and Ojukwo by another. They returned Stamper's greetings and went on with their work.

Outside, in the thin, cold, February sunshine, Stamper rapidly drew Routledge away from the open door of the shop and into the middle of the woodyard, moving him towards the bungalow. "The Father wants to see you, Routledge."

Not only was Routledge now addressed informally by the Father: he had in consequence been admitted to informal terms with Stamper also.

"Is it about that outsider?"

"Yes. The Council's in emergency session."

On entering the laboratory, Routledge saw that two trestle tables had been put together to make one large table in the center of the room. Franks was at the head, facing the main door; on his right sat Appleton. Then came Foster, Sibley, Thaine, Godwin, a vacant chair, and Mitchell. The vacant chair was Stamper's.

"Thank you for coming, Routledge," Franks said. "Take a seat."

Routledge pulled a chair from a stack by the wall. Thaine and Godwin moved apart to create a space.

The Council normally met once a week, on Friday. Its decisions owed little to collective thought. They were usually those of the Father, merely informed and refined by the contribution of his advisers. But to serve on the Council at all was to tread one of the most rarefied regions of the Father's favor, and Routledge, sitting down between two of its most prominent members, could not for the moment absorb the knowledge that he had actually been invited to join, however briefly and peripherally, in the proceedings.

No direct sunshine reached the laboratory at this hour and at this time of year. The light in the room seemed unreal, derived at second or third hand from the normal, solid world beyond the glass. Together with the arrangement of the seating around the trestles, it put Routledge in mind of some sacred medieval painting, freezing in time the gestures and attitudes, each in turn, of the apostles. But there were only seven, not twelve; and the repast consisted not of bread and wine but the ruthless, unsymbolic substance of an agenda for survival.

When Routledge was settled, Franks nodded at Appleton.

Appleton turned to Routledge. "Everything spoken here must remain in the strictest confidence," he said. "As must the fact that the Village has received a visit from an outsider. You are one of the few men to know."

"I understand."

"We have asked you here because you've been inside Martinson's hut. We need to know the layout."

Routledge wondered how all this concerned Martinson,

what the Village intended to do to him, and why; but knew better than to ask.

During his interview with Appleton on the morning after his acceptance into the Village, Routledge had been "debriefed"—that was the word Appleton had used—on his experiences outside. Appleton had been mainly interested in any names Routledge had been able to remember. He had not asked then for detailed information about Martinson's hut.

Routledge was given a pencil and paper and to the best of his recollection drew the floor-plan. "That's where he usually sleeps," he said. "This other room's the store where he keeps his weapons. The big room is the kitchen. The outer door is kept barred at night."

"Could we force the latch without making any noise?" Foster said.

"I don't think so."

"What about the walls? They look pretty sturdy from the outside."

"They're worse inside. I couldn't break out of them. I had to make a hole in the roof."

"How easy was it?"

"Quite easy. But he'd hear."

"Now, Routledge," Franks said. "I want your opinion. Do you think it would be possible for us to get in at night, kill Martinson, and remain undetected by the rest of the towners?"

Routledge took a moment for reflection and then said, "No, Father, I do not."

Franks glanced at Foster. "I agree with him. We can't risk it. Much as I'd like to."

"You're saying we ought to let Walker go?" Foster said.

"Yes," Franks said. "That was my first conclusion. Anybody got any further thoughts on that?"

No one spoke.

"All right," Franks said. "Obie can leave the Village." He nodded at Stamper, who rose and left the room.

Routledge had the feeling that he himself was just about

to be dismissed. "Forgive me, Father," he said, mentally preparing to depart. "Did you say 'Obie'?"

"Do you know him?"

"Yes. If it's the same Obie, he was one of the three who caught me."

"Martinson being another," Appleton said.

"Yes," Routledge said. Looking back, he discovered that, despite Obie's part in his abduction, he had rather liked him, just as he had developed a grudging respect for Martinson.

Franks said, "Perhaps we should let Routledge sit in for a while. He might be able to contribute something. Mr. Appleton, tell him what's at stake."

Appleton gave Routledge a concise summary of the implications of Obie's visit. As Routledge already knew, Obie had somehow found out about the boat. He wanted a place on board. In return he would provide details of a plot by Martinson to murder the two outsider chieftains and unite Old Town and the lighthouse settlement in common cause to attack the Village, kill the Father, and take over the whole island. Such a contingency had long ago been foreseen by the Father, but he had not yet decided how to deal with the immediate problem Obie had posed.

There had been two alternatives, Appleton said. The first, just rejected, had been to kill Obie right away to prevent him spreading the story any further, and for a squad to go in tonight to kill Martinson. Obie, however, claimed that he had an accomplice. He also claimed that the plot had already got as far as Houlihan's brain gang, who, living as they did inside the lighthouse, could not be disposed of so simply.

The better alternative was to let him go and to make use of whatever information he provided, unreliable as it might be. Advance warning of Martinson's plans would be of enormous value in defending the Village, if such a defense were considered practicable.

"And the ketch?" Routledge said. "May I ask what's to happen to that?"

"The Father wants to postpone the launch," Appleton said. "We're trying to persuade him otherwise."

Routledge saw why the Father would take such an attitude.

Equally he saw why, just for once, he should not be allowed to have his way.

"We come down," Franks said, when Stamper had returned, "to a choice of tactics. Straightforward defense we have already discussed. The alternatives to that are simple. One: we could give the outsiders their share of the helicopter drops. That would remove their main source of grievance. Unfortunately it would not be enough. They would want the entire drop. Then they would want everything in the Village. Finally, the Village would be destroyed anyway. Two: shall we follow the advice of Mr. Foster and certain other hardliners? Is it now the time for a cull? My objections to this, as always, have little to do with moral or philosophical considerations. From the strictly practical point of view, a cull would be worse than useless, because it would arouse and mobilize even stronger feelings against the Village than already exist and make an invasion not merely likely, but certain. Until now we have remained unmolested for two main reasons. Archie Houlihan will not risk a confrontation; and we have offered no violence to the outsiders." Franks removed his glasses, placed them on the table, and rubbed his eyes. "Three: Since Houlihan is all that stands between Martinson and us, shall we warn him that his life is in danger? What will happen if we do? The brain gang will learn that we know of the plot and in all likelihood Obie will be identified as the informer, losing us the only advantage we have. Four: shall we set Houlihan against Nackett and vice versa in an attempt to make the outsiders reduce their own numbers? Well, if we do that we shall only be playing into Martinson's hands, since he wants in any case to be rid of Nackett and Houlihan." Franks replaced his glasses and sat back. "Further suggestions, please, gentlemen. Mr. Sibley?"

Sibley shrugged. "You've covered it, Father. That's it."

"Anyone? Anyone at all?"

When none of the others spoke, Routledge shifted uneasily in his seat.

"Routledge?"

"There is something else we could do, Father."

"What's that?"

"Poison them. Poison their water. Most of the drums that get washed up seem to be marked with a skull and cross-bones. We keep all kinds of industrial chemicals in store. We'd need something colorless and tasteless and highly toxic. Then we go in at night and contaminate the wells. We might kill fifty percent, maybe more. Even if we didn't, they'd never be certain it was us. Each camp would blame the other, or they might put it down to disease."

Thaine barely suppressed a smile.

Franks also seemed amused. "That idea is repugnant and exceedingly unsporting, Routledge," he said. "Shameful to admit, I regret to say that it has already occurred to us. For some months we have even kept aside a drum of weedkiller with the exact properties you describe. But there are difficulties. If large numbers of outsiders in both camps were to die mysteriously, the Service might well break with tradition and investigate, and then we would lose the privileges we have worked so long and hard to acquire. If we restricted the poison to one camp, so making it look more like an epidemic, the survivors might well, eventually, join the other camp and an invasion would then be almost certain. So far our tactics have consisted in preserving the status quo. If, however, we come under prolonged and serious attack and all else fails, we will not hesitate to use poison." Franks looked around the table. "Right, then," he said. "We're agreed. We do nothing. We concentrate on the defense of the Community. Any dissenting voices?"

There were none.

"The final decision today concerns the ketch. Mr. Thaine, I believe there was something further you wanted to say on this topic."

Routledge noticed grease under Thaine's fingernails. His hands had been but hastily cleaned. Routledge wondered what he had been doing.

"I can't add much to what Mr. Appleton said. I just agree with him and think it would be wrong to let the outsiders dictate what we can do and what we can't. If you postpone the launch, Courtmacsherry goes and the whole project might as well be canceled. I may be biased because I'm guaranteed a place, but that's the way I see it.''

Foster, Sibley and Mitchell now voiced similar opinions.

''And what about you, Routledge?'' Franks said. ''What do you think? You're heavily involved with the work, after all.''

''I think it would be a tragedy to postpone the launch. When I first arrived on Sert and Mr. Appleton explained the advantages of living in the Community, he said that foremost among them was the opportunity to be a man. He said it was one of your sayings. At the time I didn't know what he was talking about. Once I went outside I damn soon understood. The first thing they did was try to rape me. I decided I wouldn't have it, and I didn't. Next they tried to auction me off for a gang-bang. I wouldn't have that either. Finally some caveman in animal skins forced a showdown. He was determined that it should be him or me. In the end I had a choice. I decided it would be him. That is not the way for men to live. What we have here in the Village is an oasis of peace and order. Once we let the outsiders breach the hedge we might as well forget about being men. They don't necessarily have to breach it physically. If we let them dictate to us they've breached it just the same. There's not a man in the Village who wouldn't agree, and there's not one of them who'd resent the ketch leaving, even under threat of an attack. Not one. Whatever else happens, the project must go ahead. It must.''

Routledge had surprised even himself with the vehemence of his delivery. In his argument he had somehow crystallized the whole of his attitude to the Village and the island, previously vague, formless, half-conscious. For perhaps the first time in his life he found that he cared deeply enough to get truly angry. As he finished speaking, he became aware of the startled silence in which his words had been received.

Then Thaine said, ''Bravo, Routledge.''

''Yes,'' Appleton said. ''That's it. That's exactly it.''

''Very well,'' Franks said, after a moment. ''If that's the sentiment, who am I to demur? The project continues.''

The meeting broke up. Routledge put his chair back on its

stack and was about to leave the laboratory when Franks
called out to him. "A word with you, please, Routledge."

Once the Council members had dispersed, Franks led
Routledge into the adjoining office. Routledge felt as if he
should pinch himself: he could not believe that the events of
the morning were really happening to him. It seemed not to
be an hour or two, but several days, since he had been out
on Beacon Point with Appleton and the others, since he had
plotted the positions of the lightships.

The map and its perspex sheet had been hurriedly dumped
inside the door. "Shall I put it back on the wall?" Routledge
said, almost overwhelmed by a sense of the privilege of being
invited alone into the Father's office.

"I'll give you a hand," Franks said. In his desk drawer
he found a small screwdriver.

Had it been this morning, in the laboratory, when Franks,
perhaps impressed by Routledge's single-minded devotion to
the project, had decided to mark him out for elevation? Or
had he been watching him for longer than that, for the entire
time he had been in the Community?

They laid the map on the sheet and raised it into place.
While Routledge held the perspex steady, Franks got on a
chair and fixed the three uppermost screws. Without warning, as he stood down, he said, "I want you to serve on the
Council. You will be subordinate to Mitchell. Is that all right
by you?"

Routledge scarcely knew how to answer. "I'm honored,"
he managed to say. Such a phrase had never passed his lips
in earnest before.

"You shouldn't be. Make no mistake, Routledge, if what
Walker says is true, we're up the creek. We're going to need
all the brainpower we can get. Mr. Godwin first drew you to
my attention. He thinks pretty highly of you."

"Really?"

"And I see Thaine has finally taken a bit of a shine to
you."

"He has?"

"Didn't you notice the way you were addressed?"

"I . . . yes." He remembered now.

Franks gestured at the smaller and shabbier of the two armchairs in the room. Routledge nervously sat down, wishing that the molded soles of his workboots were not quite so encrusted with the red clifftop mud.

"Drink? It's nearly lunchtime."

"Yes. Thanks."

"Beer? Whisky?"

"Whatever you've got, Father."

"Whisky, then."

As Franks went to a steel cabinet and poured the drinks, Routledge looked out of the french windows at the garden, where Godwin, balding and round-shouldered, wearing his waxed-cotton jacket, was even now heading back towards his workshop. So he had recommended Routledge to the Father. As with King, as with so many others in the Village, Routledge now felt ashamed of his first impression of the man.

"Just a general chat about the way the Council works," Franks said, once he had given Routledge a glass and sat down himself. "Normally the meetings are a bit more lively than the one you saw this morning. But, as I say, these are difficult times."

Routledge's anxiety got the better of him and he interrupted with the single most important question he wanted to ask. "Father, when you said we were going to concentrate on the defense of the Community, what exactly did you mean?"

"You're wondering how we can defend ourselves against the potential force of both the towns."

"Yes."

"You're thinking the crossbows are all we have, those and better discipline?"

"Yes."

"It's true we're in trouble if the outsiders get together. Deadly serious trouble." Franks sampled his whisky. "But all is not lost if they do. Thanks to Randal Thaine, we've got another ace up our sleeve besides that weedkiller."

6

ROUTLEDGE WAS SITTING WITH HIS FEET UP AGAINST THE edge of the fireplace, head back, half dozing, listening to the sleet on the roof and on the shutters of his house. The suggestion of a smile crossed his lips as he replayed in his mind what he could remember of the closing moves: he had finally drawn a game of chess with King. Only just. But he had drawn it all the same.

For once he had lit the fire. While playing, he and King had eaten a hot supper and drunk tea. At nine o'clock King had retired to his own house. After that Routledge had reread today's letter from Louise and examined the photos of Christopher she had sent. She had written the previous week as well, and the one before that. It seemed after all that she was going to keep her promise and continue writing. Her wedding had been three weeks ago, at the beginning of February.

In the firelight Routledge examined his watch. Ten-forty.

He looked around once more and saw that now at last he was being observed. The man in the sleeping-bag, his new ward, had regained consciousness. Twenty-six years of age, pale and gaunt, he had been convicted of murder during the execution of an armed robbery.

Routledge stood up.

The new man was regarding him with dread, but made no attempt to struggle. What was going on behind those eyes? What did he make of his host? What impression had he gained of the room, the fire, the smell of stale fulmar oil which Routledge himself no longer even noticed? As Routledge approached he was struck by the comparison between the way he himself was now and the way he must have been last July when he had awoken at King's. Had he been like this man? Yes, looking back, he realized he had. Except that he had been, if anything, even worse, even more frightened.

"It's all right," Routledge said. "Don't worry. You're safe."

The man did not reply.

Routledge said, "What's your name?"

"Where am I?"

"I ask the questions. Your name."

"Vic."

"Vic what?"

"Vic Prine."

"From where?"

"Lewisham."

"From which prison?"

"Dartmoor. Dartmoor. I was at Dartmoor."

"Well, Mr. Prine, I'm afraid to tell you you've landed up on Sert."

Prine tried not to show any reaction. "Yeah, well," he said.

He allowed himself to be removed from the sleeping-bag. A large, dark, and malodorous stain had spread from the center of the quilting. He had urinated in his sleep.

"I couldn't help myself," he said.

For a moment Routledge thought he was going to offer resistance, but then his knees buckled and he half collapsed on the floor. Routledge lifted him easily and sat him on the edge of the spare bed. "Do you want to throw up?"

Prine shook his head.

Routledge introduced himself and brought Prine a comb, the washbowl, and a pair of his own trousers, some gray corduroys long past their best.

Like patrol duty, the work of acting as guardian to new arrivals was shared equally throughout the Community. Villagers who had once acted as guardian to a successful entrant were, if they wished, thereafter exempted.

Because the new man had awoken before midnight, Appleton agreed to conduct the initial interview straight away. Routledge sat in the place Mitchell had occupied during his own first interview and delivered Mitchell's lines.

Now that he served on the Council, Routledge's eyes had been opened to the way the Village was administered. As he had suspected, outgoing mail was indeed vetted. This he regarded as a sensible and necessary precaution in the endless struggle to keep the Prison Service and hence also the outsiders at bay.

The interview procedure was part of this struggle. Having selected suitable applicants, it recruited only the cleverest, fittest, and luckiest arrivals and discarded the rest. Properly fed and clothed, armed, and with a high morale, a community of such men was more than a match for a larger and less disciplined force. Unfortunately the combined size of the two outsider camps had now outweighed even this advantage.

So far there had been only one report from Obie, according to which Martinson was lying low before attempting to assassinate both Nackett and Houlihan in the spring. Another possibility was that he was lying low because the plot had been invented by Obie purely to save his own neck. Nothing Foster had observed had given any credence to Obie's claims.

Nevertheless, for the past two months the Village had been preparing for invasion. Franks had revealed to the Council his thoughts on defense and detailed plans had been drawn up. Every second man had been issued with a prong-barbed spear, the shaft fashioned from willow or holly and the blade forged in the metalwork shop using scrap steel. Some of these weapons, Routledge learned, had been made as long as two years ago, and had been lying in store in the bungalow roof-space. Spare hoes, axes, hatchets, machetes, had been honed to extra sharpness. Thaine had designed battle-hammers made of lumps of rock some fifteen centimeters in diameter, held in barbed-wire netting attached to a couple of meters of nylon rope. Twenty of these had so far been completed.

However many weapons the Village possessed, Routledge knew, as did everyone else, that nothing could compensate for lack of numbers. This was a problem Franks had foreseen right from the start, but short of actually murdering failed applicants or risking Service intervention by launching an unprovoked attack on Old Town or the lighthouse, there had been no solution to it.

In recent weeks, though, another change in the intake procedure had been made. The period outside, at first reduced, had been reluctantly abandoned. Prine, though he did not know it, no longer faced the experience that Routledge and most of the villagers had endured. Instead, if he were otherwise qualified and if he wished, he would serve a probationary period inside the Village, working on the land, living in virtual isolation from everybody but his guardian and fellow probationers and one or two others selected by Appleton. At the end of this period the full Council would meet and decide whether the newcomer should be admitted to the Community, or expelled.

At a prearranged point near the end of the interview, Routledge conducted Prine from the room and left him in Talbot's care. When Routledge returned to the laboratory, Appleton and Stamper were already deeply in discussion.

"Well, Routledge?" Appleton said. "What do you make of him?"

As a child, Routledge had relied on his own judgment of the people he had met, forming in a matter of moments an assessment which had invariably proved right. Later in his life he had doubted the validity of these snap judgments and had suffered as a result. Since coming to Sert he had found himself slowly regaining confidence in this primitive faculty. First impressions were all that counted. In a place like this you could not afford to give anybody more than the benefit of a single chance.

"Mr. Prine's all right," Routledge said. "We'll have to keep an eye on him, but eventually he'll be trustworthy."

Both Appleton and Stamper were of a like mind. The final word would belong to the Father, who would interview him tomorrow.

"What probation shall we recommend?" Appleton said.

"Six weeks," Stamper said.

"Routledge?"

"I suggest two months."

"That sounds more like it," Appleton said. "I'll mention two months to the Father. Are we agreed, then, Stamper? Good."

One sunny Monday afternoon nearly a fortnight later, Routledge and Thaine set out with Daniels's beachcombers for the rocks below Azion Point. There were twenty-three in the party, carrying plastic sacks and lengths of cord. Under his PVC slicker raincoat Routledge, like Thaine, was also bearing a bag containing tools, water, and food.

Yesterday and last night there had been another big gale and, though the wind had now lost half its strength, it was still blowing hard from the south-south-east.

Skirting the Warrens, the group passed the thatch-roofed chapel and started along the cliffs, coming at last full into the wind.

The gale had swept all impurities before it. Today there seemed no limit to vision; the eyesight went on and on, effortless, indivisible from the brilliance and clarity of the sky. Across the huge, discolored contours of the swell Routledge could see detail and color on the heaving superstructure of the lightship. Red hull, white girders. The crew had been evacuated on Saturday; it was astonishing that the ship was still there at its moorings, riding the chains.

Astonishing too that the gulls had survived the storm. They were always here, always patrolling, evil Sert's familiars. Among the thrift and stonecrop of the cliffs they raised their young and taught them the harsh basics of the law, expressed in the pinpoint pupil of a small and merciless yellow eye. No meat, dead or alive, was too vile to be disregarded. In the snowy luxury of their plumage they seemed angels of perfect grace. Always clean, always pure, they yet made no secret of the way they lived. Routledge had come to admire them. Talbot had taught him how to identify the usual sorts: herring, common, black-headed, great and lesser black-backed, how to tell these from the gentler kittiwakes of the colonial cliffs. Glaucous and Iceland gulls were occasional visitors, and one member of the bird-watching club had last January seen a rare Sabine's gull.

Just beyond the path, over empty space, a sparse, irregular procession of herring gulls and great black-backs, adults and immatures, was drifting majestically on the updraft, spilling air, sliding across the wind. From time to time as a bird overtook the beachcombing party it might turn its head for an indifferent glance of inspection, but mostly the men were ignored.

Daniels led the way. The climb down from Azion Point was not difficult, and they were soon on the beach which, now at low tide, lay almost fully exposed. The surf was wild and violent, intensely white, broken above the rocks into sticky spray which the wind carried onshore.

The beach had been strewn overnight with dark masses of weed, their holdfasts dislodged or the stems simply snapped by the force of the storm. Scammell immediately found a broken hatch-cover, too big to be carried with the party, which he and Routledge rested at the base of the cliff for recovery later.

"Should do well today," Scammell said, bending to retrieve a capless shampoo bottle in pink, much-weathered polythene. The label, although faded almost to extinction, still bore the image of a seductive auburn-haired woman. "Wouldn't say no to a bit of that," Scammell said, showing it to Routledge.

"No. Nor me."

The image rather resembled Louise. No: it resembled her photographs. Routledge realized with a shock that he had forgotten what the real Louise looked like. He could describe her to himself, list her attributes, but when he tried to picture her face he failed. She had been, she was, the love of his life, and he could no longer even recall what she looked like.

Scammell unceremoniously flung the bottle into the open mouth of his sack.

Christopher he could remember. Christopher in nappies, Christopher at the school gate, Christopher in his pajamas, tucked up in bed after his bath and his story. "Good night, Daddy." That was the last time Routledge had seen his son, on the eve of the half-term holiday, on the Thursday before the arrest.

Whatever else happened, if Routledge did ever manage to get away from this place, he would make sure he saw Christopher once more. When the boy was eighteen or nineteen he would somehow get in touch and send him an airline ticket. Brazil. That's where Routledge had decided to go. Among the chaos and suffering of the Amazon frontier there would be complete anonymity, especially for a fugitive who no one in officialdom even knew was missing: the escapers, one by one, would be reported dead by those left behind.

In the Brazilian lumber camps, on the new highways, there would be work and money for a man who knew one end of a site from another. After a year or two of that, when Routledge had amassed some savings, who knew where he might go and what he might do?

Together with virtually everyone else in the Village, Routledge had not let his slim chances of a place on the ketch deter him from dreaming of escape. The lottery was to be held on Good Friday, April 10, which was now just over a month away. On May 1, if all went to plan, the ketch would be ready to leave. The state of the tide and the phase of the moon would be propitious then. But if the sky was clear, or the seas were too heavy, launch could be delayed until the 3rd. And that was the latest date. The next window for possible departure would be at the next new moon, and by then a new radar system at Cork Harbour would make a secret landing at Courtmacsherry out of the question.

April 10. Thirty-three days to go. A maximum of fifty-six to the launch. He knew the numbers so well he had almost begun counting the hours.

His reverie was interrupted by the sight ahead of a short length of sea-faded orange line, which he picked up and slipped in his sack.

The beachcombing party gradually followed the shore northeastwards. Some of the driftwood was oiled and good only for fuel, but Reynolds found an excellent pallet, barely stained, and Bryant uncovered a beam of what appeared to be mahogany. This, like the pallet and the hatch-cover Scammell had found, was placed under the cliffs to be collected later by donkey-cart.

When the party finally reached Star Cove the sun had long since sunk past the end of Azion Point, leaving the beach in cold shadow.

Without changing their pace, the men continued searching the shore. Ahead, less than three hundred meters away, jutted a small outcrop. Behind this the beach was relatively smoother and more sloping; behind this lay the dark, overhung entrance of the cave.

The vault of the sky, its blue yielding to the violet gray that preceded dusk, was so clear that, with a telescope, one might almost have expected to glimpse the sun reflected on the body of the satellite.

The outcrop slowly approached. To get around it the group split into single file, Thaine and Routledge near the middle, clambering over the boulders, occasionally dislodging smaller rocks with a dry, hollow clatter; on the other side their boots crunched on the shells and cobbles of the beach.

The cave mouth had come at last into view. About three and a half meters high at the middle point and five meters wide, it owed its existence to the same geological folding which had formed the cave where Routledge had taken shelter during his period outside, and which had been responsible for the vast plates and fissures he had seen on his first-ever view of the cliffs.

At the highest tides the sea almost entered the cave. Below the mouth the beach sloped fairly sharply, devoid now of any but trivial obstructions: for, one by one, under cover of fog, the larger rocks had been levered up and rolled aside to leave a narrow slipway nine meters long.

The beachcombers spread out. "See you tomorrow, weather permitting," Thaine said to Daniels, as he and Routledge ducked under the overhang.

Betteridge and Chapman were waiting inside the cave.

"How did it go?" Thaine asked Chapman, giving him his beachcombing sack.

"Like a dream."

Routledge handed his sack to Betteridge and inspected the beginnings of the ketch. Chapman and Betteridge had come down here last night, during the storm, and started the first stage in the assembly process, fitting the heavy members of the hull into the cradle of the building molds which, when fitted with wheels, would also serve as the launching trolley. The wheels had come from a Ferguson tractor found abandoned after the evacuation at the lighthouse. Until last autumn they had been on a horse-drawn cart used for hauling crops. Perished now, the tires were stuffed with turf; Thaine had made the axles and bearings in his workshop.

He and Routledge gave their coats to Chapman and Betteridge and exchanged woolen hats. The two carpenters then joined the others outside. Using a beachcombing party for the changeover had been Routledge's idea; normally all visits were restricted to conditions of bad light, low cloud, or fog.

Thaine and Routledge set down their bags and emptied their pockets of the nails, clench-rings and drift bolts required for the next stage of construction. The light was beginning to fail: Routledge hung a tarpaulin across the entrance and Thaine lit the Tilley lamps. He also lit the kerosene stove to heat water for coffee.

The back of the cave had been fitted with two bunks, a bench, and a rack for the collection of tools which, like the timbers and the prefinished parts leaning against the cave wall, had already been brought down from the Village.

Thaine cast a more detailed and critical eye over the work.

"Everything all right?" Routledge said.

Thaine nodded, running his finger over the finish of one of the scarf joints the carpenters had made.

He looked up and grinned. "Do you want to know a secret, Routledge? I'm really beginning to believe this harebrained scheme might even work."

7

ROUTLEDGE WATCHED AS FRANKS REACHED INTO THE
cardboard box and drew out another slip, which he handed
to Appleton. In total silence the assembly waited for Appleton to unfold the paper and speak the fifth name.

Routledge's hands, fingers tightly crossed, had been thrust
deep in his jacket pockets.

It was nearly noon on the first day of Easter, the ancient
festival of rebirth. Like almost everyone in the lottery, Routledge had hardly slept last night. At dawn he had conducted
Prine to the site of wall-repairs at one of the south-west pastures, where Phelps and Rothstein and a couple of others
who had not entered the lottery were today supervising the
probationers. The weather then had been clear, with a chilly
north-east wind. At mid-morning the sky had clouded over.
There had been squalls of hail, rattling the corrugated plastic
on the roof of the carpentry shop, where the final prefabri-
cated sections of the ketch were being checked.

After the hail the sun had come out again. Banks of cloud
were now drifting south-westwards, out to sea. When they
uncovered the sun its rays felt warm. Spring had returned.
In three weeks it would be the first of May. Soon after that,
Routledge might be in Ireland, heading for the airport. Heading for Brazil.

Appleton spoke the fifth name. "Mr. Blackshaw."

From his place on the veranda, Routledge saw Blackshaw

standing near the back of the crowd, among members of his congregation, which had half an hour earlier emerged from the Good Friday service. Mouth wide, Blackshaw clapped a hand to his brow, was patted and helped towards the veranda with envious but congratulatory gestures.

Three to go. Three chances left. Three out of a hundred and thirty-seven. The final figure for the draw had been a hundred and forty-two. Some had dropped out; others had changed their minds and decided to enter after all. The slips had been prepared yesterday. The tombola drum was an ordinary clothes-issue box with a hole cut in the top. The Father was being as fair as he could, stirring the slips when he put his hand inside, taking his time.

"Mr. Peagrim."

Overwhelmed, the barber came forward to the rail of the veranda and joined the rest of the chosen ones: Redfern, Carr, Thursby, Reynolds, Blackshaw.

Two chances left. Freedom, sweet freedom, two whole chances away. Probability: 0.015. It was going to take a miracle now. "O God," Routledge thought. "You gave a place to Blackshaw. Give one to me. Give one to me. Give one to me and I'll believe in you again."

The upsurge of hope in the precinct became almost tangible.

"Mr. Gunter."

It was then that Routledge knew that God wasn't listening. Knew that he didn't exist. Routledge wasn't going. One place left. He would never get it. Once chance in a hundred and thirty-five. He had never won anything in his life, never would. The judge had been right. He would remain on Sert for the rest of his days. The same feelings of doubt had already begun to afflict some of those remaining in the body of the crowd, more and more as Franks stirred the slips for the last time. He pulled one out, gave it to Appleton.

Appleton unfolded the paper and looked at the name.

"Please, God," Routledge breathed. "Let it be me. This is all I'll ever ask. I promise."

"Mr. Ojukwo."

Ojukwo's scream of delight was like the deflating slash of

a knife. The lottery, so eagerly and anxiously awaited, for so long anticipated, was abruptly over.

Routledge's thoughts returned to an evening in September, to the impending gale and the twilit carpentry shop. He thought of the housewarming party that night and of the quixotic decision he had made. And now, he reflected, thanks to his soft and foolish heart, Ojukwo had won the place that might have gone to him.

God had played his cruelest yet, his most ingenious practical joke.

Routledge's heart, or the place in his chest occupied by his heart, actually felt heavy, physically heavy. Tears prickled at his eyes. He fought them away, pressing his lips together as hard as he could, trying not to let anyone else see. He looked sideways at Foster, at Sibley, Mitchell, Stamper—at the other councilmen, none of whom had been chosen. They too were doing their best not to show their feelings. He noticed that Myers, standing on the steps, had briefly covered his face.

The fortunate eight were taken inside the bungalow by Thaine and Appleton. Franks followed them in; the rest of the Council lingered for a while yet on the veranda.

The remaining slips were emptied out on the trestle table. Appleton opened each one and called the name; the slip was then handed to its owner. When King came to collect his, Routledge gave him a commiserating glance of solidarity.

"Maybe next time," King said, in response.

"Yes. Next time."

Singly or in pairs or threes, the men in the precinct began to drift away.

Franks stood in one corner of the laboratory while each of the winners was measured and weighed. Last on the beam-balance was Ojukwo, at ninety-seven kilos the heaviest of the group. Peagrim was the lightest, registering only sixty-six. He would probably be in position four or seven, paired with Redfern, who was the next lightest at sixty-eight kilos.

After the weighing, the men sat down and Franks explained the full plan, describing the role each individual was expected to take.

He spared them nothing. "Our chances are not good," he said. "What we will be doing, in pitch darkness, during a spring tide on a coast like this, is very dangerous indeed. When she launches, that will be the first time the ketch has ever tasted water. She has no emergency buoyancy. If she leaks, that's it. If she hits a rock, we go down. If something goes wrong and we're caught inside the Magic Circle, we'll get no sympathy from the patrols. The ketch may well be rammed, or she may be taken in tow back to the mainland for examination. Either way, we can expect to be left behind. They won't risk escorting us to the island, and they won't have us aboard the patrol-boat. We have no room for life-jackets. That means we drown."

He looked from one face to another, from Thursby to Carr to Ojukwo. "But if we do succeed in crossing the Circle, our chances will rapidly begin to improve. If the ketch handles as Mr. Thaine predicts, and if Mr. Godwin's electronics behave, only collision with a ship or intervention by the armed forces will prevent us from reaching our destination. Once we make land, success is virtually guaranteed. We are going to Courtmacsherry because that is not far from where I was born. I used to sail in the harbor there when I was a boy, so we'll need no chart to get safely ashore. From the second of May onwards, my wife and some other people will be waiting in a safe house near the landing place. As you know, each of you will be supplied with a passport, the visa of your choice and two thousand punts in cash. Over a period of ten days you will leave the house and be driven to Cork, Dublin, Rosslare, or Shannon Airport, or anywhere else in the Republic you choose. After that it's up to you. Well," he said, in conclusion. "That's about it for now. If any of you are having second thoughts, this is the time to say so."

No one spoke.

"Are there any questions?"

"One question, Father," Reynolds said, hesitantly. "Why are you doing all this for us?"

"You know why. Without this number of men the scheme could never work."

"But the passports and the money. Where do they come from?"

"The money I supply. I still have some in the bank. The passports and visas will be provided by friends in Dublin, likewise the safe house at Courtmacsherry."

"But why should they do that for us?"

"Not for you, Mr. Reynolds, nor just for me. There are many political prisoners on these islands. I'll be honest. When I get to America we're going to blow the lid off Category Z."

"But all that's finished with now," Thursby said. "The European Court and everything."

"The EEC didn't give its approval to what's happening on Sert. The British are breaking their own rules here and they know it."

"Are you in Sinn Fein?" Thursby said.

"I think this discussion has gone far enough, Father," Appleton said.

"I agree," Franks said, surprised that he himself had not stopped it earlier. The truth was that, at long last, he was beginning to allow himself to believe that the attempt might succeed. Uncharacteristically, he was becoming excited; the prospect of liberty had reminded him of the wider issues involved, issues which should not concern the other escapers or interfere with the relationship they had with him. For the moment, they were still on Sert. All that mattered now was getting off. The politics could come later.

But if he were honest with himself, he knew he was not escaping for the cause: he was escaping because he wanted to see Siobhan and his children again. He was escaping because he had to have medical treatment or he might end up deaf and blind. And, most of all, he was escaping because he wanted to be free, free of Sert, of Martinson, of a future spent, like the present, in the iron grip of despair.

After the meeting, Godwin entered the bungalow and came to Franks's office. He seemed unusually withdrawn, deeply preoccupied, and sat in the spare armchair like a man condemned. Franks regarded him closely, waiting for him to speak. When Godwin remained silent, Franks said quietly,

"I understand, Godwin." He had seen this coming. For Godwin, the escape was purely an intellectual exercise. The challenge for him was to outwit the prison authorities and get away with it.

Godwin removed his glasses, covered his face with his hands, and began to weep. "I thought it would be all right. But today suddenly it's real. I can't do it, I know I can't. I'm too old. I'd let the others down. And anyway, I've got nowhere to go. My only friends are here."

"Don't be hasty, Godwin."

"I'm not being hasty. I've thought it through. I want Fitzmaurice to have my place. He deserves it."

Godwin would not be persuaded otherwise. Franks offered him a week in which to change his mind: he turned it down. Godwin wanted to tell Fitzmaurice today. He wanted Caldecote to know immediately so that Fitzmaurice's suit could be made in good time.

"Are you absolutely certain?" Franks said.

"Absolutely."

"I don't want to see you left behind. This project is yours as much as Thaine's."

"Don't make it any worse for me, Father."

Unworthy as it was, the thought now occurred to Franks that Fitzmaurice might want to come to Pittsburgh too. Franks had been prepared to testify to the world's press alone: that would have been sensational enough, but with the two of them side by side the impact would be more than doubled.

Even so, he would sacrifice almost anything to have Godwin along.

"I urge you, Godwin, think what you're doing. You may never get another chance."

"I'm resolute."

"All right," Franks said, standing up. "If that's what you really want, we'll go and tell Fitzmaurice."

For five anxious days after the 15th, the rock on Piper's Beach had stayed untouched. This morning Martinson had found it turned upside down.

That had been the signal; and tonight, bang on cue, a

small, harsh, remote segment of moon slid from wreathing cloud and flooded the landing pad with bluish, ghostly light.

Martinson gave the rope another experimental tug. "Pity it in't Christmas," he said. "Then I could've powdered my beard and worn a red coat. Still, better late than never."

"God's sake, Jim," Obie said. "This ain't funny."

"If this in't funny, I don't know what is." Martinson took a more earnest grasp. "Here goes."

"Make it quick. I don't want to get caught."

"Don't worry. First sign of bother upstairs and you leg it away, like we agreed. Meanwhile keep watching them tombs."

With that, Martinson began to climb. He had left his boots on the landing pad: his feet, wrapped in two pairs of thick white socks, found soft and easy purchase on the roughcast of the lighthouse wall. In the dim moonlight he could see well enough to avoid dislodging any loose patches of rendering. He hoped that to the guards by the tombs, if there were any, he would be invisible. During the descent of the cliffs both he and Obie had worn black. On reaching the landing pad Martinson had stripped off his outer layer of clothing, and now he was clad entirely in white.

Father Christmas did not usually come through the window; but then lighthouses didn't have chimneys, so just this once he supposed it was permissible.

Wayne Pope had been as good as his word and had left a rope dangling from the gallery. Houlihan's room was situated on the third story. He slept on the floor, on a large mattress about three paces from the window. The window was covered at night, during winter, with a firmly fastened wooden shutter. But during the spring and summer it was covered with nothing more substantial than a curtain, so confident was he that the lighthouse walls were unscalable. The door was always kept triple-bolted from the inside. On the staircase outside the door were at least two heavies armed with iron bars. More guards kept watch in the mess: Martinson and Obie had overheard them playing brag, and seen the flickering lamplight at the window.

If anything went wrong, Pope had said, Martinson would

be on his own. The directions, the rope: that was the sum
total of his involvement. Pope was presently in his own room
on the fourth floor. He had tied the rope to the gallery railings
some time earlier this evening and would take it away again
before dawn. For all the lighthousers but Pope, Martinson
was now constructing a version of the classic locked-room
mystery. Unless he were seen disposing of the rope, Pope's
alibi would be as good as anybody's. Obie's job was to as-
certain that Martinson had remained unobserved.

Martinson knew what Pope was planning and had taken it
into account. The risk to his own life, tonight, was at its
greatest. At any moment on the return climb Pope might
appear at his fourth-floor window with a knife and saw
through the rope. It was not just possible, but highly likely,
that Pope had set him up.

Martinson had considered every alternative before committing himself to this course of action. The other main routes
held their appeal, but generated a multiplicity of danger
points, most of them far worse than this, both in Old Town
and here at the light. Since Houlihan had to go eventually,
Martinson had reasoned, an unannounced night visit was the
obvious way to begin.

Houlihan had to go because he was a cunning Irish git who
had no intention whatever of jeopardizing his position by
attacking Franks or the Village. Houlihan was an obstacle,
and like all obstacles had either to be circumvented or, if that
was impossible, removed.

Martinson grimaced. His leg was hurting again. The past
winter had cost him a lot of strength. At one time he could
have shinned up a rope like this with no trouble at all. His
arms felt heavy. Sweat had broken out on his forehead. He
paused, hanging there, four meters above Obie and the landing pad, Houlihan's window another couple of meters up.
Far below, from the rocks of the promontory, came the swirling boom of the sea.

He resumed his climb.

Houlihan's curtain, the deep window-ledge, were just as
Pope had described. Martinson gained noiseless entry, tuck-
ing back the curtain to admit as much light as possible.

Looking off to the side, using the edges rather than the center of his visual field, he examined the room. There was a glimmer of fulmar light along the bottom of the door, but no sound from the stairwell. If the guards were anything like Nackett's, they were probably dozing. Martinson made out the form of shelves, a chair, a cupboard.

A faint gleam of bald skin identified Houlihan's head. As Pope had predicted, he was not alone. Both men were fast asleep, lying on their backs.

Martinson crouched down by the mattress. For a moment he thought the other man was Desborough, whose grief at Peto's passing had, it seemed, taken second place to considerations of the practical merits of remaining here as Houlihan's toss-artist; but, although fair-haired, this kid was not Desborough, but the new meat Nackett had acquired on the day of Peto's death.

From the back of his belt Martinson took a long-bladed survival knife which Tompkins had lost in the wars. In sinister Japanese steel, with a serrated spine and a half-kilo grip, the knife was Martinson's favorite, lovingly brought to scalpel sharpness and, now that the crossbow had gone, the pride of his collection.

He peeled back the bedclothes. Houlihan was wearing a vest, his little friend nothing at all. Houlihan was breathing the more heavily, so Martinson killed the boy first, placing the point directly above his heart and banging down the pommel with the heel of his right hand. Blood welled up, its animal stink filling Martinson's nostrils.

The soft noise of the blow, the victim's quick writhe, seemed to have registered with Houlihan, who uttered a dreaming groan. Being careful not to touch any blood, Martinson pulled out the knife and quickly positioned it over Houlihan's breast.

This was the bit he had been looking forward to. He paused, savoring the moment, before he struck.

Now that it was done he knew he should get out, but he remained there, crouching by the mattress, feeling curiously empty and unsatisfied. He wanted something more, something else: he did not know what.

In the heap of clothing by the mattress he found a pair of cotton underpants which he wrapped around his knife and placed in the spreading pool of blood on Houlihan's chest. When they were soaked, Martinson went to the wall. He was about to write a message, smear it in red, a cryptic message for Pope and all the world to see. *Eli, Eli.*

He stayed his hand. There was yet a part of him which would not allow it. If he were to commit that sacrilege he knew he would be condemned, finally, irredeemably, to the damnation which he already believed was his. He did not care about that; but still he did not write.

Instead he let the underpants drop on Houlihan's face, and wiped the knife clean on the bedcovers.

It was good to get outside once more into the cleanness of the night. Martinson climbed down as rapidly and quietly as he could, keeping especial watch on the window in the fourth floor. Pope did not appear.

"Anyone see us?" he whispered to Obie, pulling on his dark trousers and sweater and then, having removed one of the two pairs of socks, his boots.

"No."

"Sure?"

"I'm sure. You was gone a long time. What happened?"

"Santa delivered the goods. Don't he always?" Martinson glanced at the mess window, just above them and to the right. "Now let's get back to Toytown and cut off Dave Nackett's balls."

8

Who would lead the Village when Franks had gone? How would the new Father be chosen? At last Friday's Council meeting these questions had again been raised and again been left unsettled.

As to the means of choosing, some sort of election seemed the likeliest, contrary as this went to the way the Community had been operated hitherto. But then many changes—such as the abolition of the initiation procedure—had overtaken the Community in recent weeks and months, and many more were bound to follow Franks's departure.

Of his councillors who would remain, none possessed anything remotely resembling his personal magnetism. Godwin, or Sibley, the most senior, were nonetheless improbable candidates for an election. Routledge had already decided he would not put himself forward, even if pressed to do so, which he thought so unlikely as not to be worth further consideration. He was the most junior councilman. If Stamper and Mitchell held no chance, which common opinion had already agreed, then he could hold no more. Besides, he had no taste for leadership. He simply did not want the job.

That left only one councilman: Foster. Given his views on the outsiders, he would be a most popular choice. If Foster became the Father he would immediately declare war on the outsiders and do his best to kill them all, regardless of whatever reaction this would have on the mainland.

Routledge was too worried and frightened to sleep. It was not so much the prospect of Foster as Father that he feared; that was only a contingency and could for the moment be pushed out of mind. There were far worse, far more immediate problems facing him, facing everyone. The alliance of the two outsider camps had at last taken place. Obie had met Johnson, Foster's deputy, this morning to deliver the news: the attack on the Village would be coming tomorrow afternoon. Martinson had personally killed Nackett and Houlihan six nights ago, on April 21. On that same night there had begun a violent realignment of Old Town and the lighthouse, fought out over the succeeding days and now concluded. Although Martinson was the guiding spirit, the new leader was ostensibly a man called Wayne Pope. Pope had been one of Houlihan's most trusted advisers, a member of his brain gang, all but one of whom had eventually sided with the traitor. According to Obie, the exception was being held prisoner in the lighthouse, awaiting death by crucifixion. Martinson was planning the same fate for Franks.

Had Routledge not actually met Martinson and spent time in his company, he would have dismissed such hideous talk out of hand. But now he took it seriously, as did Franks and the whole Council. And he took seriously the warning by Obie that he himself also featured prominently on the list of those for whom special punishment was being reserved. It seemed that Martinson had forgiven neither the theft of the crossbow nor the damage Routledge had done to his house.

"Prine?" Routledge said. "Are you awake?"

No answer. How could he be sleeping?

Prine had completed his probation. At the end of last week he had been made a full member of the Community. He knew as much about the attack as anyone outside the Council, and yet here he was, fast asleep.

If the outsiders were repulsed at all, the man responsible would be Thaine. Routledge wished Thaine were here now, in the Village; but for the past ten days he had been in the cave, alone or with one or more of the carpenters, finishing the ketch. Today the sky had been clear and no one had been able to get down there to warn him. Thaine did not know the date of the attack.

The preparations for defense had been stepped up. Almost everything that could have been done had been done. Foster and Johnson and their helpers had put both outsider camps under full-time surveillance; a system of relayed signals, using Morse-flashing torches in the darkness and semaphore by day, was keeping the Council informed.

Routledge pressed a button on his watch and read the display. Three forty-eight. Less than an hour till dawn. He had not slept at all, but it was no use trying anymore. The night for him was over. Besides, he was due at the bungalow at five.

He climbed out of bed and slipped his feet into his boots. Taking his pocket lighter, he moved to the door and let himself out into the cool, sweet air drifting in from the cliffs. Except for the faint noise of a very quiet and distant jet, passing westwards at a very high altitude, and except for the whisper of waves in Vanston Cove, he could hear no sound.

Tonight it seemed there were more stars than ever. Mainland skies were always polluted, both with industrial haze and with the reflected glare of sodium streetlamps. Here the atmosphere was pure; here the full extent of the heavens was revealed to view. He looked over towards the east, towards the place where the sun would rise. The horizon there was still black.

Entering the latrine, he lit the candle, lifted it on its driftwood sconce and checked for earwigs. In spring and summer especially, the latrines attracted large numbers of these insects, active by night and the quarry in the sport of "wig-frizzling." Much too sadistic for Routledge's taste, this involved using the candle to burn them alive. His use of the candle consisted merely in making sure there were none on the seat or likely to be swept into the bag and drowned.

Rescuing the fourth or fifth earwig with a folded sheet of lavatory paper, Routledge's formless flow of thought was interrupted by a remote sound of shouting. An instant later the gong at the main gate was frenziedly struck, over and over again; there was fresh shouting, much nearer at hand, and the frantic ringing of the gate gong was taken up by the deeper tone of the gong on the bungalow veranda.

He blew out the candle and, shouting now himself, shouting to his neighbors in their beds, ran back to his house and lit the lamp.

"Prine!" he cried, pulling on his outdoor clothes. "Get up, for Christ's sake get up! Get to your station! The outsiders are coming!"

The precinct was already alive with activity when Routledge stepped up to the veranda, dodging the buckets of water with which the woodwork and floorboards were being doused. He noticed that the emergency shutters, specially prepared during the preceding weeks but kept concealed from the outsiders' view, had already been screwed into place, and the front door had been reinforced with a steel panel. Little was being said. Everyone knew his allotted task; the work was proceeding with a smoothly ominous efficiency. As he approached the doorway, Routledge almost bumped into Appleton, who, with a clipboard, was just coming out.

"We've nearly an hour yet," Appleton told him. "Johnson's signal said they were massing at the lighthouse."

"How many?"

"Worse than we thought. Two hundred plus. In one group. It looks like Foster was right. They're probably coming straight for the bungalow."

So much for Obie's warning. He knew he wouldn't be getting a place on the ketch. "Obie's betrayed us," Routledge said.

"I doubt it. He doesn't want Martinson in charge of the island, especially when any one of us might live to tell the tale. He had no choice but to be straight. Martinson must have switched the plans at the last minute. Maybe he smelled a rat." Appleton held out his clipboard and brushed past. "Oi, over here with that cart!"

Routledge had the feeling that, like himself, the Father had not slept during the night. He was unshaven and his eyes were dark with fatigue; when Routledge entered his office he saw a bottle of paracetamol tablets on the desk, a half-empty glass of water beside it. Conferring with Mitchell and Sibley, Franks seemed shorter and smaller than Routledge had hitherto believed him to be, and with a sense of alarm Routledge realized what had escaped him before: the Father was ill. He had the look of a man in perpetual pain. Somehow, previously he had been able to keep it hidden. In normal hours, when everything was under his control, that must have been possible.

"Mr. Routledge," he said, when Mitchell and Sibley turned to leave. He looked beyond Routledge's shoulder: more men were gathering at the door. "It's going to be the frontal assault, we think. You'll be taking Mr. Thaine's place. You know what to do. And I want you to assemble Mr. Appleton's squad for him. He's a bit busy at the moment. Your men will defend B2 as planned. Fall back to the gate if necessary. If they get over the boundary you come back with the rest of us to protect the precinct. I repeat, don't open up unless they threaten the bungalow, and even then not unless there is absolutely no alternative. Understand?"

"I understand," Routledge said, wanting to say something more, to express concern for his health, to convey some message of loyalty and support, but this was not the moment for that.

Before coming to Sert, Martinson, like, he supposed, everyone else, had been fully exposed to drugs. At primary school they had sniffed glue and butane; at the comprehensive and afterwards it had been crack, PCP, ether, heaven's gate, reds, grass, shit, uppers, downers, bennies, zoots, speed, heroin: the list went on and on. He had been friendless even then, but still the others had offered and cajoled. He had refused every time, despite the opprobrium and ridicule this had earned. He had not refused for his grandmother's sake, but because he had felt no need of an artificial high. Compared with the supreme, the antarctic purity of his vision, everything else was mud and shadow. Later he had become increasingly aware of its order and purpose, the deeper meanings made manifest in symbols. It had been building slowly all his life, this irresistible journey into the very heart of things, into the very center of the universe itself. He was a tuning fork. Closing on the center, he had recognized the harmony and known it as his own. And today, this morning, in this mystical April dawn, the vibrations had coincided and there was no more division between out and in:

he was the center and the center was himself. He was a giant. He was unstoppable.

It did not matter that the first attack had been repulsed, that his army had temporarily scattered. Some had fallen, hit by spears or crossbow bolts. Some had been cut down with axes and scythes. Some had fallen in the tangle of the boundary fence and been dispatched with hammers. Many had run along the border to get in elsewhere, and the chapel had been torched; but most had simply retreated and regrouped. With Pope giving the orders, they had advanced again, slightly more disciplined, and driven the villagers back through the gate, back into Franks's territory. With the Village force in rapid retreat, the real fighting had begun.

Bubbles was now in possession of the workshop under the trees. It had been ransacked; smoke was beginning to pour from the broken window. Gomm was besieging the other workshops and the Village houses.

The bungalow too was still being held. Franks was sure to be in there. The windows and the glass doors of his office had been protected with wooden shuttering, obviously prepared well in advance, just like the villagers' battle plans and their armory of spears and barbed-wire morningstars. He must have known about the attack. Someone, Obie perhaps, had been playing a double game. Martinson had not seen Obie since the first skirmish at the gate. If he were not already dead, Martinson would question him later. And if it turned out that Obie had been responsible for this debacle he would soon find himself on the top of Pulpit Head, nailed up beside Franks, Pope and Feely, facing the ocean and the broad southern sky.

Martinson, Pope, and Craddock had hastily arranged a plan of attack, taking the bungalow from the side and rear where it was most vulnerable. Pope had elected to approach the side. Martinson, leading his contingent of forty or fifty men across the garden, began making for the rear.

Almost as he reached the edge of the crazy paving, the big shutters fell or were pushed forward from the doors and hit the ground with a crash. The glass had been slid back: the furnished interior of the room was suddenly laid open, with figures in the background and some at the front, holding what appeared to be some sort of nozzle, enclosed in perforated metal, connected to a hose and then to a steel tank. At the mouth of the nozzle Martinson glimpsed a subdued and faintly sinister glow of heat, like the resting flame of a blowlamp; among those in the room he saw Franks, and among those with the nozzle he recognized Jenkins, and before he could twist and turn aside the glow exploded and blossomed into a roaring nimbus of flame. The blast pushed him off his feet and he was on the ground, half on the stones and half on the lawn. Everything had become orange. The grass blades before his eyes were shimmering slivers of bronze; heat, not air, was what his lungs now breathed. For that long, floating moment he became a salamander. The moment ended with a choking stench of kerosene and the realization that he was on fire. His beard, his hair, his clothes, were burning. Rolling over and over, away from the heat and across the dew-soaked turf, he beat at himself and managed to put out the flames.

It was then that he saw the huge silhouette of the helicopter overhead. Without his knowledge it had arrived and was hovering above the bungalow and garden. As it passed above him he glimpsed a crewman leaning out, directing another nozzle-like object downwards, black and small and threatening; in his confusion Martinson half expected this to spout more destruction, but it was only a camera, a harmless video camera. Louder even than the scream of the engines, he heard an amplified voice shouting unintelligible orders to those below.

He had been fortunate. The men who had been on his right were lying where they had fallen, islands of blazing coal. He saw Jenkins and the others bringing the nozzle and hose and tank out of the bungalow and into the garden. The fire roared again, engulfing a knot of running men. From the side of the bungalow, from the kitchen door, there came another roar and Martinson knew they had a second flamethrower there. Maybe one at the front as well.

The helicopter had slid sideways and was hanging twenty meters above the precinct. "Stop fighting!" its voice was saying. "Stop fighting or we'll use gas! Stop fighting!"

Martinson could not see Franks among the group with the flamethrower, which now was being dragged across the lawn towards the workshop under the trees. That meant he was still in the house.

As if in slow motion, as if in a dream, Martinson examined himself and found that he was whole. There was an iron bar, not his, lying on the charred surface of the grass. He picked it up and, to the blaring helicopter's refrain, started for the open bungalow doors.

"Stop fighting! Stop fighting!"

Mixed with something bright yellow to make it visible, the TK-6 began streaming from outlets in the helicopter's flanks, driven down into the precinct and dispersed by the wind from the rotors. The pilot descended even lower and flew above the bungalow roof.

Martinson had almost reached the doorway when the gas hit him. The effect was instantaneous: an acrid burning in the sinuses and throat, a feeling of needles jabbing at the eyes, disorientation, weakness, loss of control. He wanted to fall to his knees and cover his head, but he kept on, up the step and into Franks's office. He stumbled, put out his hand to steady himself on the tapestry-covered wing of an armchair, and sought in these last few seconds to find his enemy's face among those in the room.

Some of them were concealed by damp handkerchiefs. None belonged to Franks. None belonged to his brother, his counterpart, in whose name and for whose sake solely he had remained alive. Too late Martinson saw, from the right, the downward swing of the morningstar, a rock dressed in barbed wire; he could not avoid it, but rather it seemed as if he were drifting upwards into the blow. The blow that nothing could withstand.

The impact caught him squarely on the head. There was a fleeting bitterness, a sense of loss. The mystery had no conclusion yet. It remained unfinished. And because it would be going on, because it would continue hereafter, he knew at the last that he was wrong.

He had not been forsaken after all.

9

THE FOUR HELICOPTERS WHICH ARRIVED THAT AFTERNOON were not at all like the familiar Prison Service A60 which at midday had returned to gather pictures of the aftermath, and which, before leaving, had ordered the Village to prepare for a visit from the deputy governor.

These four machines were very much bigger and heavier, twin-engined Chinooks liveried in the black and gray camouflage of the Royal Marines. With a clatter that had emptied nearly every building, they had approached the island from the south-east. Franks, standing now in the precinct with Appleton and Routledge and thirty more, had heard them coming in over Beacon Point and Pulpit Head, passing directly above Star Cove where Thaine and Chapman were yet trapped with the ketch. Above the Village the helicopters broke formation and for half a minute hovered, making a formidable and effortless show of strength.

Franks did not want to look at Appleton. He felt too sick, too deeply exhausted. The Village had lost sixteen of its men. Twenty-three more were injured, some critically. Among the dead were Tragasch, Wilson, Flagg, Daniels. Among the worst wounded were Bryant, Phelps, and Fitzmaurice. Sibley and his assistants had already performed several emergency operations in the laboratory. He was still in there, covered in blood, working on Fitzmaurice, who had been speared while trying to defend the electronics workshop.

Franks had been with him when the helicopters had arrived. So had Godwin, holding him down, comforting him as if he were his own son. But, despite all Sibley's care, it looked as if Fitzmaurice was going to die too.

The fire in the workshop itself had gone out, although some of the larch trees had caught light and their remains were still smoldering. At several places on the peninsula isolated columns of smoke, more or less dense, continued to rise into the warmth of the afternoon. The windmill had been torn down and thrown over the cliff, the hut there set on fire. The chapel had burned away completely, as had two barns. The cows and horses and donkeys had been killed. Sheep and goats had been clubbed to death. The outsiders had stolen many more. Luckily they had not penetrated the precinct workshops, nor had more than one or two houses suffered any great damage. It could have been much worse. Without the gas attack it might have proved impossible to drive the invaders back, ragged and undisciplined as their onslaught had proved. And without Thaine's flamethrowers, Martinson would certainly have won.

But then Martinson, his body now lying on the lawn with the others, had won anyway. The Village would never be the same again.

Converging on the springy turf above Vanston Cove, four hundred meters away, the helicopters prepared finally to land. The point had been made. The authorities were all-powerful. Everything, but everything, was on their side.

As, one by one, the Chinooks touched down, Appleton said something and nodded out to sea, where, previously unnoticed, both the gray, lean, Prison Service hydrofoils were waiting offshore.

On landing, each of the helicopters immediately disgorged thirty-five or forty marines in combat dress. When he saw how many had come, Franks felt his heart sink still further. There were more than enough to conduct a search of the Village, of the whole island. If they used metal-detecting equipment they would find evidence of the ketch; they would find the craft itself.

Even before this morning's attack, he had given orders for

the workshops to be cleared of all tools and materials related specifically to boat-building. Any tools whose presence could not be explained in terms of land-based work had been sealed in polythene and buried in the compost heaps, as had the construction diaries, schedules, plans, tide-tables, and copies of the charts Appleton had prepared of the reefs and currents in Star Cove. The fins and suits had been too bulky to hide in this way: there had not been enough watertight plastic sacks to accommodate them. Some had been concealed in the clothing shop; mingled with the goatskins, while the rest had been distributed among the Village houses.

The advance warning of the deputy governor's visit had given Franks time to double-check these precautions. It had also given him some degree of assurance that a search was not being planned.

As the marines disembarked he looked anxiously for signs of the equipment boxes which might have contained sensors. He saw none. The marines were carrying only machine guns.

One group remained to guard the helicopters. The rest advanced on the precinct. In their midst walked a civilian in a green army-style windcheater.

Franks went forward to meet him.

"Is anyone in charge here?" the civilian said.

He was middle-aged, with spectacles and thick, brush-like gray hair. Under the windcheater he was wearing an office shirt and a tie striped in blue and red. This morning he had probably put on his suit as usual. His trousers looked like suit trousers. The windcheater was new, perhaps supplied by the military. His shoes were ordinary black lace-ups. Franks resisted the urge to stare at him, at his tiepin, at his flat, pasty, mainland features. And he resisted the urge to stare at the marines' boots and caps and machine guns, their grimly fascinated expressions. For them this was an afternoon out of the usual routine, something to talk about in the mess.

"Are you in charge?" the civilian said.

"We've got wounded men. You must take them to hospital."

"You would be Franks? Liam Michael Franks?"

"Yes."

"Are you still in charge here?"

"Yes."

"Then I want words with you, Franks." He peered beyond Franks, beyond Appleton and the others, who had slowly approached, and briefly let his eye dwell on the bungalow. "My name is John Yates. I am the deputy governor. You wouldn't remember me. You were before my time."

"Did you hear what I said? We've got wounded men. Some of them are dying."

"I don't doubt it."

"Will you evacuate them?"

"You know as well as I do, I haven't the authority to do that."

"Radio the governor."

"No one has the authority to take any prisoners off the island. You are in Category Z."

Franks felt himself close to physical collapse. "Help them," he said. "For pity's sake, what sort of people are you?"

Yates's face said "Not like you: not murderers and rapists and terrorists," but he made no reply. Instead he turned to one of the marines. "Would your medics be prepared to have a look at them, Captain?"

"Might they have AIDS or HVC, sir?"

"Quite possibly."

"They have neither AIDS nor HVC," Franks said, with all the dignity he could summon. "No one in the Village has AIDS or HVC."

"Where are they?" the officer asked Franks.

"In the house."

"Bring them outside. Into the open there."

"But—"

"We're not going indoors to treat them."

"Mr. Appleton," Franks said. "See if you can find some stretchers."

"We have stretchers," the officer said, and told two of his men to bring them. The stretchers were given to Appleton and Routledge, who, followed by several others, ran off towards the bungalow.

"Well?" Yates said.

"Well what?"

"I'm waiting for an explanation. Where did you get the flamethrowers?"

"We made them, of course. What else did you expect us to do? Sit there and wait to get killed?"

"Where are they?"

Knowing full well that the flamethrowers would be confiscated, Franks had left them on the veranda in readiness. With the marines in close attendance, Yates sternly advanced and climbed the steps. As the wounded men were brought outside, he bent to examine the workmanship and manner of construction, the valves and hoses, the air-vents, the action of the stirrup pumps. Although each of the three flamethrowers had been built to the same pattern, only one had a purpose-made pressure tank. The other two tanks had been improvised from oil drums.

"So this is what you've been using the metalwork tools for, is it?" Yates said, straightening up. "You realize you won't be getting any more kerosene, don't you? Ever. And by way of punishment all other requisitions and privileges will be suspended for two months. That includes mail delivery."

"I would remind you that the European Court—"

"Watch yourself, Franks. You're in more trouble here than you can handle already. My God, to think we even placed some trust in you. Well, from now on we stick to regulations."

"In that case I take it you were mistaken a moment ago and that you will continue to deliver kerosene. I also take it that you will be delivering the full quota of medicines we have never received, the vitamin supplements, the bedding and building materials and all the other supplies specifically itemized in Section Two of the Penal Colonies Act, 1991."

Without hesitation, Yates said, "You clearly misunderstand the law."

"Time-serving bastard," Franks thought. But what angered him most was the motive for this visit. Previous fighting among the outsiders—even the original wars—had attracted no more than a single helicopter taking video pictures for the governor's private consumption. Gas had never been used before, and there had never been a landing by troops. That was partly because the earlier fighting had been on a smaller scale, but mainly because none of it would have shown up on the routine satellite scans of the Americans, the Russians, or any of the EEC countries besides Britain, a number of which continued to oppose the penal colonies. The sudden appearance today of flamethrowers operating at several hundred degrees centigrade must have plunged the Home Office into paroxyms of political terror: the fireballs would have been detectable far out in space.

Yates turned to the officer. "Please take these things away."

"Very good, sir."

Franks watched the flamethrowers—on which so much of Thaine's time and ingenuity had been expended, and for which the men of Community had denied themselves so much kerosene over the past months—disappearing in the direction of the helicopters.

"Do you have any more?"

"No. We do not."

The gas had left him unable to think properly. He could not decide whether to placate Yates or to continue trying to annoy him. Which attitude would make him want to leave the island sooner? Talking law in front of the captain of marines might not have been such a good idea.

"You must realize, Franks, that mechanized warfare between the inmates of any penal institution cannot and will not be tolerated."

"No one regrets this morning more than me. But you in turn, Mr. Yates," Franks said, placing a subtle emphasis on the "Mr.", "you must realize what we have had to put up with from those outside our Village."

"Don't think your achievements here have gone unobserved. We well understand that you have had problems with the other islanders. But, as my grandfather used to say, there's a difference between scratching your arse and tearing it to pieces."

"What then do you suggest? Negotiation?"

"All I'm saying is that, just because this is a Category Z settlement, you men don't have carte blanche to murder each other."

"I thought murdering each other was the general idea. I thought that's why we'd been dumped on Sert, to economize on the government's dirty work and earn the approval of the press."

Yates evidently decided that this part of the conversation had become fruitless. He said, "The governor wishes me to carry out an inspection of some of the facilities you have provided." He turned to the officer. "I'll start by going in here, Captain. I don't think there'll be any trouble, but would you clear the building first?"

Was this the beginning of a search? What if they found the suits? What if they took metal detectors to the compost heaps? Franks's vision momentarily dimmed. He felt giddy. He reached out and gripped the handrail. The head-noises had grown much worse since this morning. Was it the gas, the strain, or both?

"Off here," a marine said, chivvying him and the others from the veranda, down the steps and onto the shale.

Franks saw Yates striding through the doorway into the bungalow.

Bryant, Phelps and Fitzmaurice had been laid on the shale and treated first. Five more wounded men, sitting or standing, were now receiving attention from three medics. Fitzmaurice's loud groaning had been silenced immediately with an injection, his wounds doused with antibiotics and bandaged. Beside him crouched Godwin.

"How's Fitz?" Franks asked Sibley.

With immense weariness in his eyes, Sibley turned and looked at Franks. "If they wanted to, they could have him in hospital within half an hour. Then he might survive."

Franks grasped Godwin's left shoulder and squeezed it. Godwin in turn grasped Franks's hand. If Sibley and Godwin, both British, could forgive Fitzmaurice his crimes, forgive him the carnage at Knightsbridge Barracks, couldn't Yates at least show a spark of humanity? But then Franks remembered the television pictures of the victims, the men and women and children transformed by blast and glass and shrapnel into so much raw meat, and he realized that no one could ever be forgiven for anything. What Fitzmaurice had done was still being worked out. No god could intercede on his behalf. No priest could recite a magic formula to wipe his slate clean. And what Franks himself had done, in Belfast, in Dublin, in London, in Libya, in Boston and New York and Pittsburgh, and yes, here on Sert, that too was still being worked out. And what Yates was doing today, even that would in due course have to be worked out, paid for, and settled. For Yates had a chance this afternoon to do right, to take the wounded men to hospital; but it looked as if he was choosing to do wrong, hiding behind those who called themselves his superiors.

Yates spent a long time in the bungalow. Franks became more and more afraid that he had found something to do with the ketch. Mentally he surveyed the location of all incriminating material and tried to imagine whether or not Yates would discover it. But when eventually he emerged, Yates's expression was just as it had been before. He descended the steps and told Franks he wanted to see the workshops.

Accompanied by half a dozen marines, with more standing by, they toured the precinct. Yates seemed intermittently surprised and impressed. In Thaine's workshop he halted at the lathe.

"Who made this?"

"A man named Thaine. Randal Thaine."

"Did he make the flamethrowers?"

"Yes."

"Where is he now?"

For the first time in five years, Franks was about to utter a deliberate lie. Then he said, "Under the ground."

On the shelf below the bench, sticking up among the bits and pieces in a cardboard box, Franks noticed the gleam of a metal disc marked on its circumference with grooves numbered in increments of ten degrees. A compass card! A bloody compass card! Made for one of the prototypes which had never been finished. From its size it could be nothing but the disc of a steering compass. Even if Yates knew nothing whatever about boats he could not fail to guess its purpose. In today's rush and panic it must have been overlooked.

"This drive belt," Yates said, indicating the rubber belt which disappeared through the ceiling. "I take it this connects with the windmill on the roof?"

"Yes, that's right. Shall I show you?"

Yates was looking at him strangely, as though he had detected a change in his manner. Quickly and suspiciously he glanced from side to side. Then he said, "Is there something in here you don't want me to see?"

Franks tried to remain calm. "Such as?"

"Such as more weapons. Such as another flamethrower made by the late Mr. Thaine. Or a bazooka. Or a surface-to-air missile. After what I've seen here I wouldn't put anything past you."

"Why don't you look for yourself?" Franks went to the storeroom and opened the door, then did the same for each of the cupboards.

Yates, still not satisfied, let his gaze rove over the earthen floor of the workshop. He turned his eyes to the ceiling. "Is there a roof space?"

"No."

Yates took one of Thaine's spanners and on the timber lining of the ceiling produced a dead, unresonant tapping. When he had finished he dropped the spanner on the bench. Franks replaced it in the rack.

Still Yates hesitated. He belonged after all to a species of policeman, with the same nose for evasion and deceit. But he could find no evidence to justify his misgivings, and a moment later he said, "All right, I want to see inside one or two houses now."

Once the inspection was over, Yates delivered another lecture on the evil consequences of further misbehavior by the Village. Finally, some two hours after their arrival, the helicopters and the hydrofoils departed.

Yates had refused another plea to evacuate the wounded. On a blood-soaked mattress laid on a table in the laboratory,

Godwin beside him, and without regaining consciousness, Fitzmaurice died at six o'clock.

"I've decided," Godwin said, later. "He's about the same height and build. It's what Fitz would have wanted. And it's what I want."

"Are you sure?" Franks said.

"Yes, Father. Routledge gets his place."

10

Dominating Routledge's emotions that evening was a contradictory mixture of exhilaration and fear, tempered with regret for the circumstances that had robbed Fitzmaurice of Godwin's place and given it to him. Now that he was confronted personally with the dangers of the attempt, the promise of escape held far less allure; he understood all the more Godwin's decision to drop out.

At dusk, entering the candlelit clothing shop with Godwin, the weaknesses of the scheme loomed larger than ever. Even if the ketch and her sonar worked perfectly, there was still the question of whether the men in the water could survive several hours of immersion. Except close inshore, the sea temperature in this part of the Atlantic never rose much above sixteen degrees centigrade. At eleven degrees, the present temperature, an unprotected man would last, at best, thirty minutes before unconsciousness set in. No more than an hour later he would be dead. A wet-suit could not provide adequate protection in water as cold as that. The only solution was a dry-suit, worn over several layers of woolen clothing, sealing in an insulating layer of air.

In some ways, the exposure suits Thaine had designed were even more daring than the ketch herself. They were certainly the critical element in the whole plan. If they leaked, the escape would fail and everyone would die. It was as simple as that.

There were ten suits, individually sized, and they had been made with wonderful skill by Caldecote, a short, dour, bald man who in mainland life had worked as a cutter in a firm of London furriers. In normal times Caldecote and his helpers were responsible for making the villagers' leather and sheep-skin jerkins and jackets, as well as all the other garments and objects fashioned from animal hides. For goatskin Caldecote had perfected a tanning process, using fish gruel, oak bark, salt, and human urine, which left the leather soft, supple, and virtually indestructible. His workshop in the precinct held a large supply of these skins: the finest had been selected to make the suits.

Goatskin, impregnated with grease to render it water-proof, was the best available substitute for the rubber or ne-oprene material of commercial exposure suits. Tight backstitching with dressed twine fastened the seams, which were welted and sealed with fish-glue. The suit incorporated mittens and bootees; it was donned by means of a slit from neck to navel which was then to be sewn up and sealed. The high collar fitted under and would be glued to an outer collar made from a ten-centimeter section of inner-tube rubber—saved from the front wheels of the tractor. There was also a hood, unsealed, consisting of a layer of aluminum foil sand-wiched between two layers of goatskin: this was likewise intended to minimize heat loss and hence reduce the chances not only of hypothermia but also of detection by the infrared system.

Fitzmaurice's suit was brought out for Routledge to try on. Almost black in color, the outer surface of the leather was a mass of welts and seams, so arranged as to allow free move-ment of the limbs; inside, the suit was entirely smooth. The smell of the pig grease used in the waterproofing process mingled horribly with a residual stink of the tan-liquor.

Routledge was already dressed in the woolens he would be wearing on the night itself. As he struggled into the suit, as it encased him from the toes upwards, he began to feel more and more like a monster in a horror film.

"Stand up straight, please, Mr. Routledge," Caldecote said, drawing together the temporary fastener at the throat.

He looked over his shoulder at Godwin and back at Routledge. "It'll do," he said.

"No alterations needed?" Routledge said.

"Maybe a little tighter here on the neck."

"It's not going to leak, is it?"

"Eight hours. That's the longest Mr. Thaine says you'll need to keep dry. We made up a test piece and it stayed dry for a fortnight. Mind you, you'll be swimming, and we couldn't really test the neck seal, so I suppose your guess is as good as mine, Mr. Routledge."

Routledge allowed him to fit the hood.

"This wants to come in a bit." Caldecote removed the hood and gestured at a stool by the wall: creaking softly, Routledge sat down. "Now we'll see about the fins."

These were frogman's flippers unlike any that Routledge had ever seen before. Shoes made of marine plywood fitted over the bootees of the suit and were held in place with straps. The toe of each shoe was produced into a plywood paddle, to which was fastened a longer and broader flap of rubber. This rubber had come from the legs of wellington boots, cut down the back seam and opened out. Laminated, shaped and feathered to form a swimming vane, the laminate had been fixed to the shoes with rivets and, for additional strength, sewn through with dental floss.

The fins were the right size for Routledge's feet. With minor adjustments to the straps, they would fit him exactly.

Putting on the suit and flippers, finding that they fitted, had raised Routledge's eligibility for Godwin's place from the provisional to the certain. This was the crucial moment. Unless he spoke up now, he was committed. Unless he spoke up now, he would have to play his part along with the others.

He remained silent. Caldecote removed the fins and suit.

Godwin gave a barely perceptible nod of approval.

"Can you come again tomorrow at noon?" Caldecote said, as Routledge, preceded by Godwin, thanked him and left the clothing shop. "We'll have it all ready then."

"Yes, I'll be here."

Crossing the precinct, Godwin said, "When you get back

on dry land, open a bottle of champagne for me. And for Fitzmaurice.''

''And for Fitzmaurice. I won't forget either of you.''

Godwin gave an embarrassed shrug, staving off further talk along these lines, and continued towards the bungalow, where an emergency Council meeting was shortly to be convened; Routledge first went home to change his clothes.

After the meeting Routledge called on King, who had been sitting at his table, writing a long letter to his sister.

''Well?'' King said, anxiously. ''Are you going?''

''Yes. We leave on Friday night, if the weather's good.''

King's face lit up. ''That's great, Routledge. Really great. Of course, it's terrible about Fitzmaurice, and I'll be sorry not to have your ugly mug around anymore, but all the same . . .'' He smacked his fist into his palm. ''Hell's bells, Routledge, but that's great! Three days from now you could be on your way!'' He peered around at his shelves. ''Where's my Black Label?''

As they sat drinking, Routledge gave King some of the news from the Council meeting. Sibley, Foster, and Appleton had delivered their final reports on the day's damage. With the death of Fitzmaurice the number of fatalities had risen to seventeen, but was unlikely to rise any further: Bryant and Phelps seemed to be out of immediate danger. All the dead had now been buried. Not counting those who, unseen, had been carried away by their comrades, at least forty outsiders had perished, many of them by burning. The number of injured outsiders was extremely high. Pope was dead and the rest of Houlihan's brain gang were in disgrace: Feely had been released and was now in charge at the lighthouse, while two of Nackett's men had resumed control at Old Town. It was unlikely that the attack would be renewed for a long time yet, if ever. Obie, who had supplied this information, had again asked the date of the launch and had again been fobbed off. However, as a reward for his services, and to keep him quiet on the question of future boat-building, he would, despite his past, be offered a probationary place in the Village.

Work was in hand to repair the border fortifications, the

main gate, and the electronics workshop. The windmill would be rebuilt as soon as possible. Plans to reduce the impact of the two months' suspension of helicopter drops had been drawn up and rationing of kerosene had already started.

Thaine was still in the cave. At dusk, the first available time, Betteridge had been sent down there to relieve Chapman and to take Thaine food and drink and news. Chapman had returned to the Village and reported that the ketch was virtually complete and ready to sail. All else being well, she would leave as planned.

Two factors made Friday ideal. First, it was the night of the new moon and hence, secondly, an especially high tide which would reach almost to the cave mouth. This tide was due at forty minutes after sunset, giving slack water at nightfall when the launch had to be made. Slack water would allow the reefs to be negotiated in much greater safety; a strongly ebbing tide might draw the ketch onto the rocks, while a flow tide would make the work of the swimmers very much more arduous. The launch had to be made at nightfall in order to get as far as possible from the island by daybreak. Thaine had estimated that it would take no longer than six hours to swim-push the ketch beyond the Magic Circle, giving two hours' sailing time before sunup. At a minimum cruising speed of five knots, this would put twenty-five kilometers between the escapers and Sert before the optical cameras again became fully functional. The duration of the whole voyage to Courtmacsherry would be something like forty-eight hours. Landfall would be made on Sunday night.

"That's a good time to arrive," Routledge said. "But then leaving on Friday depends on the weather. If the sky's clear we'll have to wait. The infrared would be too sensitive to risk it."

"What's the forecast?"

"Good. Cloud building from the south. Possibility of rain."

King's expression became more serious. "If this getaway comes off, Routledge, you realize it could mean the end of Category Z?"

"I know." Routledge put down his glass. His adrenalin

had run out: and that was all that had been keeping him going. He had not slept in over forty hours.

King, acknowledging this signal that Routledge was about to depart, suddenly smiled and said: "I'll make you a promise. If ever I'm transferred to the mainland and you come to see me, I might even let you win a game with that pathetic fianchettoed bishop of yours."

The speed with which Routledge had become a member of the crew had left him completely unprepared. It was impossible to adjust so quickly to the knowledge that, one way or another, he now no longer faced a lifetime on Sert.

The remaining hours and days passed so rapidly that there was not enough time for all the farewells he wanted to make: to each of the villagers, to the way of life that had become his, and even to the island itself. When, in the first twilight of Friday morning, he arrived at the cave, he found that in his hurry to be gone he had forgotten to take his leave of the house. Most of his possessions he had bequeathed to King and Prine; most of the rest had gone to the common store. As luggage he had been allowed only a few snapshots and one other item of sentimental value, the belt King had given him at Christmas. Everything else would be provided at the other end. Assuming they got there.

He was the tenth crewman down. Already waiting, sitting close to the walls of the cave, were Thaine, Ojukwo, Redfern, Peagrim, Carr, Blackshaw, Gunter, Reynolds, and Thursby. Chapman had also come down to assist Betteridge, who had been here since Tuesday: the two carpenters would retrieve the trolley after the launch and remain on hand with flashlights and a line in case there was trouble immediately inshore.

"What's the weather doing?" Thaine said.

"Still cloudy," Routledge said.

In the dim glow of a solitary pressure lamp, he acknowledged the others and took his place beside Thursby. Before him, dominating the interior of the cave, almost filling its length, stretched the dark, smooth bulk of the ketch.

She exhaled a smell of glue, timber, wax, her own special

odor of newness. With her bows tilted slightly downwards, facing the beach and the open sea, she was already anticipating her own departure; she was the source and focus of the rising sense of excitement in the cave. As his eye marveled at the clean beauty of her lines, Routledge could not help but wonder whether in some inanimate way the ketch could feel the excitement too. Her creation was complete. He could name each of her components, but he could not name what she had now become.

Almost filled as she was with water, she was imposing a tremendous burden on the trolley. The turf-packed tires had been crushed nearly flat, and for a moment Routledge doubted whether the ketch could be moved at all, still less wheeled down to the sea.

Franks and Appleton arrived five minutes later. Unlike the others, they had not brought drysuits or fins, for they would be traveling inside the hull, taking turns at the pump and the helm. Appleton had brought a packet of letters from the other villagers to their families and friends, to be posted beyond the censor's reach, and Franks, from a bulky holdall of food and water, produced a pocket radio which he tuned to BBC Radio Four and placed among the stones near the mouth of the cave.

The first weather forecast of the day came at five to six.

". . . light rain already affecting Northern Ireland will spread slowly south and east, reaching Wales and western districts of England by mid-afternoon . . ."

Franks held up his hands to silence the excited reaction to these words.

". . . a wet picture I'm afraid for the weekend, extending into Bank Holiday Monday, with temperatures rather lower than the seasonal average."

After the news bulletin and a farmers' price report came the shipping forecast. There were no gale warnings. The tinny loudspeaker, driven by a woman's voice, gave a general synopsis of falling pressure. Then came the vital information, the sea area forecasts for the next twenty-four hours. For sea area Lundy, in which lay Sert, for the neighboring areas of Plymouth, Sole, Fastnet, and Irish Sea, the story was much the same. ''Lundy, west or north-west three to four, drizzle or rain, poor.'' Light winds, rain, poor visibility. Except for the wind direction, conditions could hardly have been better.

The second shipping forecast of the day, broadcast at five to two, showed little change. Routledge did not hear it: he and most of the crew were sleeping, making themselves as comfortable as they could. By the time he awoke, at half-past five, the drizzle had begun. Twenty minutes later the third shipping forecast reported a slight northward shift in the wind, but was otherwise unchanged.

''That's it,'' Franks said, and switched off the radio. ''We go tonight. Three and a half hours to launch. We'd better have supper.''

The two kerosene stoves had been lit earlier and now Chapman handed out the coffee. This was the last hot drink Routledge would have until Sunday night. Munching on a sandwich, he looked around at Franks, who was again studying the charts of Star Cove. Routledge looked at Thaine, spooning yogurt from a plastic tub; at Peagrim and Thursby, everyone. He wanted to speak. He wanted to say that, no matter what happened tonight, even if it all went wrong and he drowned, he would rather his end came here, with them, than anywhere else on earth. He wanted to tell them how much the past ten months had meant; how the Village and the island had, completely and irrevocably, changed him and the way he viewed the world. But he could not. He was tongue-tied, silenced by the intensity of his own feelings. His future, formerly so complicated with mainland hopes and dreams and contingencies, had been reduced at last to black and white, to yes or no, on or off, alive or dead. And he was equipped for it. He had been prepared; was ready to accept whatever this voyage held.

As the hour drew nearer he recognized signs of the same fatalism in some of the others, in Reynolds, Blackshaw, Ojukwo, Franks himself. For the rest, the escape attempt was an act of desperation pure and simple, an all-or-nothing shot.

At seven-thirty they began putting on their suits, having

taken a last chance to urinate and void their bowels at the back of the cave. Each man's suit took twenty minutes to seal. Thaine and Ojukwo helped Routledge. Lying on his back, he watched as they sewed tight the open vent from navel to neck, fitted the welt and worked warm glue into the joint. When that was done he stood up and, placing a tightly fitting polythene bag over his head to protect his ears, pulled on the rolled rubber collar. Thaine spread the glue and carefully unrolled the collar, making a watertight seal.

Carr was the last to be sealed up. Chapman extinguished one of the Tilleys and turned down the other until it gave only the faintest light. He then removed the tarpaulin from the cave mouth.

Franks took a final glance outside. It was quite dark.

"You all know your places," he said.

Appleton climbed up the makeshift ladder and in through the cockpit hatch.

Franks turned to Chapman and Betteridge. "Goodbye, my friends."

"Goodbye, Father."

"Tell Mr. Foster I'm thinking of him. Of you all."

Then Franks too had disappeared inside the hull, and Routledge had taken his position at the third handgrip on the port side, ahead of Peagrim and behind Ojukwo. When each man had fastened his safety line, Chapman and Betteridge added their weight to the stern. "One," Thaine said. "Two. Three. Now!"

At that moment water began cascading from the sprinkle-bar along the ridge of the deck. The wheels of the trolley turned, reluctantly at first, and, as the inertia was overcome, more quickly. With all his strength Routledge heaved forward, trying not to trip himself over with his fins, repeating in his thoughts only the most mundane and ridiculous words: "Here goes!", and they were out of the cave, rain and fresh air on the exposed skin of his face, pushing downhill in pitch darkness across three or four meters of beach. The carpenters had dropped back. The force of a breaking wave momentarily checked the impetus of the run, lifting the bows as they smashed into the surf. Routledge, his feet and ankles and legs hampered by water, continued running for an instant longer before he lost his footing and the boat herself, dragging him forward, pulled him into a horizontal position. The trolley ropes reached their extent. The trolley stopped dead and with a brief, sickening grinding of her twin keels the ketch was free. His suit pressed flat against his skin, Routledge found himself swimming. There was nothing below him. He half rotated, so that his face was clear, and, clutching the handgrip, began furiously kicking.

The reams of calculations he and Thaine had made were coming good. The ketch was stable, almost submerged, with no more than a few centimeters of the hull exposed. Taking water now from a valve in the stern rather than the built-in tank, the sprinkle-bar continued pouring out its cold, cunning mask of sea. A second valve in the highest part of the deck supplied the cabin with air.

Once they were beyond the surf, Routledge heard Franks's voice, coming through the polythene-sealed grilles of the helmsman's two-way address system.

"Sonar's working!"

And so was Routledge's suit. No water, not even the tiniest amount, was coming in. Only his head felt wet, his face slapped by the sea and continuously washed by the rain and the heavy outflow from the deck.

"Any leaks?" Thaine called out to his fellow swimmers. There were none.

"One two three half!" Franks cried, ordering Thursby, Reynolds, and Thaine, on the starboard side, occupying positions one to three, to halve their efforts: the bows began turning in that direction.

"Reef ahead! Gap depth three meters. Range eleven meters. All half! Three four slow! Two slow! Seven eight full! All dead slow! Nine full! Nine half! Nine slow! One ten stop! All stop! Range seven meters. Five meters. Three."

Below him Routledge sensed the deadly upward thrust of the rocks. Keeping himself as horizontal as possible, riding on the swell, he let the gliding momentum of the ketch take him forward and over.

"We're through. All half. Anyone touch?"

When there was no response, Thaine said, "No touch."

The sky was so dark that Routledge could see nothing at all. Looking back towards the beach, the bulk of the cliffs seemed to form a blackness denser even than the night itself.

"All forward! Reef ahead! All slow!"

That reef passed; and another; and yet another. At the fifth there was much difficulty and delay. The swimmers had to reverse direction several times before Franks was satisfied. "Range nine meters," he said. "All half."

As Routledge began kicking again he heard a curious noise, a ventriloquial chirping, with squeaks and chatters apparently coming from several directions at once.

"What the hell?" Franks shouted. "The bloody sonar's gone haywire! All stop! One two nine ten reverse! All stop! All stop!"

The chirping grew louder, became closer, and closer still.

Routledge felt something large and insistent pushing against his flank, investigating, nudging.

"No!" Peagrim screamed, suddenly hysterical. "No! No! Keep away!"

"What's happening?" Thaine said.

Routledge extended his free hand. Beneath the goatskin palm of his mitten he felt an inexplicably smooth, gently curving surface. In the moment before he realized what it was he was still in control of himself, still a rational human being. His brain had not yet had time to understand.

And then it did.

His hand was exploring the receptively stationary snout of a killer whale.

11

THERE WERE AT LEAST HALF A DOZEN, POSSIBLY AS MANY again.

Blackshaw, the chaplain, began gibbering prayers.

"Shut up!" Ojukwo said, several times.

Blackshaw took no notice.

What was it Talbot had said? Killer whales never attacked people. Not unless provoked. It was imperative not to upset or excite them.

"I said to shut up, you stupid bugger!"

Routledge heard a dull thud; Blackshaw was silenced. "For God's sake, Ojukwo! Don't do anything sudden!"

Why didn't killers attack people? The taste, Talbot had said, or the strange feel of human skin. But the dry-suits smelled of pig grease and tan-liquor, and would make their wearers seem like nothing so much as some new and possibly edible sort of marine mammal. Were the whales waiting to strike? Were they puzzled? Did they think the ketch was one of their own kind, sick, perhaps, or injured, in need of rescue from these ten strangely finned creatures? In need of an escort ashore, to the beach?

O Holy God. It was back again, nuzzling his arm, his chest.

The chorus of chirruping had grown. There was an occasional soft report of air and spray expelled through a blow-hole.

Thaine managed to say, "They're this side now as well."

"I can't tell where we are," Franks said. "We could be moving onto the reef."

The pulse length and frequency of their sonar emissions had to be interfering with the receiving transducers. For as long as the whales remained in the vicinity of the ketch, Franks and Appleton would be blind.

There was a grating bump and Routledge felt his legs lightly touching rock. Ojukwo cried out.

"Carr and Gunter reverse," Thaine said. "Slowly. Very slowly. Now Peagrim and Redfern. Appleton, keep the pump going!"

The ketch drifted backwards. The whales squeaked and chattered.

"Are you all right, Ojukwo?" Routledge said.

"Yeah."

He didn't sound it: he sounded as though he were hurt.

"Has your suit been torn?" Thaine said.

"No."

Blackshaw began again. "Holy Father deliver us from evil! For thine is the kingdom, the power and the glory!"

Go on, you old bastard, Routledge had said, all that time ago, flinging his challenge up into the thunderstorm. *Do your worst.* It seemed the old bastard had been clever, biding his time, waiting his chance to answer such a challenge as it deserved.

He was here again tonight, among the whales. He and the whales were one. There was no distinction between them. None at all.

Blackshaw didn't understand. The whales were not evil. If they attacked, it would be because they had decided the flippered, leathery creatures could be regarded as meat like any other. But somehow, despite his brain-numbing terror, Routledge began to know that they would not attack. They were just curious. Highly advanced, gregarious, playful, they had simply been attracted here by something new in their environment. Their power, their supreme potential for aggression and speed and mayhem, was being held in check by a consciousness that was essentially benign. The selfsame consciousness that inspired the whole world; the same that had plucked Routledge from suburbia and brought him here to this point of darkness. Errant, bumptious, obnoxious children occasionally needed to be reminded exactly who was boss.

The pitch and intensity of the chirrups increased. Routledge heard a clear, bird-like whistle, repeated several times. The chattering grew louder. Again he felt the force of a blunt snout, pushed into his flanks, driving the lesson home. Then it was withdrawn.

"They're leaving!" Thursby said.

It was true. Abruptly the chorus of chirps died almost to nothing. Two, three, four blowholes sounded, moving away, parallel with the shore. The whales had gone.

"Is everyone all right?" Thaine said.

"I've cacked myself," Redfern said.

"Me too," Carr said.

"That doesn't matter," Thaine said. "You won't lose any heat because of it."

"Extra insulation, in fact," Routledge said, close to weeping with relief.

"Hey, Blackshaw," Ojukwo said. "Sorry I hit you. But when you come it with that God jazz you make me want to puke."

"My prayers were answered," Blackshaw said.

Routledge smiled and shook his head in the darkness.

"And mine," Franks said, from his place at the sonar. "Let's get back on it. Range eleven meters. Nine ten half. Eight half."

Routledge began to paddle his legs once more.

"Gap depth two point five meters. Three four five half! All slow! All stop! Range four meters! Two!"

After this there was one last reef, easy to pass. Franks relinquished the helm to Appleton and took over at the pump.

For some time the men swam in silence. Routledge found himself becoming almost warm with the effort. He could not believe that the escape was working. The flavor of the moment was so unreal that, with the regular, easy motion of his fins, he began drifting into a sort of reverie, his thoughts about the whales growing fragmented. He started thinking of the men left behind, of King and his awkward, embarrassed farewell; of the prospects for the future now that Foster looked like becoming the new Father.

He heard Ojukwo speaking, using his name.

"What was that, Ojukwo? I didn't hear."

Ojukwo's voice sounded feeble and very odd. "I said, it was you, wasn't it? It was you put that note in my pocket."

Routledge was on the verge of lying. "Yes," he said. "It was me."

"We appreciated that, Routledge."

"Ojukwo? What's wrong?"

Ojukwo did not answer.

"You've torn your suit, haven't you?"

When Ojukwo again failed to reply, Routledge knew that the attempt would have to be abandoned. The cockpit hatch would have to be opened, the lading changed: and for that to happen the ketch would have to rise and make itself known to the Magic Circle.

"Answer me, Ojukwo! Thaine! Thaine! Ojukwo's torn his suit! We've got to get him on board!"

"Did you hear that inside?" Thaine said.

"Yes," Appleton said. "I'm shutting the inlet valve now. Try to get him out of the water. We'll break the hatch seals just as soon as we can."

The handgrips were so spaced that the swimmers were set far enough apart not to interfere with one another's movements. Ojukwo's handgrip was about two meters along from Routledge's.

"Can you help me, Blackshaw?" Routledge called out. He checked his safety line and began groping his way forward along the hull.

Even before he reached Ojukwo's empty handgrip he had guessed the truth.

Ojukwo, the dying Ojukwo, had cast himself adrift.

It was no use searching. They had no ropes or lifejackets, no means of finding or retrieving him. They did not know how far away he might be, or in what direction. There was nothing to be done except open the valve, work the pump once more, and continue, guided now solely by the compass. Reynolds, who had occupied the position on the starboard side corresponding to Ojukwo's, unfastened his safety line and with great caution moved back, past Thaine and Redfern, to the stern. Taking up a position between Carr and Gunter, he tied his line to Gunter's grip.

At midnight, after two hours of paddling, the swell grew noticeably rougher. Franks said they had emerged from the shelter of the Village headland and were probably about level with the Mare and Foal. From now on they would be in open ocean.

The swimmers rested for ten minutes, rising and falling, pitching and rolling with the ketch. Routledge queasily shut his eyes. Seasickness aside, he already felt exhausted, utterly drained, and he began seriously to doubt his ability to keep up. The other men had been prepared to some extent with three weeks of special exercises; they had eaten a high-carbohydrate diet, increased in the closing stages to four or five thousand calories a day. Routledge had been on this diet too, but only since Tuesday.

A wave cuffed his face and he spluttered. He had to keep awake, to draw on his innermost reserves of strength.

The rain had become less heavy, but the night was just as dark and there was no differentiation between land and sky. Intermittently, when the wavecrests allowed, the flash of the southern lightship could be seen, red from this angle, indicating danger. Its sister flash, from the northern lightship, was as yet obscured by the cliffs of the long north-western coast.

It struck him then for the first time that he was no longer on the penal colony. The sea no longer held him captive. There was space between the island and himself. Even if he were dead by morning, he knew that now, at this moment on Friday night, he was free.

They went on again, and it soon became increasingly difficult to make effective progress. But then, off the end of Azion Point, they encountered a tidal stream which bore them west by north-west, roughly in the direction they wanted to take, and by one o'clock, when the impetus of the stream faded, Appleton said they were more or less on schedule. The northern lightship had been visible for some time. The ketch was at least three or four kilometers from the coast.

By the time Franks gave the order to use the rangefinder, Routledge was light-headed with nausea and fatigue. His whole body seemed to be lagging several seconds behind, yet his legs had continued kicking, responding to some other command than mere will. He had become an automaton, a slave to keeping going, to the forward motion of the ketch.

"Stop swimming, Routledge!" Peagrim said.

Redfern opened a compartment in the transom. He took out the rangefinder, gave it to Thaine. Just above the surface of the deck, below the sprinkle-bar, Routledge saw a faint yellow glow. It belonged to a miniature penlight, encased in transparent polythene and taped to the body of the rangefinder. The bulb was just strong enough to illuminate the white tips of the crossbar. Thaine's face remained in darkness.

Routledge waited, his head hanging, his mouth barely clear of the sea.

After an interminable period, Thaine said, "We've done it."

"Are you sure?" said the loudspeakers, Franks's voice.

"There's even a bit to spare. We must've been in another current."

The flow from the sprinkle-bar continued for a while longer, pumping out the tank. As the tank emptied, Routledge's handgrip rose a centimeter or two, three, four. From the cockpit came the thumping of a mallet. Franks or Appleton was freeing the turnbuckles.

"It can't be happening," Routledge breathed, as the cockpit hatch opened, releasing into the rain an indirect glow from the cabin and sonar lights. The hatch was twisted and drawn inside. Franks's head appeared.

Without speaking, he handed out unwrapped chocolate bars to the swimmers. Routledge could not face his. He had even forgotten what came next. Then he saw. Appleton was passing the water-filled goatskins up to Franks, one by one.

Franks rolled each of them over the side. The ketch began rising more quickly.

Peagrim was the smallest. He was due on board first. Helped by Carr and Reynolds, Franks pulled him over the stern and into the cockpit. The flow of goatskins resumed. As the skins were jettisoned so too were the timber cradles in which they had been held.

Redfern went inside next. Blackshaw. Thursby. More goatskins rolling out, rolling into the sea, rolling submerged, rolling away across the Atlantic to be washed up in Wales or Maine or Trinidad.

By now the ketch was riding high. Routledge had lost his handgrip. Only his safety line remained to preserve him.

"That's the last skin gone," Franks said.

Appleton clambered from the cockpit, wearing a safety harness, a flashlight strapped to his forehead.

Routledge could not go aboard yet. He was one of the six swimmers who had to wait while the forward deck shell came off and the mast sections were unpacked and assembled. The mizzen mast was raised first, then the mainmast. The rigging and sailbags emerged from the cockpit, were handed forward to Appleton.

"Quick!" Thaine shouted. "Kill the lights! Kill the lights!"

Routledge did not understand.

"Appleton," Thaine said, "do you hear it?"

"Yes."

Routledge listened and heard it too, the drone of aero engines coming up from the south-east. From the direction of the mainland.

Carr said, "It's the helicopter."

"They've spotted us," Gunter said.

"Can you see anything, Appleton?"

"No."

The noise grew louder. Straining to hear, Routledge persuaded himself there was another, underlying throb not possessed by the helicopter's engines. Then he changed his mind. Carr was right: this really was the helicopter. Twenty minutes ago, out in space, or on one of the lightships, somewhere in the silicon microcircuitry of the computers, a square meter of wet plywood surrounded by hooded human heads, dwarfed by the vastness of the sea, of the planet surface, had been enough to divert a flow of electrons and throw a digital switch. The ketch, a tiny glowing blip on a phosphor screen, had shown up at last.

Away to the south he saw the flashing green, red and white navigation lights, approaching at a slow but relentless rate.

"Godwin got it wrong," Carr said. "Five kilometers, he reckoned. Fifty, more like. The launch'll be here next."

"Shut up!" Thaine said. "Shut up and listen!"

"It's a plane," Redfern said, after a moment.

"That's right! It's a plane! And it's going past! Look!"

Without knowing the range, it was impossible to know the size or altitude of the aircraft, but now it seemed its course was taking it farther to the west. It was not going to come any closer than this. And, as it drew level and continued on its way, as it faded into the distance, the engine note sounded so different that Routledge wondered how, even for a second, he or anyone else could have confused it with the familiar whine and clatter of the helicopter.

"Turboprops," Thaine said.

The cabin lights came on again. Appleton resumed his work with the rigging. Peagrim helped Franks to fit the rudder. Thaine and Carr went aboard. Then it was Routledge's turn. Hands and arms reached down. The encouraging voices receded. He felt his wrists being grasped, felt the strain on his shoulder and ribcage, and it was all too much for a mind already wandering on the shores of release, craving the dead weight of the numb anesthetic that now fell in on him from above. With a soft, glad, yielding roar it pushed him downwards and back, towards Ojukwo, down into the fading depths, down and down and down.

When he awoke only a minute or two had passed. His suit had been removed and he was lying in the cramped space of the cabin, occupying the whole length of the starboard bench, looking up at the dimly lit plywood roof. Beside him Thaine was busy with the lockers, handing out sweaters and trousers.

"What happened?" Routledge said.

"You conked out. You all right now?"

Routledge sat up, leaning on an elbow. He felt deeply ashamed of his weakness. Handing out the clothing had been one of his tasks. "Yes," he said. "I'm all right. I'm sorry. What can I do?"

"Not much. Everyone's on board." Thaine squeezed himself against the bulkhead and allowed Carr and Thursby to go past, moving forward.

Routledge saw that he was in the way. He got himself to a sitting position, accepted a pair of trousers and wriggled into them. "Where's the best place for me?"

"Aft."

There was no room to spare except in the companionway next to the cockpit, where Franks had switched on the binnacle light and was holding the tiller.

On deck, Peagrim and Redfern were helping Appleton with the shackles and halyards of the mainsail. The small mizzen sail had already been hoisted a meter or so, and below his feet Routledge felt the hull and keels beginning to respond. The ketch knew what was coming next. He saw Franks's face, lit from below, the electric glow glinting in the lenses of his spectacles. "Well, Routledge," he said. "Are you ready?"

Routledge did not reply. He couldn't.

Peagrim came aft and with a squeaking of blocks hoisted the slithering expanse of the mizzen sail.

It went up into the night, and as it went up it filled with air and began exerting the first of its pressure on the mast and, through the mast, on the hull. The ketch, until now slack and lifeless, randomly tossed by the waves, had been transformed into a sailing boat.

"Swig it tighter," Appleton said. "Tighter yet."

Franks had one hand on the tiller, the other ready with the sheets.

"That's it."

With a glance at Routledge, Franks pushed the tiller hard over, bringing the boat's head into the wind. Then, to Appleton, he said, "Raise the mainsail."

PART FOUR

1

To avoid further conversation, Routledge put his head close to the perspex and looked out, past the reflections, beyond the drying concrete of the runway to the close turf where a radar dish was lazily revolving. After a dull day, the evening was sunny and warm. He watched an Amoco fuel tender driving past, manned by two Irishmen with houses and families no doubt in Ennis or Limerick, men who probably knew little and cared even less about anything but their own concerns; it struck him then that for people such as these Sert did not exist. And again it really felt as if his links with the island were on the point of being severed. He felt a sudden surge of nostalgia, of loneliness; he would never see Franks again or be able to thank him for this moment.

He turned to the right, looking across the aircraft and out through the opposite window at the terminal, still expecting a police car, a last-minute dash across the tarmac, an order for extradition.

"Are you going on after New York?" said his companion, a woman traveling alone, American, not yet middle-aged. She was dark, quite pretty. Wore perfume, a wedding ring. Had brown eyes.

Yes: he was going to Rio de Janeiro. To Brazil. "Only on an internal flight," he said.

"Where to?"

Where should he say? "Baltimore."

"On business?"

"No. Visiting friends."

Routledge looked out at the runway once more. He wondered what Franks was doing now. He wondered what all of them were doing. He thought of his days at Courtmacsherry, of Franks's wife, of the nameless man who had driven him to Limerick. Last night he had stayed in a hotel in the city center. This afternoon he had taken the bus out along the Ennis road to the airport. The terminal lounge had seemed full of priests, all going to New York or Boston. It had been hot and damp in there, smelling of wet raincoats. Routledge had sat by himself with a magazine, occasionally visiting the buffet for coffee. As in Limerick itself, he had felt intimidated by all the people, the noise and bustle. On the street outside his hotel he had nearly got himself run down by a taxi. Between arriving yesterday and presenting his boarding pass, he had spoken only to receptionists, to waiters and salesgirls, and to the clerk at the Pan Am check-in desk. And now to this woman. She had initiated the conversation. Routledge turned back and smiled nervously.

In her expression he saw that she found him interesting, even mysterious. He was not like the other men on the plane.

The engines were started.

"Your belt," she said.

"What?" he said, thinking she meant the one he was wearing.

"Your seat-belt." She nodded at the illuminated sign.

"Oh yes. Thanks."

The pitch of the engines increased and the aircraft began slowly to move. Routledge could not prevent himself from looking again at the terminal: still no gardaí, no flashing beacons or wailing sirens. The stewardesses retreated along the aisles, checking seat-belts and hand luggage, and retired to their own seats at the rear of the cabin.

Turning at first through a sharp angle, the big Boeing taxied across the concrete, the tires thumping on the cracks between the slabs. The terminal was left far behind. Routledge saw a hare running across the turf beside the runway. The aircraft halted while the pilot opened the throttles. This was the moment. The last-ever moment on Irish soil. The last-ever moment on the soil of the British Isles. He thought again of Louise, living in some house he would never see; and he thought again of Christopher, his son, who in ten years' time might also be leaving on a westward flight like this.

The engines grew louder, louder, building to a scream, and still the aircraft remained where it was. The wing below and behind Routledge's seat stayed aligned exactly with the cracks in the runway, not moving a centimeter. He clutched his armrest. Why weren't they moving?

And then they were. Gathering speed, the white and yellow markings on the concrete gradually coalesced, losing their individuality, faster and faster until, as the acceleration grew, Routledge felt a push in the small of his back and knew that he was airborne.

About the Author

RICHARD HERLEY was born in England in 1950 and educated at Sussex University. Except for a brief period in California's Marin County, he has lived in England all his life. He is the author of THE PAGANS, a trilogy consisting of THE STONE ARROW (winner of the Winifred Holtby Memorial Prize), THE FLINT LORD, and THE EARTH GODDESS.